# Queen of Mahishmathi

Anand Neelakantan is the bestselling author of *Asura: Tale of the Vanquished*, the Ajaya series and *Vanara—the Legend of Baali, Sugreeva and Tara*. He published his first book for children in 2020—*The Very Extremely Most Naughty Asura Tales for Kids*. His books have been translated into more than fourteen languages, including Indonesian.

Anand has also written the screenplays for hugely popular TV series including *Siya Ke Ram*, *Ashoka* and *Mahabali Hanuman*. He writes columns in *The Hindu*, *Indian Express*, *The Pioneer*, *Washington Post*, and Scroll.in. His fortnightly column Acute Angle, in *Sunday Express*, is very popular.

The first book in the Bāhubali series, *The Rise of Sivagami*, was released in 2017 and was the Amazon remarkable book of the year. The book was shortlisted for the Crossword Popular Award and received the Kalinga International Literary Award for the best popular fiction, 2017. The second book in the series, *Chaturanga*, was released in August 2020 and remains a bestseller. *Queen of Mahishmathi* is the third and concluding book in the Bāhubali series. Netflix has announced a series based on the Bāhubali books.

Anand lives in Mumbai with his family.

## Praise for *The Rise of Sivagami*

'*The Rise of Sivagami* captures multiple shades of the warrior mother.' —*The Hindu*

'Love, lust, greed, ambition, pride, loyalty, and more come together in this book. It's an adventure that promises to be the start of a gripping series.' —*The Sunday Standard*

'Anand Neelakantan has given wings to my imagination. I am amazed at what he has created with the few inputs I shared with him.' –SS Rajamouli

'A riveting tale of power, revenge and betrayal.' —*The Hans India*

'*The Rise of Sivagami* is a journey back to the epic realms of *Baahubali*.' —*The Times of India*

'The very first page of the book, depicting Sivagami riding in a chariot through a dark night full of looming mountains and ghostly trees is one of the most atmospheric and filmic openings I have ever read…There were, in fact, some passages and turns of phrases … that made me stop and re-read merely to savour the power of words that can create entire universes around a rapt reader.' –]aishree Misra, Author, *The Times of India*

'Anand Neelakantan's *The Rise of Sivagami* is a must-read for *Baahubali* fans.' –SIFY Com

S.S. RAJAMOULI'S
# bāhubali
BEFORE THE BEGINNING — BOOK 3

# QUEEN OF MAHISHMATHI

## ANAND NEELAKANTAN

First published by Westland Publications Private Limited in 2020

Published by Westland Books, a division of Nasadiya Technologies Private Limited in 2023

No. 269/2B, First Floor, 'Irai Arul', Vimalraj Street, Nethaji Nagar, Alapakkam Main Road, Maduravoyal, Chennai 600095

Westland and the Westland logo are the trademarks of Nasadiya Technologies Private Limited, or its affiliates.

Copyright © Anand Neelakantan, 2020

Anand Neelakantan asserts the moral right to be identified as the author of this work.

ISBN: 9789357766470

10 9 8 7 6 5 4 3 2 1

This is a work of fiction. Names, characters, organisations, places, events and incidents are either products of the author's imagination or used fictitiously.

All rights reserved

Typeset by SÜRYA

Printed at Nutech Print Services-India

No part of this book may be reproduced, or stored in a retrieval system, or transmitted in any form or by any means, electronic, mechanical, photocopying, recording, or otherwise, without express written permission of the publisher.

*To my sister Chandrika and
brother-in-law S.D. Parameswaran,
for making me what I am*

# Dramatis personae

### Achi Nagamma
The leader of an all-women vigilante army. She is fighting against the corrupt and evil people of Mahishmathi.

### Akhila
Thimma's daughter. Sivagami is very fond of her.

### Akkundaraya
A powerful bhoomipathi who is involved in the transportation of Gaurikanta. He is in charge of the forest lands.

### Ally
Brought up by the rebel queen Achi Nagamma, she is an elite warrior and spy in an all-women army. She is not shy of using her sexuality and powers of seduction to get her work done.

### Bhairava
A madman who lives near the river. He used to be Maharaja Somadeva's slave.

## Bhutaraya

He was the powerful leader of the Vaithalikas. He died during the failed coup against the Mahishmathi king.

## Bijjaladeva

The firstborn of Maharaja Somadeva, he is anxiously awaiting the day he will be declared crown prince. He is contemptuous of his younger brother and resents that their father has bestowed the title of Vikramadeva—a title given to the bravest of kings and princes—on him.

## Brihannala

A eunuch who is the head of the royal harem. She has her own secret.

## Chitraveni

The deposed princess of Kadarimandalam, imprisoned in a palace by Mahishmathi after being defeated in war.

## Devaraya

Sivagami's father, who was executed as a traitor by the government.

## Durgappa

A bhoompathi who mans the fort of Gauriparvat.

## Gomati

The wife of Kalicharan Bhatta, the son of the rajaguru, Rudra Bhatta. She is principled and brave.

### Guha

A bhoomipathi in charge of the pastoral lands and the river people. An old man, cruel and cunning, he is revered by his people. He bows only before Maharaja Somadeva.

### Gundu Ramu

Sivagami's young, loyal friend from the orphanage. Son of a slain poet, the boy adores Sivagami.

### Hidumba

The dwarf is a khanipathi, a step below a bhoomipathi, and is in charge of the Gauriparvat mines.

### Inkoshi

A young man from the Kalakeya tribe.

### Kalicharan Bhatta

The son of the rajaguru Rudra Bhatta, he officiates rituals and pujas in his father's absence. He is as immoral and deceitful as his father.

### Kalika

She is the head devadasi of Pushyachakra inn, more notoriously known as Kalika's den. She is a seductress and has half the Mahishmathi nobles under her feet. She is adept in the art of kama and supplies beautiful young women to even the maharaja's harem to entertain state guests.

## Kamakshi

She was Sivagami's closest friend in the orphanage. She was the lover of Shivappa before she was raped and killed by Prince Bijjaladeva.

## Kattappa

A slave, he is dedicated to his work and takes pride in serving the royal family of Mahishmathi. Kattappa served Bijjaladeva, the elder prince of Mahishmathi, and is the son of Malayappa, the personal slave of Maharaja Somadeva.

## Kalakeyas

The Kalakeyas are a tribe that are now considered savages, but once had the most advanced civilisation in the world.

## Keki

A thirty-year-old eunuch, she is the assistant of the famous devadasi Kalika. She is part of Prince Bijjaladeva's camp.

## Marthanda

A mercenary fighter who gains a position of power in Mahishmathi.

## Mekhala

Bhoomipathi Pattaraya's beloved and beautiful daughter.

## Narasimha Varman

The incompetent brother of the deposed princess of

Kadarimandalam, he has been placed on the throne, but real control lies in the governor's hands.

### Neelappa

The favourite slave of Devaraya, who comes to work with Sivagami after thirteen years.

### Jeemotha

A pirate, Jeemotha also trades in slaves and provides children to the Gauriparvat mines. He is handsome and uses his charm and wit to get out of difficult situations.

### Mahadeva

A dreamer and an idealist, he treats everyone with compassion and love. He is conscious of the fact that he is not a great warrior. He is in love with Sivagami.

### Mahapradhana Parameswara

The prime minister of Mahishmathi, he is trusted by the king, who considers him his guru. He is kind-hearted but a suave politician. He was also Skandadasa's mentor.

### Maharani Hemavati

The haughty and proud queen of Mahishmathi.

### Malayappa

The personal slave of Maharaja Somadeva, he is Kattappa and Shivappa's father. He is a proud man with a strong sense of duty.

## Pattaraya

A rich and ambitious nobleman, he is a bhoomipathi, a title of great importance in the Mahishmathi kingdom. He is known for his cunning and ruthlessness. He is a self-made man who rose from poverty to riches through cunning and hard work. He is dedicated to his family and loves his daughter Mekhala more than his life.

## Pratapa

The police chief of Mahishmathi, Pratapa is feared by the common people. He is a friend of Pattaraya.

## Raghava

Thimma's son, who grew up with Sivagami. He professed his love for Sivagami, but was rejected by her.

## Revamma

The warden of the royal orphanage.

## Roopaka

A scribe and the trusted aide of Mahapradhana Parameswara.

## Rudra Bhatta

The chief priest of Mahishmathi. He is a close friend of Bhoomipathi Pattaraya.

## Shaktadu

A young solider also known as Shakti.

## Shankaradeva

The cruel and ruthless governor of Kadarimandalam, he is the cousin of Maharaja Somadeva. Actual control of Kadarimandalam lies in his hands.

## Shivappa

The younger brother of Kattappa, he resents being born a slave. He loves his elder brother but is often at loggerheads with him. He was deeply in love with Kamakshi, a friend of Sivagami's, and is determined to avenge her murder.

## Sivagami

A fiery young woman, she is extremely intelligent and a trained warrior. She is the daughter of a nobleman of the Mahishmathi kingdom, Devaraya, who was executed as a traitor by the king. The wounds of her childhood have scarred her.

## Skandadasa

The deputy prime minister of Mahishmathi, Skandadasa was a man of principles. He belonged to the untouchable caste and was murdered by Pattaraya.

## Somadeva

The king of Mahishmathi. He is respected, admired and feared by his subjects.

## Thimma

The foster father of Sivagami, he used to be a close friend of her father, Devaraya.

## Thondaka

The son of Revamma, who is often drunk.

## Uthanga

A boy in the orphanage, made comatose from an accident for which Sivagami feels responsible.

## Vaithalikas

The rebel tribe that wants to take Gauriparvat back from the clutches of Mahishmathi.

# The Story So Far

YEARS OF SIMMERING resentment in the abundant empire of Mahishmathi is coming to a boil.

Orphaned at a young age, Sivagami is waiting for the day she can avenge her father's death. She hates the king of Mahishmathi, Somadeva, who accused her father of being a traitor and sentenced him to a cruel death. Sivagami's path crosses with the king's, and his family, when her foster father Thimma seeks permission from him for Sivagami's stay at the royal orphanage till she turns eighteen. Prince Mahadeva, the king's younger son, falls in love with her instantly.

Thimma leaves for a secret mission. His son and Sivagami's childhood friend, Raghava, confesses his love for Sivagami, who is taken aback and rejects him as she sees him as a brother. He leaves as well, promising that he will always help her in her mission.

Sivagami takes with her to the orphanage a manuscript that she has inherited from her father. Written in the indecipherable Paisachi language, she thinks it might solve the mystery of what led to his death. She becomes good friends with two other orphans: Kamakshi and Gundu Ramu.

Maharaja Somadeva's elder son, Prince Bijjaladeva, is anxiously awaiting the day he will be declared the crown prince. He has a frail ego and is bothered by his younger brother's popularity with the masses.

Kattappa, who has his father Malayappa's subservience ingrained in him, is a dedicated slave to Prince Bijjaladeva. Contrastingly, his younger brother Shivappa resents being born a slave and dreams of freedom. Shivappa is in love with Kamakshi, Sivagami's friend. He wants to build a new world and join the Vaithalikas, the rebel tribe that is fighting against Mahishmathi from the forests.

Besides the familial and personal, there is a political power hustle at play for the precious cave stones at the sacred Gauriparvat in Mahishmathi. This mountain is rich in Gaurikanta stones, which are used to make Gauridhooli, the magical powder that gives the weapons of Mahishmathi their great power.

The empire is ridden with political decadence and a corrupt bureaucracy, of which one of the most unscrupulous members is Bhoomipathi Pattaraya. And of the very few honourable people in the kingdom, by far the most honest is the deputy prime minister of Mahishmathi, Skandadasa. He discovers that Mahishmathi is producing Gauridhooli in an underground workshop under the palace. He starts recording the process of making this secret ingredient. Pattaraya is after this secret.

Kattappa goes into the forests in search of his brother. Shivappa, more faithful to his cause than to his brother, stabs him from behind and leaves him for dead. Kattappa is enslaved by Jeemotha, a pirate and slave trader. Jeemotha sells Kattappa to Bhoomipathi Guha as a slave. Jeemotha is hatching plans to make a fortune out of Gaurikanta stones. Ally, a member of a secret gang of women rebels led by Achi Nagamma, a mysterious old warrior, allies herself with Jeemotha to find out more about the Gaurikanta stones.

In Bhoomipathi Guha's land, the Mahishmathi government is getting a huge statue of Kali made. Every year, the Gaurikanta stones are secretly filled in a Kali statue and transported into the city. The statue is taken in ritual procession during the Mahamakam festival and immersed in the river Mahishi. The officials of Mahishmathi then fish out the stones from the riverbed and carry them to the underground workshop where they are converted into Gauridhooli.

With the help of Kattappa, on the eve of Mahamakam, Ally destroys the Kali statue and then frees Kattappa from slavery. Ally is caught by Jeemotha. Kattappa rushes to Mahishmathi where he meets Prince Mahadeva and tells him about the coup that Shivappa is planning during Mahamakam.

Kattappa then goes in search of Shivappa and stumbles on Prince Bijjala attempting to rape Kamakshi. He bears the brunt of Bijjala's wrath when he tries to stop the rape. Kamakshi commits suicide by jumping from the balcony. Kattappa immobilises Shivappa, who rushes to murder Bijjala.

Sivagami's treasured manuscript is confiscated and handed over to Skandadasa. When she sneaks into his office to retrieve it, she witnesses Pattaraya murdering the deputy prime minister. She is chased by Pattaraya's men. Sivagami flings her father's manuscript to her friend Gundu Ramu, who is waiting on the other side of the fort wall. Gundu Ramu is caught by Hidumba, a dwarf and the chief miner of

Gauriparvat, who kidnaps the boy so he can take him to the dreaded Gauriparvat mines.

Sivagami inadvertently ends up in the middle of the coup. In fighting off an attacker in self-defence, it appears as though she has saved the king's life from an assassin. The king awards her with the title of 'bhoomipathi' for her act of courage. He also confers Prince Mahadeva with the title of Vikramadeva, a title given to the bravest of kings and princes.

For unsuspecting Sivagami, the first execution she is to carry out is of her foster father, Thimma. It is believed that Thimma might have been one of the members of the Vaithalikas, and was a part of the coup. Sivagami has to do the unthinkable—take the life of her foster father. After the fight, she is appointed as a bhoompathi, but she loses the love and trust of Thimma's daughter, Akhila.

Kattappa goes to retrieve his brother Shivappa from where he buried him after using a martial arts technique to make him inert. Their father Malayappa appears as Kattappa is digging the grave. Malayappa wants to take Shivappa to the king for punishment, and in the ensuing tussle, Shivappa fatally attacks his father. As Shivappa runs away, the only thing he is focused on is to kill Prince Bijjala. As he races away, two men accost him, addressing him as the king of the Vaithalikas, and take him to the leper's village. He finds out Brihannala, the head of the royal harem, is behind his capture. Brihannala also tells him that Pattaraya and his daughter ran away from Mahishmathi immediately after Mahamakam, and that the king had ordered Bijjala to catch the fugitive.

When Bijjala finally tracks down Pattaraya and his daughter Mekhala, Pattaraya reveals to him secrets from the past and also his plans for the future. He strikes a deal with Bijjala, stating that if the prince can get him into Kadarimandalam, he will help him ascend the throne.

Ever since she destroyed the Kali statue on the eve of Mahamakam, Ally has been held imprisoned at the bottom of a well. One night, the pirate Jeemotha comes down to the well and tells her he will help her escape on the condition that she will head to where the Kali statue was sunk and be ready to help him when he requires it. He also reveals to her the secret behind the boys who mine the stones in Mahishmathi. Some of them are used as galley slaves to transport the stones to Bhoomipathi Guha's land, some are used as workers to fill up the Kali statue—and then they are ritually killed so that no one in Mahishmathi city finds out the secret.

Ally is devastated. She makes her way out of the well, and as she is running to the compound wall, the barn door opens and some boys run out. One of them is Gundu Ramu. He runs to the wall too, but clearly cannot escape the men following right behind. He pleads with Ally to tell Sivagami akka that he has kept her book safe.

In Kadarimandalam, we learn that Pattaraya and the deposed queen of Kadarimandalam, Chitraveni, were lovers. Their daughter is Mekhala. Mahishmathi had conquered Kadarimandalam and crowned Chitraveni's brother Narasimha Varman as king, with Somadeva's cousin, Shankaradeva, as governor, but the war was still being fought. Pattaraya was sent to Kadarimandalam as a junior minister, to talk sense to the defeated queen. Pattaraya immediately fell in love with Chitraveni and confessed to her the reason behind his mission. Pattaraya knows there is a special ingredient that goes into their weapon-making and tells Chitraveni he will find out what it is; in return their first-born daughter must succeed the Kadarimandalam throne.

Pattaraya has one mission in life: that his daughter become the queen of Kadarimandalam after Chitraveni. Mekhala is in Kadarimandalam too—her father has asked her to find her way into the governor's palace. She finally finds her way into his presence, using Bijjala's ring as a ruse. To her dismay, the governor, Shankaradeva, sends her to be a part of Narasimha Varman's harem.

To lure Shivappa from his hiding place, Keki comes up with a plan which involves the priest Rudra Bhatta conducting tantric rituals in a temple outside Mahishmathi. She says they will let people know that Bijjala wants to get rid of the 'ghost' of Shivappa. Shivappa would think he can corner Bijjala alone there.

Maharaja Somadeva knows that someone is plotting for the destruction of Mahishmathi. The economy is in trouble, and internal strife is increasing. Weapons have turned brittle since the production of Gauridhooli stopped. He suspects that Shivappa is alive, and if there were an uprising in Vaithalika lands, with Shivappa as their ruler, it would be disastrous for the kingdom. Somadeva decides to give Kattappa his freedom for some time and arranges for a spy to follow him. He thinks that Kattappa will lead them to whoever is plotting against the king. Somadeva knows it is a master player who is moving things behind the scene.

Meanwhile, a guru, Dharmapala, seeks permission to set up an ashram in the kingdom. Parameswara is reluctant, but the king says it will create a diversion for citizens and thus should be allowed.

Neelappa informs Brihannala that Shivappa is hiding in the orphanage, and as they are making a plan on what to do next, Ally emerges. While talking to her, Brihannala realises that she is in love with Kattappa. Neelappa tells Brihannala to use Ally to get Shivappa out of Mahishmathi. Ally manages to get a message to Sivagami, telling her Gundu Ramu is alive in Gauriparvat, and has her manuscript.

Ally meets up with Kattappa, who is ecstatic to see her again. She lies to him, saying that the leper Malla is her father and is in the colony. She kills Malla and then tells Kattappa that she wants to take him to their village and give him a proper burial as per their tribal customs. Kattappa smuggles the body out of the colony in a handcart.

Gundu Ramu has been taken to Gauriparvat by Hidumba. He tries to escape, but Hidumba sets the Garuda pakshis on him. He and the other boys are taken to the Gauriparvat mines, where he finds out that the dwarf Vamana is the one who gave the manuscript to Sivagami's father.

Keki decides to take Akhila from the ashram to the temple where the rituals are being conducted. She knows that she has been taking care of Shivappa, and feels that the slave will come out of hiding in order to save her. However, Neelappa manages to take Shivappa away to a storage house near the river. He and Brihannala hit him on his head and an unconscious, bundled-up Shivappa is interchanged with Malla's body when Kattappa is distracted. Ally, Kattappa and the unconscious Shivappa make their way in the boat downriver.

Sivagami and Neelappa go the temple where the rituals are being carried out. When Rudra Bhatta enters, Sivagami attacks him and makes him reveal why her father was killed.

He reveals that her father found out that children were used to mine the Gaurikanta stones. Sivagami is shocked. She is determined to make her way to Gauriparvat and rescue Gundu Ramu and the other children. When they hear people approaching the temple, Sivagami ties up Rudra Bhatta and takes him with her.

At the Mahamakam grounds, Sivagami ascends the stone throne, and from there, has Rudra Bhatta thrown on a burning pyre. Mahadeva arrives and orders that she be arrested for her actions.

Will Sivagami be able to save Gundu Ramu?
What will happen to Kattappa and Shivappa?
Will Pattaraya's plan succeed?

Book 3 resumes here.

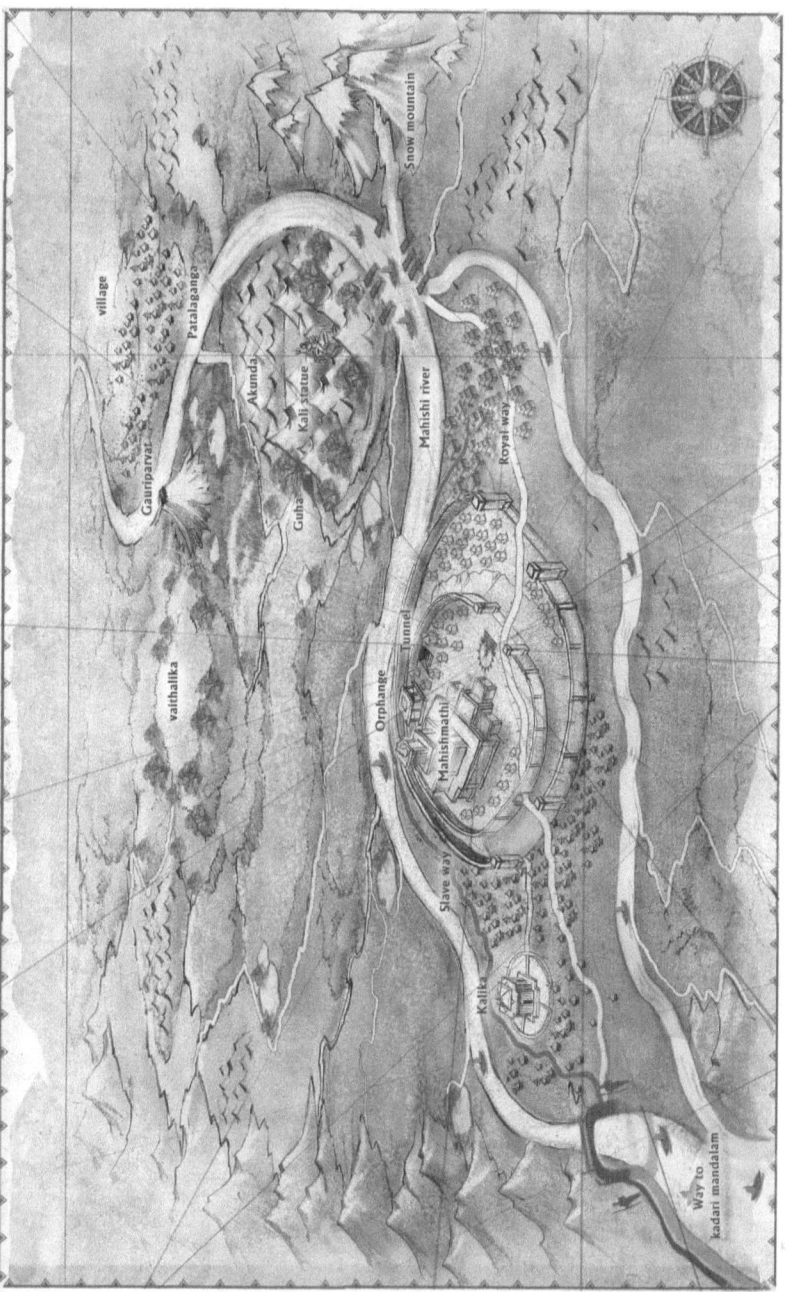

# PART 1

# ONE

# Mahadeva

MAHADEVA WAS CONFUSED and angry. It broke his heart to put Sivagami in chains. He wished she would deny what she had done. When he had seen the fire in the Mahamakam grounds, he had rushed there to see what had happened. From a distance, he could make out the silhouette of a woman with a trident in her hand, sitting on the stone throne that his father used during Mahamakam. Though the figure looked uneasily familiar, he was in denial until he had climbed the last step. He was sure the sight of Rudra Bhatta burning on the pyre and Sivagami sitting calmly on the throne would haunt him forever.

He squirmed in his chair when the soldiers walked her into the sabha in chains. Trying to calm his pounding heart, he clasped his sweaty palms and sat staring at his toes. He loved the woman and it was his fate that he had to chain her. The sabha became noisy with people abusing her for killing a Brahmin. Sivagami was unaffected by the clamour.

Outside the durbar, people from the agrahara had gathered, and they were raising slogans against her. They wanted nothing less than Chitravadha for the unpardonable sin of Brahmahatya. Mahadeva winced when he heard the crowd hailing him, the Vikramadeva, who had caught her red-handed. Some nobles came forward to congratulate him.

A horn blared and a sudden hush fell in the sabha. The crier announced the arrival of the maharaja of Mahishmathi. Mahadeva stole a glance at Sivagami. She was standing with a faraway look in her eyes, her expression bordering on boredom. Even with chains binding her, she looked more regal than anyone else in the sabha. For a fleeting moment, he wished she would weep and beg for forgiveness. He fantasised that she would plead with him for pardon, and he would magnanimously grant it.

Mahapradhana Parameswara stood up and started reading from a palm leaf, 'Sivagami devi, accused of Brahmahatya—'

The king raised his hand and stopped Parameswara. He addressed Sivagami, 'Do you have anything to say?'

Sivagami looked at him and said, 'I found out Prince Bijjala had offered ten thousand gold coins to anyone who killed Rudra Bhatta. I was doing my duty.'

'To kill without a trial? Prince Bijjala, could you please explain this?' Somadeva's tone bordered on mockery.

Bijjala stood up, defiant. 'Yes, Your Highness. People who commit such terrible crimes have no right to a trial. I have been tracking this evil man for some time after I heard complaints about children being kidnapped. The night before yesterday, I received information about the sacrifice through my spies, and I hurried to the temple. My brother Mahadeva also reached there, and I believe he too had been similarly informed. Unfortunately, the scoundrel fled before we could catch him. My soldiers would vouch for this, as would my brother. My soldiers and Mahadeva's soldiers searched for him. But it was Sivagami devi who was capable enough to find him. And I am in awe of what she did. As a warrior, I have rarely seen anyone so decisive.'

The group of soldiers who were standing at the far end of the hall cried in unison, 'It is true, it is true.'

'With your permission, Your Highness,' Bijjala said, then he bowed and walked up to Sivagami. He was holding a bag of coins, which he raised for everyone to see. 'Ten thousand gold coins. This is the reward I had announced for whoever caught Rudra Bhatta. Sivagami devi, please accept this.'

Bijjala placed the bag in Sivagami's palm. Mahadeva sprang up.

'What Sivagami devi did was wrong. The culprit deserved a trial. And what is told here is only half-truth. Nanna, they are fooling you.'

An uneasy hush fell in the sabha.

'Your Highness, Vikramadeva has called you a fool,' Bijjala said.

Mahadeva cried, 'Apologies, Your Highness. But please listen to me. This needs to be investigated. How did Rudra Bhatta get to an open place like the Gauristhalam? How did Sivagami reach there at the same time?'

Bijjala said, 'Vikramadeva Mahadeva, apologise now. How can you address a woman without the honorific of "devi"? This is the sabha of Mahishmathi. We cannot allow such disrespect to women.'

'That is not the issue here. I have always addressed her by her name. What we—'

'You always address her by her name?' Bijjala stood facing Mahadeva. 'You mean, you have always shown disrespect? You're the Vikramadeva. Your Highness, he calls you a fool. He abuses Sivagami devi, who has been so brave. I apologise for the boorish behaviour of my brother, Sivagami devi,' Bijjala said as he turned to Sivagami with folded hands.

Mahadeva knew Bijjala was diverting the issue. Frustrated and angry, he looked at Maharaja Somadeva. Why wasn't his father seeing through the farce?

The king looked at Mahadeva. The younger prince was trembling with emotion.

'Prince Vikramadeva Mahadeva, state whether you saw evidence of human sacrifice,' Maharaja Somadeva said.

His father's question startled Mahadeva. 'Ye-yes. And—'

There was a collective sucking of air.

'Did you find the victims were children?'

'Yes, and—'

An agitated murmur rose in the sabha. Mahadeva waited for the din to die down, but before he could say anything, the maharaja started speaking. 'Mahishmathi appreciates the diligent work done by Bhoomipathi Sivagami devi,' Somadeva said. 'As the ruler of this great country, I don't know how to thank you for what you have done, Sivagami devi. For many years, we have been hearing dark rumours about missing children. It wasn't the citizens of Mahishmathi who complained, but the poor tribal people in the border villages. For years, we have been trying to put down this menace. We couldn't fathom why anyone would want to kidnap children, unless they had a sinister motive. Now we know who was behind this evil. I am ashamed to say we failed to recognise the monster who was living among us. It took the enthusiasm and intelligence of a young bhoomipathi to solve the problem that was baffling senior administrators and ministers of this country.'

The bhoomipathis looked at each other and smiled. They stood up and began applauding loudly. Even Pratapa cheered for her. Mahadeva stood baffled at the sudden turn of events. A soldier rushed to him and handed over the key of the padlock to him. Mahadeva stared at the key in his hand. He wanted to tell his father his suspicions, but why was his father in a hurry to declare Sivagami a hero?

'Prince Vikramadeva Mahadeva.'

He heard his father call him and stood alert.

'Free Sivagami devi, and as a token of the appreciation of this grateful country, please hand over this veerasringala,' Maharaja Somadeva said, removing the diamond-studded bracelet from around his wrist.

'But … I have to say something,' Mahadeva fumbled.

Bijjala took the key from him and said, 'Your Highness, let me have the honour.'

He walked up to his father, bowed low and took the veerasringala—the bracelet of a hero who had done great service for the country—and marched towards Sivagami. He unlocked the padlock and the chain fell away with a clang. As the durbar erupted with applause and cheers, with the maharaja leading it, Bijjala placed the veerasringala in Sivagami's hands. Their eyes met, and Mahadeva felt a pang in his heart when he saw it.

Maharaja Somadeva declared, 'From now on, Sivagami devi will sit in the first row. Roopaka, lead the bhoomipathi to her new seat.'

Bijjala gestured for Roopaka to wait. He took Sivagami's hand and ushered her to the front row. It was still some distance from the king, but it was better than where she had been sitting all this time. Mahadeva watched helplessly.

Soon the sabha was dismissed for the day and the king retired to his harem. Mahadeva patiently waited for the crowd that had gathered around Sivagami to finish congratulating her. Again, he wondered why his father had been in such a big hurry to dismiss the case and felicitate Sivagami. Why hadn't he even allowed him to present all his evidence? He had to clear many things with Sivagami to put his mind at rest. When he looked next, Sivagami was climbing down the steps of the durbar with Bijjala. Neelappa brought the chariot to her and she was about to enter it when he stopped her.

'Sivagami, we need to talk,' he said.

'It seems you would have been happier if your father had ordered my hanging,' she said with a smile.

'No ... no ...' Mahadeva was at a loss for words. 'It is so generous of my father. I mean ... I ... I am confused.'

'My brother is always confused,' Bijjala said with a laugh.

'Why? You don't think the man who sacrifices children should be punished?' Sivagami asked. Mahadeva saw she was still holding Bijjala's hand and he burned with jealousy.

'Anyone who harms innocent children should be flayed alive,' Mahadeva said, anger flaring in his eyes. How could she even think for a moment that he had sympathy for Rudra Bhatta?

'I hope your righteous passion never wanes,' Sivagami said with an enigmatic smile, 'even when you figure out the entire truth. And regarding your father's generosity, I would say it is a master move. And I had expected nothing less from him—the master player of chaturanga.' She got into the chariot and indicated to Neelappa that they should move. The chariot shot forward and she gave a sweet smile and a wave at the confused prince and Bijjala.

Bijjala patted him on his shoulder and said, 'Take rest, brother. I hope the girl you took to the vaidya has recovered.'

Mahadeva didn't reply. He stood watching the chariot of Sivagami as it rattled off into the distance. The more he thought about it, everything seemed to lead to only one conclusion, and he didn't like it. Sivagami was acting on some plan, and she was hiding many things from him. The killing of Rudra Bhatta wasn't an impulsive move to deliver justice by a young and overenthusiastic officer; it was a deliberate action. He had seen the trident of Rakta Kali, taken from the temple, in Sivagami's hand. The image was vivid in his mind. The dark sky, the brisk wind that made her hair fly, and his Sivagami sitting on the throne with the trident in her hand. Like an avenging goddess. Like Durga.

As he rode back to his wing in the palace, he was sure that Sivagami had some sinister motive. Was she using him? He tried to push the uncomfortable thought away. No woman could be so dark at heart, surely. He loved her completely, and he was sure she felt the same way about him. She wouldn't have accepted his gifts if she didn't, would she? He smiled at the memory of Sivagami's face when he had presented her with Vajra. And it struck him like a flash. The horse hooves that he had measured in the bush near the temple. They were those of Vajra. He was sure. No other horse had such a big hoof size.

Should he go to his father and lay bare his doubts? Would he have the courage to tell him what he had found, thus indicting the woman he loved? Would he be able to live with himself if his father ordered Sivagami's execution? Was he morally courageous enough to bear that suffering for the sake of truth? If he didn't say what he felt, he would be lying to his father and failing in his duty. Mahadeva needed to clear his mind. He needed a long walk. Without entering his chamber, he turned back and walked towards the market.

Mahadeva weaved through the crowd, immersed in his thoughts. What did she mean by his father's 'master move'? Who was this woman who was capable of anticipating his father's actions? Why did she take the grave risk of killing Rudra Bhatta, yet have the audacity to think she could get away with it? And get rewarded for her move.

What was the game of chaturanga that his father and Sivagami were playing? And why was he feeling so jealous of Bijjala? What was Bijjala trying to do? The memory of Sivagami's hand in his brother's made him feel agitated. Mahadeva was deeply in love with her. But shouldn't love make him blind to her faults? He didn't think so. For Mahadeva, nothing was more important than the truth, or what he thought was the truth.

He walked through the streets, barely acknowledging the people who bowed and respectfully made way for him. He went to check on the condition of Akhila. The vaidya had given her some medicine, which had made the girl sleep. She was still sleeping when he reached the vaidya's home. He sat for some time, and when he left, it was well past sunset.

As he was walking, he heard devotional songs being sung from the ashram of Guru Dharmapala. Unconsciously, his feet led him into the ashram. The inmates respectfully guided him to their guru. Dharmapala was sitting in meditation at the far end of the hall. When Mahadeva saw the guru, tears flowed from his eyes. The guru was all grace and divinity. Mahadeva had an urge to unload the burden he was carrying at his divine feet. As if reading his thoughts, Guru Dharmapala opened his eyes and looked at the prince, and Mahadeva melted in the kindness of that holy gaze. Like a wounded son rushing to his mother, Mahadeva went to the guru. He fell at Dharmapala's feet and wept. He didn't even know why he was weeping, but it felt so natural. Dharmapala ran his fingers through Mahadeva's hair and started chanting the Shanti Mantra. The divine grace of the guru seemed to flow through his fingers to Mahadeva's body.

One by one, all the disciples left the room, and Mahadeva and his guru were left alone. Dharmapala made Mahadeva sit at his feet. He wiped the tears from Mahadeva's cheeks and said affectionately, 'Tell me, son.'

'I ... I love a woman,' Mahadeva said.

'Love is the greatest of all emotions, son. No need to feel guilty or shy. Talk to me about your Sivagami.'

Mahadeva was startled by the clairvoyance of Guru Dharmapala. He grasped the guru's hands and started pouring his heart out.

TWO

# Ally

'YOU AREN'T HAVING any?' Kattappa asked as he tore off a bite of rabbit flesh.

Ally shook her head. 'I had some when you were sleeping,' she said. She was standing with her back to Kattappa, eyeing the boat moored a few feet away, to check on the cargo she was carrying. The forest was silent and brooding around her. Mangroves hung low with the weight of the poisonous fruits of odallam. Ally had a slice of one such fruit in her hand. She should have ground the entire fruit and served it in the spicy curry she had made for Kattappa. The spice masked the oleander smell of the poisonous fruit. Had she used the entire fruit, death would have come silently for Kattappa. She had lost her nerve at the last moment and used only half of it.

They were on a river island, one among many that the rivulets branching off from the river Mahishi had created. They had rowed through the night, and when Kattappa appeared exhausted, Ally had offered to take over. A grateful

Kattappa had slept like a log in the boat's prow while Ally took a detour without his knowledge. She had guided the boat away from the river Mahishi to one of its labyrinthine branches that had shallow waters, and then moored the boat by this island. She had trapped a rabbit and cooked it with the poisonous fruit of the odallam, and green pepper that she had plucked from the jungle. In between, Shivappa had woken up, and she had forcefully fed him an intoxicant and laid him to sleep.

'This is too spicy for me,' Kattappa said as he licked his fingers clean. 'Where did you get so much pepper from?'

'They grow wild in these parts. I plucked a few while you were sleeping.'

'How far is your village?' Kattappa asked as he walked to the river to wash his hands. Ally looked around, trying to remember the designated island—they all looked alike.

'It's nearby.'

'Are you sure you haven't lost the way?' Kattappa asked. He leaned over to gargle his mouth and collapsed into the river with a splash. Ally ran towards him, praying that this wasn't the moment. Thoughts, morbid and evil, rushed through her. Did she spike it with too much poison? Did she miscalculate? He was sprawled out with his face buried in the shallow water. Ally threw away the shiny fruit she had kept hidden in her hand and started dragging him out of the river. He was frothing from the mouth. She frantically pressed his chest, slapped his cheeks and pleaded with him not to die. There was a shudder, and then he lay still. With trembling fingers she felt for his breath. She kept her ears to his chest and heard a faint heartbeat. He was alive, for now. Ally wasn't sure whether that brought her comfort or remorse. Brihannala's instruction had been clear: her duty wasn't just to deliver Shivappa to Achi Nagamma; she had to eliminate Kattappa without fail. The revolution hinged on the Vaithalikas regrouping under the scion of their dynasty, and Kattappa being alive would jeopardise everything.

This was her fate, she thought with grief—to kill the one she loved and live with the guilt, or to betray Achi Nagamma, the woman who had brought her up, and live with the weight of failure.

---

Ally hated every moment she spent with Shivappa in the boat. Shivappa had regained consciousness, and talked constantly. And the more he spoke, the more she felt the contrast between the two brothers. How easily Shivappa was convinced that he deserved to be the king of the Vaithalikas, though he kept declaring that he would bring Bijjala to the jungle.

Ally continued to row in silence. 'Are you feeling guilty that you poisoned him? It will pass. I once stabbed him from behind. He was saving me and I—' Shivappa said, while trying to free himself.

'Don't even try. It is futile.'

Shivappa gave a hollow laugh. 'I ... I stabbed him, Ally. And pushed him down a cliff. And ... and this adorable rascal came back. He will never die. My brother is immortal. I am his dasa, his eternal servant. Do I feel guilty for stabbing him from behind? You bet I do. But would I do it again? I would, without batting an eyelid. Ask me why? Ask.'

The boat continued to cut through the inky black water. Crickets chirped from the bushes on the shore. When Shivappa didn't get any response from Ally, he continued, 'Because not even the love I have for my brother can stand in the way of my freedom.' And as an afterthought, he added, 'And the freedom of my people.' He punctuated it with another laugh.

'So don't feel guilty. We are all working for a greater cause. This idiot doesn't get it. My brother Kattappa—what a fool. Adamant as a mule, loyal as a dog to his masters ... but there is no one who has loved me so much in my life.'

The paddle came down on Shivappa's forehead. 'Not a word more, you low life,' Ally panted, holding the paddle firm in her hand.

'You hit me?' Shivappa asked, tasting the blood that dripped down to his lips. He struggled to break free.

Ally placed the paddle on his chest. 'Silence,' she hissed. 'I have a job to do.'

'You hit your king?' Shivappa yelled.

'I am ashamed to call you the king. I don't know what Brihannala sees in you. You are too full of yourself. Justifying every despicable act you have done, even killing your father and stabbing your brother in the back. No wonder Kattappa wanted to kill you.'

Shivappa screamed, 'Not that you're such an angel. You poisoned him.'

'I don't need to explain anything to you,' Ally said. His accusation had pierced her heart and she masked it with anger.

'Oh, you think so? You're just a lowly servant. When I become king—'

'Oh, I thought I heard you saying sometime before that

you want to be the servant of your brother when he becomes king.'

Shivappa turned his face away, sulking. Ally snorted and went back to rowing the boat. The mangroves had given way to thick woods on one side. She read the time by the position of the stars and cursed. She was late by a wide margin. She hoped they would still be waiting, and renewed her efforts to gather speed. Her shoulders were sore from rowing the boat for so long, but that didn't affect her concentration. There it was, the soaring banyan tree with its many roots reaching out into the damp soil near the shore. For a moment, it took her breath away. The tree seemed to pulsate with strange lights. It was as if the tree were breathing and its reflection in the river made it look eerie.

This was the place, she sighed with relief. Ally guided their small boat into the cluster of roots that dipped into the shallow waters of the shore. As she entered the cave-like hideout created by entwining roots, countless fireflies rose into the sky. For a moment, she forgot everything and stood mesmerised by the spectacle. The cloud of fireflies throbbed like a giant eye in the sky, swirled, rose higher and floated across the river. Such moments were precious. Moments when she forgot she was a rebel fighting for a lost cause, a woman who had poisoned her lover and had almost betrayed everything she had lived for. Moments when she loved life just for the sake of it. Life may not have any meaning, but it was beautiful.

When the fireflies had dissolved into the darkness, Ally reluctantly returned to the present. She jumped down into the knee-deep water and pushed the boat into a cove. She cut the rope that tied Shivappa's feet. He stood up and stretched his legs. He held out his wrists, expecting Ally to cut the binding free.

Ally ignored him and went to check on Kattappa instead. She looked down at his innocent face and a sob caught in her throat. His eyes opened then, and she staggered back. His head slowly turned towards her; his gaze went to Shivappa and then back to her. Ally wished she would drop dead at that moment. A teardrop escaped Kattappa's eyes. He was struggling to say something.

Ally ran, splashing through water. She scrambled to the shore and started walking quickly through the jungle. Shivappa ran behind her, calling, 'Hey, hey, where have you brought me?' Ally didn't feel the need to answer him.

'You're being rude,' Shivappa said. Ally kept walking, cutting the undergrowth with her dagger, stepping over rocks and weaving through the bushes. Shivappa overtook her and stood facing Ally. She stopped and glared at him.

'Ally, I don't need to prove the love I have for my brother to you. Do you get it?' Shivappa said, shaking his bound fists before her face. 'I live for him. I will die for him,' he screamed. She side-stepped him and continued on. Shivappa followed.

'He doesn't understand, Ally. You know that. That's why you people came in search of me. You need me. My brother is a slave and will continue to be a slave. He can't lead. He can't take you to freedom. I can. He can't be the king. He doesn't have it in him. Don't you get it?'

'Yes, you will make a good king, Shivappa. Your brother won't,' Ally said. They had reached a small clearing.

Shivappa waited for her to speak. She looked around and gave a soft whistle. Dry leaves rustled, and before Shivappa could react, they were surrounded by women warriors. They were carrying spears, axes, swords, shields, bows, and quivers full of arrows. The first row of warriors clanged their swords and shields together and their leader's command rang out. The warriors parted and stood erect in a well-practised drill. From the darkness, a figure clad in white emerged. A woman in her seventh decade, with flowing white hair and a staff in her hand, she looked more regal than any king Shivappa had ever seen. The warriors went down on their knees and Ally, now kneeling on the ground, nudged him to bow. He hesitated.

'Young man,' the woman said with a laugh. 'Already playing the king? Ah, the vanity of men.' She cackled and shifted her staff from her right hand to the left.

Reluctantly, Shivappa bowed. She walked around him, observing his reaction keenly.

'You have much to unlearn and learn, young man. Lesson number one is, learn to respect those who are elder to you. Lesson number two is, learn to respect women. Now, am I elder to you? Well, am I a woman? Ah, I haven't been introduced to you. Ally, would you do the honour?'

Ally stood up and, without looking at the woman, whispered some words. The woman stamped her staff on the ground. 'Louder, girl. My ears are as old as I am. A thousand years old.'

Ally stood erect and said in a clear voice: 'Achi Nagamma, commander-in-chief of the Kadarimandalam army. The mother of the forest, the protector of orphans, the avatar of Amma Gauri, the—'

'Enough, Ally.' Achi Nagamma laughed. 'Avatar indeed. Young man, these girls are good at weaving stories. I am just an old woman. Not a queen, definitely not a goddess. I am mother for all these girls. Not a commander-in-chief. I used to be, but now, neither does the kingdom exist, nor the army. Now, young man—what did you say your name was?'

'Shivappa.'

'Ah, so the other one is Kattappa?' Achi Nagamma asked Ally, who nodded, thankful for the darkness that hid her blush.

'I hope you have done your job, girl?'

Again, Ally nodded. There was a momentary pause, and Ally felt as if Achi Nagamma's eyes were probing her heart.

'So you're the one who was trained by that fool Bhutaraya. How did you manage to escape that disastrous coup? Let me guess. You scooted. You left the coup midway to meet your girl. Men. Tchaw.'

Shivappa squirmed.

'That's what happens when a man leads a coup. But the Vaithalikas won't listen. They won't accept a woman's leadership. For more than three thousand years, the queens of Kadarimandalam ruled over them and a hundred tribes like the Vaithalikas from the snow mountains to the three seas, without interfering in their customs or religion, without bothering them except for an annual tribute, with justice to all and partiality to none. And despite that, none of the tribes see that a woman leader would be better. I would have preferred a queen for the Vaithalika tribe and for all such tribes. Why, this girl Ally would have made an excellent ruler. She is a Vaithalika woman and she would be better than any of you fools. But your men won't take orders from a woman. So we have to do with a Kattappa or Shivappa or whichever appa we can manage. By the way, I heard you killed your father. Boy, you are already a king in the making.'

Achi Nagamma grabbed Shivappa's hand and started walking into the jungle. Ally watched the group of warriors vanishing into the woods. She felt drained and dropped down on the grass. She lay on her back, looking at the countless stars in the sky. Now was the most difficult part of the plan. With heavy legs, she dragged herself back to the boat.

Ally waded through the water. It was now waist-deep because the tide was coming in. The current was strong. As she turned the bend, she froze. Achi Nagamma was sitting on the boat. Her heart stopped. 'Kattappa!' Ally screamed and ran as fast as she could towards the boat. When she reached, she threw herself on Kattappa, grateful to see that he was still breathing.

'You failed me, girl,' Achi said softly. Ally didn't move from her position on Kattappa. She would die before Achi did something to Kattappa.

'Have you fallen in love, girl?' Achi asked. Ally didn't reply. 'A terrible mistake, girl. One that you will regret later. I could've killed him, but I guessed it would break your heart. In my younger days, I wouldn't have cared about what you felt. Now I am at the doorsteps of Yamaraja's palace, I have become a bit woolly in my head. I waited for you, so that I can guide you on how to kill him. It will be a blessing for him. You have poisoned him, a half job done badly. I shall teach you how to steel your heart and cut his throat. He won't even feel any pain. Here, take this dagger—'

'No,' Ally said fiercely.

Achi Nagamma shook her head. 'There cannot be two scions for the Vaithalikas—especially if one of them is loyal to the Mahishmathi king. I need not tell you all this, daughter.

You know it better than me. Isn't it how I brought you up. Do it for your mother, darling.'

'He will not come in the way, I promise, Amma. I have a plan. Please, please ...' Ally grabbed Achi Nagamma's feet and sobbed.

Achi sat running her fingers through Ally's hair affectionately. Ally whispered her plan to Achi Nagamma.

When she had finished, Achi said, 'It would be more merciful if you killed him, daughter.'

Ally buried her face in Achi's lap and cried.

'I trust you on this. Don't disappoint your mother again. I don't want him to come back, ever,' Achi said with a heavy heart and got up to leave. 'Now begins your toughest task, girl. Make your mother proud.' Achi planted a kiss on Ally's forehead. 'I have a king to train. May Amma Gauri be with you.' Achi threw a pitiful glance at Kattappa and left. Ally pushed the boat into the current and started paddling to her destination. Around her, the river and the forest were bathed in the glory of sunrise.

'Where are you taking me?' Kattappa asked.

Ally whispered, 'Forgive me, Kattappa,' and rowed the boat with all the strength she could muster, ignoring the stream of tears that scalded her cheeks.

THREE

# Gundu Ramu

'CRAWL, CRAWL, CRAWL!'

Gundu Ramu could hear the harsh voice of Hidumba. He was at the front of the train of boys crawling through the mining shafts. Ahead of him, Vamana walked with a flaming torch in his hand. Gundu Ramu ran the plan through in his head once more. The key was reaching the waterfall as fast as possible. Despite Vamana's misgivings and warning that no one had managed to escape the Gauriparvat mines alive, Gundu Ramu had decided he would make the attempt. With the help of the old dwarf, he had broken down an abandoned mountain ram-driven crate and reassembled it in the cave behind the wooden door, near the opening to the waterfall.

'Pray you fall to the left, boy,' Vamana said. 'Half the waterfall plummets into the boiling core of Gauriparvat. I'm sure the other half falls outside the rim. Nothing else would explain the waterfall on the other side of the mountain from where the river Mahishi originates. We've never seen where the water falls in the boiling core because of the fog that rises when water hits molten rock. We can only hope that the hole through which the water escapes the mountain and plunges outside is broad enough to take you. Aim for the left. A slight mistake will take you to the molten rock and …'

Gundu Ramu shuddered at the thought of plummeting down the huge waterfall, clinging to a rickety box. The moment when he would need to make his move was fast approaching. The air was thick with purple smoke and the smell of rotten eggs. Gundu Ramu wiped beads of sweat off his forehead with the back of his palm.

'Crawl, crawl, crawl.' The hoarse cry of Hidumba was followed by the swish of a whip. Gundu Ramu stole a glance to the rear. They were negotiating a tough curve that sloped to the left in a sharp angle. He couldn't see those behind him. He nudged Vamana and the dwarf nodded. *This is it,* Gundu thought, squeezing his eyes shut.

He heard the hiss of a torch and opened his eyes. Vamana was beating the wall with the torch and the flame flared and sparked before dying down.

'What is happening there?' Hidumba shouted from the rear.

'I fell down, swami,' Vamana said. Gundu Ramu had already started racing ahead on all fours. From behind, the screams of the children rose. The rats had started entering the tunnel. He could hear Hidumba's yells, the sound of a lint being lit and the flare of a torch. The rats were scrambling back.

*Another thirty steps, twenty-eight, twenty-four,* Gundu counted desperately. The floor was damp now, and he could feel the spray from the waterfall on his face. When he broke out of the tunnel, Vamana was already there by the end, holding the box by its edge. They heard a scream. Hidumba had noticed their absence. Time was running out.

The rope that would take the box to the edge of the volcano's rim lay coiled on the floor, one end tied to a protruding rock in the tunnel wall. As he looked down at the ferocity of the cascade, Gundu Ramu didn't want to do it anymore. A paralysing fear poisoned his veins and squeezed his throat dry. Hidumba's shouts were nearing and Vamana gestured for him to hurry. Gundu checked that the manuscript was safely tucked under his waistband, and with limbs that had become as soft as a decaying banana stem, he stepped into the open box. Vamana's hands fumbled with the rope as Gundu closed his eyes tight and gripped the rugged edges of the box. *They seem so flimsy,* Gundu thought with rising panic, as images of himself falling into the lava or his head cracking open after hitting a protruding rock, flooded his mind.

*Amma Gauri, Amma Gauri, Amma Gauri,* he chanted to calm himself as the box teetered at the edge. Vamana was finding it difficult to push Gundu's weight. They could hear Hidumba's yells clearly now. Gundu's prayers became frenzied and suddenly he felt the box plunge down. He was plummeting through a sheer sheet of white. His scream was cut off by water gushing into his mouth, almost drowning him.

The plunge ended in an abrupt yank of the rope. Gundu opened his eyes as the box swayed over the volcano mouth. The heat was unbearable; smoke curled all around him, stinging his eyes. Gundu yanked the rope twice in quick succession and held his breath. It was a signal for Vamana to cut the rope. The next moment, the box plunged and the rope came down in a swirl. The box hit the edge of the volcano mouth and tottered there. Water was filling up the crate, making it shudder and creak. It balanced on the precipice, as if undecided between fire and water. Gundu leaned away from the volcano mouth and the box slid out into the water falling by the side. Gundu felt a great relief, but it didn't last long. The current caught the box and he screamed in terror as the gushing river carried him in his rickety box through rugged mountain caves. The box swirled in the current, catching the eddies, hitting one wall or another, bumping over rocks and hurtling through dark damp caves through which the river Mahishi rushed. The roar of the water muffled his terrified screams. With each collision against the rocks, the box splintered more.

Finally, Gundu could see a light at the end of the cave, from where the river took another plunge into the valley. The Mahishimukha was approaching. On the outside, the cave from which the river plunged was carved in the shape of a roaring buffalo.

Gundu Ramu braced for the next plunge of almost two hundred feet, this time without a rope to control the fall. The cave mouth widened and the box slowed down a bit, giving him some time to breathe. He checked for the manuscript again and sighed in relief. His father had taught him that to not betray someone's trust was an indicator of one's character. He hoped he had kept the trust of Sivagami akka. Hoped she didn't think he had stolen her book. He hoped she would accept his apologies for leaving Mahishmathi without informing her. Prayed she wouldn't be angry. He couldn't stand being scolded by those he loved. For Gundu Ramu, Sivagami was the only one left in the world to love; she was the one who had fed him. After leaving her, he had not had a full meal and was always hungry. He sat on the slowly drifting box, staring at the roof of the cave and salivating about a feast he'd had long ago. The thought of rice and sambhar made his belly rumble.

The cave mouth opened to a spectacular panorama. The sun painted the waters in golden hues and a rainbow arced across the valley. In the far horizon, past undulating hills and rolling plains, was the silhouette of Mahishmathi city.

Immersed in thoughts of food and his akka, Gundu Ramu hadn't noticed that his box had drifted to the edge of the fall. When the box jerked as it hit a protruding rock, he was startled. The box was hovering at the edge, with water hitting it and spilling into it, before flowing down. The box tilted down, and Gundu braced for the fall. The cave mouth grew dark for a moment and a blast of wind blew in, making the box shudder.

A blood-curdling screech filled the air, and Gundu shut his ears with his palms. He knew what was coming. The enchanting view at the cave mouth was cut off by the giant eagle. It hovered at eye level, its cold eyes staring at him, the feathers in its wings fluttering in the breeze. The Garuda pakshi let out another screech and the blast of hot air pushed the box a few feet back from the edge. The box got free of the rock that had blocked its fall. It swirled and turned in the eddies and was about to plunge down, when Gundu lost his nerve and jumped out on to the nearest rock. He had barely managed to hold on to the slippery surface of the rock, when the box spiralled down. The bird dove down and caught the box before it hit the bottom. Gundu watched it soar high with the box in its claws. It perched on a rock a few hundred feet away from him and started pecking at the box. The box splintered into many pieces and the giant eagle clawed through the splinter, as if searching for something.

A tremor passed down Gundu's spine. The bird thought he was in the box. At any moment, it would realise he wasn't there, and would come back for him. He looked down at the precipice and gulped. Closing his eyes and calling out for Amma Gauri, Gundu let go his grip. He braced for the fall, but found he hadn't moved at all. There was a crushing pain in his hand. He opened his eyes and saw that he was staring straight into the reptilian eyes of the bird, which was perched on his hand.

'It has found me, Amma Gauri, it has found me,' he cried as he tried to extricate himself from its grip. It was trying to lift him, and he held on to the rock with all his might. It raised its sharp beak and brought it down on his hand. Pain exploded through him, and he went blind with it for a moment. He had a feeling that he was falling, and when he opened his eyes he saw that the bird had lifted him up and they were flying. Blood spurted from his hand to his face. The iron smell of his own blood, the blinding pain and the speed of the bird made him dizzy. He knew his end was near.

Suddenly, he remembered the peculiar whistle Durgappa and Hidumba had used to command the bird. He twisted his tongue and gave a whistle. He didn't know what it meant. The next moment, the bird dropped him. It must have been a command for the bird to drop stones.

Gundu dropped down hard on the water surface. Everything went blank for a second. His vision blurred, the past merged with the future, and then everything was clear again. He was sitting with his Sivagami akka and she was feeding him, piling his banana leaf with steaming rice and sambhar. He smiled at the delicious food and plunged his hand into the pile of rice. Try as he might, though, he couldn't hold the rice. It fell right through his palm.

---

'He will live, but—'

Gundu Ramu heard a woman's voice. He struggled to open his eyes. There was a woman sitting next to him.

'Akka.' He sat up from his bed and pain shot through his right hand. He screamed at the top of his voice, 'My fingers, my fingers!' Three fingers of his right hand were missing. The old woman in front of him tried to pacify him.

'Achi Nagamma,' he heard the booming voice of a man. A tall, dark, young man entered the hut.

'I told you there would be a way. You never listened,' he said excitedly.

'Shh, Shivappa. The boy is in pain,' the woman admonished him.

The man ignored her and shook Gundu's shoulder. 'Tell me, boy. Did you escape from the Gauriparvat mines through the Mahishimukha?'

Gundu was scared by the man's brusque manner. The old woman tried to push him away, but he kept staring at Gundu. The boy said, 'My hand is paining.'

'Tell me, and I shall leave you alone,' the man called Shivappa said.

Gundu Ramu told him between sobs and yells of pain, how he had escaped and how the bird had attacked him. 'It ate my fingers,' the boy cried.

Shivappa ignored Gundu and went out, bubbling with excitement. Gundu heard the man shout, 'Women, as usual, I have been proved right. I have been insisting that it is better to take Gauriparvat under our control and hold Mahishmathi to ransom. The objection raised was how we could get it under our control. That has been solved today. A boy has escaped from the mines through Mahishi falls. If there is a way out, there has to be a way in. We are going to take Gauriparvat.'

A loud cheer rose, and the old woman left Gundu and rushed outside. Gundu heard a heated argument ensue outside, but it was none of his concern. He slid out of the cot. He had to reach Sivagami. Gundu Ramu checked for the manuscript and sighed in relief. He slipped out of the hut, and the people arguing with each other didn't even see him go. He ran into the jungle, trying to ignore the throbbing pain in his hand. How was he going to find Sivagami, he wondered. As he fumbled through the jungle, a terror gripped him. What if the giant bird came back? *I have lost only my fingers, not my head,* he told himself. *If the bird comes and eats my arms, I will still go in search of Sivagami. If it eats my legs, I will still crawl to Sivagami.* He owed it to the poor children trapped in Gauriparvat. *Only my akka can save them.*

Gundu Ramu ran through the jungle, falling, getting up and running again, crying with pain, but telling himself, *It is all right, it is all right,* and continuing. The forest was in full bloom. Spring had come and birdsong with it. A breeze carried the fragrance of myriad flowers. The boy ran through the meadows and jumped across brooks. He didn't know the way, but he consoled himself that he would ask someone. The world was full of good people, and someone would help.

FOUR

# Hidumba

'BASTARD,' HIDUMBA SAID, punching Vamana's face. But the old dwarf only laughed with every punch. He was tied to a pillar at the entrance of the Gauriparvat tunnel. His face was practically pulp, his lips were split open, and the few teeth he'd had, had been knocked out—but he continued laughing.

'Kill me, Hidumba,' Vamana said. He spat at Hidumba's face and howled with laughter.

'Enough, Hidumba,' Bhoomipathi Durgappa said, but the dwarf wouldn't listen.

'He has destroyed us, Durgappa. This swine,' Hidumba kicked Vamana, who coughed and winced in pain.

He recovered quickly and laughed again. 'That's what I did. Destroyed you. The boy will tell the world what you're doing here. There will be riots in Mahishmathi. The people will know what is being done to these poor kids. What you devils have been doing for decades, the world will know …' Vamana said.

The loud flapping of wings filled the air, and Vamana stopped talking. He looked up at the giant bird which slowly descended on a rock near the gate. It had something in its beak. It was time for Hidumba to laugh now. He ran to the bird and it deposited something fleshy on the ground. He picked it up and grinned. He ran to Vamana and dangled it before his eyes. Vamana stared at Gundu Ramu's finger and let out a howl of pain.

'That's what is left of your boy. Eat him. Here, take this,' Hidumba said as he tried to stuff the bloodied finger into Vamana's mouth. The old dwarf fainted. Durgappa picked up the bloodied finger from the ground and grabbed Hidumba's wrist. He pulled him away and they walked to the bird.

'I'm so relieved. I thought we were finished,' Hidumba said.

'I don't think we can afford to relax, Hidumba,' Durgappa said, pointing to the bird's belly. 'What do you think?'

Hidumba stared at the bird, which watched them with cold eyes. Durgappa gave a peculiar whistle and flung the finger in the air. The bird dove to catch it and gobbled it up in a trice.

'Hungry. He is still hungry,' Durgappa said.

'You ... you mean to say that the boy might have escaped? No one escapes a Garuda pakshi,' Hidumba said, but his voice revealed his doubt.

'I think the boy has escaped. Not all Garuda pakshis are the same. We are ruined,' Durgappa cried.

Hidumba scratched his chin. 'What if we let loose the female one. She is more powerful.'

Durgappa cried, 'No, no. She is to be let loose only when

there is extreme danger to Gauriparvat. A boy escaping doesn't fall under that.'

'You're not getting what I am saying, Durgappa. How long will we remain like this? This is our chance to make it big.'

Durgappa stared at Hidumba. 'I hope you don't mean what I think you do.'

'We are stuck in this godforsaken place. We enjoy nothing. Other bhoomipathis have their fiefdoms. They're kings in their realms. The ones in the city enjoy wine, women and riches. We live here like ghosts, feeding giant birds and finding our pleasure with sick boys. What sort of animal life are we leading, Durgappa?'

'We've been living like this for many decades. Don't tempt me, Hidumba.'

'Friend, this is a fool proof game. Mahishmathi wants the stones desperately. I doubt they will be able to recover half the stones from the river. Their weapons are crumbling. The weapons they gave us break like twigs. See this.' Hidumba took out his sword and snapped it into two.

Durgappa bit his fingers, worry creasing his forehead. Hidumba continued, 'They have no weapons. The city is vulnerable. We have all the stones now. We are safe here. We will make our own weapons using bamboo, wood and catapults. We have enough rock here. We are in a high place and storming the peak won't be easy for them. The fort that I man gives us protection. And if we release the female too, nothing can stop us.'

'They aren't supposed to be released together. If they mate, the female becomes aggressive and uncontrollable. They are called Garuda pakshis for a reason. The female one is capable of hunting elephants and can lift one in its talons. The one we have is the last of the holy bird of the Kalakeyas. We are inviting trouble.'

'Durgappa, you said it. What we need is trouble. We have enough food stocked here and can cultivate more if we need to. We have enough water. We may have to be careful about the birds, but they are tame birds. We know how to control them. See this.'

Hidumba whistled and the bird turned towards him. He pointed to a rock and arced his arm. The bird rose to the sky, circulated the rock and perched on it. Hidumba snapped his fingers and pointed to his left. With a jerk, the bird lifted off with the rock in its claws, rose high in the air, and dropped it. The rock fell a few feet away from them and rolled down the valley. The impact of the rock's fall threw Hidumba off his feet. When the Garuda pakshi came back, Durgappa took a piece of meat from his waistband and threw it at the bird. It gobbled it up.

'See. Imagine any army trying to scale the peak and fighting these birds that can drop rocks at them. And this is what this relatively small bird can do,' Hidumba said, getting up. He pointed to the Garuda pakshi that was as big as a full-grown bison. 'The female bird is three times this size and many times more aggressive. No one can touch us, Durgappa. This is our chance. Mahishmathi won't remain the Mahishmathi we know for long. Already there are minor rebellions. Famine is stalking the countryside. Our time in history has come, Hidumba. Let the kings and bhoomipathis and tribes fight each other. We don't care. We hold the key to prosperity. We hold the mines. We can rule from Gauriparvat and supply stones to the highest bidder.'

'Who will be the king of Gauriparvat? You or me?' Durgappa asked.

'Of course, you, my dear giant,' Hidumba said with a laugh. 'Have you ever heard of a dwarf becoming king? I am happy to be your mahapradhana and mahasenapathi. And I shall be the mantri for finance too. I will handle the commerce and the mines, of course.'

'You rascal. You know which part of the fruit is sweeter.' Durgappa punched Hidumba's shoulder in jest.

'You bet, Your Highness,' Hidumba said, grinning.

'So we keep quiet now, Mahapradhana Mahasenapathi Hidumba?'

'We let His Highness—*ahaa phuh*,' Hidumba spat. 'What highness and lowness. We tell the fool Somadeva that he will be dealing with Maharaja Durgappa as an equal from now on. He can give his offer for Gaurikanta stones. We can write to a few more kingdoms too. Even the white-skinned barbarians across the sea. I've heard they too have some kingdoms and some rudimentary civilisation. They are poor and wretched, but who knows, they may get rich in the future. Times change. But what doesn't change is Gauriparvat and the great king— Your Highness Durgappa.'

Durgappa smiled happily.

'Let's not delay this,' Hidumba continued. 'We should inform our first vassal king about our decision. Let us send a letter of love to Somadeva.'

'Okay.'

'So, when are we releasing the female bird?'

'No. I will do anything but that. The male birds are enough, Hidumba.'

Hidumba grunted. He had achieved a half victory, but he would persuade the vain fool to do what he wanted when the time came. 'I hope you can train her like you trained the males .'

'Of course, I can,' Durgappa said in a hurt voice.

In a short while, they had drafted a letter to Somadeva with their demands. As he watched the pigeon fly away to distant Mahishmathi, a fear gripped Durgappa and he held Hidumba's hand. Hidumba patted Durgappa's hand. 'Your Highness, everything will be all right. Everyone who has succeeded big has done so by taking giant leaps like this. Let us enjoy this somarasa.'

Hidumba fished out a silver pot from the folds of his clothes and dangled it before Durgappa. The burly man snatched it and emptied the pot in one gulp. Hidumba watched him with an indulgent smile. In a couple of minutes, Durgappa had started singing in a voice that would have made a buffalo proud.

Suddenly, Hidumba noticed that Vamana was missing. 'Where is that damn old dwarf?' Hidumba asked Durgappa.

'What … what happened, Mahapradhana, Mahamantri, Mahasenapathi Hidumba …?' Durgappa asked, his voice slurring. Hidumba stood stunned, staring into the darkness of the cave. Durgappa followed his gaze.

From the cave mouth, a man was walking out, and behind him were several women warriors. Two of the warriors ran to them and, before they could react, the dwarf and Durgappa found themselves staring at spears pointed a nail's length away from their throats.

'Bow to Shivappa, the king of the Vaithalikas and the lord of Gauriparvat!' one of the women yelled, and the blood drained from the dwarf's face.

## FIVE

# Somadeva

'DEVARAYA'S CURSE, PARAMESWARA. I can't think of anything else to explain this,' Maharaja Somadeva said as he stood looking at Gauriparvat through his window. Parameswara stood a few feet behind him, staring at the floor. His shoulders were stooped.

'It is my failure, Your Highness. I should have taken precautions.'

'Hmm. It is like the old saying in ancient Kadri. When there is an eclipse, even the earthworm turns into a cobra. The bastards had been waiting for this opportunity, it seems. What are they asking for?'

'Autonomy. Each wants to be a king without responsibility and a larger share of profit. They know we are in trouble and each bhoomipathi is clamouring for more power.'

'Who all are with us?'

'For now, Guha, Akkundaraya and a few more. The issue is with Durgappa, Hidumba and the minor officials who are loyal to them. They are refusing to handover the Gaurikanta they have mined. Durgappa has declared himself as the maharaja of Gauriparvat.'

'How much do they have, Parameswara?'

'Durgappa claims they have found a massive mother lode that would solve our demand for the next fifty years. They have already extracted a quarter of it, and the work is going on day and night. But the issue is they aren't agreeable to the same terms and conditions under which they worked for the last three decades.'

'Negotiate with them. Do we have any other choice? The workshops have become silent for quite long.'

'They think the longer they delay, the better the deal they can force upon us. And spies report that they are strengthening the forts. More mercenaries have joined their force. They have stuck a deal with the slave merchants, who have supplied them with a slave army. The situation is getting more grave every day.'

'They need to be smashed down, Parameswara. But I don't know whom to trust. What is the situation in Guha's land? Will the Kali statue come again to Mahishmathi?'

'Hardly a fifth of what we lost has been recovered from the riverbed.'

'Hmm. And on other fronts—what is the status?'

'I have kept an eye on that guru. Nothing seems to be suspicious so far. He doesn't say anything about politics. He urges people to love their country, their king and God. The usual mundane stuff, the same things that every guru says in their own unique style.'

'At least he provides a diversion to my restless public in

these hard times. Still, keep an eye on him. And any news about my favourite slaves?'

'The rumours about Shivappa's ghost is still alive among the lower classes, but Kattappa has vanished.'

'What do you mean by vanished?'

'The spy that Mahadeva had tailing him was distracted by the Rudra Bhatta incident.'

'Can my son get one thing right?'

'Hardly the prince's fault, though he should have ideally had more people tailing Kattappa. The slave escaped along with a girl, and apparently they had a body with them.'

'So, I was right about Shivappa?'

'Yes, Your Highness. I got the grave of Shivappa checked.'

'And?'

'It was empty. I think Kattappa made fools of us. Shivappa was never dead. I fear he staged the drama to get his brother away from Mahishmathi.'

'I hope things don't flare up, with the forest tribes rising in arms again. We have had enough bloodshed. And what about Sivagami?'

'Sivagami? Nothing important, except that ...'

'Except that?'

'Both the princes are enamoured with her. She appears to be more friendly with Bijjala now,' Parameswara said.

'Wonderful. How blessed I am to have sons like these. The empire is collapsing, and those two are giddy about a girl.'

'May I suggest something, Your Highness? Send Bijjala to crush the rebellious bhoomipathis in Gauriparvat. And send Mahadeva to Guha's land to bring the Kali statue. We can't afford the risk of something happening to it again. And this way, both will be away from the girl too.'

'The girl is the least of my concerns. They can have all the girls and their aunts and cousins too. But would you trust Bijjala to handle this?'

'He has a streak of ruthlessness, Your Highness. Something that is badly needed while dealing with these unscrupulous bhoomipathis like Durgappa and that dwarf Hidumba. The advantage is that the rebel bhoomipathis who are holding on to the supply of Gaurikanta at Gauriparvat are bound to underestimate him.'

'I am not confident he will be able to handle it. He is too young and inexperienced.'

'At his age, you were already an emperor.'

'Ah, but I had you with me. And I had Hiranya, Thimma and Devaraya with me, men I could call my friends. And he has that eunuch!'

'The boy will mature. He proved himself with that Pattaraya incident. Give the fruit time to ripen. And isn't it time both the princes know how the empire is run?'

The king remained silent, staring at the distant Gauriparvat. Finally, he sighed and said, 'Let me think over it.'

After a long pause, the king spoke again. 'Give me one good news, Parameswara.'

'Everything is quiet at Kadarimandalam,' Parameswara said.

'I don't know whether it is the calm before a storm.'

'Shankaradeva is someone we can trust, Your Highness.'

'I have learnt to trust no one. But I agree, at least Kadarimandalam is under control. I shudder to think what would've happened if Pattaraya had managed to escape and reach that place.' Maharaja Somadeva sighed.

## SIX

# Pattaraya

'CAREFUL,' CHITRAVENI SAID as she watched Pattaraya. The room was dark and stuffy, and with the windows shut tight and curtains drawn, the humidity was unbearable. Under the light of a lone lamp, Pattaraya was immersed in his job, unmindful of the streams of sweat that flowed down his face.

'I still don't understand what you're trying to do,' Chitraveni said. Pattaraya didn't reply. He placed the writhing viper back into the reed basket and picked up another one. He held it by its neck as it wound itself around his wrist and glared at him. He prised open its mouth and pressed its poisonous fangs to the edge of a small crystal bottle. A stream of yellow venom slithered down to raise the level of liquid that lay glistening at the bottom. Pattaraya repeated the process with more snakes until the thumb-sized crystal bottle was full. He closed it tight and then turned to Chitraveni.

'What are you trying to do?' she asked again.

'I am going to save my daughter,' Pattaraya said, and without waiting for a reply, he walked out.

---

'You good-for-nothing puppet, Narasimha Varman,' the mad man yelled. He was standing in court in chains, having been arrested for abusing the ruler of Kadarimandalam in the market. At the lunatic's words, King Narasimha Varman spluttered the wine he was drinking, and his obese body shook with mirth. The court burst into laughter.

'Mammallan Narasimha Varman, you are a fool and your bunch of rowdy courtiers are a blot on this holy land of Kadarimandalam,' the mad man continued, rattling his chains. More laughter followed.

This wasn't what Pattaraya had expected when he had dressed up in beggar's clothes and started ranting like a mad man. Things had gone as planned until he reached the durbar of Kadarimandalam. In the market that morning, he had yelled out his choicest abuses of the king. To his surprise, the people around had encouraged him, cheering and laughing at his diatribe, but as expected, he had been arrested by soldiers. Everything had gone awry after that. Narasimha Varman, instead of being offended, was entertained. He seemed to be amused by the mad man's comments.

'You're so funny,' Narasimha Varman said as he slapped his thighs and guffawed again. This evoked another wave of laughter in the sabha. Pattaraya felt like a performing monkey trapped amidst a group of unruly children.

'You are no king, Narasimha Varman. There is only one

ruler for Kadarimandalam, and that is Chitraveni,' Pattaraya said, sounding desperate now.

'The bastard princess, my sister Chitraveni?'

The sabha burst into peals of laughter.

'If your sister is a bastard, so are you,' Pattaraya said angrily.

'Come here, mad man,' Narasimha Varman said. Pattaraya didn't move. The next moment, Pattaraya was shoved towards the king. The soldiers pushed him down and made him kneel before the king. Narasimha Varman lifted Pattaraya's chin with his stubby toe. Pattaraya heaved a sigh of relief. Some part of his plan was clicking in place.

'Don't you know that we are all bastards in Kadarimandalam? Before the great Mahishmathi showed us the way, we lived a miserable life. We, meaning, the men of Kadarimandalam.'

'Hail Mahishmathi,' the men in the sabha called out as they raised their wine goblets.

'Comrades,' Narasimha Varman continued, rubbing Pattaraya's chin with his toes, 'tell this clown what we were before.'

'We were slaves to our women,' the courtiers in the sabha cried out in unison. A servant was passing on a smoking pot, and each of the courtiers jostled to get a puff of the fragrant smoke. An intoxicating smell spread in the hall.

'Who sat on the throne before me?'

'A woman,' cried all.

'Who ruled our homes, comrades?'

'Women.'

'Who fought in our armies?'

'Women.'

'What were we before?'

'Servants, slaves, child-makers, objects of pleasure for our women.'

'Who did all the work at home?'

'We did.'

'Who raised the children?'

'We, the men did.'

'How many husbands and consorts did each of your mothers have, comrades?'

'Countless.'

'Do any of you know who fathered you?'

'Mother is the truth, father is just a belief.'

'Ha, who taught you this?'

'Our mothers.'

'Comrades, who inherited your mother's property?'

'Our sisters.'

'And what did you get?'

'A slave's position in our mate's home.'

'And if your mate took a fancy for another man and had no inclination to entertain you further?'

'They would keep our mattress packed at the gate. We did not have the right to ask any questions. We were divorced without any means of livelihood. Unless some other woman took pity on us and took us in, we ended up living on the charity of temples.'

'And if your wife died?' Narasimha Varman took a deep puff of smoke from the pot and coughed.

'We had to jump into the pyre and become satyavan. They erected temples for us then, and worshipped us,' one courtier cried. The king emptied a pot of toddy, and gestured for his courtiers to continue.

'If we refused to jump into the funeral pyre of our women, then we were forced to shave our heads, moustaches and body hair, wear only a loin cloth and live in the confines of our kitchens.'

'See, buffoon. You may have no self-respect. I don't blame you. We never blame the poor men. You were all misguided. We have sympathy for men such as you. Your mothers taught you wrong. Before Mahishmathi opened our eyes, all of us, the men, were mere consorts, one among many for the women of Kadarimandalam. That makes all of us bastards. They called it our tradition. Have you heard of any land in the world where such barbarian customs existed?'

Pattaraya didn't reply. A couple of female servants came into the sabha carrying a huge roasted wild boar on a tray. They placed it near the king and he tore off a huge chunk from its belly with his bare hands. He took a bite and thrust it at Pattaraya's face.

'Want a bite? You must be hungry, talking nonsense since morning.'

Pattaraya shook his head. This was beyond demeaning, and he seethed at the insult. The king shrugged and threw the half-eaten piece at his courtiers. The courtiers fought for it like wild cats and the king sat back on the throne, massaged his huge belly and enjoyed the scene. Narasimha Varman tore another piece of meat and teased his courtiers. He pretended to throw it to one side and then threw it to the other, drawing groans and cheers.

It seemed the king had forgotten Pattaraya in the distraction. Pattaraya's back ached and he wanted this farce to end one way or another. He was on his knees, chained before this barbarian king, and even death was preferable to this. His actions had made his daughter share a bed with this barbarian. Pattaraya hated himself for what he had made his daughter undergo. He shuddered at the thought of Mekhala in the harem of this boor.

More fights ensued in the sabha and there was utter chaos. Being used to the stiff formality and decorum of the Mahishmathi sabha, Pattaraya watched the insanity of Kadarimandalam with horror. The sabha seemed more like a tavern with drunken sailors gone mad. More roasted fowl and beasts came. More wine flowed, and the sabha became foggy with the heady smoke of cannabis.

As a last resort, Pattaraya abused the king in the filthiest language he knew. The sabha grew silent for a moment. Pattaraya waited anxiously. Narasimha Varman glared at him. Then, the king fired back a colourful expletive, shocking Pattaraya. Shaking a fat thumb at Pattaraya's face, he started laughing. The sabha resounded with cheers and applause. Soon, the ministers were abusing each other and their king with expletives that would have suited any fish market.

Pattaraya had never imagined that his plan would end in such a farce. For a man who took pride in his ability to strategise, this was a big blow. He had planned with the expectation that his enemy would be as cunning, scheming and intelligent as he was. He wasn't prepared for this madness.

If he didn't take control of this situation, his carefully built plans would shatter like a clay pot kicked by a donkey. Pattaraya looked around for something that he could leverage. He must reach the reclusive governor somehow.

He saw the towering insignia of Mahishmathi behind the king's throne. Made of gilded gold and encrusted with

Gauripadmam stones, it dwarfed the ancient throne of Kadarimandalam. An idea started forming in his mind. A wild one, a last throw of dice, but it was better than standing by as all his careful planning went waste, thanks to the buffoonery of these barbarians.

He watched the king's stubby fingers tear through the fried wild boar. The plate had a layer of oil and grease, and with the half-eaten boar, Pattaraya calculated it would be heavy enough for his purpose. Pattaraya timed his move well. When the king's hand went to his mouth to stuff another chunk of meat in it, Pattaraya snatched the plate and flung it with all his force.

The plate spun in the air and smashed against the royal insignia of Mahishmathi. A shocked silence descended in the sabha. The greasy boar meat was stuck on the insignia, and it dripped down slowly, staining the royal sign with the curry. Pattaraya looked with satisfaction at the dent that the plate had created. A few precious stones had flown loose and landed among the courtiers. One among them found a diamond and held it up triumphantly. Immediately, a mad scramble ensued for the Gauripadmam stone, while the king yelled for order and screamed at the soldiers to arrest his ministers who were fighting for the precious stones.

The soldiers joined the fight and the king watched helplessly as the sabha turned into a battlefield. A few men ran out of the court hall, clutching what they had got, chased by others with drawn swords and daggers. When things settled down, a few courtiers, the sober ones among the insane, remained and the king sat staring at the damaged insignia, stained with boar meat, and a few stones missing.

'How am I going to explain this to the governor?' the king of Kadarimandalam lamented. He started pummelling Pattaraya with his grease-stained fists. 'I will kill you, bastard. Kill you, kill you, kill you!' Pattaraya choked as the stubby fingers of Narasimha Varman wound around his throat.

A minister yelled, 'Your Highness. Don't. Otherwise, the governor won't believe us. He will say we arranged this drama to steal the stones and found a mad man on whom we placed the blame. Send him to the governor and make him confess.'

The king kicked Pattaraya in fury and roared, 'Take this swine to the governor.'

It was Pattaraya's turn to laugh. He rolled on the floor, rattling the chain that bound him, and roared with laughter, enraging the king further. Narasimha Varman jumped from the throne and kicked him again. Pattaraya rolled on the carpet, still laughing, until he stopped abruptly and fell silent. The soldiers picked him up and dragged him to the governor's palace. They thought the swollen cheek of Pattaraya was the result of a kick he had received. They assumed Pattaraya was silent because the mad man knew his end was near. But at that moment, Pattaraya was feeling the leather pouch hidden in his cheeks with his tongue. He had managed to thrust it into his mouth while rolling on the carpet and being kicked by the king.

---

Shankaradeva asked Pattaraya in a calm, measured voice, 'So, you are the one who dared to insult the king and damage the royal insignia of Mahishmathi, eh?'

Pattaraya glared at him, defiant, acting more brave than he felt. Chained and handcuffed, he was on his knees before the governor. Though it was late afternoon, the chamber was pitch dark, illuminated only by a torch on the wall behind the governor's throne, a few feet above his head. That helped to keep Shankaradeva's face in the shadow always. A chaturanga board lay on the small table beside the governor's throne. Pattaraya concentrated on the board to keep his mind calm.

'Can we hang him? Or better still, stone him?' Narasimha Varman asked hopefully, standing like a wayward student trying to please his master. The governor ignored the king. Pattaraya could feel Shankaradeva's eyes boring through him, and the hair at the back of Pattaraya's neck stood erect. A drop of sweat crawled slowly down his spine.

'We can have a public hanging,' Narasimha Varman said hopefully.

The governor waved him away. Narasimha Varman's disappointment was palpable.

'My men want it,' he whined. 'We should make an example of anyone daring to insult our beloved Mahishmathi.' The king sounded desperate. What he wanted was a chance for all the men of Kadarimandalam to assemble in the grand arena, to watch the execution, drink, eat and make wild love with one and all. On such occasions, the stifling moral code of Mahishmathi was easier to bear.

The governor looked at the king of Kadarimandalam with contempt and snapped his fingers. Two soldiers marched from behind the curtains, bowed to the king in a way that was more mocking than respectful, and led him outside. The governor gestured with his index finger, and the room emptied, leaving only Pattaraya.

Pattaraya heard a snap and looked at the governor. Shankaradeva gestured for him to crawl to him. Pattaraya crawled on wobbly knees towards the governor. He had a moment of sheer terror when he fell flat on his face as he negotiated the steps that took him to the pedestal where Shankaradeva's throne was perched. The governor waited for Pattaraya to reach him in silence, neither offering help when Pattaraya fell, nor making a move even when Pattaraya was some feet away. The silence terrified Pattaraya. It was difficult to judge what Shankaradeva was thinking, because his face was shrouded in shadow. The big Gauripadmam diamond that decorated his elaborate turban cast a blue glow on the contours of his face. A lizard chattered from the roof, accentuating the ominous silence, as Pattaraya crawled to the governor. He stopped a few feet away, and Shankaradeva gestured for him to come closer with the twitch of his index finger.

Pattaraya's heart was pounding as he moved forward. They stared at each other in silence, the erstwhile bhoomipathi, chained and on his knees, and the powerful governor. The governor twitched his finger again and Pattaraya moved closer, struggling to balance on his knees. He was exhausted with the effort.

'Speak,' the governor said softly. Pattaraya remained silent, watching Shankaradeva carefully, waiting for some movement. Everything remained still, calm and the silence grew denser. The movement came like lightning, taking Pattaraya by surprise. He felt the coldness of steel at his throat and the grip of strong fingers on his chin. The governor's face was just an inch away from his. Still in shadow, but clearer, as the blue light from the diamond illuminated his eyes. The thin lips of Shankaradeva spread into a grin.

'Pattaraya.' The soft voice of the governor sent a shudder through Pattaraya. He felt a burning pain in his neck. The dagger was moving slowly across his skin. A drop of hot blood crawled down his chest. The iron smell of death pierced his nose.

'I knew you would come.' Shankaradeva's breath was stale and hot on Pattaraya's face. 'I knew it the moment you sent your daughter to seduce me.' The governor's grin became wider.

'You won't die so soon. Don't panic. I will watch you die, you low-caste swine, slowly, *slowly*, looking into your eyes while you bleed to death. *Slowly*,' Shankaradeva hissed, his nose almost rubbing Pattaraya's. 'Feeling scared, swine?'

This was the moment Pattaraya had been waiting for. He bit the leather pouch he had hidden in his cheeks hard and felt the sour taste of venom in his mouth. Like a cobra strikes, he bit Shankaradeva's nose hard, holding on to it with his teeth, even when the dagger cut haphazardly across his chest and throat. In a matter of moments, the venom of the vipers spread through Shankaradeva's veins, and soon the governor was frothing from his mouth. He fell dead on Pattaraya's shoulder, and the dagger dropped down on the soft carpet. Pattaraya wept, spitting the rest of the yellow venom from his mouth.

'Daughter, daughter,' he cried between his sobs, trying to shake away the dead Shankaradeva from his shoulder. 'Behold what I have done for you. Rejoice, for from now on, you are the daughter of the new governor of Kadarimandalam.'

The governor fell from his shoulder; the expression on his face was grotesque, as he lay in his own vomit on the carpet.

Pattaraya, still sobbing, full of pride for what he had achieved, filled with love for his daughter, crawled up on to the throne. He stretched up, stepping on the dead governor, and shoved his handcuffs into the flame of the torch. He cringed as the iron turned red and then white, scathing his wrists. 'For you, Mekhala, my daughter, for you,' he cried, and pulled his wrists apart. The handcuffs snapped into two. He collapsed on the governor and started laughing hysterically. He laughed at the chaturanga board and moved some coins to surround the king. Then he snapped the king into two, flung it into the air and continued to laugh.

---

The king of Kadarimandalam watched the woman who had stolen his heart enter the hall with tear-filled eyes. Narasimha Varman and his retinue were waiting outside the grand hall of the governor.

'I hope she comes back soon,' Narasimha Varman said to the courtiers. 'The governor had gifted her to me. If he had to take back the gift, why did he give it to me in the first place?'

Mekhala entered the hall and shuddered when the door shut behind her. She walked with heavy steps to the throne of the governor. The old man was shrouded in shadow as usual, and a lone torch flickered above him. She didn't know why the governor had summoned her, and why he wanted to meet her alone. Mekhala had hated every moment she spent in Narasimha Varman's harem, but had been slowly getting used to her fate. She didn't relish the thought of entering the governor's harem. Mekhala hated her father for pushing her into such a situation. He promised me the prince of Mahishmathi and see what—

Mekhala stopped short. Maybe the light was playing tricks with her eyes. She blinked and looked again. She saw the governor's arm slowly move up and pluck the torch from the wall. As the light fell on the face of the governor, Mekhala gasped. She covered her face with her palms and wept. After a moment, she ran into the extended arms of her father.

'Nanna, I was in hell. Why didn't you come?'

'Everything will be all right, dear,' Pattaraya said, lifting her face up and wiping her tears. She told him about the miserable life she had lead in the harem. He wept with her.

'Now I can live with you here, as the daughter of Governor Pattaraya,' Mekhala said, smiling through her tears.

Pattaraya hesitated.

'Now what?'

When Pattaraya told her what she had to do, she said, 'No. I can't go back.'

Pattaraya picked up a manuscript that lay on a table near the throne and waved it before his daughter's face. 'This has the design and the description of the process to extract Gauridhooli. I stole it from Mahapradhana Skandadasa. I had to kill him for this. I risked everything for this. You have to do what I say, daughter.'

'What will I tell the king?' Mekhala asked in a resigned voice.

'I will tell him. Call the fool.'

For a moment, Narasimha Varman wondered why the voice of the governor sounded different, but he didn't have the courage to say anything. He owed his throne to the prathinidhi, the representative of the king of Mahishmathi. He agreed to everything the governor said. When they were riding back to his palace, he leaned towards Mekhala and said, 'I never knew you were the illegitimate daughter of Prathinidhi Shankaradeva. What an honour he has given me. I understand that in Mahishmathi such things are frowned upon. Here, all of us are illegitimate. Ha ha. When is your idol coming from Mahishmathi?'

'Soon,' Mekhala said, looking away.

'Well, I shall get the foundation built the way he wants. But the design is strange, as well as the contraptions and machinery. I asked him if we can build it in the Kadarimandalam way. We have huge temples here, if you haven't noticed. But he said, no, he wants it to be done exactly the same way as he has described. Who am I to question him? I have promised to put a thousand people on the job. How big is the idol?'

'Much bigger than anything you can imagine,' Mekhala said, wondering how her father was going to pull off such an audacious plan.

## SEVEN

# Bijjala

'MAHADEVA, I DON'T want to discuss Rudra Bhatta's death now,' Bijjala fumed. The two brothers were standing in front of Maharaja Somadeva in the king's chamber.

'Nanna?' Mahadeva said without raising his head. 'What you are doing isn't right.'

'Son, Vikramadeva Mahadeva,' the maharaja said with a laugh, 'when will you grow up?'

Bijjala burned at the apparent softness in his father's voice when he addressed his incompetent brother. Bijjala's eyes flitted towards the dagger lying on the bed. For a moment, he thought of making a dash for it, grabbing it and piercing it deep into his father's heart. How would Mahadeva react? Had it been before Mahamakam, he would not have taken his brother into consideration at all. His brother was as skilful with his arms as Bijjala was, but Bijjala's confidence had always given him the edge. Mahadeva had always been a reluctant warrior, a coward in Bijjala's estimation. But, slowly, a grudging respect for Mahadeva had grown in Bijjala's mind. He was obstinate and stood strong for what he believed in.

It wasn't evident in the submissive and obedient way he was standing before their father now. His brother was hiding his real character; he was the hypocrite, thought Bijjala. It would be foolish to underestimate Mahadeva. He had almost caught Bijjala red-handed at the temple. No, he shouldn't act recklessly. He had to be patient. That was what Pattaraya had advised. If his attempt to kill the king failed, he was sure to lose his head. Bijjala looked away from his brother and fixed his gaze at the ceiling. He clasped his hands behind his back and stood with a nonchalant expression.

'I have ... I don't know. But there is more to Rudra Bhatta's death than we ... I am not sure, Nanna,' Mahadeva blurted.

'My brother doubts everyone. No one is as good as him, he thinks, but he does nothing. He just keeps thinking,' Bijjala said.

'Listen, sons.' Somadeva's voice had become grave. 'I have my reasons to do what I do. If I have rewarded that girl, Sivagami, it is because there is a reason for it. If I ordered her to duel with and kill Thimma, there was a reason for it. Understand that I am doing my rajadharma.'

'It isn't rajadharma to kill innocent people,' Mahadeva said.

'Oh? What is rajadharma then?' Somadeva asked with a chuckle.

'To protect the weak, to bring prosperity to the masses, to eradicate poverty, to ensure each citizen has enough to fill their stomachs, a roof over their heads and decent clothes to wear, to ensure women can live with dignity, to build hospitals, streets, schools, to protect trade guilds, to prevent usury, to promote compassion not only to humans but to all creations of God—'

The loud laughter of the king made Mahadeva halt. Bijjala, too, was laughing.

'Enough, son. Don't make me die of laughter,' Somadeva said.

Mahadeva drew himself to his full height. His submissive nature had vanished. He crossed his arms over his chest and said, 'Then, tell me—what according to you is rajadharma, Nanna?'

'You said nothing wrong, son. That is what you should keep saying to others, to the public. Your gurus have taught you well. But all this is for the consumption of the people. The moment you start believing in all this, your days as a ruler are numbered. There is only one rajadharma: survival. Do anything and everything to cling to power. The ruler who forgets that, is a dead ruler.'

'I don't believe in that,' Mahadeva said.

'You can believe anything you want. But the fool who believes the fire is cold will perish in it.'

'This is not the father I knew,' Mahadeva said with sadness.

'Grow up, son. You've known me only as a father. Now try knowing me as a king. Know that if you stand in my way of power, I might kill you too. And in a few years, you would also do the same thing.' Somadeva took the dagger in his hand. 'For example, your brother here was planning to plunge the dagger into my heart a few moments ago.'

Bijjala gave a start. Somadeva flung the dagger at Bijjala. Mahadeva gasped. The dagger struck the wall behind Bijjala, a hair's breadth away from his cheek. Bijjala gulped in fear. The king walked up to him.

'The only thing that prevented your brother was the thought of how you would react. He feared you, Mahadeva. He was scared you would perhaps injure him or stand witness to his patricide, thus cutting him off from the throne that could belong to either of you. He needn't have bothered.' Somadeva plucked the dagger from the wall and kept it at Bijjala's throat. Bijjala started sweating.

'Had this fool attempted anything, he would've been dead before he moved an inch. You're an unlucky man, Mahadeva. Your path to the throne would have been easy had this brother of yours gone ahead with his plan. Isn't that so, Bijjala?'

Bijjala looked down.

'But my son Bijjala seems to be growing smarter these days. He has learnt to control his impulses. He has a long way to go, but it is a good start.'

With a chuckle that sent a shiver down Bijjala's spine, Somadeva removed the dagger from Bijjala's throat.

'Mahadeva, I have a few questions to ask you.'

The king walked back to his ornate chair and sat with his right leg crossed over his left. He played with the dagger as he spoke. The lemon-sized diamond embedded in the handle of the dagger caught the light of the torches and sparkled.

'What happened to Kattappa?'

'I ... I lost him. I got distracted with the Rudra Bhatta situation,' Mahadeva said with stooping shoulders. 'My men are combing the city. We will find him.'

'There is no need. He has left the city, and so has his brother.'

'His brother is dead,' Bijjala said.

The king scoffed. 'Both of you have a long way to go

before even aspiring to be crown prince, let alone king. I freed Kattappa because I knew he would lead us to his brother. But now I am inclined to think the slave has made a fool of all of us. He has cleverly taken his brother from Mahishmathi. Most probably, as we are talking, he and his brother are planning the next rebellion in the forest.'

'What can a bunch of tribesmen do to mighty Mahishmathi?' Bijjala said, relieved both Kattappa and Shivappa had run away.

'Mahishmathi may not be as mighty as you think. Even the elephant fears the mouse. Mahadeva, I want you to find out what Sivagami has been doing. I am sure she has some kind of plan in mind. She came with the intention of killing me, but something has changed. She is aiming for something bigger, something which her father attempted and failed. The death of Rudra Bhatta is a deliberate act. It suited me well to lay rest to some rumours, so I used it to our advantage. Mahadeva, I want you to instruct your men to keep an eye on her and tell me what she is up to. She is asking around about a book, and if it is what I think it is, that book is of supreme importance to the existence of Mahishmathi. I want you to arrest her and bring her to me the moment she gets the book. That doesn't mean you tail her like a puppy. Your men should do it. Develop your network, your own loyal men who will serve you in the future. They should be able to do your work even when you aren't available. Until then, give her a free hand. Be the sweet, loving prince charming and steal her heart, but make sure your spies follow her like a shadow.'

Mahadeva didn't reply for a long time. The king observed him keenly. 'I haven't learnt such duplicity,' Mahadeva said finally.

'Then learn it now. Or forget about holding any position of power in Mahishmathi,' the king said.

'I don't care about power.' Mahadeva's eyes flashed in anger.

'Ah, what do you care about then, my son?' Somadeva said in a voice dripping with sarcasm.

'I care about the truth. I care about doing the right thing.'

'And without power, how are you going to do anything about maintaining the truth or doing the right thing, my boy?'

Mahadeva shifted on his feet and looked down. Bijjala smiled at his brother's discomfiture.

'Truth always wins ultimately,' Mahadeva said.

'Very good,' Somadeva smiled. 'Life will teach you about different shades of truth. Now I don't have the time to discuss philosophy with you. I am giving you an important task. The most important one in your life, perhaps. Don't mess this up with your misty-eyed idealism. Do you remember what Bijjala told us about the racket Guha was running, paying divers to fish stones from the beds of river Mahishi?'

'And you ignored me. Your officials are cheating you, Nanna, they are all corrupt. I uncovered such a big scam and you did nothing,' Bijjala interjected enthusiastically.

'They are working on my orders,' the king said.

'What?'

'There are things that you two should know and you will be told when the time comes. Parameswara will give you more details, Mahadeva. Your job is to bring the Kali statue from a village in Bhoomipathi Guha's land to Mahishmathi.'

'But isn't it the duty of Akkundaraya and Guha to bring the statue?' Bijjala asked.

'There won't be any Guha or Akkundaraya the moment the statue is loaded on the ship.'

'Oh, so my brother is going to eliminate them?' Bijjala asked, excitedly.

'Leave it to me how to deal with the bhoomipathis. Your job, Mahadeva, is to ensure the Kali statue is brought here. There may be things—how can I put it—there could be things that may not suit your tender mind.'

Mahadeva stared at his father.

'Learn to harden yourself, my brother Vikramadeva Mahadeva,' Bijjala said sarcastically. 'Rajaneeti is not for the faint-hearted. If you are not up to the task, take sanyas. Join that guru's ashram. What is his name?'

'Guru Dharmapala, and he is an enlightened soul. I heard you also used to visit him on new moon days, though I have never seen you there, Anna,' Mahadeva snapped back.

Bijjala was taken aback. How much did his brother know?

Somadeva said, 'You two can argue about gurus and gods later. Mahadeva, as time passes, there will be more tasks for you to carry out, that you may find abhorrent. But who said governing a country was an easy task?'

'I will do my duty diligently, but I will do nothing that is against my conscience. I will do nothing that is adharma,' Mahadeva said with a stiff bow.

'Protecting your people is the biggest dharma of a ruler. I am sure you will do a good job. Remember, if things go wrong, it will be the end of Mahishmathi. We are staring at a huge crisis, and if you fail to bring the statue and its contents, you will be tried like a traitor, and hanged like one.'

Mahadeva looked at his brother smiling at him and then at the grim face of his father. He bowed again and turned to leave. At the door, he paused and said, 'I would prefer to be hanged than live with the guilt of doing what is wrong.'

'I will hang you when I feel the need to do so,' Somadeva said. 'Now do as I ordered. It wasn't a request from a father. It was an order of the maharaja of Mahishmathi.'

Mahadeva stared at his father for a moment. Then, with exaggerated formality, he bowed deep. 'Yes, Your Highness.'

'And Mahadeva,' the king said with a thin smile. 'Here is some fatherly advice for you. What wins ultimately, will be called the truth.'

Mahadeva stepped outside and closed the door shut with deliberate politeness. Somadeva turned to his elder son.

'So?' the king said.

'I ... I am sorry, Nanna. I ... I didn't mean to ...' Bijjala's glance slipped to the dagger in the king's hand. Somadeva flung it on to the bed.

'Let me give you some fatherly advice as well. Your face shouldn't reflect what you're thinking—learn to be more deadpan. For instance, you're now wondering how you can scuttle your brother's success. You can't, because I am sending you on a different mission. I am sending you far away.'

'I don't want to go anywhere away from Mahishmathi. You're always sending me away. I spent six months in the jungles hunting for Pattaraya. It is unfair that my brother gets the easy job. He just has to transport the statue, something any boatman can do,' Bijjala protested.

Somadeva sighed. 'Always peeved, aren't we? I am sending you on a task that requires your kind of ruthlessness.'

Bijjala tried to suppress his rising excitement. Was this about the stones that Pattaraya had spoken about? The king walked to the window and gazed at Gauriparvat. A slanting beam of sunlight illuminated his face. The shadow of the king stretched on the floor. Bijjala side-stepped the shadow and moved closer to his father.

'You remember the day you came back with the severed head?'

'Yes, that of Pattaraya, Nanna,' Bijjala said.

'Hmm. Maybe it was of Pattaraya.'

'You don't trust me, Nanna?' Bijjala cried.

'I don't trust myself, son. That is why I remain king.'

'I killed him with this hand.'

'Fine, so be it. Good job. Now I am giving you a better task. Bhoomipathi Durgappa, the one who mans the fort of Gauriparvat, has joined hands with Khanipathi Hidumba, the dwarf in charge of the Gauriparvat mines.'

'We mine the Gauriparvat? Isn't the mountain holy?'

'Politics is about mining religion and selling what is holy, son. Yes, we mine it and milk it. I want you to go to Gauriparvat. The way is a secret. There will be many obstacles and you may have to persuade Bhoomipathi Akkundaraya to show you the path. He may have to be bought or forced to give away his secret. Every bhoomipathi has a fiefdom, and they guard it fiercely, so it won't be an easy task to persuade him. I leave it to your skills. Getting Akkundaraya to take you to Gauriparvat is half the task. Hidumba and Durgappa are negotiating for their pound of flesh. You have to use your persuasion skills again to make them more ... patriotic. They have a huge cache of Gaurikanta stones. Your job is to bring the stones to Guha's land, where Mahadeva will be ready with the statue. Bring the statue to Mahishmathi. The public believes the Vaithalikas sunk the statue during the Mahamakam coup. The princes of Mahishmathi will bring the statue back, and the maharaja of Mahishmathi will welcome Amma Gauri to her holy city. We'll make it a grand spectacle.'

'I'll do it,' Bijjala said, 'but, what is in it for me?'

Somadeva turned to his son with an amused smile. 'I have a feeling that you have the potential to become a good ruler. I liked your question—what's in it for you. I hate people who do things selflessly. They are so unpredictable and unreliable.'

'Like my brother?' Bijjala asked.

Maharaja Somadeva burst out laughing. 'You can't hide your envy of him for a moment, can you?'

Bijjala looked down. The maharaja said, 'Fine, here is what is in it for you. You will be the commander-in-chief of the Mahishmathi army. General Hiranya is retiring. I may make him a governor in one of the vassal kingdoms. You will succeed him.'

'Crown prince? Can I become crown prince?'

'You're in a tearing hurry, son. I will decide when the time comes.'

'The Gaurikanta stones,' Bijjala said, with growing excitement, 'are they very precious stones?'

'More precious than you can imagine. Take your best men with you. I look forward to the day when my sons bring the statue back here.'

'I will kill anyone who stands in my way. I will smash them to pulp,' Bijjala said enthusiastically.

'Son, learn not to spell out your intentions and keep your excitement in check. Never shed blood unless it is necessary,' Somadeva said with a smile and dismissed Bijjala.

The king watched his son leaving his chamber. He sighed and picked up the dagger again. Somadeva held it near a lamp and studied it. He saw a spot of rust near the hilt. When he pressed down on the spot, the dagger snapped into two. The king opened the window and threw the pieces out. Gauriparvat looked on impassively. A thunder cloud was forming at its crest and Somadeva could see flashes of lightning over the peak. A blue ring of light rose from the top of the peak and vanished into the clouds. With a shudder, he slammed the window shut and sat on the bed with his hands supporting his head, saying a silent prayer. He was haunted by a premonition. Had he just sent his elder son into a death trap?

## EIGHT

# Mahadeva

GURU DHARMAPALA'S WORDS hadn't pacified him much. The guru had advised him to be forthright. Confront Sivagami and ask her the truth. Don't let doubts fester in you, the guru had advised. Take life by its horns, don't cower in fear. The words had sounded deep in the presence of the guru, in the holy precincts of the ashram, but they lost their gravity and appeared mundane once he was out of the premises. Life had a way of knocking away all the profundity from the words of gurus and mocking at the 'truths' of scriptures. That is why religion hid in the darkness of temples and in secluded monasteries.

He was unable to face Sivagami after the events at the sabha. The more he thought about it, the more suspicious Sivagami's behaviour seemed. Why was she being so friendly with Bijjala? Why Bijjala, of all people? He was sure Bijjala was somehow involved in the whole sordid affair. Was Sivagami also involved in it? Were they making a fool of him and laughing behind his back? The image of Bijjala taking Sivagami's hand and helping her into the chariot flashed in his mind. Mahadeva felt a knot forming in his stomach. *She can't do this to me,* he thought. Mahadeva decided he would confront her, but doubts assailed him. He was scared about how she would react and was afraid of losing her forever. What if his doubts turned out to be true? *What if they turned out to be false,* another voice in his mind said. Either way, would she ever forgive him? Mahadeva felt he would go insane.

Mahadeva walked through the bustling streets, his mind in a whirl. Suddenly, he felt a tap on his shoulder. It was his spy, Trivikrama, now dressed as a street vendor and selling sweets. Mahadeva purchased a laddoo from him and, while handing over change, Trivikrama whispered, 'She is searching for someone or something.'

Mahadeva nodded and instructed him to continue to keep a close eye on Sivagami, all the time feeling like a swine for spying on the woman he loved.

'I have reports of that eunuch Keki loitering around the home of the vaidya,' Trivikrama continued.

A current of shock passed through Mahadeva. 'What?' he asked loudly, making a few heads turn. 'And you just left him there?' he continued in a hushed voice.

Trivikrama's face showed guilt. 'I saw my subject passing by and I followed her, leaving the eunuch. I thought—'

Mahadeva didn't wait for Trivikrama to complete his sentence. He hurried through the crowd towards the vaidya's home. It was stupid of him to have left Akhila there. He should have guessed something like this would happen. By the time he turned into the street where the vaidya's home was situated, he was running. He saw the chariot of the vaidya was not there, and his heart sank. Except for a few chickens searching for earthworms in the courtyard, there was no one around, and the vaidya's home wore a deserted look. Mahadeva ran in, and the chickens scattered about, clucking in protest. Mahadeva grabbed the rope of the bell and yanked it hard.

'Who is that scoundrel? Don't you have manners?' Mahadeva heard a yell from inside, and then the door opened. The junior disciple of the vaidya looked at Mahadeva for a moment in stunned silence, his mouth agape. Mahadeva ran in, ignoring his profuse apologies. He hurried through the dimly lit corridor, peeping into the small dark rooms where patients lay on mats. The disciple ran behind him, asking how he could help.

Mahadeva turned to him, shook him by his shoulder and asked, 'Where is that girl?'

The disciple looked at him without comprehension. 'The girl I had brought here?' Mahadeva's patience was running thin. The disciple pointed to the far end of the corridor. Mahadeva ran there and saw that the door stood half open. He could hear the sound of someone retching within. He pushed the door open and rushed in. There was no one on the mat on the floor. He turned around and saw Akhila cowering in a corner.

Her face had turned grey and she was in absolute shock. The girl's dress was drenched in her vomit. Ignoring the mess, Mahadeva ran to her and held her by her shoulders. 'Are you all right? Are you all right?' he asked. The girl shook her head and then looked towards one side. Mahadeva followed her gaze. The next moment, Akhila threw up, spraying Mahadeva with a foul-smelling thick liquid. Akhila broke into sobs, her eyes offering apologies. Mahadeva held her head close to his chest and pacified her. 'It's nothing. Don't worry.'

The disciple came up and said, 'Please move, Prince. The girl is sick. Allow me to treat her.'

Akhila's skin had a blue-ish tinge now. Mahadeva stood up and the disciple sat on the mat near Akhila and started checking her. Mahadeva stood behind him, tense and angry. He looked around and noticed that something was behind the curtain. He darted quickly towards it, but before he could grab it, Keki stepped out in the open.

'I can't stand the smell of vomit, Prince. That is why I was standing there.'

Mahadeva slapped Keki across her face. Keki was livid. 'You slapped a eunuch? You slapped a kinnara? Curse be upon you. Don't you know we can never be punished by anyone other than the king? How dare you slap me?'

Mahadeva slapped her again and the force of it threw her back. She lay sprawled on the floor. Keki started beating her chest and cried, 'I was trying to help. And the hero comes and beats me for no reason. Ask the girl, ask the girl. I was trying to save her, and this is how I get repaid. You, a Vikramadeva, *puh*,' Keki spat on the floor.

Mahadeva was about to grab her and drag her to the durbar when the vaidya's disciple said, 'It is fear that has made her so sick. I don't think she has been poisoned.' Akhila's body was trembling and her teeth chattered. She started screaming in terror when the disciple tried to put her back on the mat. Mahadeva asked him to stop. There was something wrong. He moved towards the mat.

Keki cried, 'Careful, my dear prince.'

Mahadeva lifted the pillow and a scorpion crawled out. Akhila screamed in terror.

'See,' Keki cried. 'I did nothing. I was about to help her. I was about to catch it when you barged in and broke my teeth, my bones, my spine—you beat a poor eunuch. You may be a big prince, but know that my swami is elder to you. I will complain to my swami. Prince Bijjala will—'

Mahadeva caught the scorpion and it stung him. He cried out in pain and shook his hand, dropping it. It ran towards a crevice. The disciple grabbed a copper vessel from the corner and threw it at it. He missed, but the water that fell made the scorpion run towards Akhila. She yelled hysterically.

Mahadeva said, 'No, no, don't kill it.' He moved to grab it again and it stung him on his fist.

'What are you doing, swami?' the disciple asked in dismay. 'It is poisonous!'

'Stinging is its dharma, saving its life is mine,' Mahadeva said, as held onto the scorpion that twitched in his fist. He ran out through the narrow corridor.

'Aha, aha,' Keki mocked, following him. 'A scorpion's sting is not fatal for an adult, but the prince wants to play the hero. The prince won't hurt a scorpion that stings, but thinks nothing about murdering a poor eunuch. Beating me is your dharma, prince? Kill me, kill me fully. Ouch, my teeth are shaking. My spine is broken.'

Ignoring Keki, Mahadeva threw the scorpion into the courtyard. He turned to the disciple. 'How did this eunuch enter here?'

'I flew in through the window. I am an angel. I can fly.' Keki flapped her arms and cackled.

'She came as a patient to see the vaidya,' the disciple said, baffled. 'I didn't know she had stayed back when the vaidya went out for his home visits.'

'Aha, is this the king's palace of Mahishmathi for me to want to stay back? The place stinks with the smell of medicines and herbs. Do you grind dead rats in the medicines, little vaidya? Why does it stink so much?' Keki sniffed. 'Hey, don't glare at me like that. I will get scared. Listen, little vaidya, tell the prince that I had no intention of staying in this Indraloka at all. I heard the girl scream when I was leaving. I called for you, but you didn't come. I have a soft heart. I hate to see anyone crying. I rushed in, and can you imagine what I found. That scorpion, ugly black thing, on her pillow. The same one whose—what is that—ah, dharma it is to sting. I was about to kill it when the great prince Vikramadeva Mahadeva barged in and started beating me. Let Prince Bijjala hear about how a poor eunuch has been treated for helping a poor girl, and we will soon see the fun. I can't even imagine how angry he will be.'

Mahadeva fumed, knowing well that everything the eunuch said was a lie, but it was also plausible. He wished the girl would talk. She still appeared to be in shock, but one thing was evident. She feared Keki. Everything pointed to something sinister, and his brother was involved in it. He was sure the eunuch had brought in the scorpion, venomous enough to kill the girl. Keki stood with an amused smile as the vaidya's disciple applied a herbal paste on the prince's hand and dressed it.

'It will pain for a few days, Prince,' Keki said to Mahadeva. 'Don't eat lemon or curd. Oh, what am I saying. That is for a bite from a rabid dog. You shouldn't eat lemon for ninety days, how much ever you wish for it, if a rabid dog bites you. After ninety days, you can't eat it how much ever you wish for it. You know why? You will be dead by then.' Keki cackled. 'Forgive my chattiness, Prince. I mean no disrespect. But you owe me a laugh for my jokes at least. I bear no ill will to you. You are the prince. You can beat us, whip us, even behead us, the poor people. If you laugh once in a while at this poor eunuch's jokes, that would make our sore hearts happy. Isn't it? Never mind. I think it must be paining too much—you look so grumpy. I am leaving now. Little vaidya, take care of the girl, eh? Namaskaram.' Keki folded her hands and fluttered her eyelashes.

The eunuch walked away with deliberate sensuality and then, at the gate, she started laughing.

'Prince, prince,' Keki called. 'You know what happened to the scorpion that bit you? The same one you saved so bravely? Come and see this. My swami Bijjala will have a great laugh when I tell him this.'

Keki left and Mahadeva stood, angry, helpless and feeling insulted. But he couldn't punish anyone for being sarcastic with him. That would be unethical. He looked at what Keki had shown him. The poor scorpion was being eaten by the chickens. The words of his father, the same words he had thought were amoral, came to him with a vengeance: there is only one dharma that is true, always—survival. Survival was the greatest dharma. The chickens were demonstrating it to him. Feeling like a fool, Mahadeva walked back in.

The girl was not safe here. He considered taking her to the palace. But if his suspicion about Bijjala and Keki turned out to be correct, the palace would be even more dangerous for her. After some thought, he arrived at a conclusion. There was only one place in Mahishmathi where the girl would be protected. A place where Bijjala would never dare to go. He went to the girl and said, 'I am taking you away from here to a place that you would like.'

The girl didn't reply. She sat in a corner, her arms wrapped around her knees, looking down at her toes. The trembling of her lips indicated her agitation. His heart went out to her. He held out his hand, and when she made no move to take it, he gently held her wrist and helped her get up. Hand in hand, they walked through the streets of Mahishmathi, ignoring curious onlookers who whispered to each other, till they reached their destination.

'Guru Dharmapala, would you give asylum to this poor girl?' Mahadeva asked the guru, who was staring at the girl with astonishment. The girl burst into tears and ran to the guru. The guru hugged her close and Mahadeva watched as both of them sobbed. The compassion of the guru overwhelmed Mahadeva. How much love he was showing to a strange girl. He wished he could muster up such love to all and everyone, without bothering whether they were his own people or strangers or foes. Mahadeva fell to the floor and prayed with folded hands, 'Guru, you are the light, you are the way. The unselfish, all-encompassing love that you show to one and all—bless me to possess an iota of it, and I shall be saved. Oh Guru, I am so inadequate. Teach me how to overcome my selfishness, my jealousy, my arrogance. I beat an eunuch in anger, without being sure whether she was guilty or not. I surrender to you, Guru. Make me a good man.'

NINE

# Sivagami

'WHAT DO YOU mean you don't know where Akhila is?' Sivagami asked Revamma. She was livid.

'The girl is missing, and I have complained to the dandakaras,' Revamma said, applying lime to her betel leaf. She foraged in her betel box, picked out a betel nut and examined it in the sun. Her indifferent demeanour infuriated Sivagami.

'Don't you have any responsibility to find her?' Sivagami fumed.

'What can I do if the girl runs away? You too ran away when you were here. Your friend Kamakshi ran away, too, got raped and killed. Someone might have raped and killed the girl. Maybe you should enquire with the dandakaras,' Revamma said, thrusting the betel leaf into her mouth and chewing it. An infuriated Sivagami rushed to her, but was held back by Neelappa.

'No point talking to the witch, daughter,' Neelappa said.

Sivagami went back to the chariot and sat there, wringing her hands. She didn't know where to search and whom to ask. There was no point going to the dandakaras. They would conduct a perfunctory investigation and hush up the incident. She thought of asking Mahadeva for help, but he had been behaving strangely since the Rudra Bhatta incident. The rajaguru's death had opened up a chasm between them. She heard the rattle of a chariot from behind, and the next moment, it was running parallel to hers.

'Devi, you look worried,' she heard the voice of Bijjala. He was standing in the speeding chariot driven by the eunuch Keki. Before she could react, Bijjala jumped into her chariot and was standing beside her. Keki's chariot fell back and Bijjala waited for her to speak. She was embarrassed by the sudden incursion and irritated that he had seen her at such a vulnerable moment.

'My sister is missing,' Sivagami said.

'Your sister?' Bijjala asked.

'The youngest daughter of Thimma, swami,' Neelappa answered from his seat. He swished the whip and made the horse run faster.

'Oh, wasn't she living with you? I don't remember her face,' Bijjala said. Sivagami didn't reply. How could she say that Akhila had refused to live with her, that she had left her in the orphanage, and she had gone missing from there?

'She was in the orphanage,' Neelappa answered for her.

Bijjala exclaimed 'Orphanage? Why should Bhoomipathi Sivagami devi's sister stay in an orphanage?'

Sivagami muttered, 'She ... hates me. She refused to stay with me.'

'Hates you? How can anyone hate you, devi?'

Sivagami stole a glance at him. Was the prince playing with her? What did he think her to be? A fool to be taken in by his fake concern?

'Yes, because I killed her father to gain the bhoomipathi post,' she said abruptly, looking in front. She expected him to come back with some homily, something mundane like 'anyone in your place would've done that' or 'that was destiny'. But there was an awkward silence, except for the sound of the horse's hooves on the paved streets and the rattle of the wheels. She wished he would say something. His lips were pressed in a grim line, as if striving hard not to comment on her plight.

'What is past can't be changed,' he said finally, surprising her. 'Let's try to find your sister.'

Sivagami was taken aback by the calm and composed voice of Bijjala. She was beginning to see him in a new light.

'My brother found a girl near that Rakta Kali temple where Rudra Bhatta was doing his sacrifice.'

Sivagami's heart skipped a beat. Was Akhila the intended victim of Rudra Bhatta's sacrifice? Why hadn't Mahadeva told her about this? What was he keeping from her?

'Where is Akhila now?'

'Akhila?' Bijjala asked. 'Oh ... is that the name of your sister? I think he took her to the vaidya's mansion.'

'Is ... is she injured?' Sivagami was feeling weak.

'Probably. Why would she be taken to the vaidya's home otherwise?'

Sivagami yelled at Neelappa to stop the chariot. 'Mama, turn back. We need to go to the vaidya's mansion.'

When they reached the mansion, the disciple of the vaidya said the prince had taken Akhila away. The prince had told him to inform the vaidya that he was taking her to Guru Dharmapala's ashram, he said.

They rushed to the ashram but were stopped by disciples at the gate.

'Guru is meditating and will not see anyone,' the monk at the gate said.

'This is an emergency,' Sivagami pleaded, but the monk wouldn't relent. Bijjala jumped out of the chariot and shoved the monk out of their way. He grabbed Sivagami's arm and drew his sword from the scabbard.

'Give way,' Bijjala growled, swinging his sword, and the monks who had come to see what the commotion was about scattered in fear. Bijjala and Sivagami barged into the room of Guru Dharmapala. Akhila was sitting beside the guru and she cowered in fear when she saw them. She hid behind the guru. Mahadeva, who was sitting on the floor, scrambled up when he saw Bijjala brandishing his sword.

Sivagami stood at the door, stunned beyond belief. It was the first time she was seeing Guru Dharmapala up close. As the princes argued with each other, she walked to the guru, who sat with a serene smile on his lips. Her lips slowly formed the word: 'Raghava.'

'Yes, daughter,' the guru said and smiled. 'But now, Guru Dharmapala.'

---

She was seated in Guru Dharmapala's meditation room, facing him. Raghava, the boy she had grown up with, with whom she had fought and played and who had broken her trust by proposing to her, was now a guru who cared nothing about worldly things. He spoke in a strange way, and he looked different—there was no Raghava left in him. But Sivagami was worried that he would feel hatred for her, like Akhila did, and hold her responsible for his parents' deaths.

'He wanted me to kill him. Uncle Thimma wanted me ...' Sivagami said and broke down.

'I am not the same Raghava, daughter. Once I left you, I wandered around for a long time until I met my guru. He showed me the path. Now I am here to lead people towards the ultimate truth. So many people live in darkness and I decided, instead of choosing moksha, I should stay back and try and show them the way.'

He continued, 'No one dies, Sivagami. We are all immortals. Only the body withers away. I am not this body. Neither are you your body. You are deeper than that, I am deeper than that. In another plane, there is neither you nor me. There is the ultimate truth, the Brahmam. We are all mere reflections of the Brahmam. In the same way that the sun is reflected in rivers, lakes, seas, we are all reflections of the ultimate truth, Brahmam. Does the sun that is seen in a pond exist? It does and it doesn't. But does the real sun in the sky exist? It does. Life is like that. We are mere reflectors of Him who pervades the universe. Mere death or birth doesn't concern me.'

'They were your parents,' Sivagami said. 'And mine too,' she added, looking away.

'Those who have gone have finished their role in this play of life. We all must act our parts in this play with all our hearts. But know that this is not real, and when it is over, the hero, the villain, the joker will go back to the real life, the eternal life, the one that dissolves in Brahmam. Those who don't know this truth will keep playing different roles again and again, before different audiences in different playhouses,' Guru Dharmapala said.

Sivagami longed for the old Raghava and not this stranger who talked incomprehensible things and upon whose feet kings and princes fell for blessings. She stared at the image of entwining serpents that decorated the wall behind the guru. With their hoods spread out and their blank eyes, the stone cobras seemed to glare at her.

'Akhila will be safe here with me.'

'She always looked up to you, Raghava,' Sivagami said.

'Daughter, my disciples call me Vishwaguru, the teacher of the universe. They are mad,' Raghava said and laughed. 'You may call me Nityaguru, the eternal teacher, if you want. Or you can call me Guru.'

Sivagami watched him as he laughed again. He ran his fingers through his waist-length jet black beard and adjusted his elaborate turban. He took a metal polished mirror from under the tiger skin he was sitting on and gazed at himself. He saw her staring at him and smiled at her.

'Daughter, Akhila will be as safe as any other inmate here. She doesn't stay here as my sister but as a fellow traveller in this unending quest for the ultimate truth. Would you join me on this wonderful journey, daughter?'

From outside, devotional songs praising Guru Dharmapala could be heard. *Guru Dharmapala, Jaya Satyachara,* the disciples chanted, again and again. Sivagami felt if she listened to it for a minute longer, she would go mad.

'I don't know what you have become, Raghava. I thought I would find my brother here, and what I have found is a strange man talking stranger things.'

Sivagami stood up. Guru Dharmapala laughed aloud. 'I am what I am, Sivagami. But for you, I shall try to be a friend and not a guru. If you want me to play that role, I shall play that role, but only for you. A self-realised soul can play any role. All right, I know you hate such "mystic musings",' he said and laughed again. 'Sivagami, the eternal rebel. So—what do you want to talk about?'

'Nothing,' Sivagami said, and started to walk out of the room. Guru Dharmapala moved swiftly and blocked her way.

'Sivagami,' he whispered, and her heart skipped a beat. She was scared that he would grab her hand and declare his love for her. She was yet to get over the shock of his first proposal.

'Don't be scared.' Guru Dharmapala had vanished and Raghava had appeared again. After a pause, staring into her eyes, he said, 'You do need a good friend, Sivagami. And this Raghava will always be there for you. I know you love someone.'

Sivagami was startled.

'Mahadeva has confessed to me about your relationship and I wholeheartedly approve of it. In the house of Mahishmathi, he is the only one with a heart. Perhaps in the whole empire of Mahishmathi, Prince Mahadeva is the only one who is compassionate, brave and kind. You need such a man in your life, Sivagami—that is, if you still want to dwell in this world of illusion. You are not meant for the spiritual path, and there is nothing wrong in that. You are destined for bigger things in this material world, Sivagami. I can see the future, and yours is entwined with that of Mahadeva. But something is troubling you. If you feel you can share it, please tell me.'

Sivagami started reluctantly, still suspicious of him. However, Raghava made her open up without her even noticing it. The transformation from Guru Dharmapala, the mystic who had spoken confounding things, to the friend and brother she had once adored, was miraculous. The fake laugh vanished, and in its place was a genuine smile.

When Sivagami was done, he sat running his fingers through his abundant beard, deep in thought.

'I can understand your dilemma, Sivagami,' Raghava said, breaking the long silence. 'I am happy that you no longer want vengeance against the king, but rather to fulfil your father's dream. Your actions should make the sacrifice of Devaraya and Thimma meaningful. From what you said, I believe this empire is built on adharma. What is built on untruth can never last; it will collapse on its own.'

'A boy who trusted me is trapped in Gauriparvat along with, I fear, hundreds of innocent children. I want to reach there but I don't know how.'

'Hmm ... I hope I am not breaking the confidence of Mahadeva by telling you this. The poor prince confided in me that he is worried his father has given some crucial responsibility to his elder brother. It wasn't jealousy that made Mahadeva worried. Mahadeva fears that if his father chose Bijjala over him to do this task, it could be because it involves something immoral, something that Mahadeva would refuse to do.'

Raghava paused for a second, and then said, 'Bijjala. Prince Bijjala. He is the key. The king has asked him to go to Gauriparvat. And beware of Mahadeva.'

'What?'

'Don't get me wrong. Mahadeva may have sincere love for you, but that won't prevent him from arresting you if you take one step against Mahishmathi. Why do you think he has been behaving strangely with you the last few days?'

'What should I do now?'

'Follow your heart. That's the advice I give everyone. If you think your love for Mahadeva is more important than the vow you took in your parents' name, the path is easy. You need only say "yes" to Mahadeva and lead the rest of your life as the beloved of the prince of Mahishmathi. The king may even get that boy who has been taken to Gauriparvat freed as a wedding gift. Who knows, you may even be the maharani one day, if Mahadeva succeeds to the throne. The other path is difficult. If you believe you have a duty to fulfil, then you need to do whatever it takes to redeem your father and live or die to accomplish what men like your father and my father dreamt about. Taking the difficult path will be full of heartbreak. It is trial by fire. You may be scorched to death, or you may rise out of the ashes. But whatever is the result, it will change you.'

'I may become a revered goddess or an accursed devil,' Sivagami said and laughed, trying to make light of the rising tension in the pit of her stomach.

'Or perhaps both.' Raghava smiled back. 'But promise me you won't retreat if a situation arrives, which it is sure to sooner or later, when you will have to hurt those you love for the sake of victory.'

'If you mean whether my love for Mahadeva will stand in my way—'

'It won't be about just Mahadeva. We don't know how the dice will fall and how the opponents will move their pieces in this game. You may be forced to do unpalatable things, utter unspeakable words and be ruthless, perhaps even cruel. Read about the Mahabharata war again and again. How even the honest had to lie, the noblest had to cheat, the cruellest had to be kind and the purest had to be evil—for the game changes everyone. There is no going back. We are at the cusp of history. A mega empire is tottering. An empire that spread like a giant banyan tree, that withstood many storms and which didn't allow a blade of grass to grow underneath—its roots are being cut. You are going to strike at its roots. The tree may collapse on you and crush you and many more. When it falls, the earth will shake, the termites and snakes and scorpions that hid in its crevices will crawl out. The birds that made nests in its branches will find their homes destroyed. The landscape will change forever. But the banyan has to die for the grass to grow. Do you have the heart for it? Will your hand be steady when the time comes to shoot the arrow that would perhaps pierce a loved one's heart? Or would you be like Arjuna, who felt at the beginning of the great war that it isn't worth killing his cousins and relatives, and that he would rather take sanyas?'

'If I feel so, ever, be my Krishna,' Sivagami said and smiled.

---

Gomati stood before Guru Dharmapala with folded hands. The comatose Uthanga lay in a palanquin next to her. The guru read the scroll she had carried from Sivagami. It read, 'Please take care of this poor woman and the boy Uthanga, whom I was caring for. It is a long journey I am going on. If I don't come back, please protect them. This woman's husband is out to kill her and you can see for yourself the boy's condition. Both owe their misfortune to me.'

The guru gestured to a disciple to take Gomati and the boy in. Gomati thanked him profusely.

'I am willing to do any job, swami,' she said.

'"Serve" is the right word, daughter. Here everything is done by volunteers. Each is a servant of another. No one expects payment, no one is given one. I don't offer a few copper coins. I offer the world to anyone who takes asylum in me,' the guru said.

'As you say, swami,' Gomati said and bowed.

She was thankful to Sivagami for arranging this safehouse for her, to protect her from her murderous husband. The only thing Sivagami had asked in return from Gomati was to become her eyes and ears inside the ashram. Gomati couldn't understand why Sivagami wanted a spy in a holy place, but she was ready to do anything for Sivagami.

# TEN

# Kattappa

KATTAPPA WAS TIED to the prow of the boat and barely able to move his limbs. He still wouldn't say a word to Ally. In the initial days, Kattappa had refused to take food from her hands. Later, when she had stopped crying and pleading with him to have something, and said she would leave it to him to choose whether to live or starve to death, he allowed her to feed him once every two days. When he asked where she was taking him, she would not answer; and she ignored his pleas that she kill him. She rowed the boat in silence, and he withered under the sun and rain. He endured with dignity the pain in his wrists where the rope cut into the sores that had developed, the numbness in his limbs from sitting in the same position, and the splitting headache. What broke his spirit was the shame of depending on her for his bodily needs. When she refused to free his hands so he could relieve himself, his love soured into hatred.

Kattappa's heart sank when the boat took a turn. He could see the crown of the Kali statue peeping out of the jungle canopy. As the boat moved, the statue became more visible. The sight was spectacular. Amma Kali in her most fierce form, with coiling snakes forming her hair, her eyes glowing in the sun, tongue drawn out, dozens of arms carrying various weapons—swords, trishuls, spears, bows. It towered over the jungle. Hundreds of men milled about like ants, drawing carts filled with stones over a ramp that extended to the riverbank, where divers were piling up stones that they had recovered from the riverbed. The rhythmic *hey-hos* of the slaves became clearer as the boat approached the site.

The Kali statue was much bigger than the one Kattappa had destroyed a year ago. He was terrified to see Amma Kali standing tall again. He silently begged for forgiveness for what he had done the last time. After the destruction of the Amma Kali statue, his life had become worse. Kattappa wept as the boat glided towards the shore. 'Forgive me, Amma. Don't punish me again,' he cried silently. 'Why, Amma, why me? But who am I to question your will? If possible, forgive this sinner,' Kattappa pleaded with the distant Kali statue. Its head seemed to touch the clouds, but even from that height, he felt as if mother Kali were glowering at him, the sinner who had dared to destroy her statue once. Kattappa shuddered with fear.

The slave turned his head when he heard a commotion. A group of soldiers were hurrying down the ramp. Beside him, Ally stood in waist-deep water, watching them. As they neared, Kattappa resigned himself to his fate. Amma Kali had no intention of forgiving him, he understood. The worst was yet to come in his life. He closed his eyes and bent his head in guilt and humility. 'I accept, I accept,' he whispered.

He heard the crack of a slap, and the next moment, Ally had fallen on him. The boat shook and he opened his eyes.

'Bitch. How dare you cheat me? I told you to come here, and you vanished somewhere?' The man was slapping Ally repeatedly.

'Stop. Stop. See what have I brought you,' Ally cried, trying to stave off his hands. The man turned and looked at what Ally was pointing at. Kattappa watched him: he had never thought he would see those accursed eyes again.

'Bhalle besh, sabash, sabash. Who do we have here?' Jeemotha waded through the water and came up to Kattappa. He lifted Kattappa's chin. 'My favourite slave. Kattappa.'

---

Ally's scream pierced the air. She was in the grip of Bhoomipathi Guha. She fought fiercely and managed to slip from his clutches. Guha swung his sword and missed. Jeemotha cursed and dove at Guha. For a brief moment, they both disappeared under water. They came back up, struggling, fighting each other. Jeemotha had caught hold of the sword and his palm was bleeding, but he refused to let go. The two men continued to fight like alligators.

'Guha, Guha, stop!' Jeemotha cried in between gasps.

'Leave me. I will cut that bitch into pieces,' Guha groaned.

Jeemotha punched Guha and he collapsed into the water. 'Stay there until some intelligence seeps in,' Jeemotha said, pushing Guha further down into the water. The guards of the bhoomipathi rushed in to save their master. In a cool voice, Jeemotha said, 'One step more, and we can all attend the funeral feast of Guha tomorrow.' The guards stopped. Jeemotha pulled Guha out of the water and the bhoomipathi gasped for breath. Jeemotha dragged him towards Kattappa.

'See,' Jeemotha said, shoving Guha towards the boat. Guha caught hold of the boat to balance himself and looked up to see Kattappa's face.

When recognition dawned, Guha screamed in rage, 'Get my sword, get my sword. Kill this pig. Kill him!'

Jeemotha grabbed Guha by his neck and dunked him again in the water. 'It seems you need a bit more water therapy.'

When Jeemotha loosened his grip, Guha was almost unconscious. 'Has your head become soft?' Jeemotha asked Guha, who blinked uncomprehendingly.

'Here you have the best slave in the world and you blink like an owl,' Jeemotha said.

'Eh?' Guha blinked again. Jeemotha sighed.

'Chains!' he cried. When a slave came up with chains, Jeemotha had Kattappa bound across his body. When the metal clamped down around his neck, Kattappa stared at Ally, who was shaking her head and sobbing.

'Forgive me, Kattappa,' Ally whispered. 'I have to reach Gauriparvat, I couldn't find any other way.'

Jeemotha cut the ropes that Ally had used to bind him and dragged Kattappa out of the boat. He pushed and shoved Kattappa to the shore. The pirate had a huge chain wound around his shoulder, and the end of it was clamped to the chain around Kattappa's neck. Jeemotha took Kattappa to the top of the cliff and Guha and Ally followed, as did a group of slaves and divers.

Jeemotha called out to other divers, 'Jump!' and scores of men plunged into the water.

'Now look at this,' Jeemotha said. Jeemotha fished out one Gaurikanta stone from his waistband and showed it to Kattappa. The stone caught the light of the setting sun and a blue light throbbed within. 'Get me stones like this,' he said, and pushed Kattappa over the cliff. The slave plunged into the water with a splash and the chain uncoiled in Jeemotha's hands.

Kattappa saw that the riverbed, seventy feet below the surface, was scatted with a few stones—the Gaurikanta, as well as normal pebbles. The thought of holding his breath till he died crossed his mind. Then he remembered what he had done to Amma Kali. This may be his penance, the way he could wash away his sins. This was how he was going to eat the fruits of his karma. Around him, other divers were picking up one or two stones and shooting up out of the water.

Like an offering, like a sacred atonement, Kattappa started picking up the stones. When he came up with a pile, Jeemotha howled with joy and ran down to the shore. Kattappa stood still as the setting sun warmed his drenched skin. The breeze that caressed his tired body seemed to dissolve some of the weight of his guilt. Jeemotha gave a cry of joy again when he had finished counting. Taking a fistful of stones and brandishing it at Guha's face, he yelled, 'Two hundred and twenty-three!'

He shook his fist in the air and screamed at the divers, 'See, you bastards. You fools.' He pointed to a young man from Kedaram. 'You're the champion diver here. What is the maximum number you have retrieved in one dive?'

'Thirty-three,' the man said sheepishly.

'Two hundred and twenty-three,' Jeemotha said again. 'Now you know why this is the best slave in the world—and you wanted to kill him.'

A smile spread on Guha's face. A moment later, they were hugging each other and slapping each other's backs.

'Tonight we celebrate,' Jeemotha said to his guards.

'How about Prince Mahadeva? Would he agree to the celebration?' Guha asked.

'I will handle him,' Jeemotha said to scattered snickering.

'Make arrangements,' Guha said and snapped his fingers. The guard ran to convey the good news. The divers were excited and happy. They bowed to Guha and ran to tell their friends. Work was coming to a halt for the night. They could hear the slaves piling up logs on the ramp for a campfire. Drums started rolling. A slave came with a pitcher of gooseberry wine and served it to Guha and Jeemotha. They tossed it into their mouths and howled and howled with joy.

Ally was standing silently near Kattappa. Jeemotha grabbed her waist and pulled her towards him. 'This sweet girl, my darling girl, has given me the greatest gift.' With the pitcher of wine in one hand and the other wrapped around Ally's waist, he pulled her close and kissed her full on the lips. 'This merchant is very grateful, girl.'

Kattappa, burning with an envy that surprised him, averted his eyes.

'I shall wait for you, girl,' Jeemotha said, picking up the loose end of the chain from the ground and handing it over to Ally. 'Bring the slave too. We may give him some wine and make him dance like a bear. That would be fun.'

Jeemotha and Guha walked ahead towards the centre of the ramp. Ally stood with the loose end of the chain in her hand, unable to say a word. She started walking when Jeemotha called out to her again.

'Forgive me,' Ally whispered.

A derisive smile came to Kattappa's lips. 'This slave is always grateful, devi.'

'One day, you will understand,' Ally said in a voice full of pain.

## ELEVEN

# Mahadeva

'I AM ORDERING you to surrender Kattappa to me,' Mahadeva said, springing up from his seat. 'Or else I will arrest you, along with him.'

'Oh, for some crime, or just on a whim of yours, Your Excellency?'

Jeemotha's tone infuriated Mahadeva. 'For the slave trade,' Mahadeva answered abruptly.

Jeemotha placed a copper plate in front of Mahadeva. As he read it, Mahadeva fumed. How many secrets would his father hide from him?

'As you can see, that decree from His Highness Maharaja Somadeva gives me the right to get as many slaves as possible. And Kattappa is the best one I have got. Why should I part with him? Isn't that right, slave?' Jeemotha rattled the chain and yanked Kattappa towards him. Mahadeva's heart went out to Kattappa. He looked so broken.

'He is my property, Your Excellency,' Jeemotha said, and Mahadeva saw the pain in Kattappa's face when he heard the word 'property'. *There is nothing more despicable than slavery,* thought Mahadeva.

'He is a traitor, wanted by the Mahishmathi government,' Mahadeva said.

'Oh, do you have the maharaja's orders to arrest him? I would be happy to surrender him in that case,' Jeemotha said, enjoying Mahadeva's predicament.

'I ... I will buy him,' Mahadeva stammered.

'Oh, now the princes of Mahishmathi have entered in slave trade. That's tough luck for poor businessmen like us,' Jeemotha said. 'But may I submit respectfully to the Vikramadeva of Mahishmathi that I am not selling my property. This slave is too precious to be sold.'

'I will seize him.'

Jeemotha smiled. 'Of course, you can do that. Unfortunately, that would force us to stop all the work here. I will withdraw all the divers. Being the Vikramadeva, you can order the execution of all of us. It would be an honour to die by your hands. But let me warn you, my prince: Mahishmathi would be pushed to an even more precarious situation by your act.'

Kaliya, the headman sent by the mahapradhana, moved forward then and whispered in Mahadeva's ears, 'Your Highness, we haven't even reached one-third of what we want. The maharaja will not be pleased if we stop for this one slave. We can seize him from the slaver once the work is finished.'

Mahadeva knew the headman was right. He had no choice but to work with rogues like Jeemotha. His father was making him do things that he would never have imagined doing, even in his worst nightmare.

'Your Excellency, shall I take leave? We have a lot to do,' Jeemotha said, and added after a pause, 'together.'

A wave of impotent anger washed over Mahadeva. He nodded tersely, and Jeemotha bowed and walked out of the tent, dragging Kattappa behind him. Mahadeva sat with his head bowed, the image of Kattappa on a leash tearing at his conscience. He remembered how the warning of the slave on the night of Mahamakam helped Mahishmathi defeat the coup.

'Swami, if you could come near the cliff, it would encourage the divers. Some rewards announced by the prince would do wonders,' Kaliya said.

Mahadeva grunted in reply. He hated going near the statue. The vacant looks in the eyes of Guha's slaves disturbed him. Mahadeva walked out of his luxurious tent and the headman followed a few paces behind.

'We could use the soldiers of Mahishmathi to dive in and fish out the stones, but Prince Bijjala didn't agree. Could Your Excellency put in a word with the elder prince?' the headman said. Bijjala had just reached Guha's land, leading a troupe of two hundred men.

'Use the slaves of Guha,' Mahadeva said, not wanting to plead with his elder brother for anything.

'The slaves of Guha and Akkundaraya can be used only to rebuild the statue. They can't be let out of the enclosure,' Kaliya said. 'They can never be used as divers—what if they get away?'

Mahadeva didn't reply. He increased his pace to get away from Kaliya. The short and stout headman panted and puffed behind the prince, struggling to catch up. As he walked,

Mahadeva's gaze shifted to the other camp on the far side of the clearing. *Sivagami must be with Bijjala*, he thought bitterly. When he had seen Sivagami with Bijjala in Guha's land, he was shocked beyond belief. Their gazes had met briefly before she had turned her face away. How had she managed to join his brother's mission? Did his father give her permission to do so? What was she trying to achieve? Was she so ambitious that she would do anything for power?

Mahadeva had sent one of his men back to Mahishmathi to enquire whether Sivagami was part of the mission in an official capacity, or had come with Bijjala as his lover. Every day he dreaded the answer the spy would bring back. If it were the latter, she would be betraying not just him but his country too, since it meant she had no official permission to be there. His suspicions about her, that had sprouted after the Rudra Bhatta killing, hardened to a grim resolve to punish her once he had collected sufficient evidence. He found himself fantasising about punishing Sivagami for the sake of his country, his dharma. Hadn't Lord Rama done so? Lord Rama loved his wife Sita, even fought a war for her against the great Asura emperor. But when his love for his wife came in the way of his rajadharma, he had cast her away. It broke Lord Rama. It would break poor Mahadeva too, but he had to do it, Mahadeva assured himself, feeling a dread and masochistic pleasure at the thought.

Mahadeva had also instructed one of his spies to tail Sivagami. Bhanu Gupta had ingrained himself among the camp followers of Bijjala, and the reports he secretly passed on to Mahadeva weren't very encouraging. Sivagami and Bijjala had a friendly relationship, he said.

As he walked towards the statue, a vague feeling of unease gripped him. There was something sinister here. He had felt it the first day he came. Why did the teenage slaves of Guha and Akkundaraya seem apprehensive whenever Kaliya came near them? *He does have a cruel air,* Mahadeva thought. *He is a man carrying some dark secrets that have charred his soul.* Mahadeva could sense the fear that the soft-spoken Kaliya instilled in others.

Ahead of him, the Kali statue stood tall, its head kissing the clouds. Amma Kali was standing on a huge chariot with wooden wheels, and thousands of slaves were hauling up stones. The hum of their rhythmic chanting as they worked like ants reverberated in the air: *Amma Kali, Jai Kali, Bhadra Kali, Amma Kali, Jai Kali, Bhadra Kali.*

Mahadeva attempted to speak to one of the slaves but Kaliya came running up to him and said in between gasps for breath, 'Everyone is waiting for you. Please come and watch the divers.'

Mahadeva followed Kaliya. They walked towards the heap of stones on the shore and climbed up the cliff. Mahadeva slowed down as he reached the top. The familiar laugh sent a jab of pain in his heart. Sivagami was standing beside Bijjala at the edge of the cliff and Keki stood a few feet behind. Neelappa, the slave of Sivagami, gave a curt bow as the prince walked past. A few feet away, Jeemotha stood next to a pretty girl. Behind them, bound in chains, squatted Kattappa.

Bhoomipathi Guha hurried to Mahadeva and bowed. 'We were waiting, Your Excellency.'

Kaliya came up, fanning himself with his uthariya and panting. 'The prince had gone for a walk,' he said.

Mahadeva saw Kaliya and Guha exchange glances. Again, he felt troubled. Everything was shrouded in mystery.

'Akkundaraya will be bringing his ship soon. The pier from where we will load the statue on to the ship is in the final stages of completion,' Guha said as he led Mahadeva to the edge of the cliff. Other divers who were standing around came up as well. Mahadeva peered down and his head swam. He held on to Guha's shoulder to steady himself. He could almost feel Bijjala sneer, and Sivagami smile. He had always had a problem with heights.

Below, the river Mahishi roared through the gorge and the breeze carried droplets of water high up on the cliff. A few reed baskets bobbed up and down, manned by helpers who stood on them and held on to the rocks. They were expert rowers who would collect the stones retrieved by the divers and bring the basket to the shore, from where the slaves would transport them to the statue.

At a signal from Jeemotha, the divers stood in a line at the edge of the cliff on their toes. Kattappa stood up, and Mahadeva observed that the other end of the chain that leashed him was wound over Jeemotha's arm.

'Remove his chain,' Mahadeva commanded.

Jeemotha smirked and said, 'He is too precious, my prince.'

'Remove it,' Mahadeva repeated. There was an uneasy silence. Jeemotha looked at Guha, who nodded.

'If he escapes ...'

'He won't escape. He has his honour. Don't treat him like a dog.'

Jeemotha shrugged and unclasped the leash. There was no expression on Kattappa's face. Mahadeva was disappointed that the slave hadn't acknowledged his kindness with even a grateful look.

One of the divers sang an invocation to the forest spirits and river spirits. At the command of Jeemotha, twenty-three men dived. Kattappa was the first to hit the river and, a moment later, the others pierced through the waters and vanished below.

The heads of divers popped up one by one, but there was no trace of Kattappa. Mahadeva saw that the pretty girl's face was tense. Jeemotha stared into the water.

'The bloody slave has escaped,' Keki said.

'Or he's dead,' Guha said. 'There are many sharp rocks in the bottom. I hope the poor fellow hasn't cracked open his skull.'

Mahadeva stood stunned, anxiously waiting for the slave to come up to the surface. He heard a sound and, to his horror, he saw Bijjala diving into the water. After some tense moments, they saw Kattappa's head bob up. He deposited a handful of stones into a reed basket and disappeared back under the water.

There was no trace of Bijjala.

Mahadeva stared at the roaring river, trying to suppress the horrible doubt that was shaping in his mind. He knew the hatred Bijjala had for Kattappa. Knowing how his brother treated slaves, it was unlikely that Bijjala would put himself in danger to save the life of a slave. As time crawled by, Mahadeva was sure Bijjala intended nothing good for the slave.

'Something is wrong,' Mahadeva said, 'someone jump in.'

No one moved. Mahadeva peered down into the dizzying depth. Jeemotha said to him in a grave voice, 'I followed your orders, Your Excellency. I hope I will be compensated handsomely for any loss.'

Mahadeva was livid. Even at this juncture, the pirate was thinking only about his profit and loss. Fighting the fear and the nauseating feeling that came over him when he encountered heights, Mahadeva closed his eyes and plunged into the roaring water. He shot through the turbulent surface and found the river was calm beneath. He had expected total darkness, but to his surprise, he found the riverbed throbbing with an eerie blue light. Holding his breath, he swam through the placid waters, rich with turtles and schools of fishes. Above him, the river frothed in a moving sheet of bubbly white.

Mahadeva saw them a few score feet away, partially hidden by a protruding rock scaled with water moss. Bijjala was holding Kattappa by the crook of his armpit. The slave was struggling, clawing at his captor's forearm. His legs kicked up a swirl of mud. Mahadeva grabbed Bijjala from behind and his brother, taken by surprise, lost his grip on Kattappa. The slave slipped away and shot up to the surface. Bijjala turned and wriggled out of Mahadeva's grip. He flung a punch at Mahadeva's face, throwing him back towards the rock. He shot up, following Kattappa. Mahadeva's lungs were bursting for air and he followed them. When Mahadeva broke the surface, the current carried him away. He caught a glimpse of Kattappa and Bijjala again tumbling down towards the river bottom. Bijjala had Kattappa in his grip again. Mahadeva ducked in and swam against the current. He tried to free Kattappa, but Bijjala's strong arms were wound around the slave's neck with a python-like grip. Mahadeva fished out a stone from the riverbed with his toes. As it spun up from the bottom, he caught hold of it and smashed it against Bijjala's wrist.

Mahadeva had expected Bijjala to pull back his hand in pain, but his brother held on, not loosening his grip a bit, choking the slave to death. Mahadeva struggled to free Kattappa, weakened by the knowledge that Bijjala could endure unimaginable physical pain.

The chain came from nowhere. It grazed Mahadeva's cheeks as it shot through the water and wound around Bijjala's neck. Mahadeva saw his brother's eyes bulge as the chain choked him. Mahadeva saw Jeemotha swimming past him. The pirate tightened the chain around Bijjala, making the prince loosen his grip on Kattappa's neck. Mahadeva used all his force to further prise open his brother's hands, allowing Kattappa to wriggle away. The slave shot up to the surface for air, and Mahadeva followed him. Kattappa gasped for breath on the surface and the roaring current caught hold of him. Mahadeva swam behind him and managed to grasp his wrist. He dragged Kattappa to the shore, where the slaves stopped their work and ran to help them. Jeemotha came out of the water carrying Bijjala on his shoulder. He placed the unconscious Bijjala on a rock on the shore and hauled his chain from the water.

Mahadeva sat before a tired Kattappa, ignoring the commotion around his unconscious brother.

A clamp fastened around Kattappa's neck, and before Mahadeva could react, Jeemotha had the slave back on the leash. The pirate turned to the pretty woman who was crying and said in a mocking tone, 'Our slave isn't dead, Ally. Our princes saved him.'

'His neck is injured. Free him,' Mahadeva cried.

Jeemotha pulled Kattappa towards him and said, 'My

prince, this slave is too precious. This leash is not just to keep him from fleeing. It is also to protect him from evil.'

Mahadeva had no answer for that. He had failed to help Kattappa. If not for the pirate, Bijjala would have murdered Kattappa. He burned with indignation at his brother's despicable behaviour.

As the crowd dispersed, soldiers carried Bijjala to his tent. He saw Sivagami following them. Behind him, the woman called Ally was crying for the slave. Didn't Sivagami have even an iota of compassion that this woman had for a mere slave? *I could've died in the struggle along with the slave,* Mahadeva thought. Sivagami hadn't bothered to ask him whether he was all right. He might have understood had she felt something for Bijjala. But she didn't look affected by Bijjala's plight either. Was her heart made of stone?

Mahadeva walked back to his tent, determined to find a way to help Kattappa and punish Bijjala. He felt irritated when he heard soldiers whispering about how bravely the two princes had plunged into the raging river to save a slave. *Sycophants,* he fumed; *this bloody country will never change. There is no value for truth or honour. Everything is a bloody show. Everyone is selfish.*

---

When Mahadeva woke up after a night of troubled sleep, it was already dawn. He hurried to check if Bhanu Gupta had left any message for him. The spy would convey his report on Sivagami either in person, or written on a palm leaf which he would hide either in his cloth tent, or in the roots of a banyan tree that stood behind his camp. This morning, it was tucked under the carpet, in the rear of his tent.

The note read, 'We are leaving for Gauriparvat. Bijjala has convinced Akkundaraya after protracted negotiations to side with Mahishmathi. Please check your weapons. Some of our swords and shields are crumbling like dry reeds without warning.'

Mahadeva stopped reading, his heart racing. He remembered how his favourite sword, one given by his father, had shattered into pieces the previous night. But what hurt more was that Sivagami had left with Bijjala.

TWELVE

# Shivappa

'WHY DO YOU want to sort the Vaithalika children from the others?' Achi Nagamma asked Shivappa.

Shivappa continued to yell out commands to his women warriors. Hidumba was helping them. Achi moved closer and stood glaring at Shivappa. He sidestepped her and continued with his orders. When she waved her stick before his face, he turned to her and said in an irritated tone, 'I know what I am doing.'

Except for a handful of women who remained loyal to Achi Nagamma, the rest of the group had shifted allegiance to the charismatic Shivappa. The majority of Achi Nagamma's warrior women were of the Vaithalika tribe and, using his charm, appealing to their tribe pride and exploiting the fact that they associated his dynasty with divinity, Shivappa was able to wrest leadership from Achi Nagamma.

Achi Nagamma knew it was a losing battle she was fighting, and she was bitter about it. Unlike Kadarimandalam women, the Vaithalika women were more comfortable being led by a man, and Achi knew she had made a strategic mistake by inviting Shivappa. But it was too late.

'I demand to know what you're trying to do,' Achi said.

'Can't you see, Achi? I am trying to take the count of Vaithalika children.'

'I can see that very well. I want to know why.'

'I don't want Vaithalika children to suffer anymore,' Shivappa said. 'They are going to be freed.'

'And the rest who are not fortunate to be born in the Vaithalika womb?'

'They'll also be freed, but not immediately.'

'Any reason for this discrimination, Your Highness.' The honorific, instead of being respectful, sounded like an insult. Shivappa walked away without answering, and Achi Nagamma stopped him and said, 'This wasn't what we decided when we started the war.'

'I am the king. I get to decide what we do. This is my decision, Achi. I respect you and all that. But don't stand in the way of Vaithalika's destiny.'

'Oh? What is that destiny?'

'To rule the world. We have been slaves for so long, sometimes to Kadarimandalam, sometimes to Mahishmathi. Now, our time has come. This is the moment of our redemption.'

'You've gone insane.'

'Insane? I am no fool to let go of this opportunity. The Vaithalikas have always been the owners of Gauriparvat before it was taken away through deceit by Mahishmathi. Now that I have captured it back, history won't forgive me if I let it go without using it for the betterment of my people. For years, Mahishmathi ruled the world by exploiting our mountain. We were fools who worshiped this mountain as a goddess. It is nothing but a pile of rocks. If others can exploit it, become rich and make us slaves, we too can do it.'

'You're going to do the same evil thing that Mahishmathi did?' Achi was livid.

'Mahishmathi was looting Vaithalika property. We are just using what belongs to us wisely,' Shivappa said impatiently.

'Swami, swami!' Vamana, who was listening to the exchange from a distance, ran to Shivappa and fell at his feet. 'Please don't do it, swami. Unspeakable disaster will befall all of us.'

'Grandma, grandpa,' Shivappa said mockingly to Achi and Vamana. 'Don't worry. I know old people are obsessed with death and doomsday prophecies. But allow the young to live. Allow us to flourish. Don't stand in the way of progress. I promise, I will free all the non-Vaithalika children too once I negotiate a deal with Mahishmathi. I will free them once they surrender Bijjala, who raped and killed my Kamakshi. Unlike the evil Mahishmathi, I will not kill my workers when they grow too big to fit into the tunnels. I will set them free. I promise I won't do anything secretive like Mahishmathi. I will even pay good wages for the children who work. Aren't you satisfied, Achi?'

'No, I am not. You have to stop this now,' Achi said, glaring at him.

Shivappa screamed, 'You don't know what is happening here! You want to see? You want to see? Come with me.'

'Open it,' Shivappa said. They were standing outside a thick wooden door, near the tunnel outside which the waterfall cascaded. Vamana fumbled with the keys tied to his waistband, and finally found the right one.

The door opened with a creak, and the stink of something dead and decaying assaulted them. Light fell from a hole in the roof. Water trickled down from one wall, puddled on the floor and flowed out. Shivappa picked up a dead bat from the floor and gave it to Vamana.

'Go, give him a decent burial,' he said, handing the putrefying bat to Vamana. Shivappa accompanied him to the door and gently shut it behind him.

'So? What is the life-changing thing you wanted to show me. The one that will make me change my mind?' Achi Nagamma asked, crossing her arms.

'Look there,' Shivappa pointed to a corner. Achi squinted into the darkness.

'What?'

Shivappa rushed out. Achi realised what he was doing and leapt to grab him. Shivappa's slap sent her flying across the room. He stepped out and slammed the door shut. He locked the door with the bunch of keys he had stolen from the dwarf. He saw Vamana running towards him. 'I lost my keys, swami,' Vamana panted.

'Be careful, old man. I found it on the floor. I have locked the door for you,' Shivappa said, handing over the keys.

'But ... where is that old woman?'

'My grandma? She keeps fighting with me. She just went the way we came, through the waterfall. Such an agile woman for her age.'

Shivappa looked out through the window and said, 'Hope she is all right.' The waterfall roared outside. He watched the dwarf trying each key from his ring on the door of the chamber. None fit the keyhole. Shivappa took out a key from his waistband and flung it through the window.

'Come on, grandpa,' he called out, and the dwarf followed him, looking back many times suspiciously.

When they came out of the cave, Shivappa's warriors had segregated the children as Vaithalikas and non-Vaithalikas. Hidumba led the non-Vaithalika children inside. When one of the women warriors asked him about Achi Nagamma, Shivappa ordered all the warriors to assemble.

'I had an argument with Achi Nagamma. She doesn't want us to continue mining. I want to continue for the glory of the Vaithalikas. She has left us. Those who want to accompany her are free to go now. Those who believe the Vaithalikas have a right over Gauriparvat and can use this resource to build our empire, those who believe in me, those who want me to be your king, can stay with me here.'

A murmur rose among the warriors.

'I am also offering one Gauripadmam stone each to anyone who stays, irrespective of whether they are Vaithalika or not. Durgappa and his soldiers have agreed to join our cause, and Durgappa is appointed as the mahapradhana of our kingdom. Hidumba will be our mahasenapathi. The choice for you is to either become a part of the kingdom and enjoy its riches, or to continue leading a life in the wilderness, following an old woman.'

There was a tense silence. Then one of the Vaithalika warriors cried, 'Jai Vaithalikas.' Soon, others picked up the cry.

Shivappa said, 'Mahishmathi isn't going to keep quiet. Their army will reach here soon. We will fight and defeat them. We will defeat them with our Garuda pakshis. Hidumba ...'

Hidumba came forward and blew his bamboo whistle. The two Garuda pakshis rose from the valley and flew in a graceful arc over the army. When Hidumba ordered them, they picked up huge stones, soared in the sky and dropped them into the valley.

'Nothing in the world can stop us now,' Shivappa cried above the cheers and applause of his soldiers. He felt exhilarated. He had not only become king, he would soon force Mahishmathi to surrender Bijjala. He would conduct a public trial and feed Bijjala to the Garuda pakshi. Then he would march to Mahishmathi and free all his brethren. He would prove how wrong his brother and father had been. He would bring his brother here and give him all the luxuries in the world. He would rule as per Kattappa's advice. In every moment, Kattappa should feel how wrong he was and how right his younger brother was, always.

---

Vamana tried to open the door with all the keys in his possession. He could hear the squeaks of rats from inside and sounds of struggle. He knew the old woman was trapped inside. None of the keys worked. He tried to kick open the door, but it was too strong for him.

In panic, he fetched an axe and started hacking at the door with all his might. Soon, the squeaks from inside became frenzied. By the time, he was able to make a small hole in the door, it was late afternoon. He peered through the hole, and a rat jumped at his eyes. He pulled his face back, terrified. Through the hole, hundreds of rats started jumping out. Vamana ran to get the torch in the wall and waved it at the river of rodents that were flowing out. By the time, the flow stopped and the rats vanished into the darkness, he was dead tired. He crawled to the door and peered in. The room was empty. Gauriparvat had claimed another victim. The new king had eliminated his rival without leaving a trace.

Vamana sat leaning against the splintered door and wept. All were the same: Somadeva, Shivappa, Mahishmathi, the Vaithalikas. The same greed drove them all. A hiss came from the womb of Gauriparvat, and the terrified dwarf ran to his cart and whipped his rams. He rode back to the cave mouth with tears streaming down his wrinkled face.

---

Shivappa, along with two dozen soldiers, reached the northern flank of Gauriparvat by late afternoon. They stopped in front of a cave covered by a huge boulder with rusted chains wound around it. The chains ran to a huge pulley fixed to the cliff above, The pulley hung from an iron pillar secured vertically to the rock face.

On the instruction of Shivappa, the soldiers pulled the chain and the pulley rotated with great difficulty, creaking and groaning. The boulder finally rose, leaving the mouth of the cave open. The soldiers fastened the chain to the pillar, allowing the boulder to hang above the cave mouth. They waited with bated breath for the Garuda pakshi to emerge. A beak, almost four feet long, curved at the end, sharp as a sword and shining red, emerged first. A furry golden body followed, the wings twitching at this taste of freedom.

'Hide, hide!' Durgappa screamed, and dove behind the nearest rock. The soldiers scattered in fear and hid behind bushes. Hidumba ran as fast as he could and had barely made it to his hiding place before the giant Garuda pakshi emerged fully.

Shivappa gave a cry of pleasure. 'Bijjala, bastard. See what I have kept in store for you,' he screamed, and the bird turned towards him. Its reptilian eyes sent a shiver down Shivappa's spine. He cowered behind a rock.

The bird hopped to the edge of the precipice and gave a wild call. The two male birds appeared, one after the other. Big as they were, they appeared as puny as chickens before the mighty female bird.

The two male birds screeched and cooed to the female and started a ritual dance, hopping in circles and making wild mating calls. When each male came in striking distance of the other, they lashed out with their beaks.

One of the male birds gave a blood-curdling screech. The other answered with more ferocity. The men closed their ears with their palms. The birds approached each other screeching, and soon the two males were fighting, clawing and pecking wildly. The female stood, indifferent to the fight. The two males were a ball of feathers, bouncing and rolling, flapping their giant wings.

The male bird that was losing escaped from the other bird's claws and soared high. The dominant male chased it and the battle was now being fought in the sky. In their flap of wings, trees got uprooted and rocks tumbled down. After a bloody fight, the defeated male bird flew away and the victor gave a screech of joy. The female took off and Shivappa gasped at the spread of its wings, at the majesty of the giant bird.

'Hidumba,' Durgappa hissed, 'how in the world are we going to control them?'

---

It had been a month since he had handled the Achi Nagamma situation and set free the female bird. Shivappa was mighty pleased with what he had achieved. He gathered the Vaithalika children he had freed and began giving them a speech. He was their saviour, he told them. They blinked at him. He glared at his soldiers, and they gestured for the children to clap. Shivappa told them about the glorious history of the Vaithalikas. He wept when he talked about how Somadeva had cheated the Vaithalikas of their legacy. Shivappa promised them he would regain the glory of the tribe; he had been chosen by Amma Gauri to do so, he said. The children dutifully cheered. Shivappa smiled.

The attack came suddenly. A soldier was teaching the children to sing a patriotic song when there was the loud flapping of wings. A scream rang out, and a terrifying silence followed. Shivappa ran to the last row of children. A boy, his face sprayed with blood, said between sobs, 'A giant bird took both of them.' Shivappa looked at the chilling gap in the row of children and cursed.

He ordered his soldiers to take the rest of the children inside the cave for their safety. For now, Vaithalika and non-

Vaithalika children would stay together. The Garuda pakshi did not seem to appreciate the racial superiority of the Vaithalika caste. A livid Shivappa summoned Durgappa.

---

Durgappa cursed himself as he climbed the cliff with a heavy rucksack on his back. Not a job befitting the dignity of a bhoomipathi, but he had no choice. Nothing had worked according to plan. The new king had ordered him to tame the Garuda pakshi. The male birds still answered to his commands, but he had not progressed even a bit with the female. The new king was getting angry. They had lost two children and two guards to its hunger.

There was a reason why the female bird had not been let loose for many years, he tried to explain, but Shivappa wouldn't listen. He had given Durgappa a choice: he could either be beheaded or try and tame the female bird. Between the Garuda pakshis and Shivappa, the former seemed more reasonable. So here he was, with a rucksack full of slaughtered sheep. He had been saving the flock of sheep for the coming winter, and was forced to slaughter half a dozen of them to train the bird.

He reached a small ledge in the cliff, about thirty feet broad, where he could stand comfortably. He was careful to keep himself as close to the cliff wall as possible. He untied the sack and took out a chunk of meat. He walked to the edge of the ledge and gave the call for the birds. He heard the flap of wings and rushed back to the wall. He stood panting as the two male birds appeared. They sat on the edge of the ledge and waited for his treat.

He whistled another command. They took off, circled around, and returned to their perch on the ledge. He laughed. They still listened to his commands. They hadn't gone feral. 'Here,' he cried, and they hopped to him, making a gurgling sound of pleasure. Pleased, he flung chunks of meat in the air to both of them. They caught them with their beaks and waited for his permission to eat.

'Eat,' Durgappa commanded, laughing through tears. They were his boys, the only ones who still listened to him. He moved from the safety of the wall and went to stand between them. He caressed the golden feathers on their necks and they cooed in rhythm.

'My boys, my darling boys,' Durgappa said, treating them to more chunks of meat. He didn't see the shadow over him until it was too late. The sack of meat fell down as he was airborne. He saw his boys waiting for his command to eat the chunks of flesh that were spread out on the ledge. 'Eat,' he said, and saw them gobbling up his last treat.

Durgappa landed softly on a bed of twigs. It took a moment for him to realise that he was inside the cave of the female Garuda pakshi. The bird had built a nest of twigs and stones at the far end of the cave. There were six chicks staring at him with their reptilian eyes. He scrambled up, screaming in terror, and tried to climb out of the twelve-foot wall of twigs. He almost made it to the top, but the mother bird nudged him back into the nest. One of the chicks, as tall as his waist, hopped up to him and gave him a tentative peck on his shoulder. It hurt, but no blood was drawn. The mother bird reached in and Durgappa screamed as the bird tore a chunk of flesh from his shoulder. As it fed one of the chicks his flesh, the other five chicks were upon him, pecking him all over. *Four are female and two are male,* was Durgappa's last thought on earth before the mother bird cracked open his skull. The proud mother bird watched her chicks feed themselves and gave a screech of satisfaction.

## THIRTEEN

# Mahadeva

'I AM VIKRAMADEVA Mahadeva, the prince of Mahishmathi. Nothing will happen to you. Speak.'

The boy blinked but remained quiet. Mahadeva had taken the boy away from where he was working and brought him to his tent. He was sure the supervisors must have realised the boy was missing by now. But the camp of the Vikramadeva would be the last one they would check. He had been trying to get the boy to speak for the last few minutes, and his persistent silence was infuriating Mahadeva.

'What's your name.'

The boy mumbled something. 'Speak louder,' Mahadeva commanded.

The boy whispered, 'Noota Nalabhayi Ayidhu.'

'One hundred and forty-five? That is your name? That is a number.'

The boy stared at him, clearly frightened. In a gentler tone, Mahadeva asked the boy how he had gotten here. In a shaky voice, the boy started talking about his life, how he was kidnapped and enslaved, and what life was like in Gauriparvat. He couldn't remember his name: only the number assigned to him. The other boys were also called by numbers. Other than that, they had no identity and only a vague recollection of their parents.

Mahadeva was stunned. His entire world came crashing down. The empire that he had once dreamed of inheriting was built on a foundation of evil. It was built on the tears and blood of innocents. And his father had made him play an important role in this cruelty. Evil happens not because there are evil men, but because good people stand by indifferent to the deeds of the evil men. Mahadeva didn't know whether or not he was a good man, but he was determined not to be indifferent to the sufferings of the poor and oppressed.

'Don't worry, brother,' Mahadeva said, fighting hard to suppress the tremor in his voice. 'Once we get the statue to Mahishmathi, I will give you all freedom. And if my father doesn't agree, I will fight for you.'

Mahadeva waited for the boy to thank him, one part of his mind chiding him for wanting gratitude from the poor soul. The boy remained silent. Then he said, 'Our days are numbered.'

The matter of fact way it was said took the air out of Mahadeva's lungs.

'What ... what do you mean?' he asked.

'Once the statue reaches Mahishmathi, we are brought back to this place and killed. That's how it has been for many generations.'

'No ...' Mahadeva said, but he knew the boy was right.

The secrecy, the insistence that he shouldn't speak to Guha's slaves—all of it clicked into place. He now knew why Sivagami's father Devaraya had rebelled, why Bhoomipathi Thimma had rebelled. They were martyrs for a cause greater than them. Maybe it was his destiny to follow their path. The crown of Mahishmathi, at least this Mahishmathi, he didn't want.

'For the rest of my life, however short it may be, I will ensure that no human being suffers the indignity of slavery and no child is kidnapped to work in the mines. Everyone dies eventually, I will die fighting for what is right. I will fight for your freedom.' When he finished, he was disappointed to see the boy had curled into a foetal position on the floor and was snoring.

Mahadeva saw the squat figure of Kaliya hurrying towards him through the window of the tent. He quickly drew the entrance and window curtains of the tent so that Kaliya wouldn't see the boy and hurried outside. The headman bowed before Mahadeva and said, 'Your Excellency, we need to take the Kali statue to Mahishmathi soon. His Highness has sent us a message ordering us to immediately bring the statue, even if it is half full.'

Mahadeva read the message from his father and said, 'Well, make arrangements for the ramp to be raised so that the statue can be rolled onto the deck of the ship.'

Kaliya hesitated. He scratched his head and said in a low voice, 'There is a problem.'

'Now what?'

'The ship that Akkundaraya had left us has capsized, blocking the port.'

Mahadeva hurried to the river pier. Kaliya ran behind him. 'Swami,' he called out, catching up with Mahadeva.

'One of the slaves is missing. We have searched everywhere.'

'What is his name?'

Kaliya remained quiet.

'Doesn't he have a name?'

'One hundred and forty-five,' Kaliya said.

Mahadeva exploded in anger. 'That is how you call a human being? Even cows have names.'

'The cow is our holy mother,' Kaliya said, folding his hand in reverence and looking heavenward with half-closed eyes.

*There is no point wasting time talking to this fool,* thought Mahadeva. He hurried to the port. He could see the giant ship leaning to one side. His heart sank.

The pirate and his woman were standing at the edge of the pier, looking at the ship. Kattappa was squatting at one end. Mahadeva averted his eyes from the chain that extended from his neck to the pirate's hand. Mahadeva hurried to the pier.

Jeemotha bowed. 'Clearly sabotage, my prince.'

Mahadeva stared at him.

'No, not me, Your Excellency,' Jeemotha said and smiled. 'I will get my payment only when the ship reaches Mahishmathi. Why should I put a fly in my gruel? The earlier I finish my job, the earlier I get paid. I am a merchant, Prince.'

Mahadeva nodded curtly. What the pirate said made sense.

'Someone has made a hole below water level. It is on the other side. We need to empty the water and close the hole,' the pirate said. 'I can do it, but it will take a week at least, and that only if I get sufficient men. I can be paid later. No need for an advance. I trust the prince of Mahishmathi. It is a service I am doing for my country, isn't it?'

Mahadeva walked away, his hands clasped behind his back, deep in thought. He heard the distinct clang of swords from the direction where Bijjala's camp had been set up. Had Bijjala returned? Surprised, Mahadeva walked to the camp compound. A group of soldiers were practising their skill with weapons. They paused and looked at him. A familiar face broke through the crowd and bowed to Mahadeva.

'We are here for your protection, Prince,' Keki said and cackled. A few of the soldiers guffawed. Keki sauntered up to Mahadeva and whispered, 'I sabotaged your ship. No, not on a whim. That was the order of my swami. Your brother Bijjala heard that your father wanted you to leave immediately for Mahishmathi with the statue, and he didn't want you to reach Mahishmathi with Amma Kali before he achieved success in Gauriparvat. We are here, two hundred of us, to ensure that you don't leave with Amma Kali. You continue to fish in the river, find the stones and fill them in the statue. Let your anna come from Gauriparvat with his lover, Sivagami; let him come and then together we will go to Mahishmathi. Bijjala as Rama, Sivagami as Sita devi, you as Lakshmana and me, oh, I am the monkey, Bajarang Bali Hanuman.'

Keki started clapping her hands and dancing around Mahadeva, singing in a loud voice, 'Let Amma Gauri bless our prince Mahadeva, let Kailasapathi Shankara bless our Vikramadeva, let Vidyapathi Sri Ganesha bless our scholar, let—'

Mahadeva didn't wait for the farce to continue. He stormed

back to his camp. To his horror, he found the boy was missing. He knew where to look.

Mahadeva ran to the headman's tent. He found the boy tied to the central pole inside. The headman and a few of his helpers were around him. They dropped their whips when they saw Mahadeva. The boy was unconscious, and there were marks all over his body. Mahadeva grabbed Kaliya by the scruff of his neck. The headman squealed and begged for mercy. His assistants ran away in fear.

Mahadeva dragged the headman past the ramp. He had never been so angry in his life. The boy slaves watched the curious sight of the headman pleading for mercy. The prince tied him near the Kali statue.

'You must taste the bitterness of your medicine, Kaliya. You should know how it feels to be in chains.'

'I was only doing my duty, Prince. Have mercy. I am just a worker, earning my two copper coins to feed my family,' the headman cried.

His heartfelt plea shook Mahadeva, but he allowed his anger to suppress the pity. *There are many ways to earn a living. There is no need to be a devil like Kaliya—the man deserves more than what he is getting,* Mahadeva justified his anger in his mind. Letting the headman scorch in the sun, Mahadeva hurried to the river.

Jeemotha was instructing Mahadeva's soldiers on the intricacies of repairing ships. Standing in a loin cloth, his chiselled body shining with sweat, the pirate gave off an air of efficiency, competency and confidence. After a brief set of instructions, Jeemotha climbed onto the slanted side of the ship with the agility of a monkey, and the well-trained soldiers of Mahishmathi struggled to catch up with him.

Mahadeva watched the pirate's work in fascination, as a complicated system of pulleys and ropes were assembled in no time. The assemblage of ropes and pulleys was tied to a contraption that resembled an oil press mill that Jeemotha put together with logs and planks.

By evening, the capsized ship lay like a fly caught in a spider's web, with ropes and pulleys crisscrossing it in what seemed like bewildering complexity to Mahadeva. The pirate rejected Mahadeva's offer to help with a curt smile and said he would ask the prince for aid when it was required. Jeemotha yoked Kattappa to the machine and made him walk around the contraption like an oxen is driven in an oil press mill. Nothing happened. Kattappa looked like an ant before the gigantic ship that could carry a thousand men.

'What are you trying to do?' Mahadeva asked in exasperation. Jeemotha studied the complex web of ropes and, without answering Mahadeva, rushed to pull some weights and twist some pulleys. He ordered Kattappa to walk again with the yoke on his shoulders. The contraption started moving slowly, with creaks and growls.

Mahadeva watched in amazement as the ship slowly straightened up bit by bit. Before Kattappa had completed his twelfth turn, the ship had straightened fully and was bobbing up and down in the water. The soldiers cheered and the pirate bowed with a swagger.

Mahadeva was impressed. *Here is a man who is a master in his craft,* thought Mahadeva. *Even the worst of men have some redeeming qualities.* Perhaps he had judged the pirate wrongly. In a less unforgiving country, this man would have been the admiral of the royal navies. *How many such men and women are there in my vast country, whose potential remains suppressed under the tyranny of caste and class,* Mahadeva wondered. 'When I am king, I will usher in a new world,' Mahadeva whispered, and felt embarrassed by the unexpected glimpse of his hidden ambition.

Jeemotha came up to Mahadeva with a triumphant smile. Mahadeva said, 'I bow to your mastery in your craft.' He unclasped his pearl necklace and gave it to the pirate merchant.

Jeemotha took it with an air of nonchalance and, weighing it in his palm to check its worth, said, 'Now comes the difficult work. To fix the hole. We need to start the work immediately and empty the water from the bottom of the ship. Otherwise, she will capsize again.'

An idea was forming in Mahadeva's mind. Why not use the pirate to beat Bijjala at his devious game?

'We need to talk,' Mahadeva said.

The pirate looked at the prince with a smile dancing on his lips. 'Anytime and every time. Your servant forever, noble prince.' Jeemotha bowed and showed the necklace proudly to everyone. 'This prize belongs to all—not just me. With your kind permission, Your Excellency,' Jeemotha said, and he broke the string of the necklace. The pearl beads struck the ground and danced about. He swooped them up in his hand and called forth every soldier who had helped him straighten the ship. Jeemotha gave each one of them a pearl. He placed one in Kattappa's palm too, and the slave looked at it in confusion.

*This man is a born leader,* thought Mahadeva. In a world where the so-called noblemen of Mahishmathi fight for undeserved credit, this man was sharing what he deserved with even a slave. When Jeemotha called for volunteers who would dive with him to repair the hole, the soldiers of Mahadeva fell over themselves for the privilege. Mahadeva became confident that, with the help of Jeemotha, he would soon be sailing to Mahishmathi with the Kali statue.

Ally, who was watching everything, moved up to the prince and whispered, 'For god's sake, don't trust him.'

Mahadeva turned to her in surprise. Wasn't she the lover of the pirate? Why was she warning him about Jeemotha? He said, 'I don't think the world is as evil as we all think, devi,' the prince said. 'Even in the worst of men, there is a seed of goodness. We need to water it with love and nurture it with trust.'

---

The negotiation was easier than Mahadeva had expected. The pirate settled for whatever jewels Mahadeva was wearing. It was worth a lot, but no price was too high for the freedom of the poor slaves.

In the evening, they had together checked the ramp and the ship. They had timed the journey of the statue on to the deck of the ship. They had gone through the plan in minute detail several times. There was nothing that could go wrong, Jeemotha had assured Mahadeva.

In some corner of his mind, Mahadeva felt squeamish about associating with a ruthless pirate. But even lord Krishna had used many questionable tactics for the sake of dharma's victory in the Mahabharata war. This was also a war against his evil brother, Mahadeva pacified himself. *History will be kinder to me,* he repeated as he waited anxiously for the signal from the pirate.

As midnight approached, it started drizzling, making Mahadeva more worried about the success of his role. He checked and rechecked the oil barrel kept in the corner. He counted the arrows and repeatedly checked their ends, which were blunted with oil cloths wound around them. He kept peeping out of the window of his camp, fussy about the delay. The rear side of the Kali statue reflected the light from the campfire in Keki's camp. The wind carried the lewd songs they were singing.

When the signal came, Mahadeva rolled the barrel out. He cut open the wooden barrel with his dagger and dipped the first arrow in the oil. He held it to the torch and, with a hiss, the flame caught, drowning him in golden light. He shot it towards Keki's camp and watched the arrow fly past the face of the Kali statue. After a moment's tense silence, he heard a scream and saw the blaze of fire from the camp. He emptied his quiver in quick succession, showering the eunuch's camp with fire arrows. He could hear the pandemonium his arrows were causing.

Mahadeva saw the Kali statue moving towards the ramp. The slaves of Guha were drawing the chariot down the ramp. Jeemotha was urging them forward. He saw Bhoomipathi Guha screaming at the slaves to stop and rushing towards Jeemotha. In the next moment, Guha collapsed, a dagger jutting out of his throat. The pirate stepped over him and the slaves followed.

Mahadeva ran by their side, urging them to move forward. 'I promise you freedom the moment we reach Mahishmathi,' he cried over the din. The slaves continued to pull the Kali chariot. Mahadeva heard the sickening crunch of Guha's skull breaking as a chariot wheel ran over him.

Ally and Kattappa were already at the ship. Jeemotha scrambled up the contraption he had used to steady the ship. With admirable agility, he clamped the Kali statue in a web of pulleys and ropes. He requested Mahadeva to pull one rope as the slaves were commanded to board the ship. Mahadeva pulled the rope and, with surprising ease, the gigantic statue rose up in the air. *The man is a genius,* thought Mahadeva, as Jeemotha gently guided the statue on to the ship's deck.

Mahadeva could hear Kaliya screaming. He had forgotten to free him. He felt sorry for the headman.

'Board the ship, Prince,' Jeemotha yelled as he raised the anchor. Mahadeva hesitated. He heard Keki and her soldiers rushing towards them. They must have seen the statue being loaded. The sails of the ship unfurled like a giant bird waking up. Mahadeva ran towards Kaliya as an arrow whizzed past him. He could see soldiers with drawn swords and spears rushing towards him, led by Keki. Behind him, the ship was slowly turning away from the dock.

Mahadeva reached Kaliya and quickly cut the ropes that bound him. 'What have you done, Prince,' Kaliya fell on his knees and wept.

'Run before they get you,' Mahadeva yelled and raced towards the departing ship.

The ship had left the dock. Mahadeva scrambled up a pulley contraption as arrows and spears whistled past his head. He swung on a rope and landed on the deck of the ship, at the feet of the Kali statue.

He broke down in relief. A wave of ecstasy swept through him. He had beaten his wily brother. He had executed his plan to perfection. Mahadeva could now face his father proudly. He would demand freedom for all the slaves of Guha. His father would have to answer all his questions. He turned when he felt a tap on his shoulder.

'Jeemotha, my friend,' Mahadeva said and smiled, opening his arms to hug the pirate. 'Thank you.'

The pirate bowed. The slaves were rowing the ship in unison, and their song rose in the air. Wind fluttered the sails. The drizzle turned to rain.

'But why are you going south?' Mahadeva asked.

'That is where Kadarimandalam is, my prince,' Jeemotha said.

'What?'

'The instruction of Pattaraya is to bring it where he is. A prince is one cargo too much on this poor ship.'

A dagger flashed in Jeemotha's hand. 'Sorry, Prince. You are a good man, and hence a liability to the world.'

Mahadeva stood stunned as the gravity of what he had done sunk in. He saw that none of his soldiers stepped forward to help. Jeemotha's dagger arced towards him. He stood stoic, with no will to block it, nor to live anymore.

Jeemotha swayed to one side, crashed down on the deck and slipped a few feet. Ally had kicked him. She took the hand of a dazed Mahadeva and jumped overboard. The chain in her hand took Kattappa too into the swirling waters.

When they surfaced, they saw the pirate standing at the rear of the ship's deck. 'Good riddance,' he yelled, and his laughter merged with the roll of thunder in the sky. Mahadeva watched the ship rushing away, thousands of oars rising and falling in rhythm and dissolving into the darkness like a spectra. For some time, the fierce eyes of the Kali statue seemed to glare at him from the darkness. That, too, soon vanished. He had failed miserably. He wanted to die, before his father's soldiers caught him and hung him. Thankfully, the river Mahishi was willing to cradle him in her bosom.

FOURTEEN

# Jeemotha

JEEMOTHA SAW THE ancient city of Kadarimandalam rising at the mouth of river Mahishi, and urged his slaves to row faster. The wind wasn't favourable and the tide was moving in from the sea, which slowed down the movement of the ship, but he couldn't contain his growing excitement. Here was the culmination of months of planning. This would wipe away all his debts and would launch his career as a respectful merchant in Kadarimandalam.

Jeemotha looked forward to nothing less than a ministerial position in the ancient kingdom. With a sea port that attracted merchants from all over the world, an independent Kadarimandalam was sure to regain her famed prosperity. Jeemotha would once again be the lord of the seas, the admiral of the royal navy and the minister of commerce. Who knows, perhaps a favourable play of destiny would get him the position of prime minister itself. And if destiny wasn't favourable, well, he had always forced destiny's hand before, and he wouldn't mind doing it again.

The only thing he might miss was Ally, he thought. He hated himself for the jealousy he felt at her closeness to Kattappa. It was against everything he thought he was. 'Good riddance,' he said loudly, as the ship approached the dock of Kadarimandalam. What would she be doing now? He shouldn't have let the slave escape. She would have followed him like a dog if he had the slave. *I will get hundreds of girls like her,* he told himself, *once I have enough money.* He was proud that he had never had to force himself on a woman. They came to him, every one of them, attracted by his charm and good looks. Ally was the only one who played the same game he played on women. Physically she used him as much as he used her, but he knew she never felt attracted to him. It was an insult, a blow to his ego. And then to add fuel to the fire, she had fallen for a lowly slave. The more he thought about it, the more angry Jeemotha became. He shouldn't have let the slave go. He should have killed Kattappa.

The huge cheer of the crowd brought him back to the present. He was curious about how Pattaraya had been able to arrange such a reception. Wasn't he a fugitive, and Kadarimandalam a vassal kingdom of Mahishmathi, ruled by a ruthless governor? He saw that the governor's covered chariot was already at the dock. The king, a huge man with a curly beard, was standing like a decked elephant near the governor's chariot, surrounded by his servants. It amused Jeemotha that they were giving him such a welcome. Life would be good in Kadarimandalam. He looked for the famed bastard princess, Chitraveni. He had heard a lot about her dusky beauty. Uninvited, the thought of Ally came to his mind, and he cursed. *I won't find satisfaction with any woman until I have made Ally beg for me,* he rued.

The king Narasimha Varman welcomed Jeemotha with great pomp and show. Jeemotha eyed the beautiful young woman by his side. She looked familiar, but he couldn't place her. The king appeared to be besotted with her.

The Kali statue was unloaded and Jeemotha walked by the side of the king while the slaves pulled the chariot through the streets. The governor's chariot followed the Kali statue. They reached a huge ground near the new palace of Kadarimandalam, where a freshly made structure glinted in the sun.

Jeemotha wondered where Pattaraya was, and why the Mahishmathi governor did not emerge from the chariot. He got the answer soon. The moment the consecration ceremony of the statue began, the priest asked all the Mahishmathi soldiers to lay down their arms before the Kali statue for the puja. The swords, spears and shields were piled up before the statue. Jeemotha reluctantly gave his weapons away. He was sure this was some elaborate ruse, but to what aim, he wasn't sure.

Some of the governor's soldiers appeared restless, but they didn't want to disobey the order. The young woman asked for the king's sword and walked to the statue. She placed it at the feet of the giant Kali statue and folded her hands in prayer. She walked to the covered chariot of the governor and knocked on the door. The door opened and, to Jeemotha's surprise, instead of the governor getting out, the young woman stepped inside the chariot and shut the door. Something was wrong. His instincts were screaming for him to run.

He saw a flock of birds approaching rapidly and frowned. It took an instant for him to recognise that they were arrows, not birds. The Mahishmathi soldiers panicked. Arrows were flying from all directions, taking them down. Some rushed to retrieve their weapons from the base of the statue, but were shot down. Some took off but were hit before they could reach the river. Jeemotha saw the king of Kadarimandalam standing there, stunned. The soldiers who stood around the king had already fallen. Jeemotha dove to the ground, but arrows kept falling like rain. He cursed and ran to stand behind the king of Kadarimandalam, reasoning that if he was still standing, it wasn't because the attackers were unable to hit his bulky frame. They wanted him alive. To stay alive himself, Jeemotha had to use him as a shield.

When the last of the Mahishmathi soldiers had fallen, the chariot door opened and from it emerged the young woman, smiling at the king. Behind her, was Pattaraya. *Bastard,* Jeemotha thought, smiling at the man's ingenuity. *He bribed the governor.* Pattaraya was waiting for someone else to come out of the chariot. To Jeemotha's surprise, a dusky woman stepped out, and Pattaraya bowed low to her.

Jeemotha heard the king whisper, 'Chitraveni', and everything suddenly fell into place. Pattaraya hadn't bribed the governor. He must have eliminated the governor and impersonated him. As Jeemotha stood, filled with awe and admiration for Pattaraya's evil genius, Chitraveni walked towards a trembling Narasimha Varman. From all sides of the ground, women warriors armed with bows and arrows marched towards them. Chitraveni stood before Narasimha Varman with a smile. The king, shivering with fear, fell at her feet and pleaded, 'Don't kill me, sister.'

Chitraveni stepped over his bent body and walked towards the statue. As if it had been planned, four women warriors carried in the throne of Kadarimandalam and placed it at the feet of Kali. Chitraveni ascended the throne and the priests started chanting mantras. Narasimha Varman was bound in chains and dragged to the queen. They shoved him down and he fell to his knees. The chief priest took the crown from Narasimha Varman's head and placed it on Chitraveni's as soldiers shouted, 'Jai, jai, Maharani Chitraveni!'

Pattaraya stood by her side with his arms crossed over his chest, his right palm closing his mouth—a position of abject surrender—which surprised Jeemotha. In contrast, the young woman was sitting on a smaller throne at the left of Chitraveni. The priest placed a smaller crown on the young woman's head, and the soldiers cried, 'Jai, jai, Yuvarani Mekhala Devi.'

Jeemotha saw Pattaraya wiping his tears. The young woman got up and touched Pattaraya's feet and called him 'nanna'. 'Ah, Pattaraya's daughter,' Jeemotha whispered. When Mekhala touched Chitraveni's feet and called her 'amma', Jeemotha was taken aback.

Chitraveni placed her left foot on Narasimha Varman's head and the deposed king didn't even flinch. He sat on all fours, obedient like a pet dog. The ceremony of rewarding those who had helped Chitraveni win her crown back went on and on, while Jeemotha waited patiently. He had waited all his life to gain respectability, he could wait a little more. When his name was called, he moved forward and gave a cursory bow. It was difficult to bow before a woman, and it would take some getting used to.

A cloth bag hit his face and fell to the ground. He picked it up, surprised. He hurriedly opened its strings. There were some gold coins and a ruby the size of a lemon. Precious, no doubt, but not what Jeemotha had expected. The usurer was already calling out other names, and a soldier gently tried to lead Jeemotha away.

'But this isn't what Pattaraya promised!' Jeemotha protested. He pushed away the soldier and stepped before the maharani of Kadarimandalam. He flung the cloth bag at her feet and said, 'Devi, I was promised a minister's position.'

Chitraveni smiled at him. 'A minister?'

'Yes. Pattaraya gave me his word,' Jeemotha said hotly. Chitraveni turned to Pattaraya, who looked away.

'A man as a minister?' Chitraveni laughed, and the entire sabha roared with laughter. Jeemotha's face flushed with anger.

'Do you think this is Mahishmathi, for men to hold positions of importance? You're young and handsome. Join my harem,' Chitraveni said.

'Pattaraya, you crook,' Jeemotha screamed. 'You betrayed me!'

The assembled women roared with laughter again. Blind with anger, Jeemotha screamed at Chitraveni, 'You bitch, you—'

Before he could complete the sentence, he was held by soldiers. He tried to resist, but they bound him in chains.

'Behead him,' Chitraveni said. 'And put his severed head at the gates of the city as a warning to any man who dares to disrespect women.'

Jeemotha knew he had made a huge mistake. He fell to his knees and cried, 'Spare me, Your Highness. I apologise. Pattaraya, we were friends, help me. I beg for my life. Have mercy.'

Pattaraya whispered something in Chitraveni's ears.

'I have decided to spare your life,' Chitraveni said, and Jeemotha sighed in relief. 'But I don't want you to go unpunished for your disrespect. Castrate him.'

Jeemotha screamed, 'No! Kill me, kill me—that is better.'

Chitraveni laughed. 'Sisters, see the stupidity of man. See what he values over his head.'

The sabha was filled with the laughter of women. Jeemotha wept, in despair over the betrayal, and in fear of what was in store.

Chitraveni said, 'You're a bull of a man. A fine specimen. I don't want you to be wasted. Take him to the oil press. Let's make use of your muscles.'

Jeemotha knew what it meant, and his shoulders sagged in defeat. They would yoke him to an oil press mill like a bull, and he would go round and round, squeezing oil out of sesame seeds till the end of his life. A life more miserable than that of a galley slave. Of the three options, death was the kindest one. But if he died, how would he get back at this vile woman? Around him, he could hear the chuckles of derision among the women soldiers. *If I get out of this, I will make each of them pay for this humiliation*, he promised himself. He had come with the hope of gaining the respectability he had always yearned for, and he had ended up worse than a draught bull. The deposed king, who was kneeling before Chitraveni, on whose head her left foot rested—even that fool was laughing at his plight.

As they dragged him from Chitraveni's presence, Jeemotha heard her say, 'Pattaraya, I need to rest my right foot too. When will Somadeva give company to Narasimha Varman?'

'Devi,' Pattaraya said, bowing low. 'Soon.'

# FIFTEEN

# Sivagami

'SUCH A FOOL. I knew Mahadeva would mess it up. I will kill that pirate,' Bijjala said, slamming his fist into a nearby tree. A chunk of the hard wood chipped off.

'I'm sorry, Prince,' Keki sobbed. 'I tried my best to protect him. I advised him to wait till you returned, but he trusted the pirate more than his own brother. Jeemotha stabbed the prince and flung him overboard.'

Sivagami stood stunned, unable to believe her ears. A sob escaped her throat and Bijjala turned towards her.

'I am sorry, Sivagami,' Bijjala said. 'I am devastated too. I loved him, though I am not the type who can be openly affectionate. He ... he ... was my much-loved younger brother.' Bijjala's voice cracked.

The past tense Bijjala used gave an air of finality to everything.

'No, he can't die just like that,' Sivagami whispered. She knew she was exposing herself to Bijjala, but she wasn't in a state to care. She had faked love for Bijjala so she could get to Gauriparvat. She had a grudging admiration for Bijjala's brute strength, his commanding power and the rapport he was able to build with his band of soldiers, who were ready to die for him. But she could never love him. There was something phony about Bijjala. Perhaps, after being in love with Mahadeva, no one could measure up to him.

'He may not be dead, Sivagami. I hope he isn't. He is my little brother,' Bijjala said, putting an arm around her shoulders and lifting her chin with his other hand. She turned away, unable to hide her tears.

'I saw him drowning, Prince,' Keki said.

Sivagami rushed to her tent. She didn't want to hear more. She sat in a corner, burying her face in her hands. She felt Bijjala's presence near her and shrunk into herself. She wanted to be alone. Alone with her thoughts of Mahadeva.

'Sivagami, we will avenge my brother's death. He was a fool, but he didn't deserve this—'

'Please go,' Sivagami said, without lifting her face.

'Siblings do fight, Sivagami. But I always liked him.'

'Go,' Sivagami said again.

'I know you loved him, Sivagami, and he loved you. I was jealous of him for that. But I would never have wanted it to end like this. I know I don't measure up to him. He was noble, brave, intelligent and learned. I am just a soldier. A better soldier perhaps, but that is it. I am not complicated like him, Sivagami. I am a plain man, a simple prince. When you've gotten over this tragedy, when all of us have gotten over this terrible, terrible calamity, I will ask you something,' Bijjala said, holding her elbow. She shook him away, but he held on. 'I will ask you something, Sivagami. Please don't say "no" then.'

Before she could reply, he had gone, leaving her to her misery. Outside, Vajra neighed. Did he know? Did the horse know the one who had gifted him to her was no more? Sivagami rushed out and put her arms around the horse's warm neck. It nudged her with its nose. She rested her face on his smooth mane and cried. Vajra's breath on her neck reminded her of him and brought back a thousand memories. She wished she had explained everything to him. She wished she had told him how much she loved him. It was late, too late now.

Darkness crept in from the bushes and covered her with a veil. She stood alone under the turbulent sky, hugging a mute creature that understood her perhaps more than she understood herself. It offered itself, a love without conditions and just stood with her, for her.

As mist rose from the grass and the crickets started their symphony from the bushes, she fought the sense of relief descending on her. Now she was free to pursue her goal. Nothing stood between her and Mahishmathi now. The hand of fate had removed the only obstacle. She was now equal to any of the unscrupulous players in this game of chaturanga. She would use deception, employ any tactic, to win the game and fulfil her father's dream. She felt guilty for the sense of relief. Mahadeva deserved better. Perhaps he had deserved someone far better than her. Someone who could have loved him back with the same sincerity, with the same innocence; someone who, like him, could find the best even in the worst of people. That was what had done him in, finally. The world didn't deserve Mahadeva, just as it didn't deserve Skandadasa or Devaraya.

'Akka.'

Sivagami thought she was hallucinating. Gundu Ramu's face was staring at her from the bushes. *Oh God, how much guilt should I carry? Anyone I love or admire is snatched away by fate*, she thought.

'Akka.'

She felt a hand envelop hers. She blinked in disbelief as she looked up to see Gundu Ramu.

'Gundu Ramu, Gundu Ramu,' she clasped his face in her hands, still unsure whether or not she was dreaming. Gundu Ramu stood there, battered and bruised, but alive. Sivagami showered him with kisses and the boy hugged her tight and wept on her shoulder. When they had cried their hearts out, the boy fished out the tattered manuscript from his waistband.

'Akka, here ...' Gundu Ramu said, but Sivagami had caught sight of his hand.

'What happened to your fingers?' she asked in shock, and Gundu Ramu hid his hand behind his back, ashamed of his missing fingers.

'Oh God, oh God,' Sivagami took his hand by force and looked at it in horror. 'What happened, Gundu?'

'Bird ... big bird ... ate it,' he said.

Sivagami could not stand it anymore. She didn't deserve such a sacrifice from anyone, let alone this innocent boy. She had trusted him with her book once, and he had gone through hell, and yet hadn't broken her trust. She sat down, feeling weak and broken. The horse sniffed her, as if assuring her of its unconditional love. Sitting by her side, Gundu Ramu kept his disfigured hand in hers and started telling her about the hell on Gauriparvat.

## SIXTEEN

# Bijjala

KEKI READ THE stone carving aloud to Bijjala: 'The braveheart Bijjaladeva, the crown prince of Mahishmathi, the beloved of gods, the darling of people, the blessed of saints, the one who defeated the Vaithalikas during the third Mahamakam and saved his father and the country, orders thus. Let all men treat each other as brothers. Let all men treat women as their sisters, mothers or daughters. Let each one be compassionate to the other. Let there be no killing, no violence, no jealousy or anger. The prince desires everyone live in peace and happiness.'

Bijjala scratched his chin. 'What is all this?'

Keki pointed to another slab and read aloud, 'Prince Bijjala, the beloved of Amma Gauri, the cherished son of Maharaja Somadeva, commands thus. There is no difference between men and women, higher caste and lower caste, animals and birds. All are equal before God. Let everyone conduct their lives accordingly.'

'Have you gone mad?' Bijjala asked angrily. 'I was enjoying my drink and you drag me here to read these? What is all this?'

Keki ignored the prince and said to two soldiers standing there, 'Bury them at least ten feet deep, at three-hour travel distances on the forest path.' The soldiers bowed, took the stone slabs and left.

'Are you crazy, eunuch? We don't have sufficient men and you waste them in such silly pursuits.'

'Silly pursuits?' Keki said. 'I've written only good things about you, dear prince.'

'Then why bury them like a cat buries its shit. How will people know about my greatness if you bury them?'

Keki smiled at Bijjala. 'Those who live now will know the truth one way or another. We can bribe enough bards and poets to sing about you for now. But what about the future? Those stones are for future generations to read about Bijjaladeva the great.'

Bijjala scoffed. 'Why should I care what people think about me after I am dead and gone?'

'My guru Pattaraya often says that good rulers control their present and better rulers control both their past and present. Great are the ones who control their future too, along with rewriting the past and writing the present. I have buried similar stones at various places in Guha's village. Soon, such stone engravings will be buried across the entire Mahishmathi.'

'Whatever,' Bijjala said with a shrug. 'Tell me this. Did you really see my brother die?'

Keki hesitated and then said, 'I saw it with these beautiful eyes.'

Bijjala said, 'Somehow, I have a feeling that he will come

back. Or haunt me as a ghost, as that slave haunted me for some time.'

'Oh, I forgot to mention this,' Keki said. 'A pigeon carried this message from Maharaja Somadeva to Akkundaraya at dawn.'

Bijjala snatched the message. 'Why did he give it to you?'

'You were sleeping, Prince.'

Bijjala read the message and stared at Keki. 'I don't understand. Why has my father asked me to abort the mission and rush to Mahishmathi with my soldiers? There is going to be a war with Kadarimandalam, which has declared independence? I don't understand.'

Keki laughed. 'It just means that the statue Mahadeva lost has reached its destination. Remember what Pattaraya told you in Muthayya's inn? This is the signal we have been waiting for. We won't go back to Mahishmathi, but to Kadarimandalam where Pattaraya would be waiting for you to fulfil our dream.'

'But how will I answer my father?' Bijjala cried.

'Prince. Future historians will write that Prince Bijjala rushed to Kadarimandalam without wasting time when he heard about this insult to Mahishmathi. Unfortunately, the brave prince lost the war and got caught by Pattaraya.'

'You want me to lose?' Bijjala asked. 'I will lose no battle. Never. I would rather die—'

'Prince, Prince, Prince. Please. The game isn't just about winning some battles. The game of chaturanga is about guessing what the opponent will do for the next twenty moves and play one step ahead, each time, every time. The game is more about weakening the opponent mentally. With the grace of my guru Pattaraya, I know something about this art of war. So please follow my instructions. Unless we play this drama, how would we trap—?'

'Trap my father?' Bijjala completed.

Keki smiled.

Bijjala was excited. 'Let's leave now.'

Keki held his hand, 'Not so soon, not before we do something important.'

'What now?'

'Your brother is dead ... but suppose he isn't,' Keki said.

'You keep talking in riddles, I will flay you alive, eunuch. You said he is dead and now you're saying something else. Is he dead or alive?'

'Swami, hear me out. He is dead, but what if he is alive? We need to think about that possibility too. What if you go to Kadarimandalam and Mahadeva takes Gauriparvat. You become the king of Mahishmathi, but Gauriparvat is with Mahadeva.'

The graveness of Keki's words slowly sunk in. 'But he is never going to breach the defence of Durgappa,' Bijjala said. 'He is no warrior. The fool couldn't even save the Kali statue.'

'We must think ahead, my prince. What if Mahadeva bribes Durgappa and Hidumba? What if he gets them over to his side? With Gauriparvat in his hands, he will have Mahishmathi dancing to his tunes. We need to pre-empt him. This game isn't as simple as you think.'

Bijjala was silent, deep in thought.

'The one who holds both, holds the empire, swami.'

'But Mahishmathi hasn't fallen yet.'

'Ah, its fall is imminent, swami. Do you think Pattaraya is a fool to declare independence? He knows he has an advantage.

We have all this worked out, Prince. Just follow my plan, which is nothing but Pattaraya's plan. Relax and rejoice. You will be the emperor of Mahishmathi soon.'

'But how can I take Gauriparvat and yet go to Kadarimandalam at the same time? How can I pre-empt Mahadeva?'

'Prince, this is our plan ...'

SEVENTEEN

# Sivagami

SIVAGAMI SAT WATCHING Gundu Ramu eat. The boy was struggling to put the food in his mouth as rice slipped through the gap where his fingers should have been. Without a word, she moved closer to him and started feeding him.

'Why are you crying?' she asked.

'Why are you crying?' he asked back.

'I'm not crying, you are,' she said, as she fed him another bite. She wiped her tears with the back of her hand and smiled.

Keki's voice startled her. 'The prince is calling you, Devi,' Keki said. 'I shall feed the boy. Please go. The Brahmins have come.' Keki squatted beside Gundu Ramu.

'Brahmins?' Sivagami asked, placing herself between Gundu Ramu and the eunuch. The boy had stopped eating and looked scared.

'This is the last village on the way to Gauriparvat. Once we leave here, we won't be able to do the rituals. This is the last place where you will get priests. After this, it is all wilderness.'

'Rituals? What rituals?' Sivagami asked. Gundu Ramu was staring at Keki with revulsion, his mouth wide open. 'Gundu, eat dear.' After hearing the tales of cruelty in Gauriparvat, she wanted to leave without any delay. It was a journey of perhaps three months or more to Gauriparvat from where they were camped.

'Devi, I shall feed him. Don't worry,' Keki said, taking the vessel from Sivagami. 'Please hurry. Have you forgotten? Today is the forty-first day after Prince Mahadeva's unfortunate death. We have already missed all the rituals. We don't want his soul to go to hell, do we? Bijjala is arranging for the feeding of Brahmins, giving alms, donating cows and many more things for the sake of his dead brother.'

Sivagami froze. The finality of everything crushed her heart. She got up and slowly walked out of the tent.

The rituals had already started when she reached. Bijjala was sitting cross-legged before three Brahmins who were chanting mantras. On a plantain leaf were balls of rice, along with balls of sesame seeds. In one corner, another Brahmin was preparing the feast. Villagers had assembled in great numbers and some of them were crying. A rectangular sacrificial pit was in the centre. She stood watching, her heart growing heavier with each passing moment. The grief was overwhelming. Bijjala looked as affected as she was; she could see his eyes were brimming with tears.

*Mahadeva, why did you come into my life, when all I wanted was to destroy your family,* she thought. *I came with hate and you filled my heart with love. I always thought I didn't deserve you. Destiny knew it too, and took you away from me.*

The smoke from the altar pit curled heavenwards. *Wherever you are, be happy,* Sivagami thought, suppressing a sob.

Bijjala gifted the Brahmins cows, cloth and pouches of gold coins. They blessed the elder prince to live for a hundred years and to one day be crowned emperor of Mahishmathi. As villagers ran to take their seats for the feast, Bijjala walked towards Sivagami. He looked tired and haggard.

He stood before her without saying anything, staring into her sad eyes for a moment. Then he held her close and whispered in her ear, 'I am sorry. I too loved him.'

Sivagami broke down. Gundu Ramu looked at them with his mouth agape. Finally, Sivagami gathered herself and released herself from Bijjala's consoling embrace.

'We need to hurry to Gauriparvat. It is worse than we thought,' Sivagami said. Before Bijjala could react, she narrated the news Gundu Ramu had brought her.

'Shocking,' Bijjala cried. 'I can't believe it. My father would never do so.'

'He escaped from that hell, Prince,' Sivagami said, pointing to Gundu Ramu. 'We have no time to waste. We need to go today. Please ... so many children.'

'I agree, Sivagami. We have to stop this cruelty. We will go to Gauriparvat one day.'

'One day? What do you mean by one day?' Sivagami asked. Bijjala handed over the letter from Maharaja Somadeva. She ran her eyes over it. The first sentence itself was devastating. It killed the small glimmer of hope she had dared to nurture in her mind. 'Since the death of your brother Mahadeva, I am not keeping well, son,' Maharaja Somadeva had begun. She sighed and read on.

'But ...' Sivagami stammered as Bijjala took back the letter.

'It is Maharaja Somadeva's order, devi. I need to go. Our country is in grave danger.'

Sivagami turned away, biting her lips, struggling to control her anger and frustration. She was so close to achieving her father's dream.

She turned back and said, 'Give me some soldiers, Prince.' She sounded desperate.

'Soldiers? What do you plan to do?' Bijjala asked.

'I am going to complete this mission,' Sivagami said. She forced a smile on her lips and added, 'For you.'

'Why, Sivagami?'

'Because it is important for our country. You follow the king's orders. I haven't got any orders.'

'In fact, my father had sent me many orders to arrest you and send you back to Mahishmathi. You came without his permission. It was only my ... my consideration for you that saved you, Sivagami. But now ...' Bijjala said, his tone conveying his helplessness.

'I am thankful for everything you have done, Your Excellency. But please ... give me a few soldiers. Allow me ...'

'Sivagami, I am going to fight a war. I need my soldiers. I promise, together we will come back with a huge army and end the mining at Gauriparvat.'

'That is never going to happen. Do you think the maharaja will spare me for joining your mission without his permission? I will be arrested, stripped of my bhoomipathi position and perhaps hanged,' Sivagami said. This was her last chance to fulfil her father's dream. She had been worried about trusting the unpredictable Bijjala, but he was her last hope. She had clung to it, despite all the misgivings that haunted her. If she went back to Mahishmathi, she would most likely follow her father to heaven.

'At least give me half your soldiers,' Sivagami pleaded. Bijjala turned away, shaking his head. 'At least a thousand of your soldiers, five hundred ... please.'

When Bijjala walked away, Sivagami collapsed to her knees and wept. All she had worked for had collapsed.

---

The next morning dawned with the Mahishmathi soldiers standing in rows in their battle gear. Bijjala cantered up and down on his horse, and Sivagami followed on Vajra. Bijjala, dressed in armour, drew his sword from its sheath and held it high. The rising sun caught its tip and it glimmered like a diamond.

'Jai Mahishmathi!' he cried.

The cry echoed from the three thousand throats of Bijjala's loyal soldiers. They clanged their spears against their shields, and thousands of lances, swords and maces bobbed up and down in the air. Bijjala turned his horse so he faced the army, Sivagami by his side.

'Comrades!' he called out. 'My beloved men. We have been challenged. We have been insulted. The pride of Mahishmathi is at stake.'

A roar of anger greeted this proclamation.

'Kadarimandalam, a small, pitiful vassal kingdom that was once ruled by amoral women and meek men has dared to challenge our beloved Mahishmathi.'

Another wave of indignation went through the ranks and Bijjala waited for it die down. He raised his voice again, brandishing his sword in the air.

'My father, His Highness Maharaja Somadeva, has ordered us to return to Mahishmathi to defend it. No disrespect to my revered father, but it is shameful that we have to defend it against an insignificant kingdom.'

'Shame, shame,' echoed his soldiers.

'My father is devastated by my younger brother's death and fears for my safety. He wants me back inside the forts of Mahishmathi. Understandable for a father. But as a king, I wish he had ordered us to sack Kadarimandalam. Friends, can't we do it?'

'We can, we can,' roared the army.

'Don't you trust the sharpness of your swords, the power in your arms, the speed of your steeds and the courage in your veins?'

'We trust you, Bijjaladeva. We will ride to hell with you,' cried an emotional young soldier.

'Yes, we will. We will,' echoed the others.

'Should we hide like rats in the safety of our fort or should we march like warriors and—'

'Smash Kadarimandalam!' cried the soldiers, completing his sentence for him.

'Jai Mahishmathi!' Bijjala shook his sword high in the air and the army's echo was electrifying.

With grudging admiration, Sivagami watched how Bijjala was able to inspire his loyal soldiers. As one soldier said, they would ride to hell with him.

A horn sounded and a captain walked to the centre of the clearing. 'Divide into two!' the captain called out, gesturing to either side. There was a confused murmur, but the army column divided itself into two. Sivagami frowned. What game was Bijjala playing?

'Those on my left will ride with me to Kadarimandalam,' Bijjala said. 'Those on my right will ride with Bhoomipathi Sivagami devi to recapture Gauriparvat from Durgappa and Hidumba.'

What had made him change his mind, Sivagami wondered, as she watched the effect of Bijjala's words. The soldiers who were to ride with her began voicing their protest, and soon it became an uncontrollable din.

'We can't fight under a woman.'

'She is just a bhoomipathi. We are the elite soldiers under the prince.'

'She is a traitor's daughter. Why should we trust her?'

The soldiers merged into one column and Bijjala screamed, 'Who defies my orders?'

The soldiers responded with a cry in unison, 'Jai Mahishmathi!' But they stood defiant, unmoving, angry.

'I command you to divide into two and the right wing will follow—'

'Jai Mahishmathi!' The roar shook the sky. The soldiers were in no mood to relent. The moment Bijjala opened his mouth, the shout of Jai Mahishmathi drowned out his voice. After a couple more attempts, when the soldiers began to clang their shields amidst their chants of Jai Mahishmathi, Bijjala turned to Sivagami.

'It is beyond my control, devi. I am sorry.'

Sivagami fought her tears. They saw her as just a woman, a traitor's daughter, and no soldier was willing to fight for her.

'There is a way out, but ...' Bijjala hesitated.

'What is it?' Sivagami asked, though all her instincts were warning her that she was being led into a cleverly laid trap.

'It is too early to ask, after the great loss we have both suffered. But I am going to a war, Sivagami. I don't know whether I will come back alive. If I don't ask now, it may be too late. And it may perhaps help you too. I am the crown prince of Mahishmathi, being the only surviving son of the maharaja. My soldiers may not follow an ordinary woman, but they have no choice but to follow a rani. Are you ready to become the maharani of Mahishmathi one day? Will you marry me, Sivagami?'

The words fell like thunder on her ears. *No, no,* her conscience screamed, and she nudged Vajra forward. The horse began to trot, and she sat on it with her head bowed. Bijjala galloped to her and rode by her side. He grasped her hand and leaned towards her. 'I won't ask again, Sivagami. But this is your only chance to ride to Gauriparvat and save those children. As you know, if you go back to Mahishmathi as a mere bhoomipathi, you will be tried and hanged. As my wife, no one would dare touch you. Without shame, I am asking again. Are you ready to be the maharani of Mahishmathi one day?'

Sivagami shook her head. It was a betrayal to the memory of Mahadeva. Bijjala was everything that she hated about Mahishmathi. She knew his sympathy was false. And yet ... if she didn't grab this chance, she would be betraying her father and all that he stood for. She would be betraying the sacrifice of Thimma. She would be abandoning those children.

If she could save those children, if she could stop the mining in Mahishmathi ... Better men and women had given their lives for the cause and, compared to that, her sacrifice was nothing. It was her body Bijjala lusted for. And, in all fairness, he had waited till Mahadeva was no more before voicing his interest. He had never misbehaved with her. This would be her sacrifice, her offering to the memory of the great men who had died for the cause she was fighting for. 'Forgive me, Mahadeva,' she whispered, and with tearful eyes she raised her head.

Bijjala had already returned to his position. She nudged Vajra to his side. And, looking into the distance, whispered, 'Yes.'

Bijjala turned towards her in surprise. A smile rose on his lips and he reached out and squeezed her fingers. She cringed, but smiled at him.

Bijjala shouted, 'Listen, oh fools! Hail Rani Sivagami devi!'

The din died down to a surprised silence. Bijjala scanned the army with glowering eyes, and the soldiers who had been rebelling looked down.

'Which fool said he wouldn't march under the leadership of my beloved, Sivagami devi? Who dares to call my betrothed a traitor?'

The soldiers looked at each other in surprise.

'Sivagami devi is no mere bhoomipathi. She is going to become my wife this evening. I am the crown prince of Mahishmathi. Tomorrow, I will be king. And the one you called a traitor, a mere woman, will be maharani of Mahishmathi. Who dares to defy her orders?'

'Jai Sivagami devi, rani of Mahishmathi!' a soldier cried, and after a moment's stunned silence, the cry rose from three thousand throats. Sivagami stood feeling guilt at her betrayal of Mahadeva and Bijjala, but in a corner of her mind, she found to her horror that the word 'rani' gave her an immense thrill. She remembered Mahadeva's accusation that she had killed Thimma for power, and she quickly pushed away the uncomfortable thought. She allowed Bijjala to grab her hand and raise it in the air, much to the enthusiasm of the troops.

That evening, the Brahmins who had conducted the death rituals of Mahadeva the previous day supervised the marriage of Prince Bijjaladeva to Rani Sivagami devi, and the villagers were treated to a great feast again. Hundreds of lambs were slaughtered and many peacocks roasted. Wine flowed and the celebration was raucous. Bijjala came to her bed stinking of wine and gold leaf smoke. She lay like wood, bearing his weight and the guilt of double betrayal stoically, as Keki sang bawdy songs outside.

Later that night, she woke up with a strange feeling that Mahadeva was lying beside her. In the moonlight that seeped in through the window, she found to her relief and dismay that it was Bijjala who was snoring in her bed. She walked outside and looked at the distant Gauriparvat. Moonlight melted over her slopes and spilt over to the jungle below. With bleary eyes, she looked at the mountain that had shaped her destiny. Suddenly, she noticed something strange moving near the peak. She blinked and waited. It was a speck from this distance, but it appeared to be flapping its wings. Then another one followed it, and another one followed the first two. They couldn't be birds, she reasoned. No bird could be big enough to be seen from such a distance. She sighed and went back to her tent.

The next day, Sivagami applied vermillion on Bijjala's forehead like a dutiful wife as he stood before her in his armour. He kissed her goodbye and jumped onto the saddle of his war horse. He raised the war cry and half his army joined him. To the cheers of the other half that stayed back under the command of Sivagami, Bijjala's army galloped behind their leader to crush the Kadarimandalam rebellion. Keki went with them. Akkundaraya stayed back. He had promised to take Sivagami to Gauriparvat.

Rani Sivagami devi turned to her men and said, 'Tomorrow, we start our campaign to get Gauriparvat back.' And the air shook with that strange but pleasant cry from about fifteen hundred men, 'Jai Maharani Sivagami devi, jai Mahishmathi!' She was just a rani, not a maharani, but she let the small detail pass and went to take a bath. She needed to cleanse away the smell of Bijjala's stale breath from her body.

## EIGHTEEN

# Somadeva

THE OFFICIAL SEAL of his son stared back at Somadeva from the scroll he held in his trembling hands. Queen Hemavati was standing beside him, wailing. 'I lost my son Mahadeva to your foolish plans. Now I will lose my Bijjala too,' she lamented.

Somadeva didn't understand why Bijjala had defied his orders to return to Mahishmathi and instead attacked Kadarimandalam. Was Bijjala a bigger fool than he thought? A grain of suspicion started forming in his mind.

He stormed out of his private chamber. Parameswara and General Hiranya were waiting for him, their foreheads creased with worry.

'I think this is a trap,' Somadeva said. 'I have received news of a great massacre at Kadarimandalam. Three thousand of our soldiers were murdered. Pattaraya is alive. It is a total intelligence failure. What were our spies doing? You two have failed in your duty.'

Parameswara and Hiranya stood in silence, their shoulders stooped with guilt. The king shook the scroll in their faces. 'My foolish son has attacked Kadarimandalam and has become a captive of Pattaraya.'

Hiranya looked up and said, 'There is something wrong. As per the reports I have just received, Bijjala's army split into two and one half turned to Kadarimandalam. But there are no reports of the army having reached there.'

'He went with half the strength?' Somadeva asked. 'And the other half?'

Hiranya hesitated. 'I think he ordered the other half to follow his wife.'

'Wife? What are you blabbering about?'

Parameswara intervened. 'Your Highness, it seems the prince has married Bhoomipathi Sivagami devi.'

Somadeva stared at them in shock. The maharani stormed out of the chamber and said, 'I don't care who my son has married. I want my son back now.'

'Devi,' Somadeva said, 'please, would you let us—'

'No. If I don't get back my son soon, you will never see me alive. I lost my Mahadeva and I don't want to lose my other son too.'

The queen started sobbing and an embarrassed Parameswara and Hiranya turned away. The king sighed. He said, 'Nothing will happen to our son, I promise. I will bring him back, devi. Please allow me to sort this out.'

When Queen Hemavati had walked into her chamber and closed the door, Somadeva turned to his mahapradhana.

'Why would my son do such a foolish thing as to marry that girl? She was under watch. We were discussing whether she had some secret plans against us—and he goes and marries her? I knew she was shrewd, but she has played her game really well. She is now a princess of Mahishmathi. Wonderful,' Somadeva said bitterly.

'I don't think you need to worry so much about her, Your Highness,' Parameswara said. 'There was an attack, and her army was decimated at the foot of Gauriparvat.'

'Who attacked them?' Somadeva asked.

Hiranya hesitated.

'Who?'

'Garuda pakshis. It seems Hidumba and Durgappa have freed the female bird.'

The blood drained from Somadeva's face. 'Do those morons know what they have done? The male and female aren't supposed to be released at the same time!'

'They were preparing their defence perhaps, when they heard about Bijjala's army moving towards Gauriparvat,' Hiranya said.

'The girl has probably been killed,' Parameswara said. 'Tribes report of a great massacre in the jungles of Gauriparvat, and bodies of slain soldiers still float in the upper Mahishi.'

Parameswara continued, 'Prince Bijjala was lucky that he didn't follow Sivagami to Gauriparvat. Thank god he is still alive. We can negotiate with Kadarimandalam and get him back. Even if we are forced to give Kadarimandalam independence now, we can always bring them under our fold later.'

Somadeva sat down. 'How are we going to get back Gauriparvat?'

'That is a problem we will tackle once we ensure the crown prince is safe, Your Highness. Without Bijjala, what is the use of this kingdom to us? He is your only remaining son,' Parameswara said softly.

'I have a bad feeling about this,' Somadeva said, handing over the scroll from Bijjala. 'Do you think it is genuine?'

'The royal seal of Bijjala is genuine enough. We can't take a chance, Your Highness. I suggest you take the army to Kadarimandalam. They have our prince. Negotiate a truce with them and get Bijjala back to safety.'

'The Kali statue has reached there, Parameswara. Most probably Pattaraya would have started making Gaurikhadga and other weapons. He knows the process.'

'I doubt that, Your Highness. They might have the stones, but if they had the weapons, they would have already attacked us.'

'The mahapradhana's assessment seems to be correct,' Hiranya said.

Somadeva stood up; there was a determined expression on face. 'Pattaraya thinks he is smart. He is sly no doubt, but so am I. I will do exactly as he asks. But my army will wait at the borders. The moment I get back Bijjala, we will attack. We won't give Kadarimandalam time to produce Gauridhooli. We will destroy their facilities. Hiranya, how many hands do you require to defend the city in my absence?'

'Your Highness, I will go to Kadarimandalam. It would be dangerous for you to leave Mahishmathi.'

'The letter is clear, Hiranya. They want me. Pattaraya and the bastard princess want me to beg them. They want to humiliate me. I will bear everything for my son. But I will pay them back with interest. However, I go leaving the city in trusted hands. Hiranya, you and Parameswara are the only friends left. I lost Thimma and Devaraya. I hope I can trust you.'

Hiranya fell to his knees and said, his eyes blurry with tears, 'Your Highness, my heart is broken by your doubt. Should you just hope you can trust us? My life is for you. I have always lived for Mahishmathi. I don't need many soldiers. The fort of Mahishmathi which Devaraya designed can withstand any attack. I can hold on for months even if the entire Kadarimandalam army attacks us. I will hold the fort under the command of our guru and friend, Mahapradhana Parameswara. Bring back the crown prince, Your Highness.'

Holding him by his shoulders, Maharaja Somadeva raised him up and hugged him. He included Parameswara in his embrace and said, 'We are brothers.'

Parameswara smiled. 'Mahabharata was the war between brothers. No, Soma, let us remain friends.'

Later that evening, Maharaja Somadeva left for Kadarimandalam with the major part of the Mahishmathi army and all the good weapons.

In Mahishmathi, Hiranya once again inspected the security of the fort and went home with the satisfaction that he had plugged all possible breaches.

NINETEEN

# Mahadeva

ALLY FOUND THE bard at the steps of the temple. Devotees were pouring in for the evening puja. The smell of incense and the sound of chants filled the air, with the occasional tinkling of the temple bell. She glanced at Kattappa, who was busy feeding Mahadeva the temple prasadam. She had to be discreet. She lead the bard towards the river and made her demand.

'Our art is the blessing of Lord Shiva. We don't lie, Amma,' the bard said.

'How much?' she asked, not in a mood to negotiate.

After the devastating loss of the Kali statue, Mahadeva had allowed himself to sink in the river. Ally had hauled him up and dragged him to the shore. With the help of Kattappa, she had restrained him and taken him to a village that was a two-day journey on foot, in the northern border of Guha's land.

Since then, for three months, they had been holed up in the village temple, which gave free food. The villagers had been told that Ally had brought her insane brother for a pilgrimage to the temple to cure him, a story she had cooked up when she saw other mentally ill men in the temple premises. The temple was old, the village was poor and survived on what they earned from pilgrims coming to the temple, and no one questioned her story. The appearance of Mahadeva, unwashed, unshaven, hair matted, gave credence to her story.

Ally was frustrated. She should have attached herself to Bijjala and Sivagami's army. Her aim was to reach Gauriparvat, yet she had frittered away her chance by attaching herself to Jeemotha. She hadn't wanted to leave Kattappa, driven more by guilt than love, but now it seemed everything she had worked for had vanished into thin air. She was at the same place she had started. Her own deteriorating relationship with Kattappa added to her woes.

Ally didn't know anyone who could take them to Gauriparvat. Many had dissuaded her from attempting the journey without an army. Her only hope now hinged on Mahadeva taking a decision to follow Sivagami. Being a prince, Mahadeva could arrange for men and resources, perhaps summon a regiment from Mahishmathi. But he was in the grip of a depression, often lamenting, 'I lost it all, I lost the trust of my father. I failed.' He worried about the fate of the slaves Jeemotha had carried away, and was morose about Sivagami leaving him. The better part of Ally's time and effort went in coaxing Mahadeva back to life. She kept a close watch on him, afraid he would harm himself. Finally, Ally had decided to try a ploy that might pull the prince out of his self-pity.

The bard arrived three days later after composing the song as Ally wanted. Mahadeva was sitting, leaning against a pillar, a far-away look in his eyes. Kattappa was standing near the Nandi statue in the temple courtyard, his eyes closed in prayer.

On Ally's cue, the bard started singing about Prince Bijjala's brave exploits. A few old men gathered around to hear him sing. Ally stood in the crowd, eyeing Mahadeva as the bard sang. Mahadeva continued to sit with no expression on his haggard face. When the name Sivagami was mentioned, he looked at the bard with a start. Ally breathed a sigh of relief. Her bluff might work.

The bard sang about the tragedy of Sivagami. She was on her deathbed somewhere in the jungles, he sang. The change that came over Mahadeva was astonishing. He grabbed the bard by his shoulders and shook him, questioning him about Sivagami. The bard said he had heard Sivagami attempted suicide when the news of Mahadeva's death reached her. The bard cried that no one knew where she was. Perhaps Sivagami was already buried or cremated. Mahadeva jumped up from the temple mandap and hurried away. Ally ran behind him.

'Where are you going?' she demanded.

'In search of my Sivagami,' Mahadeva said, like a man possessed.

'But how do you know where she is? Do you know the way to Gauriparvat?' Ally asked.

He shoved her out of his way and continued to walk quickly through the ridge that separated the paddy fields. 'I know, I know ...' he mumbled.

Kattappa caught up with them just as Mahadeva reached the path that would lead them into the jungle. Mahadeva stopped abruptly and studied the bark of a tree closely. Then he started running again. Ally caught his wrist and said, 'How can you be so sure? We will lose the way. And no one goes to Gauriparvat without an army. The way is full of perils.'

'We have no time. Sivagami is dying. Sivagami is dying,' he said, his eyes fixed on the distant mountain that stood covered in mist. Kattappa tried to restrain Mahadeva, but the prince knocked him down and carried on. When Kattappa tried to chase after him, Ally stopped him. They followed Mahadeva at a discreet distance as the prince walked like a man possessed. In a couple of days, he had led them to the abandoned camp where the Kali statue had once stood.

The prince stopped a few score feet away on the path leading to Gauriparvat and studied another tree carefully, after which he began running again. A hare darted across the path, but Mahadeva had no eyes for anything that would have enthralled him a few months before.

'He has someone in Sivagami's army. Maybe a spy, who has marked the way for the prince,' Ally whispered. She knew they were taking a grave risk going to Gauriparvat like this. If the fantastic tales she had heard about the mountain had any substance, they were rushing headfirst into grave danger.

Kattappa and Ally began following the prince. Night was rushing in on them. A brisk breeze rustled the tree leaves. Now and then, Ally could hear Mahadeva's forlorn cries, calling for Sivagami, and it filled her with unease. A superstition from her childhood came back to her. Be careful what you think, for the world has a way of making your thoughts come true. She hoped Sivagami wasn't really dying.

TWENTY

# Sivagami

'WHAT DO YOU mean, you won't go any farther?' Sivagami was livid.

'I have never gone farther than this. From here, you are on your own,' Akkundaraya said and smiled.

'That wasn't the deal. You were supposed to take me till Gauriparvat.'

'Rani Sivagami devi, from this valley onwards, it is Bhoomipathi Durgappa's territory. No one enters the area without his permission.'

'But he is the one who has raised the flag of rebellion.'

'That's your problem, Rani Sivagami devi. You have a truce with him, defeat him, kill him—that's up to you. I should warn you, entering his land without his permission is dangerous. He has his method of protecting his place.'

'You're supposed to assist me in this war,' Sivagami said, exasperated.

'No. The agreement was that I would show you the way. My ships can't sail any farther up, but they will wait for you.

We shall wait for either you to come with the stones or to take your dead body, if something of it is left. In either case, I would need the payment promised.'

'How dare you, Akkundaraya. You're talking to the rani of Mahishmathi.'

'Devi, never have I gone beyond this. Every Mahamakam, Bhoomipathi Durgappa and Hidumba brought the stones here and loaded them onto my ships. I don't even know what perils are there en route. I just know that it is all wilderness from here, and that it will probably take around three months for you to reach the fort, if you keep up a rapid march. I can only pray for you. I shall wait for six months and then return to civilisation. As an elderly man, I dare to give you this advice. Arrive at a truce, Rani. There is a reason why Gauriparvat has remained impregnable all this time. Devaraya, bless his soul, designed the defences well.'

Sivagami, though seething at the betrayal, knew it was of no use arguing with the sly bhoomipathi. She gave a curt bow to Akkundaraya and ordered her army to continue marching. As they started the gentle climb down to the verdant valley that stretched till the foot of Gauriparvat, she knew there was no going back now. Either she would perish here or she would redeem her father's name and come back victorious. The irony of breaking the famed defences her father had designed, to redeem him, wasn't lost on her.

Over the next two months, they marched without any major incidents, except for encountering and killing a man-eating tiger, and being surrounded by a herd of hyenas that they had to chase away. She began to wonder what the big deal was about Gauriparvat's defences.

Then they crossed a brook that flowed into the river Mahishi, and the terrain changed from shrubby bushes to thick forest. The river flowed over rocks with swirling rapids and whirlpools on one side and wilderness stretched out on all sides, except for Gauriparvat in the distance.

Three months after she had left Akkundaraya, they were traversing through a forest where trees, many score feet tall, towered over them. 'Halt,' Sivagami said, raising her hand. The long file of her army came to an uneasy stop. Neelappa, riding behind her, tried to say something, but Sivagami hushed him. She was feeling an inexplicable tension, a premonition of something sinister coming their way. There was agitation in the movements of Vajra too. Shafts of moonlight pierced through the canopy of trees, casting a dizzying checkered pattern on the forest floor.

Vajra snorted and tossed its head. It stomped the ground with its hoofs, struggling to turn and bolt. Sivagami patted the horse's neck and looked around. Even the drone of the crickets, that constant sound of the jungle, had ceased. It was as if the forest was holding its breath. Not a leaf stirred.

Gundu Ramu weaved his way forward to reach Sivagami, but a soldier held him back. The boy tried to speak, but he clasped the boy's mouth with his palm.

Sivagami unclasped her bow from her saddle and loaded an arrow. She could hear her soldiers following her lead. Were the enemy soldiers camouflaged in the bushes, waiting to ambush them? She pulled the bowstring back and slowly moved her aim, scanning from left to right. A sudden breeze made the trees murmur and sheaves of leaves spiralled down from the canopy.

Sivagami let go of the arrow, hoping to provoke anyone waiting to attack them. Following her action, the core group of two dozen soldiers, who had followed closely behind her, shot arrows in all directions. At least one would find its mark and the ambusher would give away their position by his screams. All they got was an uneasy silence.

Then a whistling sound came from far away. A moment later, a huge rock crashed through the canopy. Vajra bolted; Sivagami was thrown off the saddle, but her left foot was still caught in the stirrup. The horse dragged her as it ran in panic. Her head hit the ground many times and her shoulders collided against trees as she struggled to free herself. By the time she had him under control, she was battered and bruised. When she tried to sit up, she felt dizzy and she held Vajra tight. Gundu Ramu crashed through the bushes and ran to her crying.

'Ga … ga … gaa …' he stammered. His face was contorted with terror, and Sivagami wasn't able to make out what he was saying. The boy pointed to where the stone had fallen. She turned, and her blood froze.

'Garuda pakshi,' Gundu Ramu finally managed to say. A bird the size of a cow was perched on the rock that had fallen from the sky. Lit by a beam of moonlight, the bird looked like something out of a nightmare. It spread its wings, looked up at the moon, and gave an eerie cry. After a moment, from somewhere in the distance, a similar cry, but more shrill, echoed. Sivagami's soldiers had scattered. She tried to ride towards the bird, but Vajra refused to budge. She jumped off the saddle and a sharp pain shot up from her ankle. She had twisted it, and it was swelling fast.

Ignoring the pain, she limped towards the bird, unsheathing her sword as she approached it. The bird hopped down from the rock, looking at her indifferently. Sivagami saw Neelappa, bloodied, struggling to lift himself up. The bird watched him like a rooster would look at a worm before gobbling it up. With a flap of wings, it took off, holding Neelappa in its talons. Sivagami rushed towards the bird, yelling at the top of her voice and swinging her sword wide, but by the time she reached, the bird was soaring high with its prey. Sivagami had no time to think. She climbed onto the rock and flung her sword at the bird. And missed. Gundu Ramu, from his hiding place, gave a whistle. The bird dropped Neelappa like a stone.

Sivagami limped up to Neelappa, terrified that he was dead. He was lying face down and was motionless. Sivagami saw the huge wound that the bird's claws had caused on the old man's back. Then, Neelappa wheezed. 'Mama, mama,' Sivagami cried, cradling the old man to her bosom.

'Run, run,' the old man struggled to say between breaths. 'The bird will come back.'

She tried to lift him up, but he was too heavy for her. Gundu Ramu came up and tried to help her.

Sivagami cried to the wilderness, 'Are you men? Cowards? Leaving your queen to danger and running away? Where have you gone, you fools? Fight!'

One by one, the soldiers who were hiding came out of the woods. They walked slowly to her, their heads bowed as she chastised them. They started lifting the injured Neelappa and other soldiers who were crushed by the stone.

The next stone fell with a thud, crushing more people.

Sivagami looked up in horror and saw the bird was back. Behind her, another rock crashed down. She turned and saw the second bird. Her soldiers scattered again in fear. The birds swooped down towards them in a coordinated attack and snatched a soldier each before flying away.

The soldiers stood silent, angry. Sivagami was miserable: she didn't know how to protect her men, and the birds were sure to come back soon. Without looking at the soldiers who were approaching her, Sivagami helped Neelappa stand. The old man had broken his leg and was squirming in pain.

'Devi.' A captain named Karthikeya stepped forward.

Sivagami braced herself for what was coming.

'We are going back. We have a family waiting at home.'

'Are you soldiers or poets?' she scoffed, trying to hide her desperation with scorn. 'Your country is in danger and you refuse to obey your queen.'

'We can't fight that creature,' one of the soldiers yelled.

'Had any of you cowards helped me, we could've slain it easily. Instead you dug holes in the ground and buried yourself like cowering rats. Shame on you. My husband will chop off your manhood and make you eunuchs.'

'You girl, how dare you?' Karthikeya said.

Sivagami turned to the soldiers and said, 'Whip him. Let him learn how to talk to a queen.'

She knew the next few moments were crucial. If the soldiers refused, she was finished. Neelappa, dragging his broken leg, went up to Karthikeya and caught him by the scruff of his neck. With a strength that belied his age and injuries, he flung the rebel to the ground. That did the trick. Two soldiers rushed forward and picked up the captain. They tied him to a tree and whipped him. He bore it with dignity, and Sivagami raised her hand when she had counted ten lashes.

They spent some time burying the five soldiers who were crushed under the rocks and carried the injured ones, including Neelappa, on a hastily assembled stretcher.

As they were walking, Sivagami ruffled Gundu Ramu's hair affectionately and said, 'You're so brave.'

'I am not brave. I'm scared,' Gundu Ramu said.

'Why? You escaped that big bird, isn't it? Only someone brave can do that.'

'This is a small bird,' Gundu Ramu said. 'And I know a bit of its language.'

'What?' Sivagami laughed. 'You mean they are tame?'

'They are the guardians of Gauriparvat,' Gundu Ramu said, 'and they obey commands.'

*Oh God, oh God,* Sivagami thought, wondering how she was going to hold her army together when the birds attacked again. She had no clue how she was going to storm the mountain. She had to trust that Gundu Ramu could control them.

That night, they camped out in the open, in a meadow that gently slopped down to the river. She ordered the men to set up numerous fires. This meant that anyone watching from the fort near the mines could easily spot them. But that was better than being eaten by the birds. Her men were hardened fighters, and they could handle human enemies, she reasoned.

The army vaidya had made a brace for Neelappa's leg with wood, and had applied herbal paste on Sivagami's bruises. Sivagami knew from the way the soldiers conducted themselves that their attitude towards her had changed. Seeing her fight against the bird and stand up to the captain had raised her in their estimation. They had a grudging admiration for her now, and she could sense it. She hoped she would not lose it.

Despite the pain in her ankle, she completed her inspection of the security arrangements around the camp and then retired to her tent. Gundu Ramu came to sleep next to her. Neelappa refused to rest, but sat at the entrance of her tent, his sword by his side. Sivagami had ordered sentries to keep the fires running through the night, with the hope of keeping the birds and other wild animals away. She drifted into a dreamless sleep, with Gundu Ramu snuggled against her.

The fires kept the birds away that night. But the assault that came just before dawn was terrible. Sivagami woke up to Neelappa's screams. Outside, the camp was burning and the air was filled with the screams of dying soldiers.

TWENTY-ONE

# Gundu Ramu

'GUNDU, WAKE UP!'

Gundu Ramu opened his eyes and started coughing uncontrollably. Thick dark smoke made breathing impossible. 'Someone has set fire to our camp,' Sivagami said. Outside, Gundu could hear the screams of men and the clanging of swords

'Run out and hide in the forest,' Sivagami said as she pushed him out through the rear side of the tent.

'Akka,' he screamed and tried to get back in. The tent was suddenly ablaze, and it was impossible for him to make his way in. He ran around the tent, and heard her scream. He was unable to place the direction it was coming from.

'Akka,' he called, disoriented by the smoke and heat. He heard her scream again. He ran blindly and found himself in the open ground, where they had set up the war camp. Around him, several tents were burning and the charred bodies of men lay in grotesque positions on the ground. Some had spears thrust through their hearts, some had their limbs severed and some bodies were headless. Gundu ran, crying for Sivagami. 'Akka, Akka,' he cried in fear. A hand grasped his ankle and Gundu fell on his chest.

'Water,' a man covered in blood whispered. The terrified boy watched him as he extended his other hand. Then the man gave a shudder and died. Sobbing, Ramu extricated himself from the dead man's grip. Then he heard someone cry out. *Sivagami akka!* Her cry rose above the crackling of the hundred fires that were devouring the tents. He got up and ran, stumbling over weapons and the charred bodies of horses, weaving his way through the burning tents.

He found her by the river. Gundu Ramu froze when he first spotted her. She wasn't moving. Then, slowly, he crawled up to her, too shocked even to cry. He gasped as his hand came down on something sticky. The smell of blood made him gag. An arrow jutted out of Sivagami's left shoulder. Gundu Ramu fell on her, screaming, 'Akka, Akka, wake up, wake up!'

Sivagami's eyelids flickered. She wasn't dead, not yet. Gundu Ramu screamed, 'Ayyo, ayyo, someone please help, help!'

Except for the crackling of the fire that was devouring what was left of their camp, the forest was silent. Gundu ran around the field, trying to find someone who would be able to help him save his akka. But there was not one person alive.

Gundu felt his body grow cold. The mist had now covered most of the camp ground and the air was thick with the intense smell of charred flesh. By the time he had achieved some semblance of calm, the mist had swallowed the jungle.

*There had been more than fifteen hundred soldiers with them,* he thought. But he hadn't seen more than a few hundred bodies. Where had the others gone? Had they run away? If they had run away, they couldn't have gone far. There had to be someone around who could save his akka. He ran into the jungle, calling for help. For a moment, the fear of the giant bird flashed in his mind. He pushed it away. There was no time to be scared. 'Amma Gauri, Amma Gauri,' he chanted between cries for help to ward off his fear. Behind him, the mist had placed a blanket of white over the devastated camp, and the dying fires of the tents shone like the eyes of crouching beasts.

---

Gundu Ramu found a few soldiers by dawn. They were crouching in a dilapidated temple near a pond, deep inside the jungle. He ran to them, crying for help. A few of them sat up, surprised by his voice. Gundu Ramu saw that most of them were injured.

'Sivagami akka is dying. Please help, please help,' Gundu cried.

'All of us are dying,' a man groaned.

Gundu Ramu continued to plead, and when no one moved, he yelled at them, 'Cowards! You leave your queen to die. Shame on you!'

'Go away, boy.'

Gundu, helpless and frustrated, looked around, and his gaze fell on the idol of a multi-armed Goddess, half covered in termite mould. The Goddess had the face of a wild boar. Varahi, the Goddess of the Kalakeyas, Gundu Ramu remembered from the tales that his father had told him. Kalakeya country was far away, almost six months' journey by foot. Gundu Ramu pushed away the thought. The curse of knowing too much, his father used to say, is that trivia will pop up in your mind uncalled for. Ashamed at being distracted, he started praying to the Goddess. There is only one God and all gods are the manifestation of the one. *Save my akka,* he cried.

Someone tapped his shoulder. 'Boy, lead me to her.'

Gundu turned, wiping his tears and thanking the Goddess. It was Captain Karthikeya, the soldier Sivagami had got whipped the previous day. He had a wound on his chest and thighs, and blood oozed through a dressing. He commanded a few other men to follow, and half a dozen joined them, cursing their fate. Gundu led them to where Sivagami lay. She was struggling to breathe, but was still alive. The captain knelt next to her and said, 'There is not much we can do for her.'

'Please, save her!' Gundu pleaded.

'I am no vaidya, boy. And the vaidya died some hours ago. The only thing we can do is to wait for—'

A loud flapping of wings cut off the captain's words, and the soldiers ran and jumped into the river. Gundu Ramu fell on Sivagami, protecting her with his body, and closed his eyes shut. He was ashamed of the warm wetness that trickled between his thighs. When he heard the flap of wings again, he opened his eyes and saw the bird vanishing with the carrion of two dead soldiers.

The captain and his six soldiers came out of the river, dripping wet. Gundu Ramu stood up, looked down at his wet dhoti and started crying.

'I peed. I was so scared,' he said between sobs. The soldiers looked at each other and came to him with their heads bent, not looking in his eyes. They started attending to Sivagami while Karthikeya stood with his hand on Gundu Ramu's shoulder.

'I don't like that woman, boy. You know what she did to me. But I will give her this. She is braver than all the men she was leading. She could have saved herself, but she went back to save her slave.'

'My akka is very brave. Please save her,' Gundu Ramu said.

'I am afraid you have to brace your heart. You are a brave boy.'

'I'm scared,' Gundu Ramu said.

'Not half as much as we are, boy. We all joined the army not because we love our country more than everyone else, or because we are braver than the others. We joined to fight the enemy. You know the name of that enemy, boy?'

Gundu Ramu, worried about Sivagami, was barely listening. But Karthikeya pressed on.

'No, not the enemy you think. We fight and kill or get killed by the enemy that our rulers identify for us. That isn't our real enemy. The real enemy is hunger, boy. We joined the army so we could feed our families. We know no one cares whether we live or die. We may get a veerasringala, maybe some pompous official will visit our grieving family if we are martyred, but then we will be forgotten in a blink.'

'Save my akka, please.'

'We need to return home, boy; we need to end this mad expedition under an insane woman. We could've returned yesterday, and I told her so. She got me whipped in front of my men. I bore it, because I was scared. I was scared about what would happen if she ordered my execution. My family wouldn't even get the meagre pension. These are big people, they have our lives in their fists. I have six kids, my boy. One is younger than you. When I think of them, I forget my honour. I remember, she isn't my enemy, the bird that comes to eat us isn't my enemy, the ones the big guys want me to kill aren't my enemies. The real enemy is stalking each of our lives, mine, the lives of these men you saw jumping into the river. All of us are scared of that enemy called hunger. So don't expect us to be as brave as you.'

'Please, save my akka,' Gundu Ramu sobbed, not comprehending what the captain was saying and afraid that he was refusing to help Sivagami.

'The only thing we can do is to wait for the end and give her a decent funeral. That much I owe to the woman for being crazily brave while we ran for our lives.'

'No, she can't die!'

'Maybe, she won't, boy. The gods favour the rich and important. See those hundred men? The ones who were running away from hunger, the fools who died for two fists of rice? They weren't so lucky. Maybe the gods who didn't care a damn for those poor men will favour your akka. That's how this screwed-up world works. But I have seen enough wounds in my life as a soldier, and seeing her condition, I think it would be a blessing to her if she goes soon.'

Gundu Ramu continued to cry. The captain said, 'I am sorry, boy. Rani Sivagami devi deserves all our respect. The fires we lit to keep away the birds attracted our enemy. The attack was brutal and swift. She could have run away with us, but chose to fight. One against twenty women.'

'Women?'

'Yes. I'm ashamed to say it, but we were beaten by an army of women, led by a man called Shivappa. We thought he was dead, killed by his brother during Mahamakam. But we saw him in flesh and blood and the women addressed him as their king. He attacked thinking Prince Bijjala was leading the army, and left when he found out the prince wasn't with us. I saw Sivagami fighting like a tigress, but something Shivappa said about Prince Bijjala devastated her. The fight went out of her, and we were ruined. I think she gave herself up. After hearing what Shivappa said, she lost her will to live. So, allow me to relieve her of her suffering and we can go home. Otherwise, we will have a rebellion within the ranks.'

Gundu Ramu fell at Karthikeya's feet and sobbed, 'If Amma Gauri wants to take Sivagami akka, let her take her when she chooses. Promise me you won't hurt her. I am sure she will come back to life.'

Captain looked at the boy and then at Sivagami. *She won't last long anyway,* Karthikeya thought, and reluctantly agreed to wait. They moved Sivagami to the shelter of the dilapidated Kalakeya temple. The bodies of the fallen soldiers were left to rot, with Karthikeya justifying it as a safety measure. He hoped the birds would be satisfied eating the carrion and wouldn't bother the survivors.

While the soldiers waited for Sivagami to die, Gundu Ramu stood guard over her, afraid someone would hurt her in his absence. With every breath, he prayed to the fierce form of Varahi.

TWENTY-TWO

# Brihannala

A FEW MOMENTS after midnight, Brihannala left the harem and hurried to the river as had been her routine for the past few weeks. It surprised her that there had been no communication from Achi Nagamma or her army so far. Her network of spies was unable to tell her anything except that the army had last been seen at the foothills of Gauriparvat peak. The rumours of the Garuda pakshis filled her with unease. Where had Achi Nagamma gone? Brihannala had done her duty of getting Shivappa to her. The consolidation of the jungle tribes must have taken place by now, but there was no indication of a rebellion.

When she reached the fort gate, she was stopped and the soldiers sent her away despite her loud protests. Brihannala knew how vulnerable Mahishmathi was, with neither the king nor Prince Bijjala in the city, and almost the entire army away. The old general Hiranya had been given the responsibility of protecting the city with a limited army of five hundred people. In his meticulous, old-fashioned way, the general had set up sentries and watchers to man the fort. Catapults and giant arrows were mounted at the citadels, oil barrels and fire arrows were put in position on the fort walls and all the gates, except the main ones, which were double locked and fortified with sacks filled with rocks and sand. The general had sharpened the spikes in the fort gate and had them coated with fresh iron caps, so no army could use elephants to break the gate open. The drawbridge over the moat remained lifted always, and was levelled only when the movement of carts was absolutely necessary.

By morning, a worried Brihannala watched soldiers beating their drums and walking around the city streets, urging people to stay indoors and to report any suspicious activities or strangers to the nearest dandakara office. An atmosphere of fear hung in the city and the market was deserted. From the ashram of Guru Dharmapala, one could faintly hear mantras being chanted. Armed guards stood at the gate of the ashram and the palanquin of Maharani Hemavati could be seen. The guru was conducting a mahamrityunjaya yajna, a sacrifice for the safety of Prince Bijjala, at the request of the maharani.

Back in her chamber, Brihannala fretted and fumed. She had found a way to breach the fort, something that Hiranya had missed. If only Achi Nagamma would respond to the messages she had sent, she thought. This was the time to attack; where was Achi?

From her balcony, she saw a figure arguing with the palace guards at the inner fort gate, where the offices were located. She frowned. The woman looked familiar, and something in her manner aroused her suspicions. She hurried out of her chamber, stopped at the threshold, cursed and hurried back to look in the mirror. She adjusted her hair, wore a nose ring and earrings, fixed her saree and rushed out, hoping to catch up with the woman before she was turned back.

The woman was still arguing with the guards, who were resisting her determined attempts to enter the inner fort. As she neared the gate, Brihannala recognised the woman. It was Gomati, the estranged daughter of the mahapradhana.

'Who stops the mahapradhana's daughter?' Brihannala shouted, and the guards, seeing the chief eunuch of the maharaja's harem, hurriedly let Gomati in. The woman gave her a cursory namaskara as thanks and hurried to the mahapradhana's office. Brihannala caught up with her.

'You seem to be worried,' Brihannala said with a dazzling smile. 'Your father has gone with Hiranya on rounds of the fort.'

She stopped, looking defeated, and wiped the sweat from her forehead.

'Devi, may I help you? I too am an official of the government. Should I convey something to your father when he comes, or would you like to wait in my chamber until he returns?'

Gomati looked at her and said, 'Mahishmathi is in grave danger.'

'There is nothing to worry about—the fort is safe, and no one can invade it from outside.'

'It isn't from the outside that the attack is going to come. Guru Dharmapala isn't the man we all think he is.'

Brihannala stared at her in shock.

'I found the catchments of arms today,' Gomati said. 'They

have arrested Maharani Hemavati, and his disciples are moving to take the palace.'

Brihannala's brain was in a whirl. She knew what was coming. She had to get out. Gomati ran behind her and grabbed her wrist. 'Where are you going? Raise the alarm. They must be stopped.'

'Devi, I suggest you get out of the fort. *Now!*'

'This is your help?' Gomati raised her voice. 'My father is here. Where will I run to without him? My people are in danger. My country is in danger.'

'That is up to you,' Brihannala said, prising her hand off and hurrying away.

'I know what to do,' Gomati yelled. Brihannala didn't wait to hear more. She ran to the gate.

The guards stopped her. 'If you go out, you won't be able to come in again without General Hiranya's permission,' the guard warned.

She nodded. Which fool wants to come back in, she thought as the gate opened. She ran towards the outer gate, drawing her dagger from the folds of her saree and hiding it in her hand. When she was just a few feet away from the outer fort gate, she heard the bell tolling from the palace. Gomati had raised the alarm. Brihannala yelled at the guards to open the outer gate. They were standing stunned at the sudden alarm from the inner palace. They ignored Brihannala, and instead rushed to pick up their weapons from their offices at the fort gate. Some soldiers emerged wearing their armour and armed to the teeth. The gate remained closed. When Brihannala tried to force her way out, a soldier pushed her back. The cavalry was assembling at the gate, and the soldiers huddled in confusion, waiting for their orders to march. The bell continued to toll. Brihannala stabbed the guard at the gate, and his dying screams attracted the attention of the soldiers who had been looking towards the bell.

Brihannala was struggling to open the heavy fort gate when she heard the infantry captain ordering his men to charge at her. The foot soldiers rushed to her, but Brihannala managed to open the fort gate a few inches and slipped through the crack. She cursed when he saw that the bridge across the moat was drawn. The gate behind her opened and the soldiers rushed out, yelling at her. She jumped into the moat, scattering the crocodiles that were sunning in the sand. Before they could react, she had scrambled up onto the opposite shore. A few soldiers followed her into the moat, but the crocodiles were better prepared this time, and they pounced on the enthusiastic soldiers who had jumped in. Brihannala kept running towards the river. She could hear swords clashing and death screams from the fort.

She reached the ferry and found Bhairava standing, confused, staring at the fort. Brihannala yelled, 'Hurry, Bhairava. Where is your boat?'

'My boat was stolen long ago,' Bhairava said.

'Get another one!' Brihannala ordered, and cursed under her breath. They ran towards the dock where the boats of the rich were moored. Brihannala punched a surprised boatman into the river while Bhairava untied one of the boats. They jumped into it and started to row furiously. The tolling had stopped by now.

'What happened? Has everything ended?' Bhairava asked when they were a sufficient distance from the city.

Brihannala removed her earrings and nose ring. She flung them into the river and her saree followed. The need for disguises was over.

She was no longer a eunuch, but her transformation didn't surprise Bhairava a bit. Brihannala stood at the prow of the boat, his sculpted body glistening in the rays of the sun. He shook free his long hair and said, 'Our resistance has just begun, Bhairava. We are still at war against Mahishmathi, but this time against a more ruthless enemy.'

The screams and the sounds of battle inside Mahishmathi fort became fainter as the boat moved. The river Mahishi flowed, timeless and eternal, unmindful of the games men played in their brief lives.

TWENTY-THREE

# Sivagami

SIVAGAMI WAS RUNNING through the palace, scared and crying. She could hear the evil laughter of a man. She entered a room and stood in a corner, panting. The man rushed in and stood at the door. His face was in shadows. Sivagami cowered in fear. The man stepped in with a sly laugh. He grabbed her and tugged at her clothes. She fought him as things tumbled down in the room. She hit a brass lamp and it fell down, igniting the curtains. In the light, she saw his face. Bijjala. With a shock, she turned and saw herself in the mirror. Kamakshi. She looked like Kamakshi. She was Kamakshi. When Bijjala lunged for her, she jumped through the window. She felt herself fall for a long time—till finally she crashed down in a courtyard. A pair of eyes were staring at her. Immobile, expressionless, as if they were dead. She saw it was Shivappa's.

With a start, Sivagami woke up, covered in a cold sweat. It was dark and musty. Except for the croaks of toads from the bushes, it was silent. She felt worthless. She had married a man who had raped and killed her best friend. More than the loss of her men, more than the wound in her belly that had started festering, the words of Shivappa hurt her. He had spat in her face and said, 'You married a man who raped and killed your best friend. Living with that knowledge is more of a punishment to you than dying by my hand.'

Sivagami wished Shivappa had killed her.

'It will be all right, dear. Everything will be all right. I am here, I am here.'

'Mahadeva?' She got up with a jerk. Mahadeva's strong hands gently pushed her back. She felt his fingers run through her hair. She grabbed his hand and started sobbing. She didn't want to let it go. She knew she was dreaming. Perhaps she was dying. Perhaps she was already dead and united with Mahadeva.

'I am sorry, father,' she sobbed. 'I failed. I have gone without giving you redemption. The evil has won. Or, maybe, I was the evil. I don't know.'

'Sleep,' Mahadeva's soothing voice said in her ears. She held his hand tight to her bosom and slept.

---

Sunlight filtered through the roof. Sivagami lay watching a spider weaving a cobweb in the corner. When Gundu Ramu came in with a pot of water, she smiled at him.

'I had a dream,' she said. 'Mahadeva …'

The pot of water fell from Gundu Ramu's hand and crashed. The boy jumped out of the temple and ran, howling with joy. He ran past the soldiers who were sleeping, cut through the ground where corpses were rotting, and found Mahadeva near the river. He was talking to Ally, while Kattappa stood a few feet away, like a granite statue.

Gundu Ramu grabbed Mahadeva's hand and kissed it. 'You saved my akka. You saved her,' he said. He turned and began to run back. He stopped a few feet away and called out, 'Akka spoke,' and darted back to the temple. Mahadeva scrambled up and hurried behind him.

When he reached the mandap, Gundu Ramu was sitting near Sivagami. The boy pointed at Mahadeva. 'Akka, see,' he said and beamed.

Sivagami froze, staring at Mahadeva in disbelief. Mahadeva walked up to her with a smile and sat beside her. She touched him, felt his face with her fingers. His eyes filled up. In the sunlight that caressed his curly hair, he looked so handsome. She pushed back the unruly strand of hair that fell on his forehead and smiled.

'I came yesterday night,' he said awkwardly, but all that was to be said was in his eyes. 'I came to you and you were sleeping.'

'How ... how ... I thought you were ...'

'Dead?' Mahadeva laughed. 'I was dead, Sivagami. I lost everything. But when I heard you were dying, I regained my will to live.'

Sivagami turned away, bitter and angry, her shoulders shaking with emotion. Mahadeva said in a soothing voice, 'Forgive me, Sivagami. I am ashamed of what I did. I had a spy in your army. One poor Bhanu Gupta, who I presume died in the attack. Bless his soul, for without his marking the way, I would never have found you.'

Sivagami didn't reply. It was too overwhelming for her. She had thrown away this man for a rapist. Could there be a bigger fool than her? She couldn't imagine living with Bijjala anymore, knowing what he had done to Kamakshi. She turned back to Mahadeva and held his hand. He kissed her forehead. He leaned over to kiss her lips, and she forgot all her pain and waited in anticipation.

'Your Excellency.'

Mahadeva stood up. Karthikeya and a group of soldiers bowed deep.

'We are pleasantly surprised. We didn't know you came yesterday night.'

'I reached the ground where the massacre took place. The boy led me here,' Mahadeva said, pointing to Gundu Ramu.

'We are relieved, Prince. We heard the dark rumours …'

'That I was dead? Bards do exaggerate. As you can see, I am alive.'

The soldiers bowed.

'Where is my brother Bijjala?' Mahadeva asked.

Karthikeya said, 'His Highness Maharaja Somadeva recalled His Excellency Prince Bijjala to Mahishmathi.'

Mahadeva was perplexed. 'I don't understand. Why are you all still here?'

'We marched under the command of his wife, swami.'

'Wife?' Mahadeva laughed. 'My brother has a wife?'

'We marched under Rani Sivagami devi, Your Excellency.'

It took a moment for the meaning of the words to sink in. Mahadeva turned to Sivagami, and she turned her face away and shut her eyes.

Mahadeva dismissed the soldiers and stood without moving. Gundu Ramu knew things had gone horribly wrong and, feeling nervous, he scurried away. A thick silence had built a wall between Sivagami and Mahadeva.

Sivagami looked up at Mahadeva. Then she crawled to him and touched his feet. 'I am sorry.'

'Devi, you are my sister-in-law. You shouldn't be touching my feet. It is I who should do that.' Mahadeva bent to touch her feet.

'I thought you were ...' Sivagami said, pulling back her feet. The wound in her stomach throbbed with pain.

'Dead? Were you waiting for that?'

Sivagami sobbed. 'I had no choice.'

'Did my brother force you to marry him, devi?'

Sivagami shook her head. She covered her face with her hands. She wished the earth would open up and swallow her.

'You married of your own free will, devi. I respect that. I am a fool. I heard you were dying and ran for months through the jungle, barely sleeping, barely eating, so that I could see your face.'

'Please ...'

'I should have drowned in the river Mahishi when the pirate betrayed me.'

'I have never loved anyone other than you.'

'Devi. I am shocked to hear that. You married my brother without loving him? And you dare to say you still love me? You betray me, you betray your husband and you betray yourself. I have nothing more to say.' Mahadeva folded his hands in a namaste.

'Please don't go.'

'Go? Where will I go, devi? I will be around, in service of my sister-in-law, the wife of the crown prince of Mahishmathi,

Rani Sivagami devi. But this will be the last time I will look at your face and talk to you. You are my sister-in-law and, by custom and tradition, it isn't proper for me to talk to you directly when my brother is not present.'

Helplessly, Sivagami watched Mahadeva walk away. She lay back on the bed, listless, and looked at the slice of sky through the crumbling roof. Her mind was empty, drained of all emotions. A butterfly flitted into the temple and danced around her face. It fluttered away and, the next moment, it was caught in the beautiful cob web. The spider moved towards the struggling butterfly and spun its web around it in a trice. It rolled the ball to the centre and started devouring the butterfly. An overwhelming sadness descended on Sivagami as she watched the butterfly being eaten. How full of life it had been a moment before, and how easily the spider had trapped it.

*I don't want to live anymore,* Sivagami thought. With a strength that belied her grievous injury, she stood up. Varahi, the patron Goddess of the Kalakeyas, stared at her from her pedestal in the sanctum. One of the arms of Varahi held a rusted trident. Sivagami rushed towards the fierce Goddess, intending to fling herself on the trident.

'Akka!'

She was yanked back by a strong grip. Gundu Ramu was holding her by her waist. She struggled to free herself of his grip, but he held her tight, screaming, 'Akka, Akka.' She yelled as pain shot through her. He had grabbed her where she was wounded. She fainted in his arms.

When she opened her eyes, Gundu Ramu was sitting beside her. Without a word, he placed her father's manuscript next to her. With trembling hands, she picked it up and looked at Gundu Ramu. The boy had reminded her about her life's purpose. There were children like him waiting to be freed from their slavery. She had sacrificed everything to fulfil her father's dream. The loss of Mahadeva, painful though it was, wasn't a reason to end her life.

'Gundu Ramu, bring Kattappa, the slave of Prince Mahadeva here.'

Gundu Ramu ran to fetch Kattappa. When Kattappa entered the temple, she was sitting on the dusty pedestal at the foot of Varahi.

'Tell Prince Mahadeva to prepare for an attack on Gauriparvat tomorrow. I am making him the nayaka of the mission. He shall command it under my leadership. Tell him this is the order of Rani Sivagami devi.'

Kattappa bowed and left.

Sivagami asked Gundu Ramu, 'Where is Neelappa?'

Gundu Ramu looked away. Tears filled Sivagami's eyes. The old slave, the only one who was part of a slice of her life that was so dear to her, her father's favourite slave, was gone.

TWENTY-FOUR

# Mahadeva

*The mountain path*

Mahadeva looked through the manuscript of Sivagami's father. 'I can't read this strange language,' he said to Gundu Ramu.

The boy took the book and flipped through the pages that had strange drawings and fantastic creatures. There were maps of cities and temples, but nothing made any sense, except the position of Gauriparvat.

'It is obviously a map of Gauriparvat, but where are the cities, the palaces, the market and the temples that are marked in this?' Mahadeva asked.

Gundu Ramu turned the book sideways. 'Maybe this language was read from top to bottom instead of left to right. My father has told me about such languages, even languages that are read from right to left, or left to right and right to left for alternating lines.'

But even after turning the map every which way, nothing made sense. Then, Captain Karthikeya said, 'Forgive me,

Prince. I am not a scholar. But doesn't this sign of a wild boar resemble …'

They turned to look at the dilapidated temple of Varahi. With that as the key, suddenly things started making some sense.

'It is so overwhelming to think that the wilderness around us was a bustling city many thousands of years ago. And this temple was the centre of some civilisation.'

'But how did it become like this?'

'This earth we walk upon is a graveyard, son,' Mahadeva said to Gundu Ramu. 'The very soil we tread hides countless civilisations from yore. They are all buried, hidden by the earth in her bosom. Like us, men would have dreamed in those cities of the past; they would have fought, loved, died. Who knows, we could well be standing on the grave of a majestic city that was destroyed long long ago by the hands of destiny.'

'Vamana mama kept saying that the end is near,' Gundu Ramu said.

'Who is Vamana?' Mahadeva asked.

'The dwarf in the mines. He knows everything about Gauriparvat.'

As if on cue, a low rumble rose from the earth. An edifice of the Varahi temple crumbled down. The breeze carried the smell of rotten eggs. The soldiers looked at each other in fear.

Sivagami, who was standing a few feet away, remarked sarcastically, 'Are we going to do something or are we waiting for the world to end while we talk philosophy? I need the mines to be taken by tomorrow.'

Something strange had happened to Sivagami. It was as if all the tragedies combined had made her cold and stone-hearted.

Mahadeva, red with anger, stood up and clapped his hands. He started giving instructions, dividing the soldiers into different groups. When Karthikeya said that the soldiers were afraid of the giant birds, Mahadeva declared, 'Nothing, I repeat, nothing will stop us from taking Gauriparvat. This is a war against evil. No sacrifice is too much for the victory of what is dharma. Dharmo rakshati rakshitaha. Dharma will save those who protect dharma.'

Karthikeya gave a curt bow and left. Sivagami suppressed a smile at the captain's acquiescence. Had she said the same thing, Karthikeya would have argued. The gender of the leader matters a lot, she rued. The captain, who was walking past her, stopped and turned to her.

'Rani Sivagami devi, kindly tell the prince that in my five decades of life, I have never seen good winning over evil, or vice versa. Whatever wins is called good. But there is someone who always loses, someone whom no dharma saves. Ordinary soldiers like us.'

'You have a choice not to fight, Karthikeya.'

'No, I don't. Not unless I want to be whipped again or beheaded.'

Sivagami called the old soldier closer. 'You have children, Karthikeya?'

'Six of them.'

'How old is the youngest?'

'Eight. We hadn't planned to have him, but when you go home once in two or three years, these things happen.' Karthikeya smiled sheepishly. 'But he is my prince.'

'How would you feel if someone kidnaps your child?'

'I would strangle him with my bare hands.'

'And what if someone makes him work in a mine?'

Karthikeya stared at her. 'But they aren't the children of people like us. They are tribal children.'

Sivagami stared back at him, and he looked down, ashamed. 'It has always been like this, Rani. Even if you capture the mines, it will continue like this.'

'Karthikeya, this fight is for them. They will be the last children to be enslaved in Mahishmathi. When you are fighting, keep your youngest one—what is his name?'

'Narayana.'

'Keep your little Narayana's image in your mind. Fight like you are fighting for him. So far you have fought for money, for yourself. Now, for once, fight for your Narayana.'

'Devi,' Karthikeya said, 'don't try to trick me. I am not one who will fall for such things. I have lived long enough, fought enough wars under your husband and your father-in-law. I have sympathy for those tribal kids, but I am not a teenager to dream about saving the world or becoming a hero or any such thing by risking my head. My aim is to get back alive, earning whatever pittance you people throw at us. Forgive my selfishness, forgive my forthrightness, but life has taught me that the biggest victory for an ordinary soldier in any war is to come out of it alive. You can whip me again for this, devi.'

Sivagami smiled at him and waved him away.

The preparations for the attack were going on. The fear of the giant birds was palpable in the air. To add to their woes, many weapons had become brittle and were useless. The more they waited, the fewer swords and arrowheads they would have. On Sivagami's order, soldiers were making stone clubs, bamboo spears and wooden arrows under the supervision of Kattappa.

Sivagami tightened the dressing over her wound and picked up her sword. She started swinging it, wincing at the pain each movement brought. She saw Ally watching her. She gestured for Ally to join her. As the men drew up a strategy for the final assault, the two women practised with their swords in the courtyard of the Varahi temple, while Gundu Ramu cheered for his akka.

---

Mahadeva led the army from the front. The hailstorm had intensified, and huge pebbles of ice exploded on the ground around them. The path that wound up to the cave mouth of Gauriparvat was strewn with bodies, severed limbs and blood, and the air was filled with angry battle cries and screams of pain.

Mahadeva was careful to protect Sivagami, who tried to gallop forward. He cut across her path, not allowing her to be carried away by her enthusiasm. The most difficult part of the assault was coming, if their interpretation of the map in Sivagami's manuscript was to be trusted. The path narrowed as they advanced.

Mahadeva gave the order for the army to march in a single file. From here, the path hugged a rugged cliff on its left with a sheer drop on the right. The soldiers kept looking skyward, waiting for the giant birds to attack. An advance party was moving forward to remove the boulders blocking the path. In some places, Shivappa had got the path chipped away, creating a yawning gap many feet wide. Mahadeva had anticipated this, and arranged for bamboo poles to be carried with them for this reason. He tied them together to ford the gap.

It was as if the enemy had anticipated this too. The moment the bamboo ford was placed for Sivagami's army to march on, the fording was blown away by rocks rolled down from the clifftop, taking men and horses with it.

Mahadeva commanded the army to halt for some time. A group of archers were deployed to continuously shoot arrows to the top of the cliff, giving brief cover for the army to cross the gaps in batches.

'Karthikeya, I suggest we be cautious. Hidumba hasn't deployed the birds yet, which means he is waiting for the right time. Do we have a plan to cover the last three hundred feet to the fort gate when we won't have the cover of the cliff?'

Mahadeva knew Sivagami's question was directed to him.

'Karthikeya,' Mahadeva yelled over the din of the war. 'Concentrate on what is to be done now. The future will take care of itself. Jai Mahishmathi!'

Karthikeya's answer was drowned out in the shouting of soldiers who cried, 'Jai Mahishmathi!'

From the cliff, burning oil splashed down and balls of fire burst in their midst. Hidumba's men were running at the top of the cliff and pushing down oil barrels on the marching army. Rocks rolled down, bouncing off the path, some of them taking a few soldiers with them as they plunged down the cliff.

'Stick to the cliff wall! March sideways,' Mahadeva yelled, raising his sword. The path was narrow, barely three feet wide, and on their right lay a huge chasm. Keeping their back to the cliff wall and facing the abyss, the army inched up sideways, holding each other's hands and carefully leading their horses.

'Prepare for hand to hand combat,' Sivagami screamed as she saw men rappelling down the cliffs ahead of them. A group of men rushed at them, arcing over their heads, holding onto the ropes fastened to their waists from the top of the cliff. They swung towards the marching army with their spears pointed at them. Mahadeva watched helplessly as the enemy soldiers impaled his men with their spears.

'Archers forward,' he screamed, and the Mahishmathi soldiers had to move to the edge of the cliff. With one foot dangling over the side leading to the abyss, they shot arrows at the men swinging from the ropes. The arrows pierced the enemy soldiers or cut the ropes that held them, and Hidumba's men plunged into the ravine.

'Kattappa,' Sivagami yelled. She was the first to see the bale of cotton soaked in oil rolling down the cliff and bouncing amidst their soldiers. A fire arrow followed, and the bale became a ball of fire, incinerating many around.

By the time the second one was hurled from the top, Kattappa's urumi—the twenty-foot long whip sword that could be worn around the waist like a rope—had caught the bale of cotton in the air and deflected it away from his men. The soldiers followed Kattappa's suit and swung the burning cotton towards the valley before it could land amidst them. Hidumba changed tactics. Scalding hot oil flowed down the cliff wall and splashed on their heads. Holding their shields above their heads, the army rushed through the narrow path, clinging to the cliff, smashing the defences Hidumba had put up on the path.

Mahadeva could see the fort now, and the three hundred feet of open ground before it. The mountain had been chipped away to create a flat surface. On one side, the mountain continued to rise. On the right side, on the southern flank, it was a sheer drop. To the front was the fort gate, beyond which, after another open area of almost six hundred feet, lay the cobra mouth cave.

On the southern side, the fort skirted the edge of the cliff and ran up the mountain in the north. It was impossible to scale the cliff from the southern side. Any army attacking the fort had to traverse the open ground. With a normal fort, this would have been a strategic blunder—attackers could bring elephants to storm down the fort gates. In Gauriparvat, the open ground was a work of strategic genius. The narrow path leading up to it ruled out the possibility of elephants; attacking armies could only come on horse or foot and could therefore scarcely carry ramming rods or siege engines. They would have to brave the fire of arrows from the fort with no cover. For the Mahishmathi army, in their Gauridhooli-coated armour, arrows might not be a major deterrent. But that was not the only way the open ground was useful. There was a reason why Hidumba had held back his Garuda pakshis.

Mahadeva saw Hidumba running around on the ramparts of the fort, screaming instructions. Then, a shrill bamboo whistle blew a tune and the terrified soldiers of Mahishmathi backtracked. Everyone knew what was coming. Mahadeva had a plan worked out, though. He wanted to send his soldiers on in batches. Even if the bird got a few, the rest could reach the fort wall, where they could skirt it and be protected from the stones that the bird would hurl.

Mahadeva ordered the first batch to charge. No one moved. They could see the bird approaching. Mahadeva cried again for the first batch to move. But all eyes were fixed on the approaching bird, and the soldiers were petrified.

The horses neighed, stamping their hoofs, restless; some tried to bolt. From behind, the rest of the army that were still negotiating the narrow, winding path pushed forward, while the front ranks panicked, trying to flee back. A stampede was developing at the middle. The bird gave an ear-splitting screech. The soldiers gasped when they saw the huge rock it was carrying in its claws.

'Shoot,' Mahadeva yelled, and the archers emptied their quivers at it. Arrows whizzed towards the bird, and it evaded them with chilling ease. It swooped down over their heads and dropped the huge boulder. It crashed down in the middle of the army, crushing many, before rolling down the cliff. Karthikeya cursed, turned his horse around and fled. His men followed.

Mahadeva yelled at them, 'Forward, forward. Jai Mahishmathi!'

No one listened. The soldiers had lost their morale. The whistle rose again from the fort. They could see the tiny figure of Hidumba on the turret, gesticulating wildly. The bird made a huge arc above them.

Surprising Mahadeva, Sivagami cried, 'Forward,' and galloped towards the fort gate. The army which was fleeing, stopped.

'This woman,' Karthikeya cursed under his breath. The lone figure of Sivagami, with her sword raised and pointed at Gauriparvat, cut through the swirling dust. Hidumba set his archers at her. From the sky, the bird was approaching. Sivagami reached the fort gate and pulled back Vajra's reins.

The horse raised its forelegs and pounded on the fort gate. She turned the horse around and galloped back as the bird dropped the rock. The boulder fell behind her, missing her by a few inches, but she didn't even look back. The boulder rolled to a side of the ground and settled in a cloud of dust. The bird soared away. Sivagami reached her army and yelled, 'That's how you do it. Attack!'

Inspired by her raw courage, the Mahishmathi army rushed forward. 'No, no. Don't. Halt, halt!' Mahadeva screamed. They were doing it all wrong.

But the army rushed past him, screaming, 'Jai Mahishmathi!'

Sivagami haughtily turned her horse around again, giving Mahadeva a look of disdain. She was about to follow her army, when the bird swooped down at them from the air. It had no boulders this time. Instead, it scooped up dozens of men in its claws and, following the whistles of Hidumba, dropped them down the cliff. Men were dying like flies. From the fort, Hidumba moved his catapults and started shooting huge iron balls at the army.

Despite this, Karthikeya and a few men managed to reach the fort gate. They tried scrambling up the wall. Mahadeva was screaming for them to retreat. Sivagami stood there, her face pale. She had committed a great mistake by shaming her men with her courage and sending them to sure death. Mahadeva was right. They should have attacked in batches, not offering the enemy one single target. Still, her men were fighting well. Ally and Kattappa, with their swirling urumis, had succeeded in keeping the bird at bay. It circled around them, trying to claw them, knock them down with its flapping wings, yet Kattappa held on.

Gundu Ramu, hiding in a rock crevice at the entrance of the open ground, tried to imitate the dwarf's whistle in an attempt to distract the bird. But the sound that emerged from his mouth was feeble and didn't carry through in the din of the battle. A blood-curdling sight made Gundu Ramu scream.

'Akka, Akka!'

But his voice wasn't strong enough. Gundu Ramu watched helplessly as the dot in the sky grew bigger and the second Garuda pakshi appeared, carrying a huge boulder. It dropped it in the middle of the battlefield, crushing scores of soldiers. That changed the tide. The bravery that Sivagami had inspired evaporated at that moment. The Mahishmathi army made a hasty retreat while the two birds attacked in tandem. Horses collided with each other, people tumbled over each other, many fell victim to the ferocity of the birds, while many ran blindly, only to fall into the abyss.

The battle was lost with heavy casualties as the sun set. Sivagami was devastated. Karthikeya, with an ugly gash on his forehead, was threatening to march back even at the cost of execution.

'We aren't prepared for this, Rani Sivagami devi. The defences were designed by a genius. There is no way we can breach it. I have worked under him as an ordinary soldier, when he used to make amazing contraptions for our army to use.'

They were on the narrow path, soldiers squatting or lying down in a long line. Exhausted and rebellious, they were clamouring to return home. Night had fallen, and Hidumba had withdrawn the birds. A cold wind swept over them.

Mahadeva pleaded with the soldiers to fight, and as the argument went on, an arrow came down and struck the ground. A scroll was tied to it. Mahadeva picked it up and read it.

'Shivappa, the king of the Vaithalikas, the rightful owner of Gauriparvat, in his greatness, offers a truce subject to the following conditions. That Gauriparvat should be declared an independent country and Mahishmathi should treat Vaithalika Veera Maharaja Shivappa as an equal to Maharaja Somadeva. That Mahishmathi will purchase Gaurikanta stones from the Vaithalikas at a rate decided on by His Highness Vaithalika Veera Shivappa. That Mahishmathi will surrender Prince Bijjala to the court of His Highness Vaithalika Veera Shivappa to face trial for the rape and murder of Kamakshi.'

Mahadeva looked up at Sivagami when he finished reading the last condition. Sivagami looked away, her face burning with shame. The soldiers murmured to each other. Mahadeva looked at Kattappa. 'Is this true?'

Kattappa, nursing an injury on his right shoulder, looked down. Mahadeva flung the scroll down in disgust.

Karthikeya stood up. 'We are marching back, Rani Sivagami devi.'

The soldiers stood up one by one. In the narrow path that coiled like a snake, hugging the cliff, the cries of the soldiers rose in unison, 'We want to go back home.'

'Even if I am the last person standing, I will take this fort and end the mining,' Sivagami said, clutching her belly. Karthikeya saw that her wound had reopened and blood was oozing out of the dressing. She swooned and lost her balance, almost falling. Mahadeva instinctively grabbed her wrist and pulled her back. She pulled her hand out of his grip and held herself steady, holding on to the cliff wall.

'All I ask, you cowards, is half a day and one more assault. If we don't breach the fort by tomorrow afternoon, you may all go.'

'But the Garuda pakshis ...' Karthikeya said.

'We will take the fort tomorrow. Go and sleep,' Sivagami said. Karthikeya bowed and retreated to his soldiers.

As the night wore on, Kattappa sat sleepless, his back to the cliff wall. His mind was in turbulence at the audacity of his brother. He felt someone come up to him. He turned and saw Sivagami. He was about to get up to bow, but Sivagami hushed him. She whispered in his ears, 'By dawn, I want the dwarf.'

The cold mountain wind howled, and the drizzle turned into a torrent. A wild screech from one of the birds rose in the darkness, sending shivers down the spine of every soldier as they struggled to keep themselves warm and get some rest.

Kattappa stared into the abyss of darkness that lay before him. He looked at Sivagami and said, 'Devi, it shall be done.'

TWENTY-FIVE

# Kattappa

*The southern ridge*

Kattappa checked the strength of the climbing rope and coiled it around his shoulders. He crawled to the cliff and, holding its edge, started climbing towards the fort. Only the tip of his fingers would have been visible to a keen observer. The rain had made the edge slippery, and Kattappa didn't want to think about how deep the ravine was. Wind howled in his ears, but he pressed on.

It was almost dawn when he reached the sheer face of the fort built over the cliff. His palms were lacerated and his muscles were numb with exhaustion, but he inched on. Two sentries were pacing the fort wall. Kattappa measured their pace. He uncoiled the rope from his shoulders with one hand and squirmed in pain. His left arm was bearing his entire weight now as he hung over a sheer ravine whose bottom was thousands of feet below. He flung the rope up and got it right on the third try. The small clang of the hook in a crack in the fort wall caught the attention of a guard, who came to inspect. Kattappa hung on with bated breath, hoping the rain and the mist that rose from the valley would cover him. The soldier looked about and then continued on, and Kattappa heaved a sigh of relief.

He heard the horn blaring from Sivagami's camp. In answer to Sivagami's war cry, the horn blared from the fort. The ceasefire had ended. Kattappa knew that Hidumba would deploy the birds at any moment. He needed to get the dwarf at any cost, so that the birds could be controlled. Without that, the battle was sure to be lost, and Shivappa would slip beyond his reach forever.

Kattappa started climbing, hanging on to the rope. As he reached midway, he paused to rest. The rope that hung below him became taut. He peered down, but mist covered the rope. He pulled it and was relieved when the rope came up easily. For a moment, he had been worried someone was following him. He started climbing again.

Kattappa heard the familiar bamboo whistle and the horrified cries of Mahishmathi soldiers as the first boulder fell in their midst. A few more, and the army would run. Kattappa renewed his efforts to climb, but the strong wind was making it difficult. The blood that oozed from lacerations in his palms made his grip slippery, and the mist made it impossible to estimate how much more he had to climb. He heard a shrill whistle, but this time right above him. And from the mist, he saw a Garuda pakshi appearing like a spectra and rushing straight at him.

## Gauriparvat fort gate

Mahadeva's strategy was working. The army moved forward in batches of thirty this time. As the bird dropped boulders, the army scattered in various directions, evading the boulder, only to reassemble and advance towards the fort with their bamboo ladders and climbing ropes. He had placed six batches of thirty each near the fort and some men were climbing the fort wall, braving the scalding oil that Hidumba's soldiers were hurling down.

Hidumba changed tactics soon. The bird no longer came with boulders. Instead it swooped down on those near the fort, its talons extended. A few spears and arrows hit it, but that only helped to anger the Garuda pakshi. With the precision of an archer, Hidumba directed the bird to attack the enemy.

Sivagami directed her archers to fire at Hidumba. The dwarf's answer to her audacity was to direct the bird at her. The Garuda pakshi descended on her in a flurry of feather and wings. Vajra panicked and bolted, neighing loudly. Sivagami lost her balance and fell from the saddle.

When she stood up with her sword, the giant bird was chasing Vajra. She ignored the searing pain in her belly and the warmness of blood that trickled down. She screamed at the bird and ran to it. Just as the bird was about to lift Vajra, she flung herself in the air and, with a powerful thrust, sliced off one of the talons of the bird. It screeched in pain and rose high in the air. Sivagami mounted the saddle and brought Vajra under control. As the dust settled around her, she saw the bird was a dot in the sky.

A horn blared from the fort and she saw the fort gate open. From inside, the army of Hidumba rushed out to mow down the panicked soldiers of Sivagami. She heard a screech above and saw the bird diving towards her at high speed.

---

*The southern ridge*

Kattappa braced himself for the impact as the bird came down at him at great speed, its talons outstretched, screeching. He had warded off the first attack by swinging to the side at the last moment. He had wound the rope across his left arm and held the urumi in his right. As the bird neared, Kattappa swung his sword as fast as he could. The sinuous movement of the urumi confused the bird. On the third attack, Kattappa managed to connect his urumi with the bird's wing. A flurry of feathers rose in the air, but the bird landed on him, slamming him to the fort wall. Its talons pierced both his arms, and he was held spread-eagled against the wall.

Kattappa was unable to move his arms and the pain was unbearable. His urumi flapped ineffectively as the claws dug deeper into his arm muscles. The Garuda pakshi gave an ear-splitting screech. The stink of rotten flesh almost overwhelmed Kattappa. The bird pulled back its head and its sword-sharp, three-foot beak was pointed at Kattappa's head. Kattappa struggled to get free, and the bird flapped its wings, pummelling him with unbelievable force. It brought its beak down towards Kattappa's forehead, and the slave moved his head out of its path. A nail's breadth away from his left ear, the beak pierced the fort wall, showering his face with debris. The bird struggled to extricate its beak from the wall. The beak had dug deep into the mortar, and one of its cold reptilian eyes almost touched Kattappa's. He could see his own reflection in its terrified eye ball, which was as large as his face.

Kattappa tried to bite the bird's eye. The Garuda pakshi struggled, piercing his arm with its talons. Kattappa got hold of the edge of its eyelid with his teeth, and he bit down with force. The salty smell of the bird's blood made him gag. He spat it into the bird's eye. The bird loosened its grip on his arms and extricated its beak. It took off and Kattappa panted, trying to get back his breath. His arms had deep gashes running down them. His head swam—he had lost a lot of blood. His arm was numb where the rope was tied, and he slowly extricated himself and started climbing again. Kattappa knew he didn't have much time; he was sure the bird would be back soon.

He was four feet from the top of the fort wall, when he heard the bone-chilling screech. The Garuda pakshi was back. *Oh God, Oh God,* he prayed, gripping his urumi and twisting the rope around his arm to face the bird.

'Kattappa, you go. I shall deal with this beast.' Ally was smiling up at Kattappa, twitching her urumi, which shone bright crimson in the rising sun. Instead of her arms, she had wound the rope around her legs and was hanging upside down, leaving both her hands free to fight. In one hand, she had a shield.

Kattappa cursed.

'I followed you,' Ally said. She smiled and twisted towards the descending bird. She called out to it, 'Here, here, monster.' Ally whistled, as if calling a pet dog, and laughed hysterically.

*Crazy woman,* thought Kattappa as he struggled up.

The bird landed on Ally as she blocked its parry with her shield. It slammed her to the wall and her urumi lashed out from behind her shield as she tried to cut the bird. There was a flurry of feathers as the giant bird flapped its wings and screeched, frustrated that the shield was preventing it from tearing its prey into pieces.

Kattappa reached the top of the fort, surprising the sentry who was busy watching the carnage of the Mahishmathi army. Before he could react, Kattappa picked him up and flung him down the cliff. His scream was swallowed by the howling wind.

The other sentry saw him and froze. Instead of attacking Kattappa, he ran away. Kattappa chased him, knowing he was rushing to raise the alarm. He flung his dagger at the guard, felling him, jumped over his twitching body and continued to run without breaking his pace. Kattappa had to find the dwarf. He heard a noise from behind and turned around. A soldier swung his sword and Kattappa ducked. He swung his urumi, which caught the soldier by his neck. He pulled back the ribbon sword and the soldier's head rolled down.

Kattappa could still hear the screeching of the birds, one near Ally and other fighting with Sivagami in the grounds. He saw the bird knock Sivagami down from her horse and soar up. As she struggled to get up, the bird made a wide arc over the fort, soared in the sky and dove down towards Sivagami with an ear-splitting screech.

## Gauriparvat fort gate

Sivagami looked up at the bird; she raised her sword above her head and held it with both her hands. She may die, but she would take down the monster with her. The fighting on the battlefield seemed to freeze as everyone turned towards Sivagami.

As the bird dived down and was just a few feet above her, a shrill whistle pierced the eerie silence. The bird arrested its movement and flapped its wings gently above Sivagami. As it descended slowly and sat down calmly on the ground, she saw Hidumba on the fort. Kattappa was holding him by the scuff of his neck, like one would hold a kitten. Another bird rose from the southern ridge to perch near Kattappa.

'We surrender,' Hidumba cried, and a huge cheer rose from the Mahishmathi army.

The victorious army rushed in through the gates with cries of 'Jai Mahishmathi' and 'Jai Rani Sivagami devi'.

Ally, bruised, battered but with a wide smile, climbed the fort wall and ran to Kattappa. As she was about to hug him, Kattappa jumped from the fort wall holding a screaming Hidumba. Kattappa ran to Sivagami and flung the dwarf at her feet.

'Your orders have been fulfilled, devi,' the slave said and bowed.

'To the mines,' Sivagami cried, raising her sword. Her army's victory cry shook Gauriparvat. 'Jai Mahishmathi!'

TWENTY-SIX

# Sivagami

THE VICTORIOUS ARMY marched in, with Mahadeva following a few feet behind Sivagami. Gundu Ramu ran behind Sivagami's horse. Hidumba kept pleading for mercy, blaming everything on Shivappa. His hands were tied and Gundu Ramu led him like he was a pet dog.

Sivagami was overwhelmed by her victory. She felt a little sad, too, that her father's impregnable defences had been shattered by a determined warrior called Kattappa.

Near the inner fort wall lay hundreds of narrow carts loaded with Gaurikanta stones. They stood in a semi-circle, skirting the inner fort wall till the fort gate. Sivagami smiled: this would be her insurance. It was with these that she was going to negotiate with Maharaja Somadeva. Mahishmathi wanted the stones desperately. She would use them to extract the promise that the mines would never be opened again. She would make sure that Mahishmathi apologised to its citizens for the crime its elite had committed on the distant tribes. She would get Mahishmathi to admit that the people it had killed as traitors had not been traitors at all. She would redeem the honour of her father and mother and Uncle Thimma. A sense of pride at what she had achieved engulfed her. Every sacrifice she had made was worth this.

As they marched in, they found an army of women waiting for them at the mouth of the mine entrance. Behind them stood Shivappa.

Kattappa's heart sank. He wouldn't fight against a woman: that was a code he lived by, something his father had taught him from childhood.

'You coward,' Kattappa yelled. 'Come and fight like a man.'

Shivappa laughed. 'Slave. Talk with respect to the king of Gauriparvat. These are my warriors, my army, trained by Achi Nagamma. I know you are peeing with fear. It would be fun to watch a bunch of cowards being beaten by women. The lucky few who survive better commit suicide because, in the streets of Mahishmathi, people will spit on their faces for losing to women.'

'Attack,' Sivagami commanded, and galloped towards the army for the final assault. Kattappa watched both armies rushing towards each other, fuming. Shivappa was so near, yet beyond his reach. He ducked and moved around the battlefield, using his shield to defend himself, but never striking back. Kattappa's progress was slow, but he saw the battlefront opening up. The fight was pitched and brutal, with the women warriors matching Mahishmathi's men's strength with agile swordplay and accurate shooting of arrows. However, the armour and weapons of the Mahishmathi soldiers, perhaps the last of the sets coated with Gauridhooli, gave them a distinct advantage. Shivappa's rebel army began to be overpowered. Kattappa was waiting for this moment.

When a gap opened up in the ranks, he rushed through it towards Shivappa. His brother saw him coming and directed his warriors at Kattappa. Unmindful of the blows his armour received, ducking the sword thrusts and the blows, Kattappa weaved through the defence without shedding the blood of any women.

When he neared Shivappa, Kattappa saw him turn around and run. 'Coward!' Kattappa screamed, and chased him into the mouth of the tunnel. Shivappa stopped abruptly and turned towards Kattappa.

'Anna, look back,' Shivappa said, laughing and pointing to the ground outside. 'See the feast I have arranged for you fools.'

Kattappa turned to see why there was a silence behind him. The armies on either side stood as if in a tableau, looking towards the north. Then he saw it. A woman warrior was running towards them, holding something in her hand. She put it in the middle of the ground and stood there, panting.

'My suicide warrior. These women are ready to die for their king, Anna,' Shivappa said.

Kattappa saw it was a chick, almost five feet tall, but featherless. It screeched miserably. Kattappa ran a few feet to see what was happening and was almost blown back by a gush of wind. A Garuda pakshi, almost three times the size of the one Kattappa had fought, descended on the woman who had brought the chick. Both the armies scattered in fear as the bird tore the woman into two pieces and gave an ear-splitting shriek.

'Go, become the breakfast of the Garuda pakshi, brother. A mother bird defending her chick. Good luck and goodbye.' Shivappa cackled.

Kattappa saw Shivappa jump into a cart. A dwarf's head popped up in the front and the cart, drawn by mountain rams, began to speed through the tunnels. Kattappa hesitated. Should he stay back with his army and fight a losing war against a giant bird, or fulfil the promise he had made to his dying father?

At the bird's next screech, Kattappa made his choice.

TWENTY-SEVEN

# Kattappa

*The Gauriparvat tunnels*

Kattappa ran behind the speeding cart. The rattle of its metal wheels echoed in the tunnels, creating an unbearable din. As Kattappa ran, the tunnels became narrower and the cart continued to gather speed, screeching around the curves, careening on its side wheels, jolting back to the ground and once again moving forward with speed. Kattappa had to bend his head and run, but he never took his eyes off the torch that burned at the back of cart. His angry yell at his brother to stop echoed through the tunnels, and Shivappa's mocking laughter was his response.

Breathing heavily in the damp air, jumping over puddles, skidding, falling and scrambling up on the slippery, moss-covered floor, Kattappa chased the fast vanishing cart. He knew this was his last chance to get Shivappa. He ran past the dim torches, now on all fours, ignoring the pain in his arms. The path twisted and turned steeply, with many ups and downs, but invariably spiralling down. The last of the torches died and Kattappa was now running through pitch darkness, with only the distant glow of the cart light for guidance.

Over the rattle of the cart wheels, he heard squeaking sounds. Something ran over his arm. He ignored it and continued to run, yelling, 'Coward, face me like a man.' The tunnels took up his cry and threw it back as echoes. His brother's laughter came back in waves. Kattappa became aware of the stink. *Rats; this place is full of rat shit,* a stray thought came uninvited in his mind.

The next moment he lost his balance and fell on his face. Something bit his left cheek. He heard the cacophony of squeals and before he could get up, he was drowning in a wave of rodents. They jumped on him and clung on, fighting for the little skin on his face and hands that was not protected by armour. He slammed his body against a wall, crushing the rats on that side. The wall cracked and more rats poured in from the gap. He held his shield to his face, putting both his hands behind it. He knew no rat could pierce the armour coated with Gauridhooli. He had only to win over his squeamishness and disgust. Kattappa continued on his path, protecting his face, wading through the sea of rats that continued to multiply, pouring through every pore in the roof and the walls of the tunnel. The squealing, the stink and the slipperiness of the floor, all made him disoriented. A couple of rodents had managed to squeeze into his leather foot guard, but he was scared to remove his hand from the protection of the shield that he held close to his face. Rats continued to fall around him like rain. It was only the fire of vengeance that kept him going. He had reached so far and was determined not to be defeated by a bunch of rodents.

Kattappa found the ground below his feet giving way, and he fell into a cave. His eyes took a moment to adjust to the bright light of torches on its walls. Shivappa was standing in a corner.

'Ah, the power of Gauridhooli. You might be one of the first people to escape those rats. They cut through almost anything.'

Kattappa looked around, looking for ways through which Shivappa could escape. The rats had vanished, but he knew they were waiting in the shadows. He could smell them.

'Don't get scared, brother. They don't like the light.'

'Scared? You talk about fear, you coward?' Kattappa said, unsheathing his urumi. The ribbon sword swayed like a cobra.

'Coward? Me, a coward? I am a king, brother. But I am just warming the throne for my dear anna. You are the first-born. Sit on the throne of the Vaithalikas and I shall serve you like a servant. I brought you here to show you how safe we are here. We shall negotiate with Mahishmathi. We shall have our own independent kingdom. The Vaithalikas would be the richest race. You would be the most wealthy king in the world with this Gauriparvat under you.'

'I am Malayappa's son. You think you can bribe me, coward?' Kattappa swished his urumi and advanced towards his brother.

'Ah, a slave will always remain a slave. I knew it. To assuage my guilt, to be sure, I was determined to give you one chance. A chance to throw away your yoke of slavery and be a king. But as the old Vaithalika saying goes, a swine always chooses the gutter over the silk bed.' Shivappa clapped his hands. From the shadows, four women warriors appeared and stood before Shivappa.

'Ah, brother. Now you must fight and kill them before you can reach me. But, of course, the great Kattappa will never fight a woman. A chivalrous vow. Wonderful. Break one vow and you can break many. Or you can stay here while I escape to fight another battle another day. After giving me sufficient time to escape, during which time they will stare at you and you will stare at the roof or the floor, they will chop you into pieces and feed the rats. They haven't taken any vow that they won't kill a man.' Shivappa gave a low bow to Kattappa. 'That is the last time my head will bow before anyone, Anna. I am sorry we have to part like this. I have always loved you and still love you. Goodbye.'

TWENTY-EIGHT

# Gundu Ramu

*The cobra gate*

'It ... it can't be controlled. It is a female,' the dwarf stuttered in fear.

Sivagami watched helplessly as the female Garuda pakshi brought about unimaginable destruction. The bloody war they had fought just a few minutes before looked like child's play before this queen of Gauriparvat.

The spears thrown at it, the arrows shot at it—nothing seemed to affect the bird. It was a force of nature, untamed, unassailable, and beautiful in its own terrifying way. It was like watching a storm of monstrous proportions. The weapons of Mahishmathi and the women soldiers were like twigs thrown at a typhoon. The bird didn't discriminate between Mahishmathi soldiers or Shivappa's women warriors. It was determined to kill everything in sight. The forest belonged to her. It was her realm. The humans were like ants to be crushed, to be eaten like a sparrow would devour a worm, pests. Nothing would stop her from claiming her territory. The bird was asserting that the mountain didn't belong to Mahishmathi or the Vaithalikas or any other arrogant human. It belonged to her and her heirs.

Sivagami's army had scattered, once again running away in fear. Where had Kattappa gone? The man who could do the impossible? Where had Mahadeva gone? For the first time since the war had started, Sivagami found herself scared to the marrow of her bones. The fury of a mother, be it human or a beast—there was no power in the world that could face it. Sivagami felt bitter about Mahadeva. When he was needed, he had slunk away with the excuse that he couldn't fight women.

Then she saw him. Before she could figure out what was happening, Mahadeva had approached the chick. The mother bird was screeching and chasing a group of terrified men around the inner fort wall. It saw Mahadeva waving a rope knotted into a lasso. *Is he crazy,* Sivagami thought as she galloped towards him, struggling to control a terrified Vajra.

The bird flapped its giant wings, took a graceful arc, and with terrifying speed dove towards them. Sivagami reached Mahadeva as the giant shadow grew bigger and bigger, covering half the ground, and the bird's sharp claws descended towards them. Mahadeva threw the lasso and it caught the bird's claw. He ran, tightening it and screaming at his men to catch it. It was insane, but Sivagami could see what he was trying to do. The bird didn't touch the ground but instead soared up, taking Mahadeva with him. Several men dove to catch the rope and held on tight. They were experienced in catching wild bison like that and, for a moment, it seemed they would succeed. The bird struggled to fly higher, and more men and even some women warriors of Shivappa ran to catch the long rope.

The Garuda pakshi screeched in anger. With a mighty flap of its wings, it lifted itself and all those who were holding the rope. Many tumbled down, some heroically held on as the bird slammed the human chain into the fort wall. Sivagami knew it was a lost cause. The bird would drop them over the cliff. She whipped out her bow and struggled to take aim. It was pointless shooting the bird, but she could at least save the men from sure death. Sivagami shot the arrow, cutting the rope, and the men tumbled down. She saw Mahadeva falling down on the fort wall. Sivagami jumped off the saddle and ran to the ramparts, her heart thumping, praying no harm had befallen Mahadeva.

She heard the bird screeching and saw it arcing back towards the fort. It seemed angrier than it had been earlier, and when she heard the screams behind, she saw something that made her blood freeze.

Gundu Ramu had the screeching chick on his shoulders and the boy was running as fast his chubby legs could carry him towards the north. The mother bird flapped its giant wings and shot down towards the boy.

TWENTY-NINE

# Kattappa

*The womb of Gauriparvat*

Time was running out. At any moment, the warriors who were guarding him would move in for the kill. Kattappa gritted his teeth in frustration. Shivappa had put him in a quandary. His brother knew well that Kattappa would rather die than break the code of warrior ethics that prevented him from fighting women. *He must be fleeing now,* Kattappa thought, *and will remain alive, to tarnish their family's name.* Shivappa's life was a negation of everything their father had lived and died for. For all his sacrifices, Malayappa would forever be known as the traitor's father.

There was one way out of this, Kattappa thought. He felt sorry for the women, though he had no intention of shedding their blood. *If I get this wrong, it will be them feeling sorry for me,* he thought wryly.

The warriors were watching his every move. The stuffy room and the tension were making him sweat. He gripped his urumi tight; his move had to be accurate and lightning fast. The women stiffened and they too tightened their grips on their swords. As warriors, they had sensed Kattappa was about to make a move.

He moved forward, swishing his ribbon sword, and they moved backward, away from its reach. The next moment, he danced backwards and whipped the urumi towards the torches. It swooped all three from their pedestals on the wall, throwing them high in the air. One of them hit the roof and sparks showered down on them before the torch fell and extinguished. Before the women could blink, he had dropped his urumi and caught the other two flaming torches in his hands.

The women rushed to him and he slammed both torches against the wall. They flared and died spectacularly, filling the chamber with the thick smell of smoke. The darkness that rushed in blinded them all, and Kattappa swooped up the urumi from the floor. He jumped over the surprised women, rushed to the door through which Shivappa had escaped, and slammed it shut from outside. He could hear the screams of the women as rodents rushed in for their feast. He said a silent prayer for their souls and started running through the tunnels. Though he hadn't used a weapon against the women, he felt angry that his brother had made him do such a thing. He ran towards the light emanating from afar, guessing that Shivappa would have used a torch to light his path.

Kattappa reached the end of the tunnel, outside which the waterfall roared. The floor was wet and slippery. He could see footprints on it. A lone torch was sputtering on the opposite wall. In the shadows, he saw the old dwarf, trembling with fear. Kattappa lifted him up. 'Where is he?' he asked.

The dwarf pointed to the waterfall. Kattappa stared at it. Had he jumped down? Then he saw the rope. It was still taut. Shivappa must be climbing down. He tied the urumi to his waist and caught hold of the rope. The force of the water took his breath away. As he rappelled down, he could feel the heat of the molten rock emanating from the jwalamukhi. It became difficult to breath. From below, the eye of the volcano throbbed, sending thick spirals of coloured gas and geysers of steam upwards. He landed on a rock and held on firmly to the rope as water tried to drag him away. In the thick mist and the spray of the waterfall, the only thing he could see was the dull orange throb of the volcano eye. Where had his brother vanished?

Kattappa slowly inched away from the waterfall. Once his eyes had adjusted to the mist and smoke, he saw a shadow trying to enter a cave through which the roaring water flowed.

'Shivappa!' he screamed, and ran towards it. The moment he reached, he found the figure had vanished.

'Anna.' He heard a call. He turned around.

'You escaped from them? I knew you would. I could have escaped now, trusting the river to take me out. But what is the use? You would come after me again. We need to settle this here. Where are you looking, Anna? Look here. Here.'

Kattappa turned on his heels, his urumi untied. The voice seemed to come from everywhere, rising above the roar of the waterfall and the hiss of the volcano. A few feet behind him, a geyser shot up and showered him with scalding hot water. The smell of rotten eggs intensified. Shivappa's laughter echoed above them all.

'Anna, remember how we used to play hide and seek when we were small? You could never find me. I know you used to act as if you could never find me. You wanted me to win always, so that I would be happy. Make me happy like that, Anna. Just one more time. Lose for me, Anna. Here, here, where are you looking? I am here, Anna.'

'Come out you coward, father-slayer, traitor,' Kattappa screamed.

'You can add brother-slayer too, in that list, Anna. I was born to win. You, to live and die a slave. What a shame. A man who should have been a king—'

Kattappa found him, hiding behind the sheet of water. He swung his urumi and Shivappa jumped out, evading Kattappa's blow, his own urumi sizzling in his hands. Another geyser shot up between them. The waterfall roared, changing its pattern and rhythm. From behind, the heart of Gauriparvat bled fiery red.

They clashed, their ribbon swords hissing and entwining like cobras making love. The poison wasn't in the swords, but in their hearts, brother against brother, the most intense of all wars. The most primeval of rivalries, the poetry of love putrefying to hate. The river roared and the volcano hissed, fire against water, both sons of the same mountain.

A geyser caught Kattappa by surprise. He lost his footing for the blink of an eye and Shivappa flew at him, taking him down. They fell on the slippery rocks, in a deathly embrace. They rolled towards the rim of the volcano. A thousand feet below, lava bubbled, waiting in anticipation. Kattappa slipped and Shivappa escaped his grip. Despite his best efforts, Kattappa found himself falling into the waiting mouth of the beast, which licked him with its tongue of fire. He gripped the edge, holding on desperately for his life.

Shivappa scrambled up and stood above him. Kattappa held on to the rim as death blinked its red eye from far below. Shivappa grinned. He kept his foot on the fingers of Kattappa and said, 'Anna, once more I am asking you. You are the scion of the Vaithalikas. I shall serve you like a slave. Be our king.'

Kattappa, struggling to keep himself from falling, stared back at his brother. Shivappa repeated the question, and Kattappa spat at his face. Shivappa gave a cry of anger and stomped down on Kattappa's hand. 'Die, die then, you fool,' he screamed.

The second time the foot came down, Kattappa let go his hold and grabbed Shivappa's leg. Before Shivappa knew what was happening, Kattappa had pulled himself up and was back on the rim. Now, it was Shivappa standing at the edge of the volcano. Kattappa stood there, his urumi glittering in the fiery red light. The volcano spat out purple smoke, burning their eyes. A geyser exploded behind Kattappa. The brothers stood frozen. Both of them knew the end was near.

Kattappa's urumi swirled in the air and wrapped around Shivappa's throat. With a scream of anguish, Kattappa pulled it back, severing his beloved brother's head from its body. The headless body of Shivappa tottered at the rim for a moment and then toppled down. The mountain, with fire in its heart, gobbled it up. *Give me more,* it hissed.

Kattappa's heart-wrenching cry rose above the roar of the waterfall. He threw the urumi on the ground and crawled to the severed head of his brother. He took it in his hands and looked at it. Shivappa, his beloved brother who wanted to be free, who wanted to be king, had died with a sad smile on his lips. Kattappa cradled it to his heart and screamed in anguish.

'My brother, my brother. I wish you had won this time too, my boy,' he cried. 'You have gone. I am alone in this miserable life of a slave. I am sorry, I am sorry, Shivappa.

'Nanna,' he screamed. 'Are you happy now? I have killed your son as you wished. We are no traitors. We are loyal, as loyal as dogs. Dogs, Nanna. Are you happy? Are you happy, you fool. Are you happy? But why am I not happy, Nanna? Why? Why?' He burst into sobs.

The river roared in laughter; the volcano smirked.

## THIRTY

# Gundu Ramu

GUNDU RAMU RAN as fast as he could, knowing death could descend on him at any moment. He had wet his dhoti again. When the battle started between the women warriors and Sivagami, he had run in fear to hide behind the outer fort gate, leaving Hidumba. Horrified, he had watched the giant female Garuda pakshi wreak havoc on the two armies.

But when he noticed that the chick was screaming in terror amidst the din of the war, he started crying. He had eyes for nothing else but the helplessness of the chick. He could identify with it. He was like that, in Gauriparvat, abandoned by all, surrounded by danger. He had been like that since his father's death. Except for Sivagami and then, later, Vamana, no one had shown him any sympathy. He could understand what the small bird was going through. Though terrified of the mother bird, he could even understand her anger. Had his mother been alive, she might perhaps have fought like that. Finally, he could stand it no more. Swallowing his fear,

Gundu Ramu ran to the battlefield and grabbed the terrified chick.

Gundu Ramu ran, staggering under the weight of the chick. He had never imagined it would be so heavy. The terrified chick cried for its mother.

'I am taking you home,' Gundu Ramu cried against the wind. The chick, scared of the alien sound and smell, pecked Gundu hard on his head. Gundu screamed in pain. 'I'm helping you. Please ... please ...' The bird pecked him again. Gundu Ramu knew he had no choice other than to bear the pain. The poor bird didn't know he was helping it. 'You're just a baby, but it hurts. Poke me softly,' Gundu Ramu pleaded, and the chick bit his ear. Tears of pain blurred Gundu Ramu's vision. The terrain was uphill, rocky and slippery. As he ran, loose pebbles rolled down and vanished into the abyss. He could hear the mother bird screeching from behind, feel the gust of wind from the flap of its wings.

'Drop the chick and escape, you fool,' Gundu Ramu heard someone say and turned to look. He saw Karthikeya fighting the bird. His men were shooting fire-tipped arrows at it. Though the arrows barely hurt the monster, they managed to annoy it. More arrows shot towards the sky, creating a temporary wall of fire as hundreds of fire arrows blazed up, blocking the bird's trajectory. The bird was confused and angry.

Ignoring Karthikeya's instructions, Gundu continued to run with the chick. He had seen the cave where the nest lay. As Gundu entered the cave, his heart sank. The nest was at the far end of the cave, and was almost twelve feet high. He scrambled up the nest, carrying the chick on his shoulders, panting and puffing under its weight. He dropped it down into the nest, and the chick turned around. There were five other chicks, and they hopped up and down, squeaking, screeching, fluttering their featherless wings at him. He was exhausted, drained of all his strength. He lay on his chest, looking at the six chicks, and his mind filled with happiness. He smiled at the chicks and called them to him. They hopped towards him, screeching and jumping. A slap on his back brought him back to his senses.

Karthikeya towered over him. 'Run, you fool,' the captain screamed, and before Gundu could react, the cave mouth had darkened.

Karthikeya picked up Gundu and ran towards the opening as the giant face of the mother bird rose parallel to the mouth. It gave an ear splitting screech and shot in.

Gundu found himself in the air and then he landed hard on his back, on the rock outside. He saw the mother bird enter the cave and, the next moment, the boulder came crashing down, closing the cave.

'Karthikeya mama,' Gundu screamed as he ran to the boulder. He could hear the screams of Karthikeya and the screech of the angry bird. He pounded on the rock and yelled at the soldiers who had brought the boulder down.

'Open it, open it.'

The soldier who had untied the chain and closed the cave came down and said in a soft voice to Gundu, 'The captain had instructed us to close it when he entered the cave. That was the only way to control the bird.'

Gundu Ramu sobbed. 'Save him. He wanted to go back home. He has six kids. The last one is younger than me.'

The soldier, whose name Gundu never found out, who Gundu would never meet again, said to him, 'We are soldiers, son. His family may starve, but they will understand.'

'How can you be so brave?' Gundu Ramu cried, pounding the boulder with his hands.

'Brave? We aren't brave, son. We are as scared as anyone else. But do you know what he said to us yesterday, when all of us were planning to go back. We were worried about our families, our children, our old parents. None of us was sure we would get back alive. Captain Karthikeya said—we have fought so many wars for men as unscrupulous as Bijjala and the king. We have fought so that they could rule, they could have their revenge, they could earn their loot, win their kingdoms. We have died like fireflies in hordes in the fire of other men's ambitions. We have so far seen only selfish men and women urging us to fight and die, fool us with slogans of patriotism or religion, fill our minds with hatred for those who are marked as enemies. This is the only battle we are going to fight for the sake of a few children, expecting nothing in return. We were fighting for the future of our country, our children too. Captain Karthikeya pointed to you, son, and said, when you are sacred just look at him. You weren't aware of it, but every soldier looked at you when he said it. If that boy can brave the dangers in the mines, if that boy can escape from the giant birds, traverse the wild for days to meet his Sivagami akka, and have the courage to return to the battlefield so that he can save other children, we can bloody well afford to fight another war. He said our children's futures were safe as long as a few among those we rescue from the mines are as noble and as brave as Gundu Ramu. We can then afford to die in peace. That is what he did, son. We fought this battle neither for Rani Sivagami devi nor Prince Mahadeva. We fought it for you.'

The screams in the cave had died down. Gundu Ramu pulled himself away reluctantly. His heart heavy, still sobbing, he dragged himself to the fort ground. As he walked, soldiers lined up on either side and bowed deep as if he was a conquering emperor. Gundu Ramu didn't even see them. His eyes were blurred with tears. 'Poor man has six children. The last one is younger than me,' Gundu Ramu kept mumbling, wondering what would happen to them now. Would they be cast away as orphans, like he was when his father died?

THIRTY-ONE

# Sivagami

THE FEW WOMEN warriors who had survived the battle surrendered their arms before Sivagami. After Shivappa had fled, and the bird had been removed, the Vaithalika army had frittered away. The presence of Ally in Sivagami's ranks added to their confusion. When the last of the warriors had surrendered, Sivagami ordered for all the children held captive in Gauriparvat to be brought to her.

Gundu Ramu appeared from the north, sobbing uncontrollably. He ran to Sivagami and hugged her thighs. He sobbed and repeated what had happened to Karthikeya.

'He will be rewarded, Gundu,' Sivagami said.

'But he is dead,' the boy cried.

'His children will be taken care of, don't worry,' Sivagami said and smiled, bringing some calm to Gundu Ramu's mind. Yet, he had expected Sivagami akka to be more emotional. The calm way she took the news of Karthikeya's death made him uneasy.

Gundu Ramu looked around and started retching at the sight and smell of all the blood and gore. He squatted down, closed his eyes tight and mumbled prayers.

Soon, hundreds of children were brought out into the sun. They squinted their eyes in the glare. Some started laughing, others sobbed uncontrollably. One of the boys spotted Gundu Ramu and gave a cry of joy. Gundu Ramu's friends, with whom he had shared almost two years of captivity, ran into his wide open arms with squeals of joy. They jumped on him, knocking his bulky frame on the ground, and piled up over him. More children rushed to jump on him, screaming his name.

Sivagami watched with tear-filled eyes. It was as if, for the boys, no one else existed. He was their hero, the first one to escape, the one to give them hope when all hope had died. He was everyone's hero, though he didn't know it, she thought. 'I hope you remain as you are, my little brother,' Sivagami whispered, wiping tears of joy from her eyes.

By the time Gundu Ramu was extricated from the pile, he was battered and bruised, but laughing happily. He called each boy by the name he had chosen for them, causing them to squeal with pleasure. It was an honour to be remembered by him. For Gundu, it was nothing extraordinary. He cared for them, and when they fussed over his lost fingers, he shrugged as if it was nothing.

Sivagami turned to her army and congratulated them, announcing tax-free land for the martyr Captain Karthikeya. She promised rewards to each of the soldiers who had participated in the battle. Ally, standing beside her, whispered, 'What if Maharaja Somadeva doesn't agree to your promises?'

Sivagami said, 'We have the stones, enough for the next twenty years perhaps. We will find alternate ways to run the empire. If he doesn't agree to the promises that his daughter-in-law has given, I will withhold this stock of Gaurikanta stones. Mahishmathi needs them desperately to put its finances and military back on track. He has no choice other than to agree. It isn't just the promises I have given. He has a lot to answer for. I will make him declare the truth about my parents. Devaraya was no traitor, and I will make Maharaja Somadeva declare that in public.'

Ally nodded. The soldiers were celebrating the victory with slogans hailing Sivagami. She looked at the Gauriparvat peak and felt a sense of profound satisfaction. The reality of the victory was sinking in. She said a silent prayer to her father and mother. The shouts of joy from the emancipated children were a tribute to her father. *Nanna, you may not have approved of my methods, but I did what you wanted. Forgive me for not always walking the straight path. But I achieved this thanks to you, Nanna. I will clear the blot on your name, and that on my poor mother. I owe this to the many who showed me the way. Uncle Thimma—I killed him; Skandadasa—a man I am learning to admire more every day. So many people who helped me, I remember with gratitude. Neelappa, who sacrificed himself for me. My little brother, Gundu Ramu, the bravest of all. Kattappa—a man of such strong values and fierce loyalty that one can scarcely believe such a man exists. And my Mahadeva ...* A sob escaped her, startling Ally, who was standing beside her. *I married not for love, but for strategic reasons. I sacrificed my happiness so I could do the right thing.*

A tap on her shoulder brought her back to the present.

'Girl ...'

Neelappa. Sivagami stood there, stunned. Then a wave of happiness overwhelmed her. He was alive! She turned with open arms and a wide smile.

'Mama!' Sivagami cried. 'I thought you were—'

'Dead?' Neelappa said. 'I also thought so, girl. It wasn't Shivappa who stabbed you that night. It was me.'

'Mama?'

'Don't move,' Neelappa said. He pressed the tip of his sword at her neck. 'I spent my whole life dreaming of a free Vaithalika. When Shivappa came with his army that night, I was happy that my dream had been fulfilled. But I was scared of you. I was afraid you would destroy everything. I stabbed you that night, hoping you would die. I made a mistake. I should have cut off your head. My fears have been proved right. You shattered the dreams of our people.'

'Mama.' Sivagami's voice trembled. 'How can you do this? Am I not the little girl you brought up? Weren't you my father's favourite slave?'

'Slave,' Neelappa said with a laugh. 'Our people are just slaves for you. Good slaves, pet slaves if we grovel before you. Evil slaves, if we rebel like our Shivappa. But slaves, always. You come to our forests and grab everything, kill us, capture us, sell us like cattle. Your merchants burn our villages, rape our mothers, daughters and sisters and kidnap our children. And if we make the slightest noise of protest, we are traitors, we are enemies of the state, we are dangerous criminals.'

'Mama, when have I considered you as a slave? How can you betray me like this. I am your Sivagami. You've been like a father to me, Mama.'

'*Like* a father, girl. Never your father. Never anyone to you. You know why?' Neelappa extended his left hand towards her. 'See your skin colour and mine.' And he started laughing hysterically. 'Once in a while, let us also win, girl. Let history record Neelappa as a man who killed the rani of Mahishmathi. Your bards may call me a traitor, but I shall be a hero to our people. Die, my little girl.'

Neelappa's sword rose high in the sky. Sivagami stood frozen at the enormity of the betrayal. The sword didn't reach her neck. Mahadeva had gripped it. With a roar, Neelappa pulled the sword back, cutting Mahadeva's palm. He kicked the prince and Mahadeva fell on his back.

'You die first, Prince,' Neelappa said and leapt at Mahadeva with his sword held high above his head, its tip pointed at Mahadeva. Sivagami drew her sword from her scabbard and brought it down on Neelappa's back. The old slave fell on Mahadeva and rolled away. He lay wheezing on his back, holding Sivagami's sword running through his chest.

Sivagami knelt down near him, sobbing, 'Oh God, what have I done, what have I done.'

'You have stabbed me in my back, girl. What is so new?' Neelappa gave a shudder and died with a derisive smile on his lips.

Sivagami fell on the old slave's body and wept. Why was her every victory tainted with the blood of someone she loved? The betrayal of Neelappa was too overwhelming for her to comprehend. How could he, of all people, deceive her, plot against her? And then she remembered his last words. It was she who had stabbed him in the back in the end. She lay on his inert body, losing sense of time, losing the desire for life, wishing she was the little girl waiting for her father to come from Gauriparvat, while holding the hand of Neelappa.

*I killed him for Mahadeva*, she thought. He had saved her, again. Without him, the victory she had achieved—however hollow the death of Neelappa had made it—wouldn't have been possible.

She had not thanked him. She may never live with him, but he would always have a special place in her heart. She felt she should cry before him, pour her heart out for all the wrongs she had done, for all the sins she had committed. Where was he? Sivagami looked around. 'Where is the prince?' she asked Ally, who had come to pacify her.

A loud crash reverberated in the air. Sivagami saw Mahadeva at the top of the fort. As she watched, the prince pulled another cart filled with stones and toppled it over the edge. The cart vanished into the ravine and the prince hauled the next cart to the edge.

Sivagami ran to him, screaming, 'Are you mad?'

'We aren't here for the stones,' Mahadeva said toppling another cart of Gaurikanta stones into the valley. 'These stones are evil. We will have nothing to do with this, sister-in-law.'

'Prince Mahadeva, the stones belong to the people of Mahishmathi. It is our duty to protect them. We have stopped the mining. We have freed the children. We are sealing the mines.'

Mahadeva said, 'There is no end to human avarice. Does my learned sister-in-law think that people wouldn't be tempted to restart the evil if they find out how rich these stones can make them? They belong to this mountain and we shall leave them here.'

Sivagami was exasperated. 'Prince Mahadeva. Be practical. All of us are fugitives from the law of Mahishmathi. We are all traitors. I, you, Ally, Kattappa, everyone here. We have defied the maharaja. Can't you see that only the stones will protect us from your father? Mahishmathi wants the stones desperately. We will use them to ensure our safety. We will use it to extract the promise that the mines will never be opened again.'

'Devi, I will not be a party to blackmail.' The next cart toppled over the cliff.

'Your father will hang you. Try to understand, Prince.'

'Devi, I would happily die in the gallows rather than live with this sin. You will take the stones to Mahishmathi over my dead body.'

'Why can't you stop being so stupidly idealistic for once?'

Mahadeva smiled at Sivagami. 'Because I am like that, devi. I am not practical. I am a fool. You can kill me, but I will not allow these evil stones to enter Mahishmathi. It will destroy us all.'

As Sivagami watched helplessly, Mahadeva pushed another cart over the edge.

THIRTY-TWO

# Kattappa

KATTAPPA STOOD UP, holding his urumi and the head of Shivappa. His face contorted with anger, he started climbing the rope. He reached the window and jumped into the tunnel. The dwarf was startled to see him with the head of his brother in his arms. Without a word, Kattappa started running. Vamana plucked the torch from the wall and ran behind him, 'Swami, swami,' he called, but Kattappa had no ears for anyone. He ran without hearing the pleas of Vamana who followed him in his ram-lead cart.

Kattappa burst through the mouth of the cave into bright sunshine. He lost his balance and fell on his face. The head rolled down. He picked it up and, patting away the soil from its hair, he kissed it as he howled in anguish. Kattappa saw Sivagami and the others at the top of the fort. He ran up the fort wall and went up to Sivagami. He hesitated a moment, undecided whom to address. Sivagami was the rani, wife of the crown prince. Kattappa fell on his knees and showed Shivappa's head to her.

'I have killed the traitor. I killed him. I am not a traitor. I am not a traitor, devi. I live and die for Mahishmathi.'

Sivagami stood, too shocked to move. Kattappa took it as a sign of her displeasure.

'Rani Sivagami devi, I am your slave forever.' He caught her feet. 'I am the slave of Mahishmathi, Amma.' He picked her right foot and pressed it to his bald head. 'The slave of Mahishmathi forever.'

Sivagami tried to gather him up. He crawled to Mahadeva, weeping inconsolably. 'I am your slave. The dog of Mahishmathi. I will do anything you order.'

'Kattappa, please …'

Kattappa reached Mahadeva, standing at the edge of the fort wall overlooking the cliff.

'Swami, swami. I am the slave of Mahishmathi, swami. I have killed the traitor in my family.' Kattappa knelt before him and tried to put his feet on his head.

'Kattappa,' Sivagami called.

'Amma,' Kattappa said as he turned.

'Arrest Prince Mahadeva,' Sivagami said. 'Bind him in chains.'

THIRTY-THREE

# Ally

ALLY ACCOMPANIED SIVAGAMI as Vamana took them through the mines. The conditions there pulled at their heartstrings. This was where two generations of poor children, kidnapped from their tribal hamlets, slaved away so that a few in Mahishmathi could be rich. An empire was built on this evil.

As soldiers systematically sealed the mine tunnels, Ally eyed Kattappa walking behind Sivagami. She was feeling bad for Mahadeva, who was chained and bound to a horse. Ally's admiration for Sivagami knew no bounds. What a woman! Ally wondered whether she would be able to behave the same way to Kattappa as Sivagami behaved to Mahadeva. Then she remembered how she had betrayed him and made him a slave to a devil like Jeemotha.

Vamana's cart stopped before a wooden door.

'Shivappa imprisoned Achi Nagamma here,' the old dwarf said.

Ally was startled to hear this. Sivagami made the soldiers break open the door.

'I am sorry. There are rats, plenty of them,' Vamana said apologetically. When they entered the room, Ally could see clots of blood. A sob escaped her throat. Achi Nagamma, the former commander-in-chief of a great empire like Kadarimandalam, the woman who, for three generations, had kept the fire of revolution alive against the mighty empire of Mahishmathi; the mother of all revolutionaries; the only person Ally was fortunate to call mother—she had died a miserable death. Ally collapsed to the floor and wept. Achi Nagamma wasn't there to see her dreams fulfilled, ironically, by another woman.

Ally kissed the floor and stood up, paying her tribute to the fiery Achi Nagamma. The way Achi died, eaten alive by rats—Ally didn't want to think about it. She deserved better.

'Ally,' Sivagami said, when she came out. 'Go and inform all the Vaithalikas that they are free. You shall be the queen of the Vaithalikas. We shall return Gauriparvat to your tribe on the condition that it will never be mined again. That was the wish of my father.'

Ally bowed low to Sivagami. 'Our queen, we shall always remain your obedient servants.'

'I need friends, not servants, Ally,' Sivagami said and smiled.

Ally was bursting with joy. She looked at Kattappa. The kingdom belonged to him. She fell back to keep pace with the slave, who walked behind Sivagami with expressionless eyes.

Ally touched her belly and smiled. She then touched Kattappa's shoulder and said, 'Kattappa, I am pregnant.'

Ally watched a wave of pleasure wash over Kattappa. She whispered in his ears, 'You are going to be a father. I will bring him up to be worthy of you. He will become the king of the Vaithalikas. The lineage of Malayappa isn't meant to be slaves,' Ally said happily, as memories of the beautiful evenings she had spent with Kattappa on the banks of the Mahishi came back to her.

With trembling hands, Kattappa touched her belly, and she looked at him with a teary smile. She waited for him to pick her up and shower her with kisses.

'Ally,' Kattappa whispered.

Ally looked deep into his eyes, half crying, half laughing. From the fort grounds, they could hear the rolling of drums for the victory procession to march towards Mahishmathi. The sounds of whistles and cries of merriment filled the sky. Ally hugged Kattappa and kissed him. But slowly, Kattappa's body became rigid, his posture became stiff. She saw his lips were drawn in a thin line of grim determination as he looked over her head, into the distance.

'Kattappa?' she said. He pushed her away and took a step back.

'Is it that you suspect the child is not ...' She couldn't complete the sentence. Was he hurt because he had seen Jeemotha kissing her? Was he suspecting her? She could bear anything, but not that. She struggled for words to explain her love for him. It sounded ridiculous, after taking away his freedom and making him a slave again, but it was the truth. There was no one she loved more.

'Kattappa,' she said again. 'Is it that you suspect me?'

Kattappa looked at her and she shuddered at the hatred in his face. She touched his shoulder.

'I have always been loyal to you, Kattappa.'

Kattappa raised his wrists, showing the marks that the handcuffs had made. 'My father gave his word that his descendants would be slaves. I can't go against my father. I don't want any child of mine to be born into slavery. It should end with me.'

Kattappa started walking to catch up with Sivagami. Ally stood rooted, weighed down by the enormity of his words. She could feel the baby in her womb moving for the first time. The drums had become frenzied outside. She rushed past Kattappa and Sivagami. She had a kingdom to build for Kattappa's son. Kattappa would come around sometime, she hoped against hope.

Later that night, he came to her. She was lying on the grass, enjoying the wetness of the night dew and staring at the sky, filled with stars. He came and sat by her side. She looked at him without moving. There was sweetness in the silence that stretched between them. She did not want him to speak. His presence was enough. When desire fired her veins, she traced her fingers over his hand. He turned and grabbed her in his arms and kissed her. She could feel his love in his breath, but it had something more, something she could not understand. She saw his eyes glittering in the starlight.

'Don't,' she said. He was Kattappa, the only man in her life, the only one she would ever love, and she couldn't bear to see him cry. He had come, and that was enough for her. They sat for an eternity that was shorter than the blink of an eye, melting into each other's arms, watching the morning star rise. Then he was gone, leaving his warmth in the grass beside her, and an aching cold in her heart. Something glittered where he had sat.

Ally picked it up. A raw mango. She smiled and touched her belly. The first gift for her son from his father. She took the first bite and it was delicious. There was an aftertaste of something sweet, something that did not belong to a mango. The craving in her stomach made her take another bite. And then another. She sat there watching the eastern sky turn crimson. For a moment, everything went blank. A dagger of pain shot up from her underbelly. She clutched her stomach and the pain intensified. She felt a sticky warmth on her thighs. When she touched them, it was as if the sky had bled onto her hand. She gasped. A wave of panic swept over her. She tried to get up, but collapsed on the grass. She lay there, writhing in pain. But that was nothing compared to the heaviness that was crushing her ribs.

'Kattappa!' she screamed, more angry than heartbroken at the betrayal.

Ally now knew what she had sensed in Kattappa's kiss was his guilt for a crime he had been planning to commit. His first gift to his unborn son was death. 'Kattappa!' Ally screamed between gasps. 'Kattappa … If I survive today, I will come for you, you bastard.'

THIRTY-FOUR

# Sivagami

AS THEY SAILED towards Mahishmathi, Sivagami's mind was in turmoil. She hadn't answered any of the curious questions of Gundu Ramu, and the boy had drifted to Mahadeva, who stood as far away as he could from Sivagami in the cramped ship. Sivagami sighed when she caught a glimpse of his handsome face. He was still in chains, and he stood with a stoicism that broke her heart. He didn't deserve this. She had lost Mahadeva forever, even as a friend, even as a brother-in-law. She was the wife of a man she didn't love, a man who had raped and killed her dearest friend. The price she was having to pay for her victory was terrible.

Somadeva had agreed to all her terms. The message with the royal seal of the maharaja of Mahishmathi that she had received while camping on Guha's land assured her of a warm welcome. She felt a surge of happiness as the Gaurikanta stones were loaded on Akkundaraya's ships. This would be the final lot of these stones to reach Mahishmathi, ending an era of mindless commerce and cruelty. 'Not anymore, never again,' she whispered, as her heart filled with pride. The victory she had earned was sweet as well as bitter. *The greatest loss is him,* she thought, as she heard Mahadeva's soft voice explaining something patiently to Gundu Ramu.

Sivagami assured herself that once they entered the city, she would free Mahadeva. Sivagami could understand why he had not wanted to take the stones back to Mahishmathi. Her father would have done the same thing. That was what an idealist, a man of conscience would do.

But Sivagami was no idealist. Most idealists end up in gallows, she thought bitterly—like her father, like Skandadasa. Had she been an idealist, she would have never married Bijjala. It was her hard-nosed practicality that helped her achieve her father's dream, and she had sealed the Gauriparvat mines for ever. Never again would a child be kidnapped and made to work in the mines. Her idealism ended there. To survive in this ruthless game, she must be practical, she assured herself once again. Sivagami needed the stones to be displayed before the public of Mahishmathi. She must shame Somadeva for his duplicity. But the stones were precious. She knew they were required to make weapons. Until Mahishmathi developed a different technology, the country would be vulnerable to invasion. The country belonged to her as much as Somadeva. Her fight was with the system and not the people of Mahishmathi, an empire which her father helped build.

The face of Kattappa standing near her filled her with apprehension. Would this man, who had killed his brother to prove his loyalty to Mahishmathi, who had replaced Neelappa, turn out to be a betrayer like the old slave? His act of abject surrender after killing Shivappa made Sivagami squeamish. His sincerity was touching, but Sivagami couldn't digest anyone doing what Kattappa had done. She could sympathise with Neelappa, but Kattappa was unfathomable. Kattappa had kept her foot on his head and wept, and he had no qualms following her orders to arrest Mahadeva. Was his loyalty to her or to the throne of Mahishmathi? Or was his loyalty a rebellion in itself?

As the ship reached the dock of Mahishmathi, Sivagami surveyed the city with pride. This was the moment she had been waiting for. The journey she had started on, four years ago from Thimma's home, had culminated in a huge success.

The children she had rescued were looking at the city with wonder-filled eyes. Customs officers boarded the ship and welcomed her, saying the ruler of Mahishmathi was waiting for her and the prince. She ordered Mahadeva to be unchained. The prince stood with no expression as Kattappa unclasped the chains.

As they walked through the streets of Mahishmathi, she felt something was amiss. There was no cheering among the public that had lined up on either side of the road. She had expected a warmer welcome. The Gaurikanta stones, loaded on several bullock carts, trailed behind her procession. They passed Guru Dharmapala's ashram. Why was it so silent? She thought of meeting Akhila. The girl would be a teenager now, and she looked forward to telling her the secret she shared with her father Thimma, and why she was forced to kill him. Maybe the girl would forgive her finally. But ... why were the people not looking her in her eyes, not responding to her smile? Had something happened to Bijjala? A glimmer of relief and hope sparked in her mind and she chided herself. He was her husband.

They reached the inner fort gate and Sivagami became aware of a faint stink. Pratapa was there, waiting to welcome her. He gave her a cursory bow, but ignored Mahadeva. Pratapa was the last man she had expected to see, but she acknowledged his salutation. Behind her, she heard Mahadeva gasp and followed his gaze. Her blood froze. Staring at her were two severed heads on pikes, placed on either side of the palace gate. Flies buzzed around them. They looked familiar, but the putrefying faces were beyond recognition.

'Parameswara and General Hiranya,' Pratapa pointed to the heads and said with barely concealed glee. Sivagami stopped in her tracks. No king could be so cruel. They were Somadeva's last followers. They were his friends. The founding fathers of Mahishmathi were the five friends: Somadeva, Devaraya, Thimma, Hiranya and Parameswara. Somadeva had got rid of the first two. Had he finished off the last two among his closest friends? How cruel and power-hungry could a man get? Sivagami was burning with indignation as she entered the durbar.

The sabha was surprisingly empty. The throne of Somadeva, with its pearl-stringed umbrella and the two roaring lions as its hand rests, shone in all its majesty. The lions glowered at her with their ruby eyes. A large Gauripadmam diamond adorned the headrest. Everything was how she had remembered, but something was amiss. She could see the same apprehension on Mahadeva's face. Only Kattappa, who stood behind them, had no expression on his face. It was as if he were indifferent to everything, as if something had died within him, and he existed in a purely animal-like state. Gundu Ramu was looking around at the luxury of the sabha with awestruck eyes.

Roopaka entered with a sly smile. 'Welcome Rani Sivagami devi,' he said and bowed to her first before wishing Mahadeva. Sivagami felt uneasy, though Roopaka had done the correct thing as per protocol. She was Mahadeva's sister-in-law and the wife of the crown prince, a future maharani.

'Where is my father?' Mahadeva asked.

'He will be coming,' Roopaka said. The absence of an honorific for the maharaja sent a shiver down Sivagami's spine. What had happened when she was away? The children she had rescued—a bolt of fear passed down her spine. She had left them to wait at the palace courtyard. She turned on her heels and yelled to Kattappa—'*The children!*'

The slave's sword was out of its sheath in an instant. The shrill sound of a horn pierced the air, stopping them in their tracks. A drum started booming. The courtiers appeared one by one and took their seats. Mahadeva greeted them, but none of them looked him in the eye.

A crier announced the arrival of the royal priest and Kalicharan Bhatta walked in. Sivagami couldn't believe her eyes. The last she had heard, he was a fugitive. How had he become the royal priest? The announcement for the upapradhana, the deputy prime minister, came, and she watched with shock as Guru Dharmapala, in his flowing white robes, walked in with a smile. He winked at Sivagami as he passed her.

She braced herself for the next announcement, and the crier called for the mahapradhana. The entire sabha stood up and bowed. Pattaraya, decked in silk and pearls, his turban glistening with the largest of Gauripadmam diamonds, strode in with a train of attendants. Sivagami inhaled sharply. Was he not dead? Bijjala had lied about this too? She could sense Mahadeva's shock as well. Pattaraya gave a cursory bow to Mahadeva. The prince took a step forward in agitation, but Sivagami restrained him.

'Where is my father?' Mahadeva asked.

Pattaraya merely smiled before taking his seat. Sivagami burned with indignation, unable to withstand the perversion of seeing Pattaraya occupying the seat that great men like Parameswara and Skandadasa once had.

'Where is my father? Where is His Highness Maharaja Somadeva?' Mahadeva screamed, taking out his sword.

Pattaraya kept smiling, infuriating the prince. The next cry of the announcer sent Sivagami into a state of confusion. At first, she thought she hadn't heard the crier's words properly.

Bijjala walked in, holding the hand of a beautiful woman. Clad in a black saree and glittering necklaces, carrying a peacock feather fan, Keki strutted behind them. Gundu Ramu cowered in fear and hid behind Sivagami, but the eunuch didn't even glance their way. A long train of female warriors marched behind them with unsheathed swords and glistening shields.

All the seated dignitaries stood up and bowed low as the entourage passed. The royal pair went past Sivagami and Mahadeva, ignoring them completely, and climbed the steps to the throne. They stood at the dais and greeted the sabha. Keki stood behind them, fanning them with the peacock feather fan.

Sivagami was frozen with despair and fear. Confused and

angry about what was happening, she worried about the children she had rescued.

Mahadeva yelled, 'Where is our father, Bijjala?'

Bijjala stared at him for a moment. A cruel smile distorted his face. He snapped his fingers and the women warriors marched towards Mahadeva. Before the younger prince could react, they had chained him. He struggled to get free.

Sivagami yelled, pointing her sword at the captors, 'Free him!'

Bijjala's voice startled her.

'Sivagami devi, my wife,' he said and laughed. 'Still in love with my brother?'

Sivagami turned towards him. 'You coward,' she said.

Bijjala laughed. 'Dear, dear. You are setting a bad example for your co-wife. Is this how a wife should address her husband? Wrong dear, absolutely wrong. Learn to respect your husband and his senior wife. Bow to Maharani Mekhala, Sivagami.'

The words scathed her, but she stood defiant. She knew whatever she had struggled for was crumbling around her. Whatever she had achieved was vaporising before her eyes. The husband she had wedded, against her conscience, had taken another woman. *You did it for practical purpose, Sivagami, you smart woman,* a voice mocked her. *Now pay the price.* Soldiers moved in to chain her, but Bijjala stopped them.

'Oh no, Sivagami is my junior rani. Spare her,' Bijjala said. 'Why Sivagami? Why are you glaring at me like that? You wanted my army, so you agreed to marry me. You thought, anyhow Mahadeva is dead, why not enjoy the power of being the wife of the crown prince of Mahishmathi and become maharani one day. Ha ha, wife you became, but you will never be the maharani, for you are just a junior wife. I had married Mekhala long ago.'

'Where is my father?' Mahadeva struggled to get free.

'*Our* father, brother,' Bijjala said. '*Our* father. Of course, from the way he always favoured you over me, I understand why you think him as your own. Our father is safe. He is in Kadarimandalam, serving as the footstep of the empress Chitraveni.'

Mahadeva gave a cry of anguish. 'How dare you?'

'How dare I? Our father prided himself on being a great player of chaturanga. We know what happens when someone becomes overconfident about their abilities—they forget there are better players than them. He thought the letter my beloved wife Mekhala wrote was from me. He thought I was being held captive in Kadarimandalam and came to play the hero, to rescue me with his army. Instead, he got trapped between the army of Kadarimandalam and my army. We squeezed him from either side, Pattaraya and Bijjala. And our great father had left Mahishmathi's safety to his stupid general and mahapradhana. Their severed heads hanging at the fort gate is the reward for their foolishness. They made the fort impregnable from the outside. Not even a fly would enter the fort, Hiranya boasted. He had no idea that an entire army was camped *inside* Mahishmathi under Guru Dharmapala, the man Pattaraya had placed many months ago. That is how ace players play the game of chaturanga, Vikramadeva Mahadeva.'

'You backstabbed our father!' Mahadeva cried.

'What is rajadharma without some backstabbing, brother?' Bijjala said. 'Our father backstabbed many to build the empire.

Now he is paying the price. Our father killed my junior wife's father. I was taking revenge for my Sivagami. Does that please you, brother—that I care for your lover?'

'Shut up, you unscrupulous man. Don't involve my father in this,' Sivagami hissed. 'He lived and died for this country and for what is right.'

'Ah, my junior wife. You are indeed the right one to speak about righteousness.' Bijjala's laughed loudly. 'Sivagami, you sold yourself for power. Do you know the word for someone who sells themselves for a reward. Whore. That's what you are.'

Mahadeva screamed, 'You brute, how dare you insult her!'

'Ha, Sivagami, your lover is suffering. He can't bear to see you being insulted. I shall fix that,' Bijjala said in a voice that chilled Sivagami's blood. He turned to a woman soldier near him. 'Blind him so that he won't suffer seeing his lover as my wife anymore.'

'No!' Sivagami screamed, rushing towards Bijjala with her sword. She swung it at Bijjala, but he caught her wrist with ease. 'Kattappa!' Sivagami yelled.

The slave didn't move. Bijjala laughed. 'He owes his allegiance to the crown and not to any one person. Whoever sits on this throne will be the only one who can command him. If you sit here, he will obey you. If I sit here, he will obey me. That dog has been trained like that, my junior wife.'

Sivagami struggled to free her wrist from his grip. Bijjala smiled. 'This right hand of mine can crush elephants. You think you can escape me? Keep struggling. I like your fighting spirit. You're entertaining. I shall entertain you too. Let us watch your lover going blind.'

Mahadeva was standing with his head held high, his eyes wide open, not even showing a trace of fear. A woman soldier of Kadarimandalam approached him with a red hot needle. Sivagami screamed, 'No, no. Have mercy.'

Bijjala glanced at Mahadeva and then turned to Sivagami and said, 'Your lover isn't crying, my wife. He is acting brave. Let him plead with me, and I shall think of being a bit—a little bit, that's all—I shall think of being a bit compassionate.'

Mahadeva stood without blinking, proud and dignified even when the red hot needle was a finger's length away from his eye.

'Do what he says, Mahadeva,' Sivagami cried, struggling to get free of Bijjala's grip.

'Be practical, you mean, Sivagami devi.' Mahadeva's words stung Sivagami more than Bijjala's grip.

'I'm not you, devi. I am Mahadeva—the fool, the coward, the idealist. I will never bow my head to evil. Not at the cost of my sight, not at the cost of my head.'

Sivagami sobbed; her heart felt like it was being torn open. Bijjala whispered in her ear, 'It looks like it hurts you more than him. If I blind him permanently—that is, if I pop his eyes, plop, plop, like this—he would cry for two days and everything will be back to normal after that. Isn't it? We will all be reconciled with what can't be reversed sooner or later—death, for example. What's the fun in that? You'll get strange ideas of revenge. I won't be able to sleep peacefully after that. Ah, who wants such a life? I want you to be under my thumb, dear. I want you to live with the fear that I can harm him anytime I wish.' Bijjala commanded the soldier, 'Don't put that needle in his eyes. Just sew his eyelids together.'

Bijjala turned to Sivagami. 'Do you know what that means, dear? He will be blind for as long as I wish. Whether or not he gets his vision back is in my hands. You behave well, I may think of asking my vaidya to remove the stitches. You act funny or he acts funny, I will blind his eyes. Plop, plop and he is blind forever. Don't I have you like a worm in my hand now? In this hand, my powerful hand. Bahubali—the one with the most powerful arm, that would have been an apt name for me. Our grandfather's name. Instead, my stupid parents gave me the name Bijjala. Ah, let be it so. I am happy with the name Bijjala too. What's in a name? But my dear wife, do you think you can ever escape my grip? Do you think you can escape the power of my hand? I shall crush you like one would crush a fly.'

'You don't know me, husband,' Sivagami spat. 'You won't have any arm left soon. Better you kill me now or you will regret it.'

Bijjala laughed. 'Oh, and the world would call me a thankless person. I am grateful to you, Sivagami. You and your lover boy got back Gauriparvat and killed the traitors. You brought back all the stones from the mountain. You revealed the secret and now there is no need to do all that nonsense my father used to do—bringing a Kali statue, hiding the stones inside it, immersing the statue in the river and retrieving the stones from the statue clandestinely from the riverbed. Ah, what duplicity, what a way to fool our own subjects. I am a straight man. There won't be any secrets in Mahishmathi. We are mining Gauriparvat, and those who have a problem with that can leave this country or be hanged here. We aren't going to be lenient with any antinationals. And the kids you brought here, they are going back to the mountains. If we want more children to mine the mountain, we aren't going to bother about secretly kidnapping them from faraway tribes. Every citizen must give at least one child in their family for the nation's cause, irrespective of whether they are Mahishmathi citizens or some tribe in the deep jungles. That is the order of the empress of Kadarimandalam and we are just a vassal state, my wife. Now, stop trying to burn me with the fire in your eyes. You are no Shiva to open your third eye and turn me into ashes. You are just a woman. There. Look there. Watch how beautifully your Mahadeva's eyes are getting stitched.'

Sivagami turned to see Mahadeva standing without moving as a soldier sewed his eyelids together. The prince didn't even flinch as lightness vanished from his eyes. Suppressing her sobs and gathering all her anger, Sivagami said aloud for the sabha to hear, 'My husband has chosen to spare my life. He is being foolish. This is Sivagami's oath. I will do anything to ensure the end of my husband's rule—nay, misrule. I promise that I will make Vikramadeva Mahadeva the maharaja of Mahishmathi before I die. This is my oath on my father Devaraya. This is my oath on my foster father, Thimma. This is my oath on the man I consider as my guru—Skandadasa. This is Sivagami's oath—that I would dethrone my husband and make Mahadeva sit on the throne.'

The sabha stood in stunned silence. She turned back to Bijjala, who stared at her. She prised open his grip from her wrist. She walked down the steps with her head thrown back, defiant and angry.

'Wife,' she heard Bijjala calling. She turned back. Bijjala started laughing. 'How are you going to dethrone me, when I am not the king at all? You are so amusing,' Bijjala said. He reached out and held the hand of Mekhala. Pattaraya was grinning.

Bijjala made Mekhala sit on the throne and stood by her side. 'I am a humble servant of the maharani of Mahishmathi, the vassal kingdom of Kadarimandalam. Don't you know that in Kadarimandalam, it is the woman who rules? And their laws apply here too. Now, bow to your ruler, Sivagami. Bow to Maharani Mekhala devi, the sovereign of Mahishmathi, and the senior wife of Bijjaladeva.'

## THIRTY-FIVE

# Achi Nagamma

*A few months later*

The old woman crawled through the cave. She had a bleeding rat in her mouth which twitched in the throes of death. She had been trying to find a way out, but wherever she crawled, she had found it sealed with mortar and rocks. Twice she came back to the cell where she had been imprisoned by her unscrupulous protégé. The silence in the mines made her uneasy. Where had all the child slaves gone? Where were the dwarfs? Why was there no rattle of the cart driven by rams? The only sound was the breathing of the mountain, which hissed and sputtered. The fire in the belly of Gauriparvat kept flaring up. The caves often filled with the smell of rotten eggs. Sometimes, she got near the waterfall, but even the window that used to open to the mouth of the volcano was sealed. There was no way to escape. Was she destined to die like this?

At the age of seventy-five, she should have been dying in her deathbed, surrounded by her grandchildren. But some women are not born to have a mundane life or death.

The old woman crawled through a new way. She had seen a ray of sunlight slipping through a crack on the floor. She reached the spot and started digging with her bare hands. When a cold breeze carrying a beastly smell hit her nose, she frowned. 'There is hope as long as there is life,' she said aloud, and the cave echoed it back. She continued to dig. When the hole was large enough to squeeze in, she entered it.

The old woman fell into something soft. She stood up and found a giant bird and six smaller birds were staring at her.

The mother bird gave an angry, ear-splitting screech. Achi Nagamma had not been intimidated by anything in life.

She stood erect in the nest of the Garuda pakshi, thrust her staff firmly on the ground, and screeched back at the mother bird.

# PART 2

*Five years later*

THIRTY-SIX

# Akhila

AKHILA STOOD WITH her ears pressed to the wall. From the other side, she could hear muffled conversation, accompanied by Pattaraya's loud laughter. She hated it when Pattaraya visited her brother's ashram. Akhila despised everything about the new Mahishmathi, but the most challenging thing to accept was her brother's new avatar. Though Raghava had now become the mahapradhana of Mahishmathi, he had continued to live in the ashram. The saffron dress he wore endowed him with an authority that no position of power could have ever given him; it gave him the licence to do anything. Who can question the ways of mystics? Why risk the wrath of the gods by probing a man of religion?

Akhila was seventeen now, and the last five years she had spent in the ashram had been wretched. Not that her brother had been unkind to her. In fact, he was always affectionate and granted her the kind of freedom none of the other inmates in the ashram enjoyed. She had also learnt to mask her feelings by always appearing to be pious and obedient. She wondered whether he would continue to be so loving if he knew of the emotions seething within her. A tap on her shoulder startled Akhila.

'Eavesdropping?' Raghava folded his arms across his chest and smiled at her.

'I ... I ... Do you need refreshments?'

'My sister is welcome to sit in on the council meetings,' Raghava said, leaning towards her.

'I hate them,' Akhila blurted out.

'I, too, hate them,' Raghava said in a hushed voice.

'How could you, Anna? After our father ...'

'Our father was an idiot, Akhila. What business did he have to join the low caste Vaithalikas and rebel against the king?'

'The king is no saint. He killed Devaraya, our nanna's dearest friend,' Akhila said hotly.

With an amused smile, Raghava said, 'Are you trying to turn into another Sivagami? She killed Nanna, sister. I left Mahishmathi for her. I came back, meaning to help her. But when I returned, she had killed our father, and our mother had died. I don't blame her for what she did, but that opened my eyes.'

'Opened your eyes? You sided with them—'

'Hush.'

In the other room, Pattaraya said something and Keki burst out laughing.

'You abandoned Sivagami akka,' Akhila said, dropping her voice.

'I don't care about Sivagami. I don't care about anybody other than you, my sister. They have spared you because I sided with them. Imagine if I had stood with Sivagami? Look at her plight now. The much-ignored second wife of Bijjala. And look at where I have reached. I am respected as a saint and feared as the mahapradhana.'

'But Anna, we are now slaves colonised by a foreign empire. Doesn't it affect you that our people are living under such wretched conditions?'

'Our people? Who are our people? The filth that live in the slums of Mahishmathi? The slaves of Mahishmathi? As if Mahishmathi was heaven during Somadeva's reign. Bah! I care about your safety—nothing else matters to me.'

'God will not allow evil to flourish for long,' Akhila said angrily and Raghava burst out laughing.

'God?' he said. 'The one who allows evil to flourish for thousands of years and finally takes on an avatar to vanquish it? Evil is perpetual, Akhila. Avatars happens once in an eon.'

Akhila turned her face away, flushing red in anger. 'I don't like these people. Why have they come?'

Raghava said in a low voice, 'Prince Mahadeva.'

A shiver passed through Akhila and she averted her eyes. 'What ... what can the poor blind prince do to them? Aren't they satisfied by their savagery towards him?'

'It is a rumour, spreading through the lower ranks of society, that is worrying us. Bards are singing about the coming of a vikramadeva to free Mahishmathi. And the only vikramadeva alive is Mahadeva. There is the stirring of a revolt, and we need to crush it.'

Akhila's throat went dry. Was her brother aware of her role in spreading the rumour? 'Are ... are you going to kill Prince Mahadeva?' she asked.

'Isn't it time for you to oversee the food distribution?' Raghava said, changing the topic. Akhila nodded and hurried away. She ran through the meditation hall, where ochre-clad disciples of Raghava were chanting mantras, and past a group of bhaktas acting as if evil spirits had possessed them, so they could put up a good show during Guru Dharmapala's exorcising ceremony.

The day was hot, and the air was heavy with the smell of incense. As she walked to the kitchen, Akhila thought about visiting Sivagami. Her sister had become remote and unapproachable, yet Akhila thought of Sivagami as her only true friend; if only she could bring herself to ask for help. It was Sivagami who had withdrawn from Akhila, and she realised guilt plagued her akka. But what her brother had said terrified Akhila. Should she inform Sivagami?

The inmates of the ashram were waiting for her orders. Several copper vessels covered with banana leaves stood before them. She had to tell them which streets they should take these to, for this was the food for the destitute. That is how the ashram maintained its popularity. Give some charity and there would always be people to defend you, even if you committed a series of murders. It didn't matter that the ashram was giving away only a tiny part of what it was earning.

People would fight with each other for a morsel of this food. It was considered special because the 'avatar of God', Guru Dharmapala himself, had blessed it. Akhila, however, took part in the philanthropic acts as they were close to her heart. She instructed the inmates of the ashram on where to take the food, and picked up a vessel and walked towards the palace.

When she reached the prison gates, the guards playing chaturanga looked at her indifferently. She was the sister of Guru Dharmapala, and she often came to feed the prisoners. They opened the doors and let her in, impatient to get back to their game. Akhila's heartbeat increased as she descended the irregular steps towards Mahadeva's dungeon. She walked past the cells of the other prisoners, pausing only to hand over some food, and hastened to the far end. She waited a few feet away, listening to Mahadeva sing. She wouldn't interrupt him until she had memorised the lyrics he was singing. His mellifluous voice soothed her like a cool breeze.

The prince sang about the divine love of God for his creation, but she liked to imagine he was singing for her. Akhila stood listening, overwhelmed by her love for him. Who, she wondered, would not adore a man who, despite the tribulations he had faced, went on to spread light in the world? When she had heard him sing the first time, she was a girl of twelve. Now, at seventeen, she was the greatest admirer of his poetry. She had resolved that Mahadeva's lyrics would not die in the dampness of this dungeon. The prince, however, wasn't even aware of her love for him. In all this time, Akhila had barely said a word to him.

Akhila stepped forward and saw him sitting cross-legged in a corner of the cell. Her eyes filled up. How could her brother conspire to kill this man? Look at him, she thought. It didn't matter to him that no one heard his poetry. The song soared through the gloom of the prison, making fragrant the musty odour that permeated the space. Like a summer shower, like the breeze of the hills, his voice soothed, caressed, breathed hope into even the most forlorn of souls. Akhila could hear some prisoners weeping, not with despair, but a joy that no words could capture. She placed his food down and walked backward. It would be a sin to interrupt his meditation by warning him about what awaited him. He did not belong to the future, nor to the past. He was suspended in the present, exuberant and eternal.

Akhila was humming to herself as she passed the guards. By the time she returned to the ashram, she knew the verse as if she had written it. It had now become hers, and soon it would belong to the people of Mahishmathi. Her brother might think throwing some morsels of food at the oppressed would keep them beguiled. He and his friends were not yet aware of the power of an idea. The Pattarayas and Bijjalas of the world were fools who thought they could imprison the wind. It was the breeze that lifted a butterfly's wings and rustled the leaves that would become a storm when the time arrived. And a storm *was* brewing—to a small degree for now—because of Akhila.

Akhila entered the aviary. There were a few parrots and parakeets here that she had bought from bird catchers. She often freed them after keeping them for a few days. For the world, it was an act of compassion. Little did anyone know it was an act of rebellion.

Akhila sang Mahadeva's poem and the parakeets cocked their heads, listening keenly. She paused and waited in nervous anticipation. A moment later, the birds sang back from their cages. She laughed and repeated the song, and this continued for some time. Every time she sang Mahadeva's songs, she felt he was sitting by her side, singing with her. To be alive in the same world as Mahadeva was a blessing in itself, she felt. When she was satisfied with the way the parakeets were singing, she opened the cages. She had let loose hundreds of parrots in this way, over the last few years.

'Go—spread the message of hope, the spirit of love, the fragrance of freedom,' she said to them. The birds circled around her head, and through the gaps in the roof, vanished into the sky. They would go to the distant corners of Mahishmathi, singing the words of Mahadeva. Soon, the song would echo from the lips of humans and birds, awakening a nation.

With her heart racing with inexplicable ecstasy, she came out of the aviary and inhaled the fresh air. She felt one with the world. Akhila could feel Mahadeva's words of hope in the breeze, shining in the blades of grass, throbbing in the melody of birdsong. Mahadeva was immortal; no one could harm him, she told herself.

When she entered her brother's chamber, Raghava was reading the Upanishads. He set it down when he saw her. 'You were eager to know whether we would kill Mahadeva,' he said. 'He is more valuable to us alive than dead. We are going to parade him, along with Somadeva, through the streets of Mahishmathi. People should see how powerless he looks. If you want to know something, don't eavesdrop, my sister. Just ask, and I will tell you. Why should I deny you anything?'

Akhila quickly turned to go before her face could betray her pain, when Raghava suddenly asked, 'Are you in love with someone?'

She rushed to her brother and hugged him. She sobbed on his shoulder and said, 'I want to marry Mahadeva. Please save him.'

Raghava flinched and stared at her for a moment. 'Why do you want to marry that blind fool? I can get you any prince or king. Many are my disciples. I will arrange your marriage with the choicest of men.'

A look of determination came over Akhila's face. 'What you will be arranging will be my funeral.'

Raghava was speechless. Then, pointing a trembling finger at her, he managed to ask, 'Are you behind those songs that are spreading through the kingdom? How did—' Raghava stopped as realisation dawned on him. 'The parrots.'

'I'm so sorry, Anna.'

'What you have done could get us both killed, Akhila. You are spoiling everything I have built.'

'I will die, Anna. I won't let any blame fall on you. I have no will to live anyway.' Akhila broke down and Raghava stood stunned, as the enormity of what his sister had done dawned on him.

## THIRTY-SEVEN

# Ally

ALLY LOOKED AT the undulating hills stretching before her. Mist curled up from the valley, and the jungle looked as if it held some terrifying secret. Ally could hear the Vaithalikas working on building the temple for Amma Gauri. It had been a task for her to unite all the Vaithalikas who were hiding in the jungles.

It had been raining incessantly for the past few weeks, and wherever she could see, there were waterfalls. As if the mountains were bleeding, the water gushed down, rusty red in colour, roaring towards the valley. From a distance, Gauriparvat looked hauntingly beautiful. No wonder it generated a feeling of awe in people in the valley and the plains. But, up here on the peak, it was hell. The wind howled around her and jabbed her with its icy fingers, making her shiver. She was drenched from head to toe but couldn't afford to leave her post. Rumours had reached her that the Kalakeyas were marching from the far north towards Gauriparvat.

When the clouds moved, she could see the glimmer of the golden pagodas in distant Mahishmathi. The river snaked its way through the jungles towards Mahishmathi, and even from this distance, Ally could see that it had eaten away the shores on either side. This had been a miserable year of flood and torrential rains. Somewhere in the distance, thunder rumbled.

The Vaithalikas paused in their work and looked fearfully at her. They had heard something. They lay down their tools and started chanting prayers. Vamana, the old dwarf who was sitting near the chained Hidumba, scrambled up.

'Devi ... devi ...' The old dwarf stumbled forward. He fell on his face and Hidumba burst out laughing.

'You heard it too, old fool? Ha, ha, all of us are going to die, die, die,' Hidumba said and spat out an abuse. The Vaithalikas continued to chant, but the tremor in their voices was unmistakable. Ally stood up and walked towards them. She helped up Vamana from the dirt.

'I heard it, devi. Garuda pakshi ...'

Ally listened. Nothing. Hidumba, chained to the wall, shaggy and dirty, continued to cackle, peppering his laughter with abuses aimed at the Vaithalikas. He hurled caustic caste slurs at the Vaithalikas, and when Ally's shadow fell on him, he looked up with a sneer. 'Whore, you want something?' he said with a lewd smile. In a swift movement, Ally's knee cracked Hidumba's nose, and the dwarf howled in pain.

The Vaithalikas shifted on their feet, uneasy and frightened. 'Devi, you shouldn't hurt anyone weaker than you,' Vamana reproached her, and she sighed. If not for the Vaithalikas' superstition that killing a dwarf would bring them bad luck, Hidumba would have become rat food a long time ago. At night, their frightened squeaks kept her awake. When she had reached Gauriparvat five years ago, she had been afraid rats would take over the entire mountain, but something had kept their population in check. An unknown predator prowled the ragged peaks of Gauriparvat, rustling through the tunnels and caves in the night. The Vaithalikas thought it was the ghosts of the children who had perished in the mines. Ally had her own ideas, but she kept them to herself. Though she had not seen it with her own eyes, there had been sightings of an old woman riding a giant bird on new moon nights. Achi Nagamma's ghost haunted the mountain, the Vaithalikas often whispered amongst themselves. They lit a lamp at the mouth of the cave, and kept a portion of food there to please the ghost. The food remained untouched on most days, but sometimes it would vanish, and, on those days, the Vaithalikas would go into a frenzy. They would beat their chests and heads with their hands and weep for the long-dead Achi. They prayed for her protection, to save them from the greedy hands of the civilised. For they knew, sooner or later, the new rulers of Mahishmathi would come to bore the mountain again. Ally was preparing for such an eventuality, but she knew it was a lost cause with barely a hundred men with her. If only Mahadeva had remained king. If only her brother Brihannala was with her ...

An unearthly screech filled the air, and the Vaithalikas stopped their chanting. Ally heard a flap of wings and held her breath. From the valley, another cry arose in answer, in a strange language.

'Kilikki,' Vamana's voice quivered.

Ally ran towards the fort, ignoring the pleas of her men. She cut across the ground where the bloody battle between

Sivagami and the Garuda pakshis had taken place five years ago, and ran up the steps to the top of the fort. The valley was filled with men, dark as coal and fierce as the ghosts of Lord Shiva. Ally's throat went dry. Kalakeyas, thousands of them, were screaming and yelling in their strange tongue. Their maces and spears bobbed up and down as they jumped and stomped about.

A gust of wind above her head made her dive to the ground. The wing of a humungous bird grazed her back as it glided down towards the army. 'Achi Nagamma!' she gasped.

Behind her, the Vaithalikas screamed in one voice, 'Amma!'

Unspoken words stuck in her throat, Ally stood stunned. The Vaithalikas prostrated on the ground, weeping and shouting with joy. Some were on their knees, their arms thrown skywards. Through her tears, Ally saw the glorious figure of Achi, riding the giant bird as it soared above the peak. There she was, her mother, her guru, riding the Garuda pakshi like a goddess from some ancient myth. The setting sun's bleeding rays reflected on the Garuda pakshi's feathers for a brief glorious moment, and then the bird vanished beyond the peak.

As the Kalakeyas regained their courage, a loud ululation rose from the valley. They howled like a pack of wolves that had spotted their prey and rushed up the hill, shaking their maces, swirling their spears.

The bird appeared again, this time with a massive rock held in its talons. Ally held her breath. The bird was protecting them. She shouted a command at her men not to be scared and to hold their positions. She could sense their unease; she was feeling a primeval fear in her veins as well. Suddenly, a man ran towards the fort, waving both his hands.

'Amma, it is me. Your son,' the man cried. Brihannala. Her brother.

The bird was high in the sky when it dropped the boulder. Ally screamed in terror. With a sound that shook the foundations of the fort, the rock fell a few feet away from Brihannala, and rolled down the valley, crushing several trees on its way before plunging into the roaring Mahishi river a few thousand feet down. The bird circled above them and landed gracefully inside the fort, and the Vaithalikas rushed towards their goddess.

Ally rushed to the fort gate and pulled open the doors. She ran into the open arms of her brother and sobbed on his shoulder. Behind them stood the fierce army of the Kalakeyas, grunting and growling.

Ally remarked that Brihannala looked strange in men's clothes, and her brother said he would soon borrow a sari. They laughed and cried and laughed again. Holding on to his arm, Ally walked towards their mother. Achi Nagamma was standing, caressing the feathers of the bird that had settled down on the ground and watching them with an indulgent smile. As soon as they neared Achi, they dissolved into her embrace and wept.

'There, there, Ally; you can't cry. This fool crying, I can understand. Though you were never born of my womb, wasn't it you I carried in my heart always? Wasn't it you who I trained to be my successor? Silly girl, wipe your tears.'

'I … I …' Ally was too emotional to speak.

'Thought I was dead?' Achi asked with a chuckle. 'Don't you know that I am immortal?'

'You are Gauri, Amma. You're immortal,' Brihannala said.

Achi eyed her son with affection, but when she spoke, the words were mocking, as usual—a tone she reserved for the ones she loved the most. 'What a good son you are, leaving your old mother to survive on rats and rodents.'

'That is how you survived?' asked Ally.

'For five years, girl. It took me five years to tame them, but now they obey my every command,' Achi said, running her fingers through the feathers of the Garuda pakshi. 'But my daughter and my grandsons gave me good company.'

'Grandsons?'

'She has four sons,' Achi said, and in answer, the giant bird cooed.

The Kalakeyas stood some distance away. A few of them had strayed towards the mouth of the cave, and the terrified cries of Hidumba could be heard. The breeze had turned into a gale, and the air was becoming unbearably cold.

'Amma, I got news about Mahishmathi preparing to come here, so I rushed here with the Kalakeyas,' Brihannala said. 'We must—' Achi raised her palm to cut him off.

'No. It is we who must talk war to Mahishmathi and Kadarimandalam,' Achi said. 'And then they will know this Achi is not Gauri but Kali, the Goddess of destruction.'

A low rumble emanated from the belly of the mountain. The Garuda pakshi gave a wild cry and, flapping its gigantic wings, took off towards the sky.

The next night, when the earth was wrapped in a blanket of darkness, Ally saw the Kalakeyas dancing around a blazing fire, their wild cries echoing in the mountains. They looked as if they had stepped out of a nightmare.

Achi Nagamma stood before the fire and raised her

staff. The Kalakeyas stopped dancing and watched her with curiosity. Achi started speaking in their tongue, and at the end of each of her proclamations in Kilikki, the Kalakeyas erupted with wild applause. Ally looked at Brihannala, her eyes wide in amazement.

'I didn't know our mother can speak Kilikki,' Ally said.

'Is there anything she doesn't know?' Brihannala smiled.

'Why are they so excited?'

'She just reiterated my promise that they will get their holy book back. All they have to do is to march to Mahishmathi under the leadership of Achi Nagamma, ransack the city and kill everyone—then they can take the book.'

'Book? Which book? Where is it?'

'The book that Sivagami claims is her father's. The book that the fat boy ... er ... what is his name?'

'Gundu Ramu?'

'Yes. The book he carries with him,' Brihannala said. 'The book belonged to the temple of the Kalakeyas. They used to pray to it.'

Ally laughed. 'Prayed to a book? Look at these savages. I can't imagine it.'

'I never said they read the book. They prayed to it.'

'How did it come to be in Devaraya's possession?'

'I don't know. All I know is that Devaraya spent hours in the library trying to crack the language in which it was written. Finally, he learned that it was in Paisachi, a language that was once regarded the language of culture and science in the ancient world. The Kalakeyas, who are now considered savages, were once a highly advanced civilisation. They had found a way to mine Gauriparvat. In and around the mountain and in the valley of river Mahishi, a majestic civilisation had spread. They had fantastic temples and forts, palaces, education institutions ...'

'Amma Gauri!'

'It is believed that the jungle that separates Mahishmathi and Gauriparvat hides a majestic city under its soil. The book contained some hints about the mining of Gaurikanta stones. Devaraya used that as the foundation and designed a system to recreate what the Kalakeyas had done many thousand years ago.'

'You mean to say it wasn't the evil genius of Devaraya that created this despicable system?'

'Devaraya was hardly evil; in fact, he was just the opposite. He was a scholar and a scientist, driven by the passion for knowledge. He didn't just copy what the Kalakeyas had done, but used his own genius to build something on it. It was power-hungry people like Somadeva who used it to their advantage, to hold on to power and use it as a means of oppression.'

'How did the ancient Kalakeya civilisation vanish?'

'Gauriparvat finished it.'

'What?'

'The holy mountain, the abode of Amma Gauri, exploded, spewing tons of hot lava and poisonous gas, and buried the Kalakeya civilisation. Amma Gauri has fire in her womb and nothing can stand in her path when Gauriparvat explodes. The Kalakeyas forgot this basic fact and paid a big price. In fact, their holy book was written by a Kalakeya seer who survived the catastrophe. Devaraya was trying to prevent that from happening to Mahishmathi. He had started seeing the signs of impending disaster. Nobody can predict when a volcano will erupt, but the signs are all there. The curious formation of clouds above the peak, the strange smell of rotten eggs, the tremors in the earth.'

'But the occasional tremors have been there right from my childhood, and Devaraya was killed almost two decades ago. Why hasn't it erupted even after two decades?' Ally said, fear making her voice tremble.

Before Brihannala could reply, Achi gestured to them. She had finished her speech and the Kalakeyas resumed their wild dance around the fire. 'Tomorrow morning, you two will proceed to Kadarimandalam,' she told Ally and Brihannala.

'We have heard rumours that Mahishmathi is planning an expedition here, Amma,' Brihannala said.

'I will handle them. I will take the war to their city. What I want is for you to finish Kadarimandalam. They will try to protect their colony. I want you to incapacitate their navy for some months. Once we conquer Mahishmathi, we will take down Kadarimandalam too.'

'But how?' Ally protested.

'"But how?" Is this what you learnt from me?' Achi mocked her. 'Find that pirate. Despicable he may be, but there is no one who knows ships better than he does. My son says Jeemotha is a galley slave in Chitraveni's ships. The pirate will have an axe to grind with Chitraveni. Do not return until you have neutralised Kadarimandalam.'

Achi turned and walked to the cave. The Kalakeyas continued to dance, their howls and shrieks adding to the eeriness of the night. Shivering in the breeze, but not wanting to go near the fire and share space with the Kalakeyas, Ally stood with an inexplicable fear rising in her gut. Brihannala ran to join the Kalakeyas. The mountain gave a deep growl and they all paused in fear. The revelries resumed soon, but Ally felt, in her bones, a premonition of disaster.

THIRTY-EIGHT

# Sivagami

SIVAGAMI PEERED THROUGH the curtains. It was not yet dawn, but rhythmic drum beats had woken her up. The usual daily procession was winding its way through the streets, but what was unusual today was the number of people who had lined up on either side of the royal highway, unmindful of the pouring rain.

At the head of the procession was the drummer, pounding on his drum. A dozen women soldiers of Kadarimandalam walked behind him with their naked swords held high. In the initial days after Mahishmathi's fall, many had thronged to watch this spectacle. Who doesn't like a great show? But the novelty had worn off in a few days, and the procession became routine, like the temple elephant's circumambulation of the city with Amma Gauri's idol on its back. People glanced at it and then went on with their lives. The last time so many people had assembled was to watch Somadeva's humiliation four years ago, and that was the morning after Queen

Hemavati's suicide. People had come to see whether the high and mighty cried when their loved ones died. They went home disappointed, but also a bit in awe, as Somadeva had been stoic, with only his customary contemptuous expression on his face. Sivagami's hatred for him multiplied after that. What kind of a monster was the erstwhile king that he didn't even cry on the day of his wife's funeral?

Now, as she watched her foe, the man who had killed her parents, reduced to such a pitiful state, Sivagami felt a strange satisfaction. Not that her position was too different, yet it made her feel happy. He looked up then, and raised his handcuffed hands. Somadeva knew she would be watching, and did not forget to mock her.

It was then that her eyes fell on the figure staggering some steps behind him. Guards pushed and shoved him, and the people lined up on the streets let out a cry. Sivagami felt her body going numb and her vision blurred. His scraggy, greying beard hung till his navel, and the sackcloth he wore was frayed in many places. When someone from the crowd lamented, 'Our vikramadeva, what a fate!', his eyelids, sewn together by his brother, twitched. Sivagami ran to the balcony and, as if sensing her presence, Mahadeva turned towards her. She stood like stone, letting the tears burn her cheeks. Guilt twisted her heart as the soldiers drove him—the one she still loved but had forsaken—like a beast of burden through the streets.

Sivagami ran out of her chamber, down the stairway and through the long corridor. She had to fall at his feet and ask for forgiveness. Like a woman possessed, she ran out on to the royal highway. The procession had vanished though, and entered the city. It would wind through the lanes and alleys of Mahishmathi, through the slums where the poor and the wretched lived, and would double back down the untouchables' lane to reach the main fort gate by mid-noon.

No one stopped her or gave her a second glance. The soldiers at the gate did not even raise their heads from their chaturanga game when she stormed past them. That was what five years of being Bijjala's unwanted wife had given her. She was nothing, despite all the sacrifices she had made. Mekhala ruled as queen. But the real power was with her father, Pattaraya, who was now the viceroy, with the title of mahamandaleswara of Kadarimandalam. He ruled on behalf of Chitraveni, the queen empress of Kadarimandalam. Mahishmathi was a colony of the port kingdom. After all her efforts, her foes had won. Sometimes Sivagami wished they would give her a painful death and make a spectacle of it. It was preferable to sinking into anonymity and impotence.

As Sivagami neared the port, she saw a fleet of ships anchored at the dock. She paused to watch, frowning at this unusual sight. The flag that lay limp like a rag from the lead ship's flag mast was familiar. Her eyes fell on the old man almost at the same time as he saw her. He hurried down the rope ladder with an agility that belied his age and bowed deep before her.

'Akkundaraya,' Sivagami said with a smile, grateful for his show of reverence, for a moment forgetting that he had once betrayed her. He stood beaming at her, running his fingers through the sparse hair pasted on his balding head.

'What are you doing here?' she asked.

'We will be ready in a week, devi,' he said.

'Ready for what?' Sivagami asked.

'For Gauriparvat,' the old man said, and turned to yell at a slave who was walking past them. 'Hurry,' he said, shoving the slave towards the ship. 'Lazy fool.'

Akkundaraya turned back to Sivagami, and his expression changed, seeing surprise in her eyes.

'You didn't know?' he asked in an embarrassed voice. But Sivagami was no longer listening. Her gaze was fixed on a slave carrying a bundle of long bamboo poles that had razor-sharp iron tips.

As he came up to where they were standing, she whispered, 'Kattappa.' The slave stopped. A whip fell on his back at the next moment, and Sivagami shuddered.

'What are you doing here?' Bijjala grunted and walked towards her. Kattappa hurried to the ship.

Sivagami threw back her head, defiant and angry. 'What is all this?'

'This is a ship. That is another ship. And this is your husband,' Keki said, appearing from nowhere and taking her position by the side of her master.

'You can't go to Gauriparvat,' Sivagami said, ignoring the eunuch.

'Oh, do I need your permission to go anywhere?' Bijjala asked.

'It is by order of Maharani Mekhala,' Keki said.

'Gauriparvat has been handed over to the Vaithalikas. It is their holy mountain. We cannot defile it,' Sivagami said curtly.

'Who handed it over?' Bijjala sneered.

'Prince Mahadeva.'

'Oh, the blind one,' Keki said and cackled.

Bijjala stepped towards Sivagami. 'It is not your lover who

sits on the throne. It is my wife, and she wants to reclaim Gauriparvat.'

'We have run out of the stones you brought, you see,' Keki added helpfully.

'I tried to warn them,' Akkundaraya said, and Bijjala exploded with rage.

He grabbed the old man by the scruff of his neck and said, 'You think only Mahadeva can conquer it? You think I am not man enough for it?'

'Let him go,' Sivagami yelled.

Bijjala turned towards her and said, 'Leave—go back to your chamber.'

Sivagami knew any resistance would result in further embarrassment. Already the slaves and workers on the ship had stopped their work to gape at them. Sivagami tried to stay calm despite the seething anger that rose within her. She had to do something to stop this madness. The only consolation she'd had in the past five years of misery was that she had fulfilled her father's wish of stopping the mining in Gauriparvat. Now that, too, was in danger.

Slaves went past her carrying cartons of provisions for the soldiers. Marthanda, the new general and dandanayaka of Mahishmathi, was leading a group of soldiers pushing war engines. She looked at the humungous machines towering over her, stretching forty feet towards the sky. The taut strings had massive arrows notched to them.

Trying hard to suppress her impulse to tear Bijjala from limb to limb, Sivagami rushed back to the palace. Her apology to Mahadeva could wait—she had barely a week to do something about Bijjala's plan for Gauriparvat.

Sivagami spent some time in the temple, praying for courage, praying for a way out. Her mind remained blank, though; no plan manifested. Amma Gauri had forsaken her long ago, Sivagami thought bitterly, as she walked back to her chamber. It was late afternoon, and the relentless downpour had weakened to a drizzle. The sky sagged with dark clouds, and the river was a raging rusty red, swollen with the sediments it was carrying to the sea. Crows sat drenched and miserable in trees, and a lone mynah hopped away from her path.

Sivagami paused at the door of her chamber as she heard Somadeva yelling. She closed her eyes tightly and took deep breaths to calm her frayed nerves. Of all the punishments that Bijjala had meted out to her, this one was the most bitter. She was to take care of the erstwhile maharaja of Mahishmathi, the same man she had once vowed to kill. The irony tickled Bijjala's perverted sense of humour, and Sivagami knew he hoped she would snap and harm the deposed king. She was determined not to give Bijjala or his first wife the pleasure, but the cantankerous nature of the bitter ex-king was driving her insane. Why did they not parade him for the whole day?

Sivagami entered the room, determined not to look at him. Gundu Ramu was dressing Somadeva's wounds.

'Ah, welcome, my daughter-in-law,' Somadeva said, and then cried out, 'Aah! Fool—look where your hands are.'

'Don't abuse him.' Sivagami glowered at Somadeva. 'He is serving you because it is his nature to help. You are no longer the king.'

Gundu Ramu stood up. He was clearly on the verge of tears and Sivagami wrapped her arms around him and held him close.

'I'm sorry, Your Highness,' Gundu Ramu whispered.

'He is no more a highness than you, Ramu,' Sivagami said, and Somadeva burst into laughter.

'The delusion of an old man!' Sivagami snapped.

'Just opportunists, Sivagami. You and I are nothing more than that. We are just waiting for the right time to seize power. I, at least, have the honour of being tortured by my foes. Look at you, you are just the unwanted second wife of a fool.'

'I destroyed your kingdom,' Sivagami said angrily. 'My father wanted to stop the mining in Gauriparvat, and I achieved that. I fulfilled my father's wishes, and I have destroyed you too. Look at yourself now, no better than a slave or the temple bull, being paraded every day through the streets of Mahishmathi. And you have the nerve to mock me?'

'Stopped the mining in Gauriparvat? Ah, I hope I don't die of laughter. It seems you have no idea of—'

'I know what they are planning, and I won't allow it.'

'You won't allow what? Who are you to allow or disallow anything?' Somadeva's booming laughter filled the room. As much as she despised him, Sivagami knew he was right. She held no power. She wasn't even a bhoomipathi now. She sank down on a chair and turned her face away from Somadeva. She hated the thought that he would see her cry.

Gundu Ramu stood before her, struggling to say some words of comfort. A gentle breeze played with the curtains. Sunlight streamed into the room through the window in the roof, and it illuminated a square patch near Sivagami's feet. She stared at the dust particles swirling in the beam of light. Her mind was blank. She was being forced to do something else with her life, and the sacrifices she had made were being rendered meaningless.

'Chaos.'

Sivagami frowned up at Somadeva. He had a mischievous smile on his parched lips. Was he going senile? Sivagami stood up and turned on her heel.

'There is a strategy in chaturanga. Frowned on by masters, and admired by the best players. The method is simple, though crude. When you find everything stacked against you, when your opponent has cornered you, do the unpredictable and create chaos.

Sivagami shook her head and walked away. 'My sons are the key,' Somadeva called out behind her. Sivagami wanted to get as far away as possible from this despicable man. She walked towards Uthanga, lying in the far corner of the room in a comatose state. He occupied a small corner in the cavernous room she shared with Gundu Ramu and the chained Somadeva. Sivagami started wiping Uthanga with a wet cotton cloth.

'I will do it, Akka,' Gundu Ramu said.

'No,' she said abruptly.

Uthanga represented everything that was wrong with her life. The boy had fallen into a coma a long time back, when she was still a resident of Revamma's orphanage. It was an accident, but she carried the guilt of making the boy an invalid since then. It wasn't as if that was the only crime she had committed. She had killed Uncle Thimma, caused many deaths, seen her beloved Neelappa being assassinated, betrayed Mahadeva, and yet the accident she had caused Uthanga long ago weighed more heavily than any other. Compared to what Uthanga suffered, her trials and tribulations appeared trivial. Except for the brief period when she had gone to

Gauriparvat, she had never left Uthanga's side. And when she came back, she was shocked to find that he had developed severe bedsores. Even when tragedies struck her life, she held on to Uthanga, the boy she had wronged. In a life filled with intrigue and ruthless political machinations, serving Uthanga made her feel human.

Uthanga looked several years younger than his twenty years. Emaciated and frail, he had a bewildered expression fixed on his face. His unseeing eyes and parched lips lay half open. Sivagami tried to lift him and turn him on his side. Gundu Ramu rushed to help her.

'Don't you have anything better to do?' Somadeva yelled from the far corner and rattled his chains. Sivagami ignored him. She knew the erstwhile monarch thought it humiliating to share a room with Uthanga.

'I have something important to say. Come here,' Somadeva commanded, but Sivagami ignored him.

'That boy is going to be your downfall,' Somadeva cursed.

'What do you want?' Sivagami snapped.

'I will tell you what to do. If it works, you will win a kingdom. If it doesn't, we will die like your father. The plan involves Raghava, now known as Guru Dharmapala. Some guru, he is.' Somadeva chuckled.

Flushing red with anger, Sivagami stormed out. Raghava was now occupying the position that Skandadasa and Parameswara had held. 'Traitor,' Sivagami hissed under her breath. Of all the betrayals, that one hurt the most. Raghava, the one she had adored as her brother, the one who had proposed to her, the one who had promised to help her avenge her father's death, who had gone away and come back as a charlatan and destroyed everything she had achieved.

Sivagami was angry and frustrated. She closed her eyes, trying to hold back her tears. The sight of Mahadeva had shaken her. The news of the Gauriparvat expedition was the last straw. Blood pounding in her head, she stepped out into the rain and looked skyward, droplets washing over her face.

'Akka.'

Sivagami turned, wiping her tears with the back of her hand. Ramu averted his eyes and said, 'His Highness is the only one who can help you.'

That was how Sivagami found herself sitting by the foot of Somadeva's cot, listening to the king's diabolical plan. In the game of chaturanga that Somadeva was playing, she was not sure whether she was a pawn or the dice. But she plunged into it, and that would change history forever.

THIRTY-NINE

# Ally

'I DON'T THINK you should do that, Anna.' Ally's lips quivered. She didn't like what Brihannala had suggested, but in her heart, she knew they didn't have a choice. They had managed to sneak into the city of Kadarimandalam, disguised as a eunuch and a performing girl, and were now standing by the port, which was busy with slaves loading and unloading goods from ships. As far as the eye could see, the Kadarimandalam harbour was filled with ships with multi-coloured sails. Trade was at its peak, and prosperity was in the air.

Ally and Brihannala had managed to collect information that Jeemotha was in one of the ships that piloted the trade vessels from the high seas to Kadarimandalam port. Kadarimandalam had a navy, mostly consisting of men who patrolled the seas. They would accompany the trade ships into the seas for seven days of voyage and then return with vessels coming into the harbour.

The string of Kadarimandalam's navy battleships was intimidating, and there was no way of knowing which one had Jeemotha as a galley slave. Ally counted not less than twenty ships in the inner dock and another seven boats getting ready to pilot the huge trade ships to the open sea.

'There's no other way, Ally. I'll create a diversion. I don't know how long I can hold out, and I may get killed ...' Brihannala smiled ruefully and continued, 'But don't worry. I will give you enough time and I assure you they won't capture me quickly.'

Ally said, 'This is madness—I don't trust that pirate. What is the guarantee that he will help us even if I manage to find him?'

'Do you have a better plan?' Brihannala asked.

Ally didn't have an answer. She took a deep breath, hugged her brother tight, and then vanished into the crowd. The moment she left him, she heard him yell abuses at the queen of Kadarimandalam. She looked back, and as they had planned, a mob was gathering around Brihannala, who was waving his sword in the air and challenging Queen Chitraveni. People laughed at the man dressed in a sari, with bangles on his wrists. He caused merriment rather than fear.

Ally could hear catcalls and whistles as Brihannala continued with his act. A few women soldiers passed Ally, casually chatting with each other. They were experienced in handling such madmen and drunks. A port city had its share of drunken sailors and visitors who often went berserk after having a drink or two too many. Ally paused at the edge of the dock. Everyone's attention was on Brihannala's antics. Then she heard a loud scream and people began running helter-skelter. Straining to catch sight of Brihannala, she saw that his sword was now crimson. He had stabbed someone. There was no going back. From amusement, the matter had turned to one of murder. Ally saw more soldiers running towards her brother. Fighting back her tears, she dived into the water.

At the dock, Brihannala found himself surrounded by soldiers of the Kadarimandalam army. He brought down the sword of the soldier on his left. He grabbed the shield of another who had attacked him and slammed it down, breaking the head of the soldier who had tried to plunge her sword in his back. Covered in sweat, he turned on his heel and struck a blow that sent the spear of yet another soldier flying from her hand. More soldiers were rushing at him and he braced for another attack. Around him, eight soldiers were squirming in pain. A crowd of drunken sailors had assembled, watching him fight, cheering him on.

'Break their heads!'

'Break the arrogance of the women!'

It was rare for a man to fight the dreaded soldiers of Chitraveni. Brihannala knew he was taking a desperate risk. He wasn't sure how long he could last alone. His only hope was to kill or at least injure enough soldiers for the queen to take some interest in seeing him before hanging him. If she met him, he knew, she would decide to use him as a pawn in case of an attack by Achi.

Meanwhile, Ally swam underwater, passing several trade ships before she finally came up for air. She saw Brihannala was bringing down anyone daring to approach him. She could see that even the crew in the security ships were crowded about their decks, watching the drama unfolding on the dock.

She started climbing up one of the ships. It was slippery and the afternoon sun burned her back. Finding small wedges and cracks in the ship's smooth hull, she finally managed to hurl herself onto the upper deck.

Back on the dock, Brihannala could hear the sound of horse hoofs. The mounted archers were arriving and he knew it would soon be time to stop the fight. He slammed into a soldier who tried to wrap her urumi around his neck and flung another into the cheering crowd. The sound of her splashing into the water and the enthusiastic cheers of the crowd brought a smile to Brihannala's lips.

Ally could hear the crew cheering, and knew her brother was holding on. She untied the rope of the sail and swung from one deck to the next. She ran down to the lower deck calling out Jeemotha's name. She could hear someone shouting a warning; maybe they had spotted her. She reached the slaves' deck and cried out for Jeemotha, but was met with silence. She could hear footsteps running down the spiral staircase. She slipped out through a porthole and plunged into the water. She ducked under the ship and stayed there until she could no longer hold her breath. She emerged from the water, gasping. She could still hear the cheering and shouting going on, not too far.

On the dock, the cheering soon turned into frightened cries as the mounted archers shot without warning into the crowd. The mob ran; some fell into the water and many were killed in the confusion. The captain of the mounted archers, a lean, middle-aged woman, came up to Brihannala on a majestic Arabian horse. She pressed her sword at the hollow of his neck. Brihannala dropped his weapons.

Ally swam towards the next ship, this time not climbing up till the deck but sneaking in through a porthole where she had estimated the galley slaves would be kept. When she called out, she sounded desperate to her own ears. Yet again, there was no answer. She gave up and sat on the floor filled with slime and the excrement of the galley slaves. She sobbed as she could hear the cheering above was slowly dying down.

Suddenly, Ally heard laughter and looked up, startled. That creepy laugh couldn't belong to anyone else. She ran across the length of the deck, calling out his name. No one responded. In frustration, Ally yelled, 'Jeemotha, I can free you. Please tell me where you are!' She heard a low whistle and ran in its direction. Ally tripped on something and fell flat on her face. She sat up, and in the dim light filtering through the cracks in the board, she saw him, sitting amidst the other galley slaves. She didn't know whether it was relief or revulsion that she felt.

'How can I help you, devi?' Jeemotha asked with a smirk. He knew he was in no position to help anyone—he was shackled like an animal and had spent the last five years rowing a ship up and down.

Ally went up to him. 'We will help you have your revenge against Chitraveni,' she whispered.

Jeemotha laughed. 'Who told you I want revenge? I am perfectly happy here,' he said, shaking his handcuffs in her face. She stared back at him and he turned away. Ally saw Jeemotha's back had welts running criss-cross, the marks of lashes that had fallen on him.

'Rot here then, you fool. I came with an offer to help you. I sacrificed my brother for it. And you are playing games,' Ally said.

Jeemotha turned to her. 'I have stopped trusting women. I will have my revenge, but I won't owe it to someone like you,' he hissed.

Ally felt like telling him that he had only got what he deserved, but she swallowed her words.

With desperation in her voice, she said, 'I beg you—we need your help.' She could see Jeemotha was curious now, and she pressed on. 'We are planning an attack on Mahishmathi.'

Jeemotha burst out laughing. 'We? You and your eunuch brother, or is your slave lover also a part of this master plan?'

'They are about to resume the mining of Gauriparvat, and we are determined to stop it,' Ally said. 'We have the support of the Kalakeyas and the Vaithalikas.'

Jeemotha smirked. 'I can give you the names of a few more barbarian tribes. Together, you would all form a great army. If you get the help of another two or three tribes, you might last for half an hour against Mahishmathi. Otherwise, everything will be over in a blink.'

Ally felt anger rising up in her veins, more so because what he said was the bitter truth. But he didn't know something very important. If he was going to help her, he needed to be sure that they had a chance at success. Ally looked around and whispered, 'Achi Nagamma is alive and she has tamed the Garuda pakshis. The attack would be with the help of the Garuda pakshis.'

Jeemotha was silent for a moment. Then he started drawing something with his index finger on the slime on the floor. She strained her eyes and saw that it was the diagram of a ship.

'The ships of Kadarimandalam have a peculiarity,' Jeemotha said. 'They don't use nails.'

'Why?'

'Because nails have a habit of rusting, so they tie their planks with coir ropes and apply the sticky glue from jackfruit and some chemicals to make it waterproof. This is a design unique to Kadarimandalam. Made with teakwood and tied together with treated ropes, their ships last for centuries. It is a very unique innovation, and that is their strength—and their weakness.' Jeemotha stared at Ally, as if he had explained everything worth knowing.

Exasperated, Ally said, 'I was talking about an invasion and you are showing off your knowledge!'

Jeemotha smiled. 'Women! None of you have any patience.'

Ally could hear horns blaring from the deck. The galley slaves who were dozing on their oars suddenly became alert. They raised their oars in unison. They started singing as their oars went down, and the ship moved with a jerk. Ally panicked and gripped Jeemotha's hand. He was drawing something rapidly on the floor.

He circled a portion near the prow of the ship in the diagram he had made and said in a low voice, 'Cut it.'

Ally heard the sound of boots and she knew that the slave master had entered the deck. She heard a crack and the groan of the slave on whose back the whip had fallen. 'Faster,' the slave master commanded. She had to leave quickly.

Ally was grateful to Jeemotha. Seeing his plight, she felt a wave of pity washing over her. 'Can I cut off those chains? We can escape together.'

Jeemotha shook his head sadly. 'I have a job to do. I belong here. Do this and let us see what will happen. Do it for all the ships. But don't cut through it completely—leave a strand of rope behind. And remember, there are more than twenty-one such knots near the prow. You will have to cut through each of them. If you get caught ...' Jeemotha paused, his grin saying it all.

Ally thanked him, slipped out through a porthole and dropped into the sea. She had a job to do. Her orders from Brihannala were to immediately implement any plan she got from Jeemotha, and not stay behind after that, but rush to meet Achi Nagamma.

Ally vaguely understood what Jeemotha was planning. He was incapacitating the navy of Kadarimandalam, and that would buy them time to invade Mahishmathi, conquer it, and hold the fort. Ally would have to face Kattappa, this time as his enemy, and she didn't know how he would react. More importantly, Ally didn't know how she would react. She would never forgive him for what he had done to their baby. And yet ...

It was night by the time Ally had managed to do what Jeemotha had told her. The dockyard where her brother had fought and been captured was empty now, except for a few derelicts playing a board game under a light pole. Wiping her tears, Ally started her journey back to join Achi's army.

FORTY

# Sivagami

'FOOLS, HURRY UP,' a familiar voice yelled.

Sivagami looked down from the balcony and saw Bijjala on his horse. He cracked his whip in the air, urging the slaves to move faster. As she watched him, the contours of an audacious plan formed in her mind. She whistled softly. Bijjala was about to whip a slave when he heard it. He looked up and saw Sivagami gazing down at him. She smiled seductively. Bijjala was confused. She had fought him off every time he had tried to be intimate with her, and this flirtatiousness threw him off. Sivagami continued to smile suggestively, as she ran her fingers on the balustrade of the balcony, and then vanished into the darkness. She knew he would come for her.

---

Sivagami looked at Bijjala sleeping next to her. She felt like gagging. She would need to wash herself many times to scrub away the smell of stale wine that clung to her body. She had never felt so worthless in her life. She had resisted Bijjala since the day he had betrayed her. It was demeaning to yield to him now, though it had been her last resort.

She inched towards him and slowly, carefully picked up the keys he carried in his waistband. Bijjala stirred in his sleep. She had added sufficient intoxicants in his wine, and there was no danger of him waking up anytime soon. Yet, her heart beat like a caged pigeon against her ribs as she slowly unclasped Bijjala's waistband and took out the bunch of keys from it. Bijjala didn't trust anyone and always carried the key to the dungeon with him.

Sivagami hurriedly pressed the key into a mould of lac before slipping it back on the waistband and re-clasping it. She took a deep breath and tiptoed towards the door.

'Gomati,' Sivagami whispered, and heard the woman answer. She opened the door and gave the mould to her. Parameswara's daughter, whom she had rescued from a bad marriage to Rudra Bhatta's son, was her friend and companion now. Gomati took the mould, nodded at her, and walked away. Sivagami took a deep breath. She had moved the first piece on the board.

---

A week later, Sivagami was at the docks. The day of the expedition had arrived. Though it was still raining and the river had swelled even more than before, the loading of the ships had gone on efficiently. The slaves marched in a line towards the ships, and as Kattappa went past her, Sivagami whispered, 'Maharaja Somadeva wants you here.' If the slave had heard it, he didn't give any indication of it.

Horns blared and the fort door creaked open. From the main entrance, Prince Bijjala led his regiment. The armour and spears of the cavalry that followed him glinted in the rays of the setting sun. Sivagami moved behind a pillar, trying to make herself as inconspicuous as possible. Riding a majestic black stallion, Prince Bijjala galloped towards the dock platform and his cavalry thundered behind.

'Jai Kadarimandalam,' Bijjala cried, and the soldiers repeated it in unison.

A moment later, another cry rose from the slave deck—'Jai Mahishmathi!' The response was electrifying. It was as if the entire city was answering the call. Sivagami saw Kattappa standing at the prow of the ship, raising a massive iron-tipped spear to the sky as he cried again, 'Jai Mahishmathi!'

Once again, sailors and soldiers cried 'Jai Mahishmathi' in reply. Sivagami's eyes filled with tears. The slave was once again risking his life for her, for the king, for Mahishmathi.

Sivagami could see the golden chariot of Queen Mekhala approaching the dock. Kattappa yelled the slogan again at the top of his voice and the soldiers responded. Bijjala came in full gallop to the dock and pulled his horse's reins a finger's breadth before the edge. He turned it around and yelled, 'Silence!' and the voices died down.

Mekhala's chariot rumbled towards the dock. The queen, decked in diamonds and gold ornaments that could shame a caparisoned elephant in any temple festival, alighted from her glittering chariot. A moment later, Pattaraya, the mahamandaleswara of Mahishmathi, followed. He took his daughter's hand and walked towards the dock.

As the queen and her father walked, the people and the soldiers fell to their knees and touched their heads to the soil. In the initial days, those proud Mahishmathi citizens who were reluctant to demean themselves in this fashion had paid with their lives. Now there was no need for coercion; grovelling before their ruler had become a matter of habit. Sivagami continued to stand hidden, unwilling to bow before this evil woman. She snickered when Bijjala dismounted from his horse and fell on his knees and kissed Mekhala's feet. Sivagami wished there was some way to capture this ridiculous scene for posterity. She should employ a painter who could draw this scene and place it in her chamber.

Bijjala stood up and cried, 'Jai Maharani Mekhala!' After a moment's pause, there were scattered repetitions of this slogan. Sivagami saw that not even a single slave answered the call. They have more spine than all these privileged scoundrels, she thought. Bijjala drew his sword from its sheath, raised it to the sky and repeated his war cry again, 'Jai Kadarimandalam!'

This time, the response was better, but Sivagami heard a lone cry of 'Jai Mahishmathi'. It didn't miss the attention of Mekhala either. The flapping sound of sails fluttering in the wind accentuated the tense silence. Again came a heartfelt cry of 'Jai Mahishmathi' from the deck of the ship. The people of Mahishmathi replied in unison to the call of Kattappa. Pattaraya arched an eyebrow, and like a dog taking a cue from its master, Bijjala snarled. He ran up the ramp, climbed up the rope ladder, and reached Kattappa in a trice. The slave looked Bijjala in the eye and yelled at the top of his voice, 'Jai Mahishmathi!'

Encouraged by the open defiance on display, Mahishmathi soldiers and slaves erupted with the patriotic slogan. Bijjala swung his sword to decapitate Kattappa. Sivagami saw Kattappa arching backward. The long bamboo spear in his hand flew free from his grasp and fell into the water, and a moment later, the slave followed. Sivagami saw the water turning red, and a gasp escaped her throat. A few people ran to the edge, but soldiers pushed them back. The brief revolt had ended and it was not worth wasting time on a slave.

Horns blared and drums rolled. Sails rose and anchors were lifted. The lead ship with Bijjala at the prow started moving. The boat song of the slaves rose in the air, as well as the rhythmic sound of paddles falling on water. Nobody had even bothered to check about the slave who had fallen overboard. Sivagami watched the ships passing over the spot where Kattappa had fallen. Twenty-two ships passed by and the crowd dispersed. The chariot carrying the queen and her father went back into the palace and darkness descended.

Sivagami stood at the edge of the dock, peering at the spot where Kattappa had vanished. Behind her, the servants were lighting up the Mahishmathi palace. Rain fell relentlessly, as if the end of the world was imminent.

Sivagami was getting worried when she heard the familiar voice. 'Devi …' Sivagami turned and saw Kattappa. Forgetting herself, she ran up to him and hugged him, sobbing on his shoulder.

'My brother,' she said.

Kattappa's body stiffened and he stepped back. He bowed low and said, 'I am your slave.'

Sivagami smiled through her tears and patted Kattappa's shoulder. 'We are going to save Prince Mahadeva,' she said, taking out a brand new key from the folds of her dress. She waited for some reaction from Kattappa, but there was none.

'Wait for the message,' Sivagami said to Kattappa. He nodded, stepped into the shadows, and vanished.

When she started walking towards the palace, she saw Gundu Ramu hurrying towards her.

'Akka, Mahapradhana Dharmapala is waiting for you in the king's chamber.'

'How did he manage to convince Raghava to come?' Sivagami was amazed.

'I went to the guru's discourse as His Highness instructed. I stood up and asked—if parrots sing about freedom, would they be killed? Guru Dharmapala ignored my question, but after the discourse, I was called in. I told him Maharaja Somadeva wants to consult him, and he came,' Gundu Ramu said in an amazed tone.

The last person Sivagami wanted to associate was with Raghava, but he was key to Somadeva's plan. Freeing Kattappa was step two and now they were about to move the next piece in the game.

---

When Sivagami entered her chamber, she saw Raghava talking to Somadeva. Sivagami had not met him after the fateful coup. She averted her eyes and walked towards Uthanga. Was there something different about the boy today? It had seemed as if his eyebrows had twitched. Or was it that his fingers had trembled? With a feeling of unease, she moved near Uthanga and observed him. The boy lay motionless. Maybe the flickering light of the oil lamp was playing tricks on her eyes. Gundu Ramu entered the room with a tray filled with fruits and a jug of warm milk.

'Akka.' It was Akhila. She had been standing in the shadows, and Sivagami hadn't seen her.

A wave of memories overwhelmed Sivagami and she turned away to face the wall. Without a word, Akhila embraced her from behind.

'Are you angry with me, Akka?' Akhila asked, leaning her head against Sivagami's back.

'You are the one who should be angry with me, Akhila,' Sivagami said.

'I was, Akka. I saw you killing …'

Sivagami stiffened. She didn't want to remember the duel with Thimma. Everything had been in vain.

'I was a little girl then, Akka. Now I know why you did it.'

'There is no excuse, Akhila. I—'

'Not a word more, Akka. I know how much you have suffered.'

Sivagami turned and saw tears glistening in her sister's eyes. She hugged her tight. They stood in an embrace, in silence, forgiving each other.

'Sivagami,' Somadeva called in an impatient voice. Sivagami's feet felt heavy as she approached the old king who was sitting with Raghava.

'Guru Dharmapala will help us,' Somadeva said. Raghava sat with his gaze fixed on his toes, his fingers intertwined tightly. Beads of perspiration on his forehead glistened in the light.

Somadeva said, 'I have given Guru Dharmapala—'

'Raghava,' Sivagami said. 'He is no guru for me.'

'Sivagami …' Raghava's voice faltered, and Sivagami winced. She stood staring at the lamp in the corner. In the light breeze, the flames danced, throwing bizarre shadows on the wall.

Somadeva continued. 'Your beloved brother will start the coup that will overthrow Pattaraya.'

'I can't trust him.'

'You can't trust me either,' Somadeva said and laughed. 'But Guru Dharmapala can be trusted. He has no choice other than to be trustworthy. Isn't it, son?'

Raghava continued to stare at the floor.

'So, he will use his disciples—yes, the same ones who once took the crown away from me—and arrest Marthanda. That swine, who replaced my beloved Hiranya and duelled with and killed Pratapa, will change sides in an instant. He is a mercenary and is only interested in being on the winning side. Meanwhile, you have to save my son, Mahadeva. He will be the face of the rebellion. The people of Mahishmathi will fight for freedom under my son.'

Akhila burst out sobbing. Sivagami turned towards her in surprise.

Somadeva paid her no attention. He said, 'And I will keep my word, Guru Dharmapala. My son Mahadeva will wed your sister. My Thimma's daughter will be the queen of Vikramadeva Mahadeva.'

Sivagami saw Akhila blush and smile through her tears. A jab of pain gripped her chest and a pang of jealousy shot through her veins. Raghava sat like a statue.

'But what about Kadarimandalam? They are not going to sit idle while we dethrone Pattaraya and his daughter. Besides, Bijjala might return to fight,' Sivagami said.

Somadeva laughed. 'Trust me. I know what I am doing.'

Raghava bowed stiffly and left. Akhila took Sivagami's hands in hers and said, 'Bless me, Akka.'

Sivagami closed her eyes and placed her hands on Akhila's head. This was her moment of redemption. *I am giving my Mahadeva to you, sister. I hope you keep him happy, always*, she said silently. When Akhila left, Sivagami felt something had died inside her. Instead of feeling happiness for her sister, why was she feeling envy? *What have I become*, she lamented.

Somadeva said softly, 'It seems you are not pleased.'

'How did you trap him?' Sivagami asked.

'Remember the parakeet that came to our window a few months ago? The one that sang strange songs of freedom before flying away? My son was singing the same song today while they were parading us. I have seen parrots being freed from the ashram many times, and then it was just an elementary deduction. I was not the king of Mahishmathi for nothing, Sivagami. I wasn't sure how much Raghava valued Akhila. If he was willing to sacrifice her, my plan would have failed. But Thimma's son is not evil enough—and that will be his downfall.'

'What do you mean?' Sivagami asked. Then she noticed that Somadeva was looking past her at Uthanga. When Sivagami tried to follow his gaze, Somadeva grabbed Sivagami's hand and pulled her towards him. He seemed to be trying to say something, and Sivagami put her ear to his lips.

'Chaos. I am creating chaos. It is up to you to sink or swim,' he said, and he winked, sending a chill down her spine.

FORTY-ONE

# Bijjala

'YOU CAN'T AFFORD for this not to succeed, my prince,' Keki said to a worried Bijjala. 'Else, what we have been planning for so long will come to naught. You will never become king, but will remain subservient to Pattaraya and his daughter.'

Bijjala grunted, looking past the eunuch. Keki pressed on. 'Get as many Gaurikanta stones as you can, but don't send them to Kadarimandalam. We will hold them for ransom. Declare independence from Kadarimandalam and—'

'We have discussed this a hundred times,' Bijjala snapped. 'But why should I beg that old fool, Akkundaraya. I have enough men to take over Gauriparvat.'

'We don't know what the perils are, my prince. The more hands we have, the better. We can carry back as many stones as possible. The more we have, the greater will be our bargaining power. Don't let Akkundaraya get away with his impudence. Tell the old fool no one is going to steal his ships.'

Bijjala nodded and walked towards Akkundaraya. The old bhoomipathi was standing at the stern of the ship, supervising the unfurling of sails and dropping of anchor. When he heard Bijjala's demand, Akkundaraya smiled.

'I will remain here with my men, Prince Bijjala. I did that the last time as well; I didn't go any farther with Rani Sivagami devi,' Akkundararya said, leaning against the railing of the ship deck.

Bijjala laughed aloud. 'Are you scared? Do you believe those ridiculous stories about some giant birds? My nincompoop brother has too much imagination and not enough courage. Wild giant birds indeed. Garuda pakshi! I have seen many Garuda pakshis, and they are not any bigger than ordinary vultures. A properly aimed arrow is all you need to tackle them.'

The old bhoomipathi inclined his head and said, 'I shall wait here for you to return victorious, Prince Bijjala.'

'Come on, do you believe in those old wives' tales? Bards will say anything if you pay them enough money. Keki knows all about it, isn't it, Keki? How many stories have you made the bards sing about me?'

Keki cried from the other end of the ship, 'Yes, my prince. If there is anyone more unscrupulous than rulers, it is writers. Pay them enough, and they will bark for you. Pay them less, and they will bark at you. Either way, they are dogs. If you know how to make the dogs obey, you can be whatever you want.'

Bijjala laughed. 'That is a political lesson for you, Akkundaraya, in case you want to play the game at some point in your life.'

Akkundaraya said, 'I am nearing seventy. I have no ambition but to keep the position that I have reached so far. And I have managed that by being careful. Again, I wish you luck. May you have more success than Mahadeva.'

Bijjala was livid. He was losing authority in the eyes of Akkundaraya's men, and nothing frightened the prince more than that.

'Arrest this old fool, and if any of his men object, make them crocodile feed.'

'It is you who are being foolish, Prince,' Akkundaraya said. 'These are the finest sailors in Mahishmathi. Without them, you won't be able to get back, even if you manage to bring the Gaurikanta stones down.'

In a fit of rage, Bijjala slammed his fist on a sail pole, splitting it into two. Akkundaraya looked at Bijjala, horrified by his mindless anger. Soldiers had surrounded the bhoomipathi, but were unsure of what to do next. Bijjala picked out the splinters from his skin and wiped the blood on his waistband, all the while glowering at his soldiers.

Keki swished a whip in the air and yelled, 'What are you gaping at, you morons? Didn't you hear the prince? Arrest the old man.'

The soldiers grabbed hold of Akkundaraya; he was handcuffed and tied in chains. Keki grabbed the free end of the chain and yanked him down the plank to the shore. From the lower decks and the other ships, Akkundaraya's men saw their leader shackled and began to rush to his rescue. Akkundaraya raised his handcuffed fists in the air and screamed, 'Surrender. There is no point in losing your life fighting a fool. He will lead all of us into the mouth of death.' The men stopped and reluctantly threw their arms down.

Bijjala said, 'Make them march among the slaves. That is the punishment for not obeying the king of Mahishmathi.'

'King?' Akkundaraya scoffed. 'More like the dog of the queen, the bootlicker of a foreigner.'

Akkundaraya's men cried in unison, 'The dog of the whore!'

Bijjala charged at Akkundaraya and slapped him across his face. The older man reeled back with the impact, but as soon as he regained balance, he stood up and faced Bijjala, unflinching and erect.

'Put this fool in the front. Let him lead the slaves,' Bijjala said with a smug smile. Akkundaraya spat on Bijjala's face, spattering blood on him.

'I could kill you now, you old fool, but I won't. Do you know why? Because I plan to make you regret that you were ever born. I am not my father to allow impudent men—vermin who think they can defy the king—to go unpunished,' Bijjala hissed.

Akkundaraya sniggered. 'Every dog in Mahishmathi knows that. You are not your father. You are scum, a worm, a despicable scoundrel—'

Bijjala grabbed the whip from Keki's hand and swung it at Akkundaraya. He pushed and shoved the old bhoomipathi and screamed, 'Walk!'

The grim procession towards Gauriparvat started, with old Akkundaraya in the front and his three hundred sailors walking in a file behind him, their shackled legs making a rhythmic sound as they marched through uneven terrain. Behind them walked the train of slaves brought from Mahishmathi, and the rear was formed by the ten thousand soldiers that Bijjala had brought with him. Despite his bravado while dismissing the story of the Garuda pakshis, Bijjala had taken sufficient precautions. War engines rattled at the rear, long spears notched in them, ready to shoot at anything that approached from the sky.

Bijjala was sure that, with more than ten thousand men, he would be able to take back enough Gaurikanta stones to last the next three or four generations. And once he had the Gaurikanta stones, he would declare independence from Kadarimandalam. He would kick Mekhala and her despicable father Pattaraya from the throne, and would sit on it.

Finally, Mahishmathi would get the king it deserved. People of Mahishmathi would marvel at his cunning for years to come. Centuries after he had gone, they would speak of the clever Bijjala, who had moved his pieces discreetly on his board of chaturanga, and emerged the surprising winner. He would bring in the next golden age of Mahishmathi. With the kind of treasure he was about to capture, he could buy all the mercenaries in the world. Men like Marthanda would serve him loyally. He could have the greatest army that history had ever seen. Who knows, perhaps he would sail to the distant barbarian lands and conquer them too.

People would finally see Bijjala for who he truly was—a decisive king, a great leader and a brilliant man who knew when to fight and when to play the submissive husband. Once he had the crown of Mahishmathi firmly on his head, he would get his revenge on Mekhala and Pattaraya by including them in the daily parade that his father was taken on. He would have loved to get rid of Mahadeva altogether, but Keki had advised him against it. Even now, the people of

Mahishmathi loved Mahadeva. They had not risen in rebellion for fear of Mahadeva's life. An incapacitated Mahadeva, a blind Mahadeva in the dungeons, was safer for Bijjala than a dead one.

But that would be his next course of action. Once he assumed kingship and had freed Mahishmathi, he hoped he would replace Mahadeva in the hearts of people. And if he was successful, then he would arrange a show. The Chitravadha of Mahadeva. Long ago, he had watched how his father had killed Devaraya. It was such a bloody spectacle; it still gave him goose bumps. And the way in which Sivagami's mother had been burnt ... Why not arrange such a spectacle again? Burn the daughter this time. He could always say that she and Mahadeva had an immoral affair. It wouldn't be a total lie; the two did love each other. That could be a good way to turn public opinion in his favour.

Keki touched Bijjala's shoulders and he came out of his daydream.

'What is the problem?' Bijjala asked, irritated. He realised the procession had stopped. 'Why aren't the men moving?'

Not getting an answer, he made his way to the front and saw Akkundaraya standing still, as if frozen. The men in the front looked terrified. Bijjala rushed to Akkundaraya, wanting to bring his whip down on the old man's back, but when he saw what Akkundaraya was looking at, he felt the blood become ice in his veins.

Their way was blocked by what looked like a hill. There was a rotten smell in the air that made Bijjala gag. Drawing his sword, he slowly walked towards the hill, the noxious smell becoming more intense as he neared it. As he got closer, he saw that the hill was made of bones. The bones of beasts, but not bison or deer, he knew. With a shock, he realised that they were the bones of elephants. What could be eating elephants and piling up their bones like this? Bijjala turned towards his soldiers and was about to command that they ignore such things and carry on, when he heard a distant screech. A long and blood-curdling cry, as if it were emerging from the folds of antiquity. The forest went deadly silent. The soldiers looked skyward and Bijjala followed their gaze. In the azure sky, something was circling above them.

'It is an eagle, you fools. Walk,' Bijjala said, and the next moment, with another terrifying screech, the bird dove down at them. It was as if a mountain was coming at them. At that moment, Bijjala understood that writers do exaggerate, but not always.

FORTY-TWO

# Sivagami

IT HAD BEEN three months since Bijjala had left, and every day Sivagami waited for the promised rebellion to begin. She couldn't understand the reason for delaying the coup they had planned with Raghava. Bijjala could return any day now. In a corner of her mind, she nurtured a hope that he would perish in Gauriparvat. There had been dark rumours of a carnage at the holy mountain.

If they had to carry out the coup, there couldn't be a better time, Sivagami thought. It had been raining relentlessly for the past six days, and she knew that many villages were cut off from each other, as the Mahishi river had swollen and spread across the valley. The untouchables' path that skirted the fort was already underwater. People from distant villages were migrating to the city, as they had lost everything in the flood. They had not seen anything like it for a century.

'You are going to catch a cold,' Somadeva said from inside. Sivagami didn't answer. She hated sitting in the same room as him. The imprisoned king's sarcasm was beginning to get on her nerves. She could smell the broth that Gundu Ramu was preparing in their kitchen, and she felt like gagging. Sivagami was pregnant and had concealed it from everyone.

'Be patient. It will happen soon,' Somadeva cried from inside.

She continued to ignore him as she stood in the balcony, desperately waiting for the signal.

If she didn't free Mahadeva soon, she might never get the chance. All her sacrifices, deception, all the things she had done against her conscience, would be a waste. *I will not live, if that happens*, she told herself. There was another danger too, which she was trying not to think about. Queen Mekhala would soon know that an heir was arriving. Pattaraya would never allow it, which meant her life was in danger.

She saw a figure approaching their wing of the palace. His face was obscured in the pounding rain, and she squinted her eyes, trying to make out who it was. 'Raghava,' she gasped. He had covered his face with his turban and was dressed in plain clothes. Her heart started beating faster; perhaps today was the day. He walked past the balcony and disappeared into the darkness. But Sivagami had got what she had been eagerly waiting for. He had paused for a moment and looked towards the main wing of the palace, where Pattaraya and Mekhala lived. That glance was the pre-arranged sign. Sivagami touched the duplicate key she had made, concealed in the folds of her saree. She dashed inside and grabbed her sword from where it hung on the wall.

Somadeva cried, 'All right. It starts now. Cut off my chains and go. Sivagami … Sivagami …'

Without bothering to reply, Sivagami ran out, ignoring Somadeva's curses. The two soldiers posted to guard the former king were sitting and chatting by the landing of the staircase and Sivagami caught them by surprise. One of them scrambled up, but Sivagami hit his head with the hilt of her sword. She kicked the other one, who toppled down the stairs and lay unconscious. Now there was no going back.

She took a deep breath, plunged into the rain and cut across the garden, careful to keep to the shadows. The wind had blown out most of the torches in the veranda, but if someone saw her walking with her sword, they would be suspicious. The five years she had spent not making even a whimper of protest had caused them to let down their guard, but she wasn't foolish enough to underestimate Pattaraya. He had outplayed an ace opponent like Somadeva. Such a man would be prepared for any eventuality.

Sivagami stood behind a tree, studying the guards at the entrance of the dungeon. The small stone mandap wasn't giving them much protection from the lashing rain. Somewhere in the distance, thunder rumbled. The roar of the distant river felt like mocking laughter to her ears. Crouching in the shadows, Sivagami slowly inched towards them.

FORTY-THREE

# Somadeva

AS SOMADEVA SHOUTED curses at Sivagami and shook his chains, Gundu Ramu came running up to him.

'Free me, you fool,' Somadeva roared, looking at where Uthanga lay. Gundu Ramu fumbled with the chains, but could not see how he could unshackle the old king.

'Are you going to bite through the chains, idiot? Never mind. There is no time. Get a palm leaf. Fast.'

Ramu ran, scared by the urgency in Somadeva's tone. He came back with one and Somadeva yelled at him for not bringing a stencil. Ramu rushed off and came back with a stencil, panting and puffing.

'Draw a rectangle, divide it in the middle. Draw two intertwined cobras. Draw lines for water, fish.' Gundu Ramu had many doubts assailing him, but, terrified of Somadeva, he tried to draw as best as he could. He showed it to Somadeva, who cursed under his breath.

'I can't draw well,' Gundu Ramu whimpered.

'This is no time for drawing lessons, you fool. Run to Skandadasa's abandoned mansion and fling this palm leaf over the wall. Come back immediately after. Do not look back, whatever happens.'

Ramu ran out, pausing a moment near Uthanga's cot. His eyes widened in fear. The cot was empty.

FORTY-FOUR

# Pattaraya

PATTARAYA WOKE UP when he heard the loud knocks. He pulled open the door, irritated, and saw two soldiers there, holding on firmly to a boy.

'Your excellency, this boy was trying to sneak in,' one of the soldiers said.

Pattaraya grabbed the boy by his hand, pulled him in and slammed the door shut.

'It has started,' Uthanga said.

Pattaraya stared at him for a moment, cursed under his breath and then ran out.

'Call to arms! Tell Marthanda to arrest Mahapradhana Guru Dharmapala!'

Uthanga could hear Pattaraya screaming instructions and the sound of soldiers running. For many years, Uthanga had been a spy for Pattaraya. He had gained consciousness a long time back, when Sivagami was fighting the Garuda pakshis in Gauriparvat. When Pattaraya took over Mahishmathi, his soldiers had caught Uthanga trying to sneak away. Pattaraya had given Uthanga a choice: either he would have a painful death or he could spy on Sivagami and earn rich rewards. Whatever qualms Uthanga felt on betraying Sivagami, who he realised had taken care of him for years, vanished with Pattaraya's question: she stole your childhood and made you an invalid; you still want to be loyal to her? The choice was an obvious one for Uthanga. From that day onwards, he had been the eyes and ears of Pattaraya, passing on cryptic messages to him in the bowls of food sent from the royal kitchens to Somadeva and Sivagami.

It was through Uthanga that Pattaraya had kept track of the impending coup. He had toyed with the idea of arresting the guilty parties immediately, but it was dangerous with Raghava being so popular. Who knew how people would react to a guru being incarcerated? They had to be caught red-handed. Pattaraya also knew Sivagami would attempt to free Mahadeva, and then the fun would begin. In conservative Mahishmathi, this was a perfect opportunity for Pattaraya to get rid of Mahadeva forever without risking a revolt.

Pattaraya returned to his chamber and began putting on his armour. He noticed Uthanga was still there.

'What?' growled Pattaraya.

'My reward,' Uthanga said, scratching the back of an ear.

Pattaraya raised his hand to slap Uthanga and the boy cowered in fear. A smile came to Pattaraya's thin lips and he caressed the boy's hollow cheeks. 'Double of what I offered if you do this too.'

When Pattaraya had finished telling him what he wanted done, the boy whimpered in fear. 'It is a sin,' he mumbled.

Pattaraya picked up a dagger from the table, put the sharp tip against the boy's chin and said, 'Eh?'

'I will do it,' Uthanga said.

Pattaraya gave him a menacing look before he flung the dagger on the floor and rushed out. Uthanga picked it up and stared at it. Its serrated edge glimmered in the lightning. A window slammed shut somewhere. Uthanga stepped out.

Soon, he was leaping over the unconscious guards whom Sivagami had knocked out and running towards his room. He paused at the door that was half shut, catching his breath and gathering courage. Water pooled at his feet. The wind howled through the corridor and made him shiver. He pushed the door and it opened with a creak. A sudden breeze snuffed out the lamp, plunging the room into darkness. Uthanga tip-toed towards Somadeva's bed.

## FORTY-FIVE

# Sivagami

THE BELL AT the fort ramparts started ringing frantically, indicating an emergency. The coup had begun. Sivagami heard shouts that the palace had caught fire. Good, she thought. Gomati and Akhila were doing their part. Sivagami could hear the clash of swords and screams from people now. A distance away, she could see a pitched battle being fought by Raghava's men and the Kadarimandalam soldiers.

Outside the palace, people were pounding on the fort door. It sounded as if the entire city had risen in rebellion. Guru Dharmapala's disciples were leading people to the fort.

This was her chance. She ran towards the mandap and the soldiers who were watching the city burn were taken by surprise. Before they could even draw their swords, Sivagami cut them down. With trembling hands, she fished out the key and tried the lock. It did not fit. In frustration, she pounded on the door with the hilt of the sword.

Behind her, the battle had intensified. Marthanda's commands rose above the din and soldiers lined up in the garden to shoot down people climbing over the fort wall. Many fell to the arrows, but a few managed to get inside. They opened the fort gates and a flood of the city's citizens poured in. The fort complex was now lit by the burning roofs of the palace wings. Lightning washed the fort in blinding whiteness every once in a while.

Sivagami knew she didn't have much time—she could see soldiers running in her direction. She had to get in before someone spotted her. But the torches in the mandap had been blown out during her fight with the soldiers, and in the darkness, she wasn't able to see the keyhole. Blindly, she continued to try and fit the key in the hole.

'Guru Dharmapala has been caught,' Sivagami heard a soldier yell, and just then the key turned and the door flung open. Sivagami took a deep breath and walked in. It was pitch dark, and the damp smell made her feel giddy. The wall she held on to as she walked seemed alive—slimy and breathing. As she walked past a cell, a hand grabbed out at her.

'Save me,' a gruff voice echoed in the darkness, making Sivagami jump. She slammed the hand with the hilt of her sword, and the man howled in pain. She ran down the corridor, stumbling on the uneven floor.

'Mahadeva,' she called out, and heard the clank of chains.

'Sivagami?'

She took a deep breath and pursed her lips tight. Despite herself, tears welled up in her eyes and her shoulders shook. She backed up a few steps and found the cell, the bars rusting, sharp with shards. She pressed her cheeks to them and extended her arm inside. Sivagami wanted to just hold him for a moment, feel his face, dissolve in his embrace. But he remained beyond her reach.

'Mahadeva, there has been a coup—we have to escape. I have come for you.'

'What for?' His cold words sent a chill down her spine.

She felt a sob rise up in her throat. She saw the latch on the door had no lock and she pulled it open, not bothering to wonder why there was no padlock. She rushed inside, stumbling on a step and falling on her knees. A dull light filtered in from a window high in the wall, and it showed Mahadeva crouching like a cornered rat in the farthest end of the cell.

'I am not coming anywhere with you,' Mahadeva said. Sivagami knelt before him and tried to touch his face with her trembling hands.

'Don't worry. We shall carry both you lovers.'

When she turned, the cell was flooded with the golden light of torches. Pattaraya's laugh echoed through the dungeon.

FORTY-SIX

# Kattappa

KATTAPPA LOOKED AT the palm leaf. It had come flying over the fort wall, tied to a stone that plunged into the water. Kattappa had quickly recovered the stone and untied the leaf around it. He had been waiting at the same spot, every day, for the last three months since the night he had last met Sivagami. He had been hiding in the lepers' colony since then, making his way through the untouchables' path every night. The path had become perilous—the river had submerged it after the incessant rains and made it its own. But every night for the past three months, Kattappa had stood at the designated place, waiting for the message, and today, he was rewarded.

He squinted in an effort to read the note, waiting for flashes of lightning to light it up. Kattappa couldn't understand the drawing. He wracked his brain to crack the code. He could hear the sounds of fighting inside the fort and was tempted to hurry there and join the fight. What if Sivagami devi was in trouble, or they were trying to execute Mahadeva?

Tempting though it was to join the coup, Kattappa would never take a step away from his duty. The king had ordered him to do something, and it was for him to find out what that was. Kattappa furrowed his brow, deep in thought. The rectangular lines indicated a door under water. The king was ordering him to open a door under water. Where could such a door exist? He looked nervously at the river flowing by swiftly. Could it be under the river? How would he find it? He didn't even know where to look. And why would there be a door under the water? When the next lightning bolt blazed, he saw the two coiled snakes. Devaraya's emblem. Kattappa paused to think.

So, the door was designed by Devaraya. Was it somehow connected to Gauridhooli? Now that there was no need for it to be a secret, everyone was aware of the workshop under the palace where Gauridhooli was extracted from Gaurikanta stones. The door must have something to do with that, but why was it underwater, Kattappa thought.

He remembered that, when Somadeva ruled, they brought in the Gaurikanta stones hidden in the Kali statue. Kattappa had himself filled stones into the statue in Bhoomipathi Guha's land. If they had brought the stones in the Kali statue and they didn't want the people to know about it, they would have extracted the stones after the statue was immersed in water—ah yes, the Kali visarjan spot in the river!

Kattappa took a deep breath. Blood pumped through his veins. It was a mission of extreme peril, but the king had asked him to do it. Kattappa started wading through the water, against the current, towards the spot where the Kali statue was always immersed. The river Mahishi roared and raged in the rains; it lashed at the shores, frothed and swirled as it rushed to the distant sea. Holding on to a crevice in the fort wall, Kattappa looked at the spot where they immersed the statue. If he had to dive to the bottom of the river, he had to go farther.

Kattappa kept pulling himself upstream, and when he had reached close enough to the visarjan spot, he took a deep breath and dove into the churning waters. He allowed the current to carry him while he paddled down towards the bottom. The flashes of light from the lightning barely penetrated the river. Kattappa swam down, trying to spot a door. The bottom of the river was muddy, though, and the darkness made it all the more difficult. Kattappa swam close to the bottom, where the current was not as strong as it was on the surface. His legs grazed the rotting structures of earlier Kali statues, and he knew he had reached the visarjan spot.

At a distance, he could see a faint blue light. The light wasn't constant, but lit up whenever there was lightning. Maybe these were stray Gaurikanta stones that were catching the light from the lightning, he thought. He swam towards it, but before he could reach the spot, he was out of breath. He shot up to the surface, only to be carried away by the current. But now he had his mooring, and he swam back.

The water was biting cold, and he felt his strength draining away, but he held on. 'Nothing should stop a slave from obeying orders,' his father's words echoed in his mind, giving him courage. He made his way to the shining Gaurikanta stones and started searching for the door. When his right foot hit a handle, he cried out in happiness and swallowed some water. Choking, he shot up to the surface, gasping for breath.

A huge tree that the river had probably uprooted somewhere upstream swirled from nowhere towards him. Instinctively, he ducked underwater to the bottom of the river, and this time he didn't have any difficulty in finding the trapdoor. He tried to pull it, but it seemed stuck.

Kattappa knew he would need something to ram down the trapdoor. He shot up to the surface and cast his eyes about. He saw the carcass of a dead elephant floating past him. Then something hit him on his head, almost knocking him unconscious. When he came back to the surface, he saw the river carrying a coconut tree, and he frantically swam to catch up with it. He grabbed the trunk of the tree and tried to dive down with it. But the river fought back, its buoyancy keeping him and the tree afloat.

Gathering all his strength, Kattappa pushed down the tree trunk and shot towards the trapdoor. It was a battle of wills between the slave and the river. The river threw him back, contemptuous of this puny human trying to win against its strength. Its roar sounded like mocking laughter to Kattappa. Years of bottled-up rage bubbled in the slave's veins, and gathering the last of his strength, he dove down with the tree, ramming it against the trapdoor. This time, a crack appeared on the door. Kattappa was encouraged, and while he allowed himself to be carried to the surface, he didn't let go of his grip on the tree. On the seventh attempt, the door cracked open, and Kattappa was sucked into a whirlpool.

FORTY-SEVEN

# Gundu Ramu

GUNDU RAMU WAS rushing back after throwing the message over the mansion wall when he saw the commotion. The soldiers had captured Guru Dharmapala. Another group, led by Pattaraya, emerged from the dungeons, dragging Sivagami and Mahadeva in chains. The rebels surrendered as soon as they saw Guru Dharmapala captured.

Gundu Ramu looked around at the carnage that the failed coup had resulted in. The ground was a mire of blood and rainwater. Headless torsos lay strewn all over. The soldiers of Kadarimandalam and the Mahishmathi soldiers who had remained loyal to Pattaraya had rounded up the common citizens who had joined Guru Dharmapala's rebellion. The procession wound its way towards the Gauristhalam pyramid, and Gundu Ramu followed, sobbing quietly.

Rain continued to pour down without a pause, and there was almost knee-high water in the arena. People stood and watched Sivagami and Mahadeva being dragged by Pattaraya's soldiers. No one wanted to be associated with the failed coup anymore. Soon, people's survival instincts kicked in—though a majority remained silent, merely watching the procession with hostile eyes, Gundu Ramu could see that more and more people were joining in with Pattaraya as he abused Sivagami and Mahadeva. 'Whore!' Pattaraya cried, and his soldiers repeated the chant.

Queen Mekhala's chariot arrived, splashing water on the onlookers. The pyramid steps were illuminated with torches that were fighting a losing battle with the rain. The arena was filling up with people. By the time the soldiers had dragged Sivagami and Mahadeva to the Gauristhalam, Queen Mekhala had taken her seat on the stone throne.

Pattaraya announced over the sound of rain and thunder, 'We have caught the second wife of the queen's consort in a compromising position with Prince Mahadeva. The punishment for immorality is death. People should remember that Sivagami is the daughter of Kadambari, who was punished for a similar crime. It is sad to see how such things run in her family. Her father was executed for treason, and her mother for immorality—the daughter follows their family tradition.'

Gundu Ramu screamed in protest. He tried to push through the crowd and reach the place where Sivagami stood in chains. Soldiers were now raising massive tripods before the pyramid. A cart trundled in, bringing two iron cages. The cages were hoisted and the soldiers tested their strength. Sivagami and Mahadeva stood, drenched in rain, but in the flickering light of the torches, Gundu Ramu could not see even a trace of fear on their faces.

Gundu Ramu saw soldiers dragging Raghava up the steps. How was Guru Dharmapala betrayed? No one outside the walls of their chamber had any inkling of their plans. Suddenly Uthanga's empty cot flashed in front of his eyes, and something clicked in his head. Somadeva's frantic call for him to come back as soon as he finished his mission rung ominously in his ears. Torn between Sivagami and the call of duty, Gundu Ramu hesitated. Perhaps Somadeva could still do something to help Sivagami, he reasoned, and began running across the massive palace garden. He had to get back to their chamber before it was too late.

Gundu Ramu ran through the veranda and leaped from the main wing to Sivagami's wing in the palace. He slipped and fell a couple of times, but he didn't pay attention to the pain—all he knew was that he had to make it back in time. When he entered the chamber, he was shocked to see his worst fears unfolding before his eyes.

Uthanga, the one who had lain unconscious for almost a decade, was now attacking the king. With a roar, Gundu Ramu threw himself upon Uthanga. Blood spattered on Gundu Ramu's face as Uthanga turned, a bloody dagger in his hand. The king was writhing in pain. Gundu Ramu stood stunned, gaping at the stab wounds in Somadeva's belly. The next thing Gundu Ramu knew, he felt a stabbing pain in his shoulder. He staggered back as Uthanga made a beastly grunt and swung his dagger again at Gundu Ramu.

'You fool! He is going to kill you too. Run, boy, run,' Somadeva screamed. Gundu Ramu took off towards the door, but out of the corner of his eye he saw Uthanga turning back towards the king. He rushed back towards the assailant. Ramu threw himself on Uthanga and together they collapsed on Somadeva. Gundu Ramu felt the dagger piercing his back many times, but he didn't let go of his grip on Uthanga. Slowly, he felt Uthanga's arms go limp, and the dagger fell to the floor with a clang. Covered in sweat and blood, Gundu Ramu stood up and saw Uthanga lying dead on the king's chest.

'Oh God, I have killed him!' Ramu cried out and collapsed on the floor, sobbing.

'Idiot, fool ...' the king growled. 'You didn't kill him, you moron. I killed him and I know that he has killed me.'

Gundu Ramu couldn't comprehend what the king was saying, and then he saw the chain wrapped around Uthanga's neck. The king had used his shackles to strangle Uthanga. Gundu Ramu grabbed the king's feet and cried, 'Thank you for saving my life, Your Highness.'

'Idiot,' the king said. 'I didn't save your life. You saved mine. Now run and ring the bell. Three short rings and one long peal. That is the code for the king's death ... I hope my trust in Kattappa was not in vain. Hurry now and don't die before you reach the bell tower.' The command in that voice made Gundu Ramu spring up. He ran out, ignoring the pain from the many cuts on his body. A few feet away, he collapsed. A lightning bolt of pain shot up his spine.

Gundu Ramu felt faint and knew that he was losing a lot of blood. But an order from the king was an order, and he had to do what was asked of him. After all, the king had saved his life. 'Oh God, let me not die until I ring the bell,' he prayed, as he crawled towards the bell tower over the rampart.

## FORTY-EIGHT

# Kattappa

THE RIVER CARRIED the slave and the tree trunk through the underground tunnels at a great speed. It gushed through, smashing everything on the way. The walls of the tunnel collapsed behind Kattappa, new paths opened up and suddenly he found he was in a huge workshop with towering machinery. The workers sleeping inside yelled in terror as the wall of water hit them. Kattappa's tree collided with the machineries, pounding them to smithereens as the river roared through the workshop.

Water burst out through a sluice, throwing Kattappa fifteen feet in the air, and when he landed, the river was swallowing the city. Devaraya's clever design, to flood the city and fort in the event of an enemy takeover, had worked perfectly. Adrift in the rushing water, Kattappa saw people running away in terror as the river gushed through the city. Pillars collapsed, trees in the garden were uprooted, and those men still fighting threw down their weapons and tried to run away from the water, in vain. The river had been invited into the city, and she would not leave without her feast.

Carried in the arms of river Mahishi, Kattappa saw he was reaching the Gauristhalam. He could see Sivagami and Mahadeva at the top of the pyramid in chains; Pattaraya and Queen Mekhala were yelling instructions in panic, and the body of Guru Dharmapala was swinging in the wind, twenty feet above ground.

The water carried Kattappa towards the pyramid. He held on to the tree trunk as it smashed its way through the palace garden. The decorated mandaps, the ornamental trees and beautiful sculptures were all pulverised by the force of the river. People scrambled to climb the fort walls, some climbed up the trees in the garden and a stampede started in the arena. The people at the upper levels of the gallery were safe, yet fear made them run. It was total chaos. After all, there was no difference between vanquished and victor before the roaring river.

Pattaraya and Mekhala were shouting commands, but their voices were drowned in the mayhem—the roar of the water, the pounding rain, the thunder, the screams of frightened people. Their instructions could not reach the soldiers. Most of them had deserted their positions and the few still around were struggling to keep afloat in the surging water.

Kattappa knew he had only a moment as the wave that was carrying him approached the pyramid. If he missed that, the surge of water would carry him across the arena. He could hear the distant crash of fort walls. There was no difference between the river and the city now.

Kattappa saw that Pattaraya had drawn his sword and was rushing towards Mahadeva with a scream. Kattappa slammed the tree trunk at the base of the Gauristhalam and catapulted himself to the top of the pyramid. In one sweeping move, he swung the tree trunk at Pattaraya. It slammed into him with a massive force and he heard ribs cracking. With a gasp of pain, Pattaraya collapsed at Sivagami's feet and lay there wheezing.

'Devi,' Kattappa said, kneeling before Sivagami as he kept an eye on Pattaraya.

It took a moment for Sivagami to comprehend what had happened.

'Kattappa ...' Sivagami said finally, and broke into fits of sobs. It was embarrassing for the slave to see the queen crying and he turned away. He heard something rattling behind Sivagami and leapt up, just in time to grab Queen Mekhala's wrist. Had he been a moment late, Mekhala's dagger would have plunged into Sivagami's back. Kattappa prised the dagger away from Queen Mekhala's grip.

Kattappa glanced at Prince Mahadeva, who was standing without any expression on his face. It was as if he didn't care whether he lived or died, whether he won or not.

'Amma Gauri is with us. She is with what is right. This flood was a godsend,' Sivagami said. Kattappa didn't reply. He didn't want to say that the rain and the flood may have been a godsend, but it was Maharaja Somadeva who had invited it into the city, and it was the design of her father Devaraya that had helped Somadeva do so, with a little aid from this humble slave. He stood with his head bowed, waiting for the next order.

Sivagami said, 'With the capture of these two evil people, I think our path is clear. Once the flood subsides, we will make arrangements for the coronation of our new king—

Vikramadeva Mahadeva.' Sivagami looked at Mahadeva with pride and love. Mahadeva continued to stand as if none of this mattered to him.

Just then, the bell at the top of the rampart started ringing furiously. Sivagami and Kattappa looked at each other—they recognised the pattern in which the bell was ringing. Three short and furious peals, followed by a pause and then a long peal. It was repeated twice. The blood drained from Sivagami's face. Someone important had died.

Distracted by the bell, they did not see Mekhala crawling away and plunging into the raging river. And that mistake would come back to haunt them soon.

FORTY-NINE

# Sivagami

IN THE FAR corner of the room, Somadeva lay still. In the occasional flash of lightning, his face looked hideous. Sivagami approached slowly, and then she saw it. There was blood everywhere—on the floor, on the bed, on the wall behind the king's cot. She had always wanted this man dead, but now that her wish had come true, she was horrified.

'Ha, you are not late,' Somadeva said, giving Sivagami a shock. 'I am not dead, not yet, but don't worry, I will be gone soon.' Sivagami moved towards Somadeva and stumbled on something on the floor.

'That is your favourite boy, the one you have been serving like a slave. The beggar almost got me. No, he actually did get me, but I got him too. See the irony of it. The last act of Somadeva, the emperor of Mahishmathi, is to kill an orphan. How cruelly will history judge me? To hell with history. I have lived my life,' Somadeva said with a laugh, which ended with a bout of coughing. He spat blood on the floor and continued to laugh. A wave of revulsion swept over Sivagami. Somadeva rattled his chains. 'I pleaded with you to free me before you went, but you wouldn't. I hope you feel that you got your revenge.'

'But ... how did he wake up?' Sivagami asked, bending down and checking Uthanga's pulse.

'He is dead, I told you. But as usual you are more concerned about him than a dying king. I don't blame you though, for no one should trust a ruler. And the downtrodden are always noble.'

Sivagami said, 'Don't talk and exert yourself too much. We'll get the rajavaidya here.'

'The rajavaidya can do nothing for me or that poor bastard I killed. But get him. He can help that fool who almost got killed.' Sivagami looked at Somadeva perplexed.

'Gundu Ramu. The boy had gone to the bell tower to announce my death. He was in a bad way when I last saw him.'

Sivagami rushed to the bell tower and found Ramu there, covered in blood, lying unconscious under the bell. With a gasp, she ran to him and picked him up. Gundu Ramu struggled to open his eyes.

'Akka ...' he said, swimming in and out of consciousness.

'What happened to you?' Sivagami said.

'Uthanga ... he almost killed me. But His Highness saved me.'

'Ramu ...' Sivagami choked with emotion. 'Stay right here while I get help,' she said and rung the bell again frantically. When soldiers arrived, she asked them to lift Gundu Ramu and take him to her room. She ordered one of them to fetch the rajavaidya immediately.

When she reached her chamber with the soldiers carrying Gundu Ramu, Kattappa was already there, holding Pattaraya in chains. Mahadeva was kneeling beside his father's bed. Something stabbed at Sivagami's heart. She looked away, unable to stand Mahadeva's grief. The blind prince ran his fingers all over Somadeva's face and an animal cry rose from his lips, shattering Sivagami. She felt responsible for his pain.

'Ah. Mahadeva, my son.' Somadeva's voice was tender and affectionate. 'Vikramadevas should not cry,' he said with a chuckle.

A soldier entered with the rajavaidya, who rushed to Somadeva. 'Your Highness.'

'Ha, I thought you were dead. I haven't seen you for the last five years. Now I'm "your highness" once again. I feel so proud.' Somadeva laughed. The vaidya started mumbling apologies.

'Leave me alone, you fool. Treat that boy; he has many more years to live. Let me spend some moments with my son and my daughter-in-law. I have the affairs of a kingdom to settle,' Somadeva said in a weak voice.

The rajavaidya looked at Uthanga and said, 'He is beyond help.'

Somadeva started laughing uncontrollably, and blood oozed out from his stab wounds. Sivagami couldn't stand it anymore. First the death of Raghava and now this—what use was such a victory? She snapped at the rajavaidya, 'Not that boy, this one.'

The expression on the rajavaidya's face grew grim as he checked Gundu Ramu. The rajavaidya ordered a soldier to help him, and together they lifted Gundu Ramu and moved him to the other side of the chamber. Sivagami hurried behind them, but Somadeva called out, 'Don't you want to hear my famous last words, daughter?'

Sivagami closed her eyes and a teardrop fell down her cheek. She didn't know who she was crying for, or whether she should be crying at all. She glanced at Gundu Ramu—she wouldn't be of any help to the rajavaidya anyway. It was better to let him do his duty. She turned back and went to Somadeva.

'Chaos,' Somadeva said. Sivagami looked at him, trying to understand what the king was saying. 'Don't you remember what I said a few months ago? When you give birth to Bijjala's son, you should tell him the story of his grandfather who thrived in chaos.'

Sivagami felt Mahadeva shudder at the remark. How had the king known that she was pregnant? She had tried to hide her pregnancy from everyone.

Somadeva continued. 'I knew Uthanga had regained consciousness a few months back. He and I were stuck in this room all day and night, and I had nothing better to do than keep an eye on him. He was careful to lie exactly the way Sivagami left him, but I saw the way he would move when he thought I wasn't looking. If he was still pretending to be in a coma, he was spying for someone. It had to be Pattaraya. The only way to outplay someone like Pattaraya is to play the same game. Now you might understand why I had insisted Raghava should visit us here. I wanted them to think that they had caught us again. If the coup had to succeed, I needed even nature to aid me, for I knew how Devaraya's design of flooding the city worked even on a normal day. In the middle of a flood, the impact would be devastating. The Gaurikanta workshops would be destroyed forever. Kattappa did not fail me.'

'I agree you fooled me there, Somadeva,' Pattaraya said suddenly.

Somadeva started laughing. 'Pattaraya, you old devil. See, both of us are going to die in chains.'

Pattaraya laughed. 'But I have destroyed your empire and ruled it for five years through my daughter. Not bad for someone from a low caste. I have played the game well and I will go to the gallows knowing that I did everything to deserve it. Unlike some men like Devaraya who were killed for no fault of theirs except that they were a friend to the king.'

Pattaraya's retort was delivered smoothly, and Sivagami sprang forward with her sword unsheathed.

'Sivagami, easy. Now all he has are these words. Let him have his fun,' Somadeva said.

'Fun, Your Highness?' Pattaraya said, emphasising the word 'highness'. 'Do you think Queen Chitraveni will keep quiet? The Kadarimandalam army will descend on Mahishmathi as soon as they hear the news of the capture of the queen's consort. And remember, my daughter has gotten away.'

'That is a game to be played by my son and daughter-in-law. Our game is over, Pattaraya, yours and mine, and I won it, friend.'

'You are unscrupulous, Somadeva. You sacrificed Raghava, and you almost got your son and daughter-in-law killed.'

'I have always thrived in chaos, Pattaraya, and so have you. But I have men I can rely on. I was still able to inspire loyalty in them—which you couldn't. I believed in Kattappa and that poor boy, Gundu Ramu. Isn't it sweet, Pattaraya, to know that your entire life collapsed because of such small people's love for their king?'

'Die, Somadeva. You had everything. Your birth in a royal family is an accident of fate. The loyalty is for the position you inherited. You earned nothing, friend. You were born a king and you are dying in chains like a slave. I was born poor, from a low caste, and I became the ruler. I am a better man than you.'

'Don't delude yourself, Pattaraya. You and I both are scum. We would destroy anyone for power. That is politics, and both of us were playing the game. Now keep your mouth shut while I settle the affairs of my kingdom.' Somadeva turned to Mahadeva, 'Son, I declare you, Vikramadeva Mahadeva, as the next king of Mahishmathi. But I have one condition. You will marry Thimma's daughter, Akhila.'

The king's words startled Mahadeva. He tried to say something, but his father gripped his hand. 'Speak no more, son. The people should see this victory against Pattaraya as that of their own. But know that it is Kattappa who won it for us.' He then turned to Sivagami and said, 'Come here, daughter. I have nothing against you. It was your father's design that helped us, finally. When he designed that trapdoor in the river, he told me that it would one day save Mahishmathi.' Somadeva paused. His breathing was getting more and more laboured.

'Mahadeva, your brother might come with the Kadarimandalam army. Win the war against him, and show no mercy. I hope my daughter-in-law will pardon me, but that is rajaneeti. Don't make the same mistake that Pattaraya did. He should have killed us all when he came to power, but he let his baser nature succeed. He wanted to relish our misery and humiliation. Don't make that mistake.'

Then the king turned to Sivagami and said, 'Fetch your sister.'

---

It was with a numb mind that Sivagami watched Somadeva place Akhila's palm on Mahadeva's hand. Sivagami suppressed the heart-wrenching pain, the oppression she felt as she saw her Mahadeva taken forever. In some corner of her mind, there had been a flicker of hope. She couldn't deny that she had dreamt of a future where Mahadeva was king, and she the queen, obedient and faithful to her husband. In the rush of emotions, she had forgotten that she had already achieved what she had set her mind on, in the last five years. She had freed Mahadeva, and freed Mahishmathi from the rule of Pattaraya and his daughter. To achieve it, she'd had to depend on the very slyness of Somadeva that she despised, and that made the victory bitter.

'Devi,' the rajavaidya called in a low voice and Sivagami turned to him.

'He will live, but ...'

'But what?' Sivagami cried.

'He may not walk again.'

Sivagami rushed to Gundu Ramu and hugged him. The boy was weak, and could barely open his eyes.

'Akka, how is the king? He saved me. Is he okay?' Gundu

Ramu asked. Sivagami burst into tears. Behind her, she could hear Akhila sobbing.

Then Mahadeva's trembling hand touched her shoulder. 'The king is gone.'

Ramu, who hadn't heard Mahadeva's low voice, asked again, 'How is the king? He saved my life.'

Sivagami looked at Mahadeva and turned to Ramu. 'The king is all right. I hope he will be kind, compassionate and rule Mahishmathi forever.'

'The king is kind and compassionate. He saved my life,' Ramu said, and slipped into unconsciousness.

Sivagami sat there, looking into his face, letting her tears fall freely. She barely listened as the rajavaidya told her that he might be able to restore Mahadeva's sight, for Bijjala had only got the lids stitched together. Nothing else seemed to matter, she wanted only one thing in her life—for her Ramu to walk again.

## FIFTY

# Mekhala

MEKHALA AWOKE WITH a start—someone was patting her on her shoulder. It was dark and she could hear rain pounding on the low roof above her. The last thing she remembered was plunging into the dark swirling waters from the Gauristhalam.

'Queen, my queen,' she could hear someone saying softly. A small lamp in the corner threw off a tiny glow and cast a disproportionate shadow in the room. Everything smelt of fungus and sweat.

'Where am I?' she asked, and a hand held her firm.

'Your Highness, not a word.'

Mekhala was terrified. She could see a dark figure moving towards the lamp and picking it up. When the figure turned, she thought she could recognise who it was.

'You …' she said, trying to place him.

'Roopaka, Your Highness.'

Mekhala sighed in relief. He was a confidant of Pattaraya. Then she remembered that her father had taught her that there was no such thing as selfless loyalty. Her hands went to her neck and it was bare. Her wrists were bare too, and she didn't even have her nose ring.

'I saved you from the river, Your Highness,' Mekhala heard Roopaka say, and she knew that she would never see any of her precious ornaments again.

'Where am I?'

'You are in the attic of my house, Your Highness.'

'But why am I here? I am the queen of Mahishmathi,' Mekhala said, knowing well what the reply would be.

Roopaka was silent for a moment and then said, 'Not anymore, Mekhala.'

The abrupt change in the way he addressed her sent a chill down her spine. She had gone through so much to reach where she had. And now what was to become of her? What had happened to her father?

As if reading her mind, Roopaka said, 'They have caught Pattaraya.'

'Have they—' Mekhala couldn't dare complete the question.

'Not yet, though it has been two weeks since the great flood.'

'I have been unconscious for two weeks?'

'You've had a very high fever. The few times you woke up, your words didn't really make sense. You yelled often in your sleep. I thought you were gone. But I served you loyally, and I hope you will remember …'

'Of course, of course,' Mekhala said, not wanting to dwell on it. She wondered why they had spared her father's life so far.

'Somadeva?'

'Dead,' Roopaka answered. 'Mahadeva is king now.'

Mekhala sat up, allowing the tears to flow down her cheeks. She had failed her father. He had worked hard to rise from nothing and she had lost everything. Maybe she hadn't deserved to be queen.

'And Bijjala?'

'There is no new news—only the same rumours that they were attacked by giant birds. It is said that not many have survived.'

Mekhala started sobbing uncontrollably. There was no point in living anymore. It would have been better for the river to have swallowed her.

'Mekhala, I think there is still hope. The rumours are that the Kadarimandalam army will reach here any moment.'

'And they will free my father,' Mekhala said with sudden enthusiasm.

Roopaka shook his head. 'Mahishmathi is keeping him as bait. They will use him as a bargaining tool with the queen of Kadarimandalam.'

Mekhala laughed between sobs. 'Then they are in for a big shock. My mother doesn't care for my father.'

Roopaka remained silent. With sudden determination, she grabbed his arm. 'He has only me, Roopaka. Help me save my father and I shall reward you.'

He gave a careful nod.

'Let me stay here as your guest, and when the attack of Kadarimandalam comes, we will plan our move. If my husband's second wife Sivagami thinks that she has finished us, she is in for a shock.'

Roopaka nodded, watching her carefully.

## FIFTY-ONE

# Keki

KEKI BLEW INTO the embers to get the blaze going. The leaves she was burning were damp, and her eyes stung from the smoke. Silently cursing, she looked at Bijjala who was sitting a few feet away, shivering, his face ashen.

'How much time are you going to take, you fool?' Bijjala snapped.

Keki didn't reply. She had half-carried, half-dragged Bijjala from the site of the disaster. She felt lucky that they had escaped unscathed. She had never seen anything like it in her life. Hell, she had not heard of such insanity, not even in a folk tale. Who would have ever believed in the existence of gigantic birds that drop huge rocks down at people? The memory of it made her shudder.

When the Garuda pakshi had approached, Akkundaraya had cried out, 'Free us, you fool, or we are dead—'

Before Akkundaraya could complete his sentence, the first rock had fallen, and the Mahishmathi army had scattered like mice, screaming and yelling in terror. The soldiers were trained to fight other armies, not monstrous birds. The first rock took out only a few men, but the terror it created was unimaginable.

A soldier had the presence of mind to unchain Akkundaraya, and the old bhoomipathi was able to free most of his men before the next wave of attacks commenced. While Bijjala cowered and muttered incoherent commands, Bhoomipathi Akkundaraya got his men to pick up bows, arrows and spears and placed them in strategic positions. They stood with their arrows pointed skyward.

Keki saw that Bijjala was getting angry that his commands were being ignored. He began arguing with Akkundaraya, who finally turned around and slapped Bijjala across his face. This affront, which in other times would have got him a death sentence, now drew smirks from the bhoomipathi's men. Akkundaraya, who had clearly had enough of Bijjala, ordered his men to restrain the prince. Bijjala, livid, stood swinging his sword, daring anyone to touch him. As the farce was going on, an unearthly screech reached their ears. The men looked at each other, terrified. All arguments ceased when they saw five giant birds approaching them. After that, nothing mattered.

A massive boulder dropped by a Garuda pakshi pulverised Akkundaraya and many men by his side, missing Bijjala by a whisker. Keki took off, not caring whether Bijjala was alive or not. The eunuch ran without pausing until she could no longer hear the screeching of the birds or the terrified cries of men. She collapsed near the river and lay there for some time, panting like a dog. Then she crawled towards the river and lapped up water; when she felt her belly would burst, she turned on her back and lay there staring at the sky.

Thankfully, there were neither any clouds nor any giant birds. She lay there until the sun had dipped towards the west, thinking about the precious ornaments that Bijjala wore. If he was dead, perhaps she could claim them. When her greed won over her fear, she got up and headed back towards the site of the carnage.

It was already dark when she reached the spot. A pack of jackals feeding on the corpses scurried away with short yelps of protest at their feast being interrupted. Cursing loudly, Keki started scavenging valuables from the dead. Soon, the forest turned pitch dark and it was impossible to forage further. Keki stood up, exhausted, and at that moment heard someone sobbing. The sound was coming from near an old banyan tree that stood with its fronds dangling over the river.

It was Bijjala, with not a scratch on his body. She approached her master apprehensively and squatted in front of him. Bijjala's eyes remained blank, as if he hadn't seen the eunuch. Saliva dribbled from his chin as he continued to sob and babble. Keki shook his shoulders and said, 'Prince, it's me, your humble servant Keki.'

Bijjala gave her a startled look and then started sobbing, 'I saw her. I saw her.'

'Saw who, my prince?' Keki asked. But Bijjala would only keep repeating that he had seen her, and Keki knew it would be futile to get anything coherent from Bijjala at that moment. She helped him stand up and found that he was burning with fever. 'Can you walk, my prince?'

Bijjala looked at her blankly. Keki placed his arm on her shoulders and said, 'Even if you don't want to walk, we have no choice. No one is going to send us a chariot here.'

Keki was chuckling at her own joke, when Bijjala suddenly grabbed her by the neck. He slammed Keki hard against the trunk of the banyan tree and said, 'Fool do you not understand—I saw her!'

Keki gasped for breath. Even if she wanted to ask him who he had seen, and why he should attempt to murder her for it, she was in no position to say anything. Then, as suddenly as he had grabbed her, he dropped her and she collapsed like a rag. Bijjala sat beside her and started bawling like a baby. A wave of pity and revulsion washed over Keki. The prince had gone mad, she thought. Or perhaps he had always been mad and she had failed to notice it before.

'Achi Nagamma,' Bijjala said finally. 'Achi Nagamma is the one who sent the birds. I saw her. She is a ghost, she is a devi, she is a witch,' Bijjala continued to ramble.

Keki was getting tired of his hysteria. She considered murdering Bijjala and escaping with the gold she had found, but eventually decided against it. She had been the head of Bijjala's harem for the past five years now, ever since Brihannala had vanished. It was a position she had always coveted, and if she ran away, she would probably end up dancing in some shady tavern. She had bet on Bijjala, and so far it had served her well. She decided to stay with Bijjala for now.

That was how Keki found herself trying to light a fire to cook a meal for her master, three weeks after the catastrophe. By this time, Bijjala had recovered enough to return to his usual nasty self. Three miserable weeks of hunting food for her master, eating raw frogs and tiny little birds and getting kicked and abused every day by Bijjala, had made her rethink her decision to stick with the prince. Had they not lost their way in the jungle, she would have left him a long time back. The prince, meanwhile, was furious that his plans had been foiled by some blasted birds, as he put it. He had not mentioned Achi Nagamma once since the day of the massacre—perhaps he too thought he had imagined the whole thing. He worried about his reputation—he had failed where his wife and brother had succeeded. His plans to depose his first wife Mekhala and grab the throne had been crushed, and Bijjala took out all his frustrations on Keki.

'How much time do you need to cook a bloody meal, eunuch?'

'I am the head of your harem, not a cook or a hunter,' Keki said, crying as she continued to try and light the fire. She began listing the sacrifices she had made for Bijjala, when the prince smacked her head with the back of his hand.

'Shut up you fool,' Bijjala hissed. 'What was that sound?'

In the distance, they could hear the thump of many feet marching.

'What are you gaping at? Climb that tree and look,' Bijjala said, pointing to a tree on a hill. With a sigh, Keki stood up, wiped her hands on her sari, and hurried to the hill. She climbed to the top of the tree and looked around. Against the blaze of the afternoon sun, she shielded her eyes with her hand and stared towards the northeast.

Bijjala was poking the burnt leaves with a twig when he heard Keki cry out, 'Prince, come and see this!'

Bijjala ran over to Keki. He climbed up the tree and looked towards where Keki was pointing. An army was marching through the valley. Their weapons were strange—nothing Bijjala had seen before—as were their clothes and appearance.

'Kalakeyas,' Keki whispered in awe and fear. Bijjala continued to stare, blinking from time to time, trying to understand the nightmare unfolding before him. Above the marching army, he could make out five dots in the sky. It didn't require much imagination to know what these were—Garuda pakshis.

'They are marching towards Mahishmathi,' he whispered. 'We should warn them.'

'Well, that is a noble thought, Prince,' Keki said. 'But instead, what if we let the Kalakeyas take over the city?'

Bijjala stared at her and she pressed on. 'We could go to Kadarimandalam and get the navy of Queen Chitraveni to save Mahishmathi. The hero prince rescues his people—that is what the poets will sing about.'

Bijjala's eyes sparkled, and he said in a dreamy voice, 'Yes, yes …' Then he frowned. 'But how the hell do we reach Kadarimandalam? Do we fly, you idiot?'

'We find one of Akkundaraya's ships.'

Bijjala slapped Keki's shoulder and cried, 'Yes, exactly what I was thinking.'

'Of course, Prince,' Keki said and bowed.

FIFTY-TWO

# Jeemotha

THE FOUR MONTHS following his encounter with Ally had been tortuous for Jeemotha. It had been more difficult than the five years he had spent as a galley slave. For the first time in half a decade, he had a glimmer of hope—but it depended on many fine factors.

Finally, a few days ago, news had reached him that Mahishmathi had successfully thrown off the yoke of slavery and declared independence. So whether or not Ally's barbarian army succeeded in conquering Mahishmathi did not matter. Kadarimandalam had to reclaim its lost colony. There were whispers already of Kadarimandalam preparing to launch an attack. As he rowed the ship to and back from the open seas, his mind was busy with calculations. He fretted over whether Ally had understood the precise nature of her work; he worried she might have cut too deep or too little into the ships' holding ropes. He was terrified of the ropes giving way in the high seas, before time.

Meanwhile, he had been grinding through his chains using the small dagger Ally had given him. The slave master of his deck had not noticed that one of the links of his chain had been worn down.

In the last four months, the ship had done four voyages to the open sea and back. His calculations depended on the weight they would put on the ships. Since he worked on one of the pilot ships that guided the trade vessels in and out of Kadarimandalam port, his ship was always lightly loaded. Its deck was often manned by a few women soldiers and their consorts. Their job was to protect the trade ships from the occasional pirate attacks.

Jeemotha knew all about pirates, for he had spent the better part of his life as one. He had little respect for the present lot. They were landlubbers who had taken to piracy out of desperation. Most of them were fishermen or peasants who had no other means of living since the rich merchants of Kadarimandalam had taken away their land or driven them out of their fishing grounds with their sophisticated fishing vessels that employed hundreds of slaves.

When Jeemotha and his father were pirates, there was respectability in the trade. A pirate captain was a soldier, a commander, a seaman, a strategist and a king, all rolled into one. Pirate captains were the stuff of legends, living on their wits and skills. He had to protect his people from the royal navies of various kingdoms as well as the vagaries of nature and the raging storms when at sea. Jeemotha was a hero among pirates, and to think that he had ended up as a galley slave made him seethe with anger. He felt like a fool for not seeing through the deception of the queen of Kadarimandalam. It had been a jolt to his ego that he was outplayed by a woman, and he had waited patiently for a chance to take his revenge. Every time the whip of the slave supervisor fell on his back, Jeemotha reiterated his vow to destroy Kadarimandalam.

Jeemotha prayed to a God he had never believed in. Sooner or later the Kadarimandalam navy would move to reclaim their colony. The river was the fastest way to reach Mahishmathi: it was merely a month's journey by ship, while it could take more than half a year by foot.

He didn't understand how Ally and her band of barbarians planned to take on Mahishmathi, but that was not his concern. The Mahishmathi fort had been designed by Devaraya, and it could withstand a siege for many months. It was almost impregnable through river or land.

Long ago, in one of those drunken revelries of his early youth, Jeemotha had lain on a boat with two of his pirate friends and plotted a charmingly foolish plan of attacking Mahishmathi fort. A lightning raid, a diversion to catch the soldiers by surprise, kill everyone who came in the way and dash off with whatever valuables you got your hands on was the long and short of it. Mahishmathi's wealth made this plan tempting, but when he was sober, Jeemotha actually looked at the city's defences and returned to his friends with a disappointing report—it would be suicidal to attack. The fort was perfectly designed, and unless one could fly into it, you would be caught and roasted by Mahishmathi soldiers.

Jeemotha had seen many forts across the world and had conducted raids on them with mixed success. He had come back from Mahishmathi with a grudging admiration for the man who had designed the fort. When he heard about

Devaraya's execution, Jeemotha drunk himself to oblivion for two days. He had felt a strange kinship with that genius, for the pirate considered himself to be one of the sharpest minds in the world. They might have been on different sides of the law, but ultimately the government had got them. Rulers hated extraordinary people, and he would probably share Devaraya's fate. But wasn't he smarter than Devaraya, a naive fool who believed in the goodness of all humans? Jeemotha knew there was no good or bad in the world. Only winners and victims.

'Live, don't just exist', was the pirate's motto. It had often crossed Jeemotha's mind to find a way to escape the galley ship when it was in the high seas. But that would have just brought him to where he had started: a poor pirate with nothing to show for his brilliance. If his plan worked, if his knowledge of ships was as precise as he thought it was, he would once again be at the helm, and then he would turn history upside down. 'Revenge,' he murmured, with each pull of the oar.

Everything depended on Kadarimandalam deciding to reclaim Mahishmathi. The loss of Mahishmathi would mean the loss of Kadarimandalam's trade empire. The merchants would not like that. Historians think kingdoms are run by brave kings and warriors. But the people who directed the course of history and decided the fall and rise of kingdoms were not those who held the sword but the purse. Merchants owned the world. The kings, the priests, religion, society, slaves—all were mere pieces on their board of chaturanga. And piracy was just a form of business. A business that he had run, until it had failed so badly that he was now a rat on a ship. But he had suffered enough—his luck had to turn.

It happened one day. He heard siege machines rolling towards the dock. They would soon start loading them onto the ships and then would bring on board the massive iron balls to fire with the catapult. Jeemotha's knowledge of ships was going to be tested now, and he felt a feverish anticipation. When the load on the ships was light, the ropes that tied the planks of the hull would hold, but with every passing day, the threads were fraying a bit more. That is, if Ally had done her job exactly as he had told her. To think that his fate and the fate of kingdoms depended on a girl was a delightful irony that made Jeemotha laugh. The laughter earned him a whip across his back, but he had long learnt to ignore the pain. When the first siege engine rolled onto the upper deck and the ship sank by two feet, Jeemotha held his breath. 'Now,' he muttered to himself. 'Now, bloody hell, now.' The ship creaked and shuddered. *Now, now, now.*

Jeemotha placed his fingers on the side of the ship and felt a low vibration. He could hear more siege engines being loaded onto other ships. He placed a bet with himself on which ship would give way first. He bet on his own ship, but lost. The first one to capsize was the third ship in the row before his. He heard shrieks and the delightful sound of the ship's hull cracking into two. This was the moment he had been waiting for. He looked around at his comrades with whom he had shared this dark, dingy cabin for five years. 'Poor souls. You were born slaves and now will die in chains. Goodbye,' he said as he heard the sound of his ship starting to crack. He took a deep breath as with a sudden jerk and a deafening sound the ship tore apart. With a yank of his chain, Jeemotha pulled himself free and, as the ship sank, he swam away. From a distance, floating in the deliciously warm water, he watched the beautiful sight of Kadarimandalam's navy getting destroyed.

*Good job, girl,* Jeemotha thought, giving a soft whistle of appreciation for Ally's work. His legs were still in chains, but he could float with his hands free for many days, if it were required. Five years of rowing had made his muscles bulge like that of a draught bull. He felt pride at his precise calculations and his knowledge of ships. *I deserve more in life, God, goddamn you,* he said, looking at the sky sagging with dark clouds. He savoured the caress of rain on his face, drinking the elixir of freedom.

After some time, he swam towards the shore and stood along with the few lucky crew members who had managed to escape the sinking ships. He saw a few slaves trying to swim to the other side of the river in the hope of freedom, only to be shot down by Kadarimandalam soldiers. By swimming back to the port, he had ensured his own safety. He knew that Kadarimandalam would now be in a hurry to repair the destroyed ships. If they delayed it, it would become difficult to recapture Mahishmathi. Their former colony would have time to collect enough provisions to withstand a siege. Jeemotha smiled, watching the wreckage he had caused. The river was in spate and the water was rusty red in colour. Good, perfect, he said to himself. The capsized ships had closed the river mouth and the flood was carrying massive amounts of sediments from the mountains. Soon the port mouth would fill up, a delta would form and if they didn't remove the ships quickly, Kadarimandalam port would be closed forever. Not only did they need to repair the ships, they also had to get the massive parts out of the water immediately, and there was only one man who knew the art of lifting such humongous vessels; vessels that weighed more than three hundred elephants. And that man was a genius, and that man was he, a pirate. He could not wait to see Queen Chitraveni's face as she pleaded for his help.

Jeemotha had reclaimed his world.

---

Chaos ensued after the ships capsized; some of the ships split in various parts, their hulls and planks floating away and piling up at the river mouth. As the river mouth closed with the sediments, the water level started to rise and slowly began flowing into Kadarimandalam city. The remaining galley slaves, including Jeemotha, were made to lift the parts that could be used to rebuild ships.

After four days, the shipbuilders of Kadarimandalam had barely managed to lift the pieces of only half a ship. A huge crowd had assembled to watch the process, and every time the carpenters failed in their attempt, they erupted with loud cheers. Jeemotha wondered whether they were cheering for their navy to succeed or were happy at their failure.

That afternoon, Jeemotha whistled softly as he spotted two familiar faces on the dock. It was Bijjala and Keki. Finally, someone who knew about his skills. He had to get their attention somehow. He waited until the slave master reached near him. He lunged at the poor man, and soon soldiers were jumping into the water, trying to constrain him. The crowd cheered from the shore. He put up a reasonable fight and then gave up. They pounded him with the blunt end of their spears and punched his face. He had attempted to kill a slave master after all. They dragged him to the dock and took turns to kick him.

'Hey, that is our man,' Jeemotha heard the eunuch's cry, and sighed with relief.

---

Once again, Jeemotha was in the sabha of the queen of Kadarimandalam.

Bijjala bowed low. 'He is someone who can help us,' he said.

'Do I look stupid that you expect me to believe you again? I entrusted you with one job, Bijjala, one job, and see where you are!'

Bijjala stammered, 'Your Highness, there were these giant birds and they dropped stones on us and—'

The sabha erupted in laughter.

'Next you will say there were flying elephants that showered flowers from the sky and sung your praises. Pattaraya made my daughter marry a fool.'

Jeemotha chuckled when he saw Bijjala's face turn red. Chitraveni looked at the chained pirate.

'Why are you grinning, monkey?'

Before Jeemotha could retort and make things worse, Keki intervened. 'Your Highness. Jeemotha is the best pirate captain in the world. There is nothing he doesn't know about ships.'

Chitraveni studied Jeemotha and finally asked, 'What is your demand?'

'The position of sarva nayaka of your navy,' Jeemotha said. As he had expected, his demand drew laughter from the courtiers.

'Oh, Your Highness, if it is his caste you are worried about—' Keki said.

'Bah! In Kadarimandalam, there are only two castes,' Chitraveni said. 'The superior one and the male.'

One of the ministers stood up and said, 'The eunuch thinks we are some barbaric society where men are given positions of power. But who doesn't know that men botch up most things they try to do?'

Jeemotha turned towards her and winked, drawing gasps and angry exclamations from the courtiers.

'Agreed,' Chitraveni said with a smile.

Jeemotha smiled back. 'I know what you are thinking. Let the pirate lift the ship and then we can have his head.'

There were smirks and muffled laughter. Jeemotha addressed the courtiers, 'The flood has changed the contours of the river. The riverbed has shifted and there are many dunes where the ships can get stuck. It needs an expert eye like mine to steer the ships towards Mahishmathi.'

'How the hell do you know about Mahishmathi?' one of the courtiers snapped, but Chitraveni waved off her objection.

'You are too smart for your own good, pirate,' she said before dismissing the sabha. Jeemotha stood with a broad grin on his face as soldiers unchained him.

'I will take you to your Nanna, boy. Don't cry,' Jeemotha said to Bijjala, standing pensive near him, and the prince exploded with rage. Jeemotha's laughter boomed through the ancient sabha of Kadarimandalam as Keki dragged away Bijjala as he screamed threats that Jeemotha would be beheaded for the insult.

'Give him something cool to drink,' Jeemotha yelled. 'Or better yet, pour it over his head.' Some of the soldiers grinned at the pirate's antics.

'Don't be shy, don't be coy, for I know you know, this pirate boy can bring you joy,' he said to them, and they burst out laughing. They watched him walk out of the sabha with an impressive swagger.

Over the next fourteen days, Jeemotha commanded a gang of two dozen galley slaves, and before the incredulous eyes of the people of Kadarimandalam, he achieved the impossible. Using a complicated design of pulleys and ropes, he was able to lift the massive hulls and parts of the ships out of the water with surprising ease. He could see the Kadarimandalam shipbuilders trying covertly to copy his designs and he purposely made them more complicated than required.

Jeemotha worked with a deliberate slowness, which gave the impression that he was being very thorough with his work. It took him another few months to repair the broken ships, and when he couldn't delay it any further, he gave the command to the Kadarimandalam navy to proceed. Once again, he was at the helm of a fleet of ships. But this time, he was not a mere nauka nayaka, a captain, but an admiral, a sarva nayaka. He looked proudly at the hundreds of ships and canoes that were following his ship's lead. Bijjala and Keki came to stand by his side at the prow of the ship, and Jeemotha gave them a friendly smile. Wind flapped at the sails and thousands of oars fell in rhythm. The air was filled with boat songs and sparrows flitted in and out to peck grains on the deck. All was well with the world, Jeemotha thought; he was finally commanding one of the most formidable navies in the world.

His eyes went to the crow's nest of the ship. A woman who appeared to be of gigantic size was tied there. Keki followed Jeemotha's eyes and said, 'That is for our protection. That is Brihannala, the son or daughter, whatever you prefer, of Achi Nagamma.'

Jeemotha knew that he had once again underestimated Chitraveni. She knew about Achi Nagamma's plans to attack and had the foresight to place her son as ransom. Chitraveni had calculated that Achi Nagamma wouldn't dare launch an attack on the ship where her son was kept as hostage. Jeemotha wondered whether the cunning queen of Kadarimandalam knew what he had in store for her. He must move very carefully, he warned himself, for he knew that in a single throw of his dice hung the future of many empires.

FIFTY-THREE

# Sivagami

QUEEN AKHILA SAT by Sivagami's bed, looking at the baby. 'He looks like you, Akka,' she said. Sivagami sighed. She was exhausted and didn't feel like moving at all.

'We were really scared,' Akhila said.

'I heard the rajavaidya began making funeral arrangements for me and my son,' Sivagami said, smiling weakly.

'Amma Gauri is kind, and that is why she has given such a beautiful prince to Mahishmathi.' Akhila kissed Sivagami's son.

Sivagami watched her sister through half-closed eyes. Sunlight streamed through a window, casting an almost ethereal glow over them. Sivagami looked at her son's innocent face and wondered how she had once thought of getting rid of him. She had never wanted a child, not from Bijjala, but in the nine months she had carried him, Sivagami had come to love him more than anything in life. It was as if nothing else mattered to her—the kingdom, her need for revenge, even her contempt for her husband. She could hear Somadeva's mocking laughter in her mind. *They have trapped me, the wily king and his sons, and now I am part of the family that I once wanted to destroy.*

'One day he will be the king of Mahishmathi,' Akhila said, gazing down at the baby.

That was the last thing Sivagami wanted. She looked at Akhila's swollen belly and an uncomfortable thought flitted through her mind. Soon Akhila would be a mother, and if she had a boy, the bloody feud would start once again. History was full of empires destroyed by conflicting claimants to the throne.

The seven months after Somadeva's death and Pattaraya's capture had been a blissful period in Mahishmathi. Mahadeva was an able king and a doting husband to Akhila. Sivagami was conflicted. She was happy for Akhila, but in a corner of her mind, jealousy throbbed. She had learnt to push away such thoughts, but at night, as she lay in her room alone, she felt unwanted and lonely. There had been no news of her husband, though there had been many rumours that he had survived the Garuda pakshi attack.

Kadarimandalam had not come to reclaim their colony as they had feared, and a period of peace, prosperity and hope had dawned on the battered kingdom. Spies informed them about the mysterious collapse of the Kadarimandalam ships, and many believed it was the work of ghosts or the result of some ancient curse. Regardless, it gave Mahishmathi some respite, and sufficient time to repair the fort. Slowly, they rebuilt the city ravaged by floods.

'Akka, Akka, see this,' Gundu Ramu's excited voice came from the veranda. A moment later, the boy appeared in an ornate chair with wheels. Gundu Ramu made a swift turn on his wheeled chair.

'Ramu,' Akhila called, laughing. Sivagami smiled at the boy's happiness that he could now move around. He was paralysed from the waist down in the fight to save Somadeva, but had thankfully made it out alive. Ramu went around the cot in his wheeled chair, which was beautifully carved, with pearls hanging from its sides.

'Isn't it wonderful?' Akhila asked Sivagami, who was looking at Mahadeva, leaning against the doorframe, his arms crossed over his chest, smiling at them. Akhila stood up, exclaiming, 'Look at him, Akka! Does he look like a king? He looks like a carpenter who has wandered in from the street.'

'I've been working on Gundu Ramu's chair,' Mahadeva said, walking in. Sivagami's baby started bawling.

'Did I wake him up?' Mahadeva asked, embarrassed.

'You did, my king. But it is all right. I think he is hungry,' Akhila said. Mahadeva picked up the baby who cried even louder.

'Is that the way to handle a baby? Learn fast, my king, for you will be a father in a few months,' Akhila said with a smile. Sivagami closed her eyes, unable to handle the emotions she was feeling. They were made for each other, Akhila and Mahadeva. Sivagami had never felt so lonely. Gundu Ramu came up in his wheeled chair and made faces at the baby to pacify him.

'It seems he doesn't like his uncle much,' Akhila said, taking the baby from Mahadeva's arms and handing him over to Sivagami.

'He loves me. Give him to me,' Gundu Ramu said.

'He has to nurse. All boys out of the room,' Akhila said, pushing Gundu Ramu's chair out. Sivagami looked at Mahadeva, an awkward silence between them.

'There is no news about him,' Mahadeva said. Sivagami nodded. Discussing Bijjala with Mahadeva always made her uncomfortable.

'Out,' Akhila said, as she came back in. She grabbed Mahadeva's hand. 'The baby is hungry,' she said, pulling her husband out of the room. Sivagami watched them walking out with a terrible sense of loss. The baby cried, breaking the silence. Sivagami started nursing her baby, and nothing else mattered.

---

A month later, Sivagami walked into the sabha of Mahishmathi after a long hiatus. The courtiers rose in respect and she took her place by the side of Maharaja Mahadeva and Mahapradhana Gomati. Sivagami had had to use all her wits to suppress the protests that had arisen at a woman being appointed mahapradhana, but Mahadeva had supported her decision. Since then, Gomati had served Mahishmathi as efficiently as her father Parameswara. Behind the king stood Kattappa, just as his father Malayappa had stood by Maharaja Somadeva.

Sivagami saw the middle-aged man sitting where the legendary General Hiranya once sat and whispered to Gomati, 'Why is that man still here?'

'The king says Marthanda has done nothing to warrant his dismissal; he was just doing his duty while serving Queen Mekhala.'

'He is a mercenary. We don't know where he came from and whose spy he is. He was hired by Pattaraya. If you ask me, we should hang him from the nearest tree. When will our king learn he can't trust anyone?'

Gomati shook her head with a resigned smile. 'You know the king better than me.'

Mahadeva began speaking then. 'I was waiting for Sivagami devi to come to the sabha,' Mahadeva said. 'I have an important announcement to make. I am making Sivagami the mahanayaka, the commander-in-chief of the Mahishmathi army.'

Sivagami was taken aback by this announcement. It took a moment for the courtiers to absorb the news and then the sabha erupted. 'The soldiers will revolt.' 'Isn't it enough that there is a woman as mahapradhana?' 'Is this Kadarimandalam?' 'Your Highness, we humbly request you to reconsider the decision.'

'None of you were there in Gauriparvat when Sivagami devi led the army to conquer it. There is no man to match her,' Mahadeva asserted in a calm voice.

'Am I dismissed?' Marthanda asked.

'No, you will serve under her. And you still retain the position of dandanayaka.'

'Of course, Your Highness. It would be an honour,' Marthanda said and bowed to Sivagami.

She wondered whether she was ready to take on such a huge responsibility. The least Mahadeva could have done was to consult her before making such an announcement.

Roopaka stood up to speak and the sabha grew silent. He looked around, licked his lips, cleared his throat and started in a halting manner, 'Your Highness, the matter I want to discuss is delicate.'

The king nodded and Roopaka continued. 'It is about propriety. Already many learned Brahmins are objecting to a widow...' Roopaka paused and looked at Sivagami. She gripped the armrests of her chair and glowered at him. She had been hearing the hushed murmurs about her appearing in public.

'Who is a widow?' Mahadeva asked, perplexed.

'I am not a widow,' Sivagami said as she stood up, her eyes blazing.

Mahadeva's face darkened. 'My brother is not dead. And my sister-in-law has every right to be here.'

'Well, Your Highness, pardon me, but it is nearly a year and there is no news of Prince Bijjala. The information that has travelled from Gauriparvat is that he was killed in the attack of the Garuda pakshis. Many soldiers who managed to escape have confirmed it,' Roopaka said in a firm voice. 'And the bhoomipathis and elders feel it would be better if Sivagami devi stayed away from the public gaze until we get confirmation that Prince Bijjala is alive.'

Sivagami saw many courtiers nodding their heads in agreement.

'I have confirmation that Prince Bijjala is very much alive,' Marthanda said, standing up.

Sivagami sat back down, wondering whether she was relieved or disappointed by the news. 'My son deserves his father, whether I love him or not,' Sivagami told herself.

'My spies have just informed me that Bijjala has reached Kadarimandalam and is planning to bring its navy here to attack Mahishmathi. They would have reached here earlier, but for that strange accident in the naval dockyard of Kadarimandalam. But we can expect them soon.'

Commotion broke out in the sabha. Sivagami saw that the blood had drained from Mahadeva's face. She could sympathise with him, for he hated violence and Mahishmathi was only now limping back to normalcy after the devastating flood. There were reports of famine from the distant villages. But this was expected; it was unrealistic to expect Kadarimandalam to not react.

'Silence,' Sivagami commanded, and the sabha fell into an uneasy quiet.

'Devi, I am waiting for your instructions,' Marthanda said, smiling.

'We need to strengthen our fort,' Sivagami said. 'We need to prepare for a long siege. Fill our granaries so there is sufficient food. Kattappa, you will supervise it.'

The slave nodded.

Marthanda was still standing and Sivagami turned to him questioningly.

'I have graver news,' Marthanda said, pausing for effect. It seemed like he was enjoying himself.

'The Kalakeyas are marching towards Mahishmathi.'

A dreadful silence descended in the sabha. Sivagami slowly sat down and gripped the armrest again so no one would notice her trembling fingers. Her throat had gone dry.

'Also,' Marthanda added and surveyed the sabha, as if enjoying everyone's reactions, 'Achi Nagamma is leading the Kalakeyas. They have five Garuda pakshis with them.'

'Garuda pakshis don't exist!' yelled a courtier.

'All tales by unscrupulous poets,' scoffed another.

Sivagami sat with her hands pressed to her forehead. The very mention of Garuda pakshis had brought back terrifying memories. The fear still throbbed in her veins.

'We will fight and win,' Mahadeva's calm voice cut through the din.

Sivagami wanted to scream, 'How, Mahadeva, how?'

'Send messengers to all parts of the kingdom. Everyone in every hamlet in the three ways to Gauriparvat should march to Mahishmathi fort. Every citizen of Mahishmathi should come inside the fort. Today. Now.' Mahadeva's voice was calm, determined.

'Every citizen?' Roopaka asked. 'Even untouchables, low castes?'

'Everyone, including those in the leper colony. And you will supervise it,' Mahadeva said, looking Roopaka straight in his eyes.

Angry protests erupted from various corners. 'How can untouchables come into the city?' 'Who can live with lepers?' 'How many days will the siege go on?' Mahadeva did not even bother to answer. He walked out of the sabha with steady steps.

Sivagami knew nothing would change Mahadeva's resolve now, and it would be left to her to keep the infuriated nobles in check while fighting off a two-pronged attack. 'How to protect this man from himself,' Sivagami wondered with exasperation and admiration for the idealistic king.

Sivagami was supervising the fortification as a huge train of refugees walked into the fort. Gundu Ramu approached her in his wheeled chair.

'Akka, please come with me,' Ramu said, grabbing her hand.

'Not now, Ramu,' Sivagami said impatiently. The soldiers were erecting massive spikes above the fort walls. Some sat sharpening arrows. Bullock carts sagging with the weight of grain rumbled past them. Elephants dragged in huge barrels of water. Wells were being dug in various parts of the fort.

'Akka, please. This is important,' Gundu Ramu said, and with an exasperated sigh, Sivagami followed him. As they walked, Ramu said enthusiastically, 'I have been going through various granthas in the royal library.'

Ramu fished out some palm leaves from his waistband and waved it before Sivagami. 'You were afraid about the Garuda pakshis. That got me thinking about what could scare animals away. Animals and birds are afraid of many things, but they are universally afraid of fire.'

Sivagami nodded, not understanding where this was going. They could light a fire, but what good would it do if the birds remained high in the sky and dropped massive stones on them as they were trained to do.

Gundu Ramu echoed her thoughts and said, 'And this is where the knowledge of Acharya Chanakya comes in use. Chanakya had talked about different kinds of fire, and one is vasavashakthi. It causes an explosion. Here is the mixture which I found in ancient books. You need gandhakam, which His Highness arranged from Devaraya's old mansion. I think your father had collected soil and stones from Gauriparvat when he visited it. Then you need yasada, and most importantly, laksha, the resin made by the small red bugs in the forest. The third one is to glue the first two together. If we add kala lavanam to it, it can create fire spontaneously.' Gundu Ramu rambled on, explaining the various technical aspects of vasavashakthi, half of which escaped Sivagami. When he had finished, he waited expectantly for her to say something.

'All this is fine, fire can be prepared in various ways, we can even prepare fire by simply putting hemp cotton and coconut fibre doused in some linseed oil directly under sunlight—it will combust spontaneously. I have seen my father do that. The problem is not creating a fire or an explosion, Ramu, the problem is how to tackle the Garuda pakshis.'

They were walking through the vast palace gardens, past the carpenters sharpening weapons and stitching new armour of iron nails and copper. Sivagami could see an odd contraption in the middle of the garden.

'What is that?' Sivagami asked.

Gundu Ramu smiled. 'Many hundreds of years ago, the king of Magadha, Ajathashathru, had used a mahashila yantra.'

'What?'

Gundu Ramu pulled out a palm leaf from the bunch in his lap. On it was a rough drawing of a curious mechanism.

'It was used to hurl stones to far distances. We can put the fireballs in it and shoot,' Gundu Ramu said. 'I have made some to show you.'

Sivagami's mind was in a whirl. Was there a glimmer of hope?

'Call Mahapradhana Gomati,' she ordered a soldier walking

by with a bundle of lances on his shoulder. He nodded, dropped the lances and ran to fetch the mahapradhana.

Gomati came and so did Mahadeva. Marthanda and a few courtiers, including Roopaka, had followed them, and they now all stood in a semi-circle, making Gundu Ramu nervous. He took a black ball and loaded it onto the mahashila yantra. He lit the ball, which immediately started spewing thick smoke. He then hurried to wind a handle on the contraption. When he released the handle, the fiery ball was hurled a few feet into the sky and it plummeted down in the middle of some onlookers, scattering them like frightened chicken. The ball spun and hissed, danced and bobbed, before exploding with a huge force.

'Bah, nice one to kill our own army,' Marthanda exclaimed. 'We should not be wasting our time with these toys.'

The courtiers sneered at the failed demonstration; Mahadeva patted Gundu Ramu's back and left without a word.

'Fatso, next time instead of the ball load yourself in your blasted yantra,' Marthanda said, and the soldiers roared with laughter. Ramu sat with his head bent, silently crying.

Sivagami put her arms around him and said, 'It is marvellous, Ramu. We will find a way to use it.' Fighting the disappointment she felt, Sivagami walked away, leaving Gundu Ramu in his wheeled chair, sitting with his head bent in shame.

---

A few weeks later, the Mahishmathi sabha met once again. By this time, the fort was filled with refugees.

## Queen of Mahishmathi

Mahapradhana Gomati said, 'We have a problem. We do not have sufficient stock of grains. We need to feed the people. There have been riots over food on the streets.'

'That is what happens when you allow the dregs of society inside the fort,' a courtier said, and many heads nodded in agreement.

'Lepers, untouchables, low castes ... some of them tried to storm into the temple and pollute the prasad.'

'Hungry people will do that.'

'Is their hunger more important than the purity of God?'

'This country went to the dogs the day Skandadasa became mahapradhana.'

'We need to throw everyone out of the fort.'

The pandemonium inside the sabha was unbearable to Sivagami. 'Why are you allowing everyone to speak,' she hissed to Mahadeva.

'A king has to hear everyone's side and then take a decision,' he whispered back. Sivagami shook her head in annoyance. The way Mahadeva ruled exasperated her.

Mahadeva waited patiently for everyone to vent their anger and then said in a calm voice, 'Mahishmathi belongs to everyone.'

An uneasy calm descended on the sabha. The king had spoken, and tradition demanded that the courtiers remain silent. The alternative was to challenge the king to a duel or raise the flag of rebellion. But considering Mahadeva's popularity with the public, no one dared attempt such a thing. Once again, Mahadeva had prevailed without raising his voice, without threatening violence.

'If food is scarce, all of us will eat only once. I vow to have only one meal a day. And that applies to our God too. The temple will have only one puja.'

There was an uproar in the sabha, and Mahadeva waited for the furore to die down before he said in a composed voice, 'First the people, then God.'

The king had said the unthinkable, and before the shock had subsided, Sivagami said, 'We need to discuss our defences. We are facing a two-pronged attack. We do not have enough provisions to withstand a siege by Kadarimandalam, and we have no way to prevent the attack from the Kalakeyas.'

'No one can breach the fort, Devi,' Marthanda said.

'Not even Garuda pakshis?' Sivagami said scornfully. The courtiers shifted in their chairs.

Sivagami continued. 'Our first priority is to negotiate peace with Kadarimandalam. The Kalakeyas are the common enemy and maybe we can form a joint front against them.'

'We have nothing to offer Kadarimandalam,' Mahadeva said.

'We have Pattaraya,' Sivagami said. 'I had insisted that we not execute him with such a situation in mind. Hoist him above the fort gate on a pole. Let the queen of Kadarimandalam see the plight of her husband. We will start the negotiation from a position of strength.'

There was scattered applause and the sabha began discussing her suggestion.

Later in her chamber, Sivagami asked Gomati, 'Do we have any trace of Mekhala?'

Gomati said, 'Nothing at all. Maybe she drowned in the flood. But why are we bothered about her? No one even remembers her anymore.'

'Pattaraya is one among many men in Queen Chitraveni's life. He may not be such a strong bargaining tool, for she may not even care about his life. But a daughter would be a different matter,' Sivagami said, glancing at her sleeping son.

For some reason, Gundu Ramu's defeated face came to her mind and the seed of an idea germinated in Sivagami's head. When she laid out her plan to Gomati, the mahapradhana shook her head in dismay, 'It looks so desperate.'

'Do you have anything better in mind?' Sivagami asked, and Gomati had no answer. Sivagami yelled for the guard, and when he came, she said, 'Fetch Gundu Ramu and Kattappa.'

The two loyal servants soon appeared and Sivagami shared her plan with them. 'The future of Mahishmathi depends on you,' she said at the end.

They did not reply, for the enormity of the task weighed heavily on their shoulders.

As per her earlier plan, Pattaraya was dragged from the dungeon and hoisted on a pole above the fort. But that was just a decoy. Gundu Ramu and Kattappa began working on something in the centre of the palace garden. A new mandap was rising up in full view. Away from the eyes of the people, sculptors began making fifteen wooden elephants.

---

Ten days later, the bell in the fort tower rang frantically, waking up Sivagami. Startled, her son began crying in his cradle. Sivagami could hear steps hurrying towards her room. A moment later, Mahadeva came in, along with his ministers.

'Ships ... ships of Kadarimandalam. A massive fleet is arriving. What should we do?' Mahadeva's voice was boyishly high.

She could feel the panic in the room. Everyone was looking at her expectantly.

Sivagami turned towards Mahadeva and said, 'Surrender.'

Mahadeva looked at her incredulously. 'Surrender?' he repeated.

Sivagami picked up her crying baby and patted his back. She smiled at Mahadeva and said, 'We shall not just surrender, we will pay tribute to the queen of Kadarimandalam. A tribute of fifteen elephants decked in gold, pearls and diamonds.'

# FIFTY-FOUR

# Ally

THE MIGHTY ARMY led by Achi Nagamma had overrun Guha land and was camping in the grounds where the Kali statue used to be made. Ally joined them after completing her mission in Kadarimandalam. She ran into the open arms of Achi and sobbed on her shoulder.

'They caught Anna,' Ally said, and Achi was silent for a moment.

'It doesn't matter,' Achi said finally, wiping Ally's tears.

'What do you mean it doesn't matter? They must have killed—'

'Don't worry. Sooner or later, everyone has to go. Tell me what you did there.'

Achi sat on a rock, her long staff resting on her shoulder, her eyes closed, as Ally narrated what had happened.

'When are we moving towards Mahishmathi?' Ally asked finally.

'Give Jeemotha time to repair the ships. I needed to delay them only until I brought my army to Mahishmathi. I want both the kingdoms face to face in the battlefield. Then I can destroy them both, together,' Achi said and smiled. Ally looked around at Achi's army. Two Kalakeyas were duelling with their stone clubs while the rest cheered them on. As Ally watched, one of the duellers clubbed his opponent to death. He stomped on the slain man's chest, thumped his own, and gave a wolf-like howl, while his tribesmen roared. The Vaithalikas squatted at a distance, eyeing their allies with fear and disgust.

Just then a group of Kalakeyas approached the camp dragging an elephant carcass behind them, and the entire clan ran to them with wild cries and hoots. The tribe fell on the carcass like a pack of wolves, hacking it into many pieces with their stone axes and stuffing their mouths with meat.

Ally heard a cackle and turned to see the dwarf Hidumba. He was chained to a peg, like a pig. Hidumba sneered at her. 'They are going to cook you one day, girl, and eat you. And this old hag—they will eat her alive.'

'Why have you not killed that hideous creature?' Ally asked Achi in disgust.

'Oh, he is an important official of Mahishmathi.'

'Khanipathi,' Hidumba cried, rattling his chain. 'Free me, you witch.'

'Patience, boy. Patience,' Achi said with a smile.

---

A fortnight later, one of the spies came back with news of the Kadarimandalam navy laying siege to the Mahishmathi fort.

Achi ordered that they march quickly towards Mahishmathi. But the wild Kalakeyas obeyed no command. They had a will of their own. They left a trail of destruction, scorching all the villages en route. Something struck Ally as odd as they passed hamlet after hamlet. Where had all the inhabitants gone?

'It shows Mahishmathi knows about our advancing army and has pulled everyone into the fort. It also limits their options. They will not be able to withstand a long-drawn siege; they're sure to run out of provisions soon,' Achi Nagamma said.

'Sivagami and Mahadeva have regained power. They will keep their promise never to mine Gauriparvat,' Ally said. 'I know Sivagami. She will keep her word.'

'You have told me that countless times. She may have become your friend, but she is still the enemy of our people. How does it matter who sits on the throne of Mahishmathi? Mahadeva might be a good man and Sivagami can be expected to keep her word, but what guarantee is there that the next generation will do so? The centralisation of power has destroyed humanity. It is better to return to a simpler life. Look at the Vaithalikas—they worship nature and live without causing any harm. They have no palaces, no commerce, no wealth. Compare it with the damage caused by Mahishmathi or Kadarimandalam.'

Ally looked at the massive Kalakeya army and thought that perhaps the tribal life was not ideal either. What if the world was filled with savages like the Kalakeyas? Didn't people progress from those tribes to build empires like Mahishmathi and Kadarimandalam? What good would it do to go back to being barbarians again?

As if reading her thoughts, Achi Nagamma said, 'They are just our weapons. They will go away once they get their book.

They lived for thousands of years without disturbing anyone until their holy book was stolen.'

'What if they don't get the book?' Ally asked. 'Won't they turn against us?'

'Then we would have to keep them under control,' Achi said in an irritated voice.

'You mean by force? How different would that be from what Mahishmathi and Kadarimandalam are doing? We would just be replacing the present regime with our own.'

'Don't question me, girl,' Achi Nagamma snapped. 'I know what I am doing. We are not going there for power; we are unleashing the Kalakeyas on the so-called civilisation. They will pulverise Mahishmathi while my Garuda pakshis and I take care of the Kadarimandalam navy. My intention is to destroy, not create. Now, no more questions.'

Ally remained quiet, but a premonition that nothing was going to go as per their plan gnawed at her. She didn't know whether she was more afraid of the five Garuda pakshis that Achi Nagamma had tamed or the untamed Kalakeyas. At least the Garuda pakshis remained out of sight. Achi Nagamma could beckon them with her peculiar whistle and she could control them. The Kalakeyas were a different matter altogether. The unruly tribe obeyed no orders, cared for no rules, and picked fights with each other or anyone else at the slightest provocation.

A few days later, Ally felt compelled to bring up the subject again. 'Our people are scared of the Kalakeyas,' she said to Achi.

'All of them are your people, whether they are Vaithalika or Kalakeya.'

'They hunt every game. They kill indiscriminately and often feast on the poor hunted animal before it is even dead. They have scourged the jungle. And you want to protect Mother Earth with their help?'

'It is the law of nature, daughter. The tiger hunts the deer, the mongoose hunts the snake, the snake hunts the bird, the bird hunts the worm and the worm eats the leaves—'

'No tiger empties a jungle in a day. Look at those lying dead, with their heads smashed in by their own brethren. They are fighting for the hide of a bison they hunted and we have been stuck here since morning.'

'It is their currency. They neither care for gold nor any modern luxuries. All they need is the hide of animals that they either wear or make into weapons. The more they have, the happier they are.'

'Not so much different from the people in Mahishmathi or Kadarimandalam.'

Achi Nagamma sighed. 'I can understand your fear. But what choice do we have? Rebellion after rebellion has failed to stop Mahishmathi or Kadarimandalam. A modern kingdom is very powerful. With farmlands feeding lakhs of people, they can afford to have big armies, bureaucrats who can manage their revenues and merchants' trading ships. The complications of a modern kingdom are mind-boggling, and the more complex the cities, the more trouble they create for Mother Earth. The kingdom is a kleptocracy, where a few steal from everyone else as taxes, as trade. A few live in luxury, offering protection to the common people. Our intention is to show that the modern state is incapable of protecting its people from anything. Using the Kalakeya army is my final throw of dice. The sack of Mahishmathi and the destruction of Kadarimandalam will send shivers through the various kingdoms across the world. Barbarians overrunning an established empire, ah, what could be a better argument against civilisation?'

As if in agreement, the Garuda pakshis screeched from above and the Kalakeyas paused their fighting for a moment. Then they roared in unison and Achi Nagamma laughed aloud. 'Look at them, girl. Do you think Mahishmathi will last a day? Take them and crush Mahishmathi while I and my children finish off Kadarimandalam.'

Ally had once fought shoulder to shoulder with Sivagami and knew her old friend would never give up so easily. It was going to be a clash of wills between her and Sivagami. She had Achi, the Garuda pakshis and the Kalakeyas, and Sivagami had Kattappa. Ally was not sure who would prevail. And then, there would be the wily Chitraveni, and of course the wild card—Jeemotha. 'Amma Gauri, let my side, the righteous side, win,' Ally prayed. But when she looked at the army she was leading to Mahishmathi, she was not sure of her own righteousness.

## FIFTY-FIVE

# Sivagami

IN THE SUNSHINE, the fifteen elephants sparkled with all the riches from Mahishmathi's treasury. From behind the central elephant, which was almost ten feet high, Gundu Ramu hurried towards Sivagami, pushing his ornate chair with his hands. He grinned at Sivagami. 'Don't they look alive?' Sivagami nodded with satisfaction. It was a perfect work of art.

Gomati said, 'We should put some hay and palm leaves before them to make them appear more natural.' Sivagami nodded and walked around the elephants.

Then she frowned and said, 'Ramu, these elephants are too still. To look natural, they should be flapping their ears.'

Gundu Ramu bit his tongue and said with a sheepish grin, 'I will get it arranged.'

'Hurry up, Ramu, we are going to invite the queen of Kadarimandalam soon, and these elephants need to look as real as possible.'

'The diamonds in their caparisons are real, the pearls hanging from the umbrellas are real, the cloth that covers them is inlaid with gold,' Gomati said.

'Don't underestimate Chitraveni,' Sivagami said, as they hurried to the next important part of the arrangement. Kattappa was putting the final touches on the mandap.

'So this is where you and the king will kneel before Queen Chitraveni?' Gomati asked.

A place was marked for the throne where the queen of Kadarimandalam would be sitting, and two places were marked for Sivagami and Mahadeva to kneel before her. Sivagami saw that her position was marked with the carving of two coiled cobras. Gomati stepped to the place marked for Mahadeva. They made Kattappa stand where Queen Chitraveni would be during the surrender ceremony. Sivagami knelt and slammed the hood of the carved cobra with her palm. A trapdoor opened taking Gomati and Sivagami down. They fell on a bed of cotton and the trapdoor slammed shut above them.

Gomati laughed. 'It is perfect.' Kattappa opened the latch and reached down to help them out.

Sivagami went through their plan once again. 'The king and I will fall into the safe box like we just did. And then the elephants will explode, hopefully killing Queen Chitraveni and all her nobles,' she said, as she finished going over all the details.

Gomati asked, 'How will you time the explosion?'

Sivagami pointed to the balcony of her palace wing. 'Gundu Ramu will be positioned there with a fire arrow. When he sees us kneeling, he will shoot it. None of the Kadarimandalam royals will be spared.'

Gomati exclaimed, 'If we succeed, this will be talked about for many centuries to come. It is so brilliantly evil.'

Sivagami smiled. 'Don't tell Mahadeva. He detests evil.'

Later, when Sivagami managed to get Mahadeva to put his royal seal on the terms of surrender, he said, 'I don't know what you are planning, but I believe deception will only beget more deception. Are we ready to face it?'

Sivagami looked Mahadeva in his eyes and said, 'That is war.' Mahadeva shook his head, troubled. The bedecked elephants were included in the terms of surrender. Sivagami was sure the merchant guilds of Kadarimandalam would not resist the temptation of so many riches. Sivagami had also sweetened the deal by writing an abject letter of apology, saying they had erred and would accept any punishment Chitraveni deemed fit. They would even free Pattaraya. As Sivagami had suspected, the gambit of using Pattaraya to stall Chitraveni had not worked. The queen of Kadarimandalam had merely sent a rope as a gift to hang Pattaraya with. They should have got the queen's daughter and they might have had a chance, Sivagami thought as they walked towards the fort gate to deliver the message to Chitraveni's envoy.

Gomati said, 'I am excited, Sivagami. Good always wins over evil. We will win this war.'

Sivagami smiled. 'Provided we are on the side of good. And you are forgetting that there is another player in this game. Achi Nagamma and the combined army of the Kalakeyas and Vaithalikas. We have nothing to defend ourselves from the Garuda pakshis. Not yet.'

They reached the fort gate and the gatekeeper opened the small door to let them outside.

The Kadarimandalam envoy was standing there, fanning herself. It was Keki and Sivagami winced at the sight of her. The gatekeeper announced Sivagami devi's arrival.

From above their heads, Pattaraya cackled. 'Ah, the daughter of a whore and a traitor is now negotiating treaties with queens. You will soon hang from here, bitch.'

Sivagami ignored him and stood with a confidence that belied the flutter she felt in her guts. Keki walked towards her with a swagger and said in a mocking voice, 'Have you come to surrender? Where is Mahadeva?'

Suppressing her rising anger, Sivagami said, 'Eunuch, give this message to your queen. We are inviting her into the fort, and in the presence of the people of Mahishmathi, we shall surrender. Our only demand is that, except for Mahadeva and me, no one else should be punished.'

Keki smiled. 'My master, Bijjala, will decide that. Every traitor should hang.'

Sivagami's voice grew stern. 'Your job is to pass on my message, eunuch. Either she can accept our offer, or we can fight. We may lose, but we will cause maximum damage to you all. Tell her my message is that this is the only way to avoid an unnecessary loss of life. And we shall pay tribute to her if she accepts our terms. Here are all the riches of Mahishmathi.'

Sivagami welcomed Keki to have a peek at the caparisoned elephants standing at a distance in the palace gardens, gently swaying their ears and trunks. They were out of Pattaraya's line of sight. Keki's eyes widened in awe as she saw the gold, pearls and diamonds glittering in the sun. Her eyes scanned the elephants greedily and then went to the mandap which was almost complete.

Keki smiled. 'Good that you have come to your senses. Fifteen elephants bedecked in diamonds and gold. But you think you can bribe the queen of Kadarimandalam with this pittance?'

'Convey our offer to your queen,' Sivagami said abruptly. She had seen the greed in the eunuch's eyes.

From above, Pattaraya wriggled in his chains and yelled, 'What did you say, eunuch? Fifteen elephants? It is a trap.'

Sivagami felt like rushing to the top of the fort and chopping Pattaraya into many pieces.

But Keki only rolled her eyes. 'Pattaraya, die. Enough of your advice. See where your great cunning has taken you.' Then she walked to the boat that would take her to Chitraveni's ship.

Pattaraya continued to yell at the top of his voice, as Sivagami and Gomati returned and the fort gate slammed shut. Sivagami prayed that Keki would ignore Pattaraya's warning as unimportant babbling. Otherwise, all their elaborate planning would be in vain.

FIFTY-SIX

# Jeemotha

UNDER THE SHADE of sails that fluttered in the brisk breeze, Keki conveyed Sivagami's message to the queen of Kadarimandalam. Chitraveni sat haughtily on the throne placed on the deck of the ship, listening to the eunuch. At her feet sat the erstwhile ruler of Kadarimandalam, Narasimha Varman, squatting in chains. The queen was resting a foot on his shoulder.

The eunuch talked excitedly about the tribute Mahishmathi was offering as a part of the peace treaty, and the merchant nobles of Kadarimandalam crowded around to hear her describing the riches with a gleam in their eyes. As an afterthought, Keki said, 'Poor Pattaraya is hung like a rag from a pole, to dry in the sun. He was screaming that the entire set-up is a trap.'

Jeemotha looked at Chitraveni and said, 'What do you think of the eunuch's message, my queen?'

No one replied. Jeemotha's nostrils flared and his lips

curved in a derisive smile. 'Smart!' he said. 'That woman is smart. But they are underestimating me, the great Jeemotha.'

'Stop boasting and come to the point, pirate,' Chitraveni snapped.

'Can't you smell it? They have managed to create some sort of incendiary weapon. In many wars across the world, especially in those where the yellow barbarians beyond the snow hills rule, they use such weapons. The Yavanas used gandhakam and the resin of a tree that grows in their snowy hills, and I have heard sages of our own land talking about such weapons of the past. They were called agnibanas or vasavashakthis, but that technology is lost.'

'Why are you wasting our time talking such nonsense?' Bijjala snapped. 'Let us go now. I want to see Mahadeva grovel at my feet, and this time I will blind him permanently.'

Chitraveni snapped her fingers and Bijjala fell silent. She gestured for Jeemotha to continue.

Jeemotha said, 'I can smell gandhakam in the wind, my queen. Pattaraya may be right. We should not go inside the palace or the fort. This is a trap.'

Keki couldn't control herself. 'But I saw the elephants, and we will be marching in with thousands of soldiers. They don't have as many men, and they certainly can't withstand the fighting skills of Kadarimandalam's soldiers.'

Jeemotha turned to Keki and asked, 'Did you actually see those elephants meant for the tribute?'

'Yes, that is what I described, pirate.'

Jeemotha slapped Keki hard across her face with the back of his hand. 'You will address me as sarva nayaka or swami, not "pirate".'

'You hit me! You hit a eunuch! You will rot in hell. You will—' Jeemotha hit Keki again, this time with his other hand; the eunuch reeled back on her heels and squatted on the deck, holding both her cheeks. She started sobbing and the shrill laughter of Narasimha Varman filled the air.

'Silence!' Chitraveni kicked her slave, her brother, and snapped at Keki. 'Answer him.'

Choking down tears of rage and shame, Keki said, 'I know elephants when I see them. There were fifteen of them.'

'Aha, she knows how to count,' Narasimha Varman said, and got the blunt end of a spear slammed into his ribs as a reward.

Jeemotha leaned down to meet Keki's eyes and asked, 'But were they alive?'

'Were they alive? I don't think dead elephants would be flapping their ears and eating palm leaves,' she said.

Jeemotha asked, 'Are you sure?'

Keki cried, 'What do you want me to say? They were decked with diamonds—' Keki froze and her eyes widened in realisation. 'All the ears were flapping together.'

Jeemotha laughed aloud. 'That proves it, they are contraptions filled with some sort of incendiary mixture. They are going to light it somehow when the surrender ceremony is happening.'

'Boom,' Narasimha Varman added helpfully, and looked up at Chitraveni to receive his punishment. She did not give him the satisfaction.

Bijjala scowled. 'What nonsense. Mahadeva and Sivagami have to be present when they surrender, and if they are planning something stupid like this, they would be the first to get killed.'

Jeemotha smiled. 'Eunuch, did you see anything else?'

Keki nodded. 'I saw them making a new mandap.'

'Undoubtedly, it will contain something that will help them escape,' Jeemotha said. He threw his arms up in the air and bowed, like a virtuoso seeking applause after a scintillating performance.

Chitraveni said in a grave voice, 'Eunuch, go back and give this message to those fools. We will accept their surrender but the ceremony should happen here, on our ships. And she can keep her elephants.' There were angry murmurs, but the queen had spoken and no one dared say anything.

The nobles began dispersing, clearly unhappy. Jeemotha moved up to Chitraveni and whispered, 'My queen, when they are surrendering, you should not be here on this ship.'

Chitraveni's eyes flashed. 'What do you mean? I am the sovereign of Kadarimandalam and Mahishmathi. People have to see Sivagami and Mahadeva bow before me.'

Jeemotha said, 'Trust me, my queen. Didn't I figure out their plan? Sivagami is not one to give up easily. They will plan something to take us down when they come here. We have to be ready with our own deception.'

Chitraveni stared at him. 'What do you propose, pirate?'

'Sivagami will try some nasty trick or another to assassinate you. It is my duty to warn you. You should be in a ship as far away as possible from this one, along with all your nobles. Dress this buffoon in a saree and make him sit on the throne instead of you,' Jeemotha said, pointing to Narasimha Varman. 'Let this dog be of some use.'

'No, no, no,' Narasimha Varman cried, horrified. 'I am a dog, I want no throne, I fancy no crown.'

Chitraveni was silent for some time and then, without a word, she walked away, dragging Narasimha Varman behind her. Jeemotha knew she would follow exactly what he had suggested. Now he had to wait for Sivagami.

## FIFTY-SEVEN

# Ally

ALLY AND ACHI NAGAMMA crouched behind the bushes across the river and studied the city of Mahishmathi. Docked in the river were many ships, and the sight of hundreds of multi-coloured sails fluttering in the wind was one to behold. The Kadarimandalam flag was hoisted on them, and their massive catapults were trained towards the fort. The fort gate was shut, and soldiers had taken their positions. The Mahishmathi flag flew proudly over the palace.

'It is a siege,' Ally said.

'Perfect.' Achi rubbed her hands in glee. 'Now, tell me, how are you going to storm the fort?'

'Storm the Mahishmathi fort designed by Devaraya? Do you want me to die?'

'Think.'

Ally could not figure out what Achi was implying. The fort was impossible to breach, otherwise Kadarimandalam would have attacked by now. Once, under the leadership of Thimma, the Vaithalikas had ingeniously breached the fort using deceit. Pattaraya had done it once by smuggling in soldiers with the help of Guru Dharmapala. But no one had ever taken the fort in a frontal attack.

'You will be my age by the time you figure it out, I think,' Achi said.

'Amma, will you keep quiet? Let me think,' Ally said, and Achi chuckled. Ally scanned the fort walls. The water level had receded, but it had left muddy marks on the dark granite wall which was at least twelve feet higher than the water level.

'The flood,' Ally said hopefully, and Achi nodded with a smile. Encouraged, Ally continued. 'The flood saved Sivagami. How did the water enter the fort?'

'Yes, how did it enter?' Achi asked, toying with Ally.

'The river entered because someone invited it in,' Ally said, her eyes shining.

'You are not as dumb as I thought,' Achi said with a smile.

'There has to be some underground path by which they flooded the city. But the river is now following its original course. It has been almost a year, so they would have closed that path.'

Achi said, 'They would have, for they are not fools, but the river would have breached many channels through the underground path, and they would have had neither the time nor the expertise to close them all. The fort was meant to be abandoned once they used the river to destroy it. Remember that Devaraya designed it as an emergency system if the fall of the city was imminent. Devaraya, being the genius that he was, would have never agreed to use the fort again. If the enemy could repair it and use it, then the very purpose of destroying it is lost. In short, my girl, the fort is not as impregnable as it used to be,' Achi said.

'How will we find a breach?' Ally asked.

'Look at where the flood mark is the highest and where it is the lowest. Think,' Achi said.

Ally looked at the ships and said, 'The reason why they have not abandoned the fort is because they were expecting the Kadarimandalam navy to rush in and try to regain the colony. The time spent repairing the ships gave them some time, and they would have fortified the riverside.'

Achi said, 'Let's try and look at it from another side. How do you think Sivagami expects us to attack?'

'She would expect us to come from Gauriparvat's side, and that we will attack her using our best resources—the Garuda pakshis. She would think it unnecessary to fortify the other sides of the fort when the attack is coming from the sky,' Ally said.

'Good,' Achi Nagamma said, nodding.

'Then here is what we should do. We will march upstream and cross the river to reach beyond the lepers' colony, which lies beyond the fort. They have brought everyone into the fort and we will not be spotted. We can look for the breaches where the river flowed during the coup.'

'Look out for newly repaired portions in the rear,' Achi added.

'We will dig a tunnel and enter the fort. But won't guards see us?'

Achi said, 'Wait for them to be fully involved in their fight with Kadarimandalam. When their attention is focused there, I will put up a bloody show with my children. When they see

Garuda pakshis in the sky, they will expect the entire Kalakeya army to attack from where the Garuda pakshis are. That will be your signal. You will sneak in from the rear with your fantastic friends, the Kalakeyas. Show no mercy and butcher everyone inside, whoever dares to try and stop you. Sivagami might have been your friend—'

'No one is my friend. I live for my mission,' Ally said, drawing herself up to her full height.

'And you might find people you still love there,' Achi continued, and Ally turned away.

She muttered, 'The murderer of my child.'

'When you see him, remember that and remember only that.' Ally was silent and Achi let her remain in her thoughts for a few minutes. Then, she put an arm around Ally and whispered in her ear, 'Once you have taken the fort, destroy everything while I unleash the Garuda pakshis on the Kadarimandalam ships. I sink Kadarimandalam, and you, girl, you torch Mahishmathi. This is a war we have been preparing for, for years. This is the people's war. Total revolution.'

FIFTY-EIGHT

# Sivagami

'LET US STOP these games, Sivagami. We will fight like warriors and win or die like warriors. Let us not waste time on such tactics,' Mahadeva said.

The inner council of Mahishmathi was assembled in Sivagami's chamber. They had received the message that Chitraveni wanted the surrender ceremony to take place on their ships, and Mahadeva sounded as if he were relieved that their plan had not worked.

Sivagami gazed out of the window. In the evening light, the fifteen decorated elephants, with enough power to destroy empires in their belly, stood glimmering. They looked as if they were mocking her. She felt like tearing her hair and screaming. All the careful planning, the faultless arrangements, all had been in vain. The bards would sing of her folly, even after hundreds of years, to amuse people.

Kattappa, who was standing in a corner of the room, stepped forward. He suggested a strategy, in a low voice, as if scared to give an opinion in front of the king and other nobles. Sivagami's eyes sparkled when she heard what he had to say. Even if it did not work, they would have tried their best in a desperate situation.

When they reached the ground where the elephants stood, they found Gundu Ramu fretting over a row of black balls lined up against the wall. When he saw Sivagami and the king, he started trembling, as if guilty of something.

'What happened, Ramu?' Sivagami asked, kneeling before him.

Ramu turned his face away and said, 'There is something wrong.'

A knot formed in Sivagami's belly. What could have gone wrong now?

Ramu said, 'Some of the kaala churna is missing.'

'Missing?' Sivagami asked.

Gundu Ramu pointed towards the balls made of the black paste. He started counting them, and when he reached forty-two, he started from the beginning again.

Sivagami lost patience. 'Enough, Ramu. We need your help.'

Ramu continued as if he hadn't heard her. 'One of the balls is missing, Akka. I clearly remember having made forty-three and the heap of powder I have can be used for another seven. Where has one ball gone?'

Sivagami took a deep breath and patted his arm. 'Gundu Ramu, you have done well, but these elephants won't be of any use. They are not coming here. And all these balls of fire aren't of any use without a proper catapult.' Ramu had constructed two more mahashila yantras, but neither could shoot more than a few feet. In any case, Sivagami thought, if they couldn't figure out a method to defeat Kadarimandalam, the Garuda pakshis would be Kadarimandalam's problem, not theirs.

Gundu Ramu's lips trembled and his shoulders slumped. 'I am sorry for letting you down.'

Sivagami's heart went out to him. She patted his back and said, 'Don't worry, Ramu. Kattappa has come up with a brilliant idea. I don't know whether it will work, but that is our only hope. You have to help him.'

Sivagami left Kattappa with Gundu Ramu to make arrangements for their last desperate attempt to save Mahishmathi.

---

As the sun began to set, Sivagami patiently waited before the closed chamber of Mahadeva. She could hear Akhila's sobs. She could hear her pleading with him not to go. Then the door opened and Mahadeva came out.

Akhila rushed to Sivagami and hugged her. 'Please Akka, bring him back alive,' she cried.

Sivagami said in a confident voice that belied the fear she was feeling, 'This is a war we are fighting to win.'

As Mahadeva and Sivagami marched towards the fort gate to surrender to Kadarimandalam, the people of Mahishmathi gathered to watch them with tears in their eyes. They had enjoyed almost a year of independence, but now, their country was once again going to be enslaved. Soldiers marched solemnly behind Sivagami and Mahadeva.

They reached the riverside where Kattappa was waiting in his boat. Clouds that were a deep red, as if soaked in blood, drifted by above them. There was an uneasy silence, a grave solemnity to the occasion. Sivagami and Mahadeva stepped into the boat. Kattappa handed over the torch he was holding to Sivagami, whispering to her to hold it away from the boat. She looked at the dark powder that filled the boat and shuddered. A spark from her torch would annihilate them all. On the shores of the river, on Mahishmathi's side, their army and people stood with bated breath, watching their dream of freedom collapse.

Kattappa rowed the boat towards the massive lead ship of Kadarimandalam. Sivagami prayed the breeze would not change direction and carry the astringent smell of kala lavanam, triggering the enemy's suspicions.

Since Chitraveni was not coming to the fort where they had laid out a trap, Sivagami was taking the trap to Chitraveni. Kattappa's plan was elegant in its simplicity. Mahadeva and Sivagami would climb the ship and reach the deck where Chitraveni would be waiting for them for the ceremony of surrender. Sivagami had hidden her urumi in her waistband, and so had Mahadeva.

When they knelt before the queen, they would whip it out and attack her, and at the same time, Kattappa would slam the boat on the hull of the ship and light the incendiary powder. Hopefully, it would make a hole big enough in the hull of the ship to capsize it.

After assassinating the queen, Sivagami and Mahadeva would jump into the river and swim back, away from the sinking ship. If they were able to reach the shore and enter the fort, their fortunes would have changed forever. The leaderless Kadarimandalam would be more malleable to a truce. The merchant guilds would not want war, and they could perhaps pay off the Kadarimandalam army. Then they could concentrate on a plan to tackle Achi Nagamma when she arrived.

On the deck of the ship, Sivagami could see Chitraveni sitting on her throne. She looked majestic against the backdrop of the setting sun. When they had passed a quarter of the river's breadth, Sivagami looked at the Kadarimandalam fleet that lay at a distance from the lead ship.

'Mahadeva, why are all those ships so far away?' Sivagami asked, but Mahadeva was sitting with his eyes closed, in meditation.

Something was not right. This was their last roll of the dice, and she didn't want to think that Kadarimandalam had outplayed them again. Had they guessed what she had planned?

The answer came the moment their boat reached the ship. Sivagami heard Kattappa cry, 'Maharaja Mahadeva has arrived,' and the next moment she was drenched in cold water.

A moment later, Jeemotha's grinning face appeared on the upper deck. He called out, 'One more,' and his soldiers toppled another vessel of water from the ship into the boat.

'It is good to take a bath before any auspicious thing. Welcome to our ship,' Jeemotha said and vanished.

Sivagami and Mahadeva looked at each other. Once again they had been outplayed. The kala lavanam, the incendiary paste, was as good as river mud now. The blasted pirate had neutralised their last plan.

A rope ladder rolled down from the deck and Jeemotha beckoned them to come up. 'Leave the torch with that slave. We have enough light here,' Jeemotha yelled.

Mahadeva said to her, 'I am going to kill that woman. You need not come Sivagami, I will take her down and then you fight and win freedom for Mahishmathi.' He started climbing up the ladder.

Sivagami knew they were walking into a trap. Ignoring Mahadeva's orders, she followed him to the deck of the ship, leaving Kattappa alone in the boat, holding the flaming torch in his hand.

FIFTY-NINE

# Pattaraya

PATTARAYA LAUGHED UNCONTROLLABLY from his position above the fort wall. From his vantage point, he had enjoyed watching the war games being played by either side. It hadn't surprised him that Chitraveni had not even bothered to try and save him. He had never expected any love or compassion from the woman he had chosen as his wife.

What had been worrying him until a few days ago was the whereabouts of Mekhala, but he had caught a glimpse of her a few days back on the roof of the palace. Roopaka had taken her there to show her the plight of her father. That brief glimpse of his daughter had brought him immense relief. All was not lost.

Even before Sivagami had left to board her boat filled with kala lavanam, Pattaraya had seen Chitraveni leaving the lead ship dressed as a common soldier. Her gait and carriage were unmistakable. At that moment he knew that his fate was not to die on this pole. The game had turned again.

He wanted to scream to a long-dead man who had been his master once and would be his foe always—'Somadeva, this is a game that I am playing to win. I told you, I came with nothing but I will die a king.'

Pattaraya yelled in joy when he saw Jeemotha drenching Sivagami and Mahadeva before they were brought up onto the ship. That chit of a woman thinks she is smart, but she has not seen how a real game is played, he thought.

Suddenly, an arrow struck the pole he was tied to and its feathered tail vibrated an inch away from his face. Pattaraya turned to see Roopaka and Mekhala at the far end of the fort wall. Mekhala was carrying a dark ball in one hand, and a sword in the other. The soldiers at the wall were busy watching the surrender ceremony that was unfolding on the river, oblivious to the intruders. Mekhala and Roopaka began running towards Pattaraya, slaying the surprised soldiers in their way. After the initial shock, the soldiers raised an alarm. Dozens of men ran towards Pattaraya's daughter as she stood still, waiting for them. What was she doing? 'Run, daughter, run!' Pattaraya screamed. He could see more soldiers were arriving with an officer. Mekhala continued to stand there calmly. As the soldiers approached, she grabbed a torch fixed on the wall and rolled the ball in her hand towards Pattaraya. It bounced past the running soldiers, who leapt out of its way as it continued rolling. Mekhala flung the flaming torch in the air. Time seemed to slow down. The torch flew over the soldiers' heads and hit the rolling ball. With a whooshing sound, it caught fire and began spewing dark smoke. Sputtering and spinning, it hit the pole Pattaraya was tied to with a dull thud. A fraction of a moment's silence was followed by a deafening explosion. The pole broke and Pattaraya fell to the ground. A bolt of pain shot through his shoulders and he was blinded for a moment. He was still bound to the pole. The first of the soldiers who recovered from the shock of the explosion rushed to Pattaraya. Leveraging the pole, Pattaraya swung it at his pursuers, toppling them over the fort wall. Mekhala and Roopaka reached him and cut off his chains. Pattaraya embraced his daughter.

Before more soldiers could band together to apprehend them, Pattaraya and his daughter took off, with Roopaka following behind. Gundu Ramu's missing ball of fire had found its use.

SIXTY

# Sivagami

MAHADEVA RUSHED TOWARDS Jeemotha, his sword drawn, but Bijjala moved between them. 'Finally, you have come to die at my hands,' Bijjala said.

Hundreds of archers stood with their arrows pointed at Sivagami and Mahadeva, as Jeemotha crossed his arms over his chest, with an infuriating smile on his lips, and a twinkle of mischief in his eyes. At the far end of the deck, on the ivory throne of Kadarimandalam, Narasimha Varman sat looking as ridiculous as possible in Chitraveni's saree. He scratched his beard and grinned like a monkey.

Sivagami did know what to do. All the elaborate planning had ended up as a farce, a comedy, making her and Mahadeva look like idiots. If their lives and the destiny of Mahishmathi hadn't been at stake, she could have burst out laughing at the absurdity of her situation. Amma Gauri is a prankster, she thought.

Bijjala raised his arm and commanded the archers, 'Put your bows down, I have a score to settle. Brother to brother, prince to prince. Nanna, Somadeva, you gave the title of vikramadeva to a fool. Now watch this from whichever hell you are rotting in. Last time, I sewed his eyelids together, this time I will blind him forever. I will chop his limbs one by one. Watch me do it.' Bijjala shook his sword and advanced towards Mahadeva.

As soon as Bijjala launched his attack, the two brothers were engaged in a grim battle. Like game roosters, like bulls in an arena, like bull elephants in musth, they fought on the deck. Their swords sliced open barrels of water, cut the ropes of sails, splintered poles. The women warriors of Kadarimandalam cheered and flung expletives at the fighting brothers. Mahadeva surprised Bijjala with his vigour and nimbleness. 'Oh, it seems that your lover Sivagami has taught you some tricks. But it's not good enough to match me, Mahadeva,' Bijjala said mockingly.

Sivagami knew it was a fight that Mahadeva was bound to lose, for the moment he got the better of Bijjala, the archers of Chitraveni would finish him and her. They were just toying with them, having fun like a cat playing with a mouse for a while before delivering the fatal blow with its paw.

Jeemotha came up to her and stood by her side, his eyes fixed on the two princes fighting. He said softly, 'Whom do you want to win?' A wave of revulsion and anger washed over her. Just then Mahadeva's urumi cut Bijjala's shoulder and drew blood. With a roar, Bijjala kicked a barrel that was lying on the deck. Sivagami screamed as it spun towards Mahadeva, but he deftly caught it with the urumi and flung it back at Bijjala.

Bijjala moved away, and the barrel crashed and bounced till it hit Narasimha Varman on the far side, drawing laughter from the soldiers. From the corner of her eye, Sivagami saw that Jeemotha too was laughing, and the next moment, she drew her urumi from her waist and wrapped it around Jeemotha's neck. She heard the soldiers of Kadarimandalam lift their bows and the sound of a hundred arrows getting notched into the bowstrings. She wound the urumi tighter around his neck.

'Tell them to drop their weapons or you will drop dead,' Sivagami hissed. Mahadeva and Bijjala were still fighting, oblivious to what was happening.

Jeemotha laughed. 'Soon all of us are going to be dead.' He was looking at the sky. Sivagami followed his gaze and froze in fear. In the far horizon, five Garuda pakshis were advancing towards them.

SIXTY-ONE

# Ally

ALLY HAD MANAGED to dig a tunnel into the fort with the help of the Vaithalikas. The abandoned lepers' colony ensured that their activities went undetected. After the tunnel was ready, it was difficult to keep the Kalakeyas restrained; they were itching to fight, and had already set upon and killed an unsuspecting Bhairava who happened to wander by. Ally was relieved when she finally spotted the Garuda pakshis rising high in the sky.

The final battle had begun. Ally raised her sword and the Kalakeyas rushed forward. The Vaithalika army waited for her next move, but there was no point in having half the army disciplined while the other half swarmed around like locusts. She took a deep breath and gave her orders, 'Destroy everything. Kill anyone in the way.'

Like children set free to play, the Kalakeyas crawled into the tunnel as the Vaithalikas waited patiently for their turn. Ally felt a pang of pity for the people of Mahishmathi. She prayed God would forgive her for what she was going to unleash on a city that was already besieged with problems. She also felt wretched that this was how she was repaying Sivagami, who had once made her the queen of Gauriparvat.

Mentally asking for forgiveness from Sivagami and the people of Mahishmathi, Ally plunged into the tunnel as well.

The savages advanced, butchering everyone in sight. The first people to fall prey to their attack were Revamma and Thondaka, who had just left the orphanage in order to watch the surrender ceremony. Ally tried to bring about some modicum of discipline, but it was like trying to control a herd of elephants running amok. The Kalakeyas did away with everything that hampered their advance, destroying whatever stood in their way, animate or inanimate. The pillars were toppled, trees and plants in the gardens uprooted, humans and beasts chased and bludgeoned to death. Vases were thrown out of balconies and great paintings were slashed. Wild cries and blood-curdling roars shook the earth.

Ally took her band of Vaithalika men away from the Kalakeyas. She needed to take someone of importance hostage. Achi Nagamma was confident of her plan, but Ally felt it would be good to be prepared for any eventuality. While leaving the Kalakeyas to their fate, she would try to get something that was precious both to Mahishmathi and Kadarimandalam. Though all the odds favoured Kadarimandalam, Ally knew Sivagami could still pull off some sort of miracle. *Luck always favours that woman, something I sorely lack*, she thought bitterly as she sidestepped a headless torso.

Ally hurried through corridors, with her men following close behind, praying that she would not have to come face to face with the man she loathed and loved. At the far end of a corridor, a bunch of soldiers stood ready for combat. Before Ally could register what was happening, Kalakeyas emerged from nowhere and headed towards them, shouting in Kilikki. Ally gestured to her followers to move into the shadows.

They watched as the Kalakeyas butchered the Mahishmathi soldiers, who fought with desperation. Above the din of the battle, Ally heard a baby's cry from a room.

'It must be the prince of Mahishmathi,' Ally whispered to her followers. 'We need him alive. He will be our insurance, in case Sivagami wins against Kadarimandalam. Let us not allow the Kalakeyas to kill him.'

Ally rushed out, yelling and trying to control the savages she had unleashed on Mahishmathi. The baby continued to cry as the Kalakeyas now fought the Mahishmathi soldiers as well as Ally's men. What Ally did not know then, was inside the room a pregnant Akhila lay whimpering in fear, holding the hands of a terrified Gundu Ramu. Only a door stood between the Kalakeyas and the two little princes of Mahishmathi, one of whom was yet to take his first breath of air.

SIXTY-TWO

# Keki

KEKI HAD WATCHED from the shore as Kattappa rowed Sivagami and Mahadeva to the ship. Despite what Jeemotha had said, she could not stop thinking about the bejewelled elephants that were standing in the palace garden. She looked around and slowly slipped back into the crowd. Everyone's attention was on the ships of Kadarimandalam and the surrender ceremony. Keki reached into the pouch she had hidden in her waistband. She smiled wryly at her foolishness; she had scavenged the bodies of slain Mahishmathi soldiers near Gauriparvat for a handful of coins, rings and ear studs, and here was literally a king's ransom waiting to be looted. She could buy a country if she could find a way to rob what bedecked even one of the elephants, and there were fifteen of them.

Keki inched towards the gate, and when what appeared to be a fight started on the deck of the ship, she slipped inside the fort. She kept to the shadows of the fort wall and headed towards the garden. Pressing her body to the fort wall and crawling, she reached behind the first elephant. Remembering Jeemotha's talk about the elephants being a trap, she became cautious as she neared the elephants. In the light of the torches, the precious stones sparkled, and Keki stood mesmerised with greed.

Enough of being a slave to ungrateful masters like Bijjala. With this treasure, she could get out of this accursed Mahishmathi and go somewhere else. Keki saw a soldier walking in her direction, and her heart palpitating, she crouched against the wall again. The guard relieved himself a few feet from Keki and returned to the front. Keki waited there, willing herself to calm down, to normalise her breath, telling herself, 'Only a few steps and you are made for life Keki, only a few steps ... all your problems will be solved. You can have an inn of your own. You can have dancing girls who will entertain rich clients, maybe a gambling den too ...'

Outside the fort walls, she could hear shrieks and yells and then an unearthly sound that she was familiar with—the screech of the Garuda pakshi. The dull thud of catapults being released, the loud crash of ship hulls cracking, the screams of dying men, the panicked yells from people watching on the riverside, all came in waves, making her legs go weak and pinning her to the shadows. Above her, over the fort wall, she heard someone running. A soldier landed with a thud a few paces away from her, writhed for some time, and died. The guards near the bejewelled elephants rushed to their fallen comrade and then they looked up at the fort. Drawing their swords, they scattered to all sides and left to fight whoever was on the fort wall. Had Keki gathered the courage to crane her neck and look, she would have seen Pattaraya, Mekhala and Roopaka making their escape.

Keki knew she would never get another chance. She touched the dagger at her waist and, telling herself that this would be the last murder she would commit, she started crawling towards the two remaining guards still standing at the front of the elephants. She yanked the head of the first soldier and sliced his throat. The second soldier, who had been talking to his comrade while looking beyond the fort towards the river, didn't even hear his fellow soldier fall dead. When he turned, Keki's sneering face was inches away from his, and before he could blink, her dagger plunged into his eye.

Keki wiped the dagger clean on her saree, put it back in the folds of her waistband and ran to the first elephant. She paused for a moment before the dazzling riches and clapped her hand in glee. In a frenzy that would have shamed a starving pig who had found its trough filled with food, Keki started plucking out the precious jewels. She was so engrossed in her task that she did not hear the war cries of the Kalakeyas who were circling her with their bloodied stone axes and clubs.

SIXTY-THREE

# Akhila

SIVAGAMI'S SON WOKE up from his sleep and started crying. Akhila, crouched in a corner, didn't have the courage to move towards the cradle and rock it. She could hear the screams and shouts outside and she gripped the hands of an equally terrified Gundu Ramu.

Gundu Ramu whispered in a terrified voice, 'Kalakeyas,' and Akhila felt as if a hand had reached inside her womb and was choking her baby. The pain was unbearable, and her nails dug into Gundu Ramu's hands. Gundu Ramu tried to free himself from Akhila's grip. He wanted to scream out in pain, but that would only frighten Akhila more. He knew that, in a moment or two, the Kalakeyas would rush in and they would all be dead. He had to do something. He slowly prised Akhila's fingers from his wrist and whispered, 'Akka, please.'

Akhila was in no mood to listen. She gripped him again, shivering with fear and crying with her eyes squeezed shut.

Ramu kept whispering, 'Akka, we have to do something, please stand up and pick up the baby too, please, please.'

Then Ramu saw a stone axe splintering the door, it's sharp edge visible through the wood for a moment. Then it vanished, and before it could strike again, Ramu heard a familiar voice. 'Ally akka,' he whispered. What was she doing here? Surely she wouldn't cause them any harm; or was it that she was being held by the Kalakeyas? That put Ramu in a quandary. He couldn't just sit by quietly if the Kalakeyas had caught Ally. He remembered her kindness and the things she had done for him. He looked at Akhila and then thought about Ally. He didn't know what to do, and in a helpless rage, he banged his head on the wall. 'Amma Gauri, show me a way,' he said.

The baby in the cradle continued to cry. The door rattled violently.

SIXTY-FOUR

# Sivagami

FROM THE CROW'S nest in the mast above her, Sivagami heard Brihannala scream, 'Kill them all, Amma. Destroy both Kadarimandalam and Mahishmathi!'

Mahadeva and Bijjala stopped fighting, and everybody looked up as the screech of Garuda pakshis filled the air. Sivagami saw Achi Nagamma riding on the shoulders of one of them. Something dangled from a rope she held in her hand, and it almost grazed the crow's nest of Jeemotha's ship as it swung past.

'Khanipathi Hidumba!' Brihannala yelled in joy.

Like the voice of God from the skies, Achi Nagamma thundered, 'You keep fighting, exploiting nature, enslaving poor people, and playing war games. We are here to destroy you both. Queen of Kadarimandalam, your navy is going to be history soon. King of Mahishmathi, your city has been taken over by Kalakeyas.'

Mahadeva let out a scream of agony, 'Akhila …!'

Sivagami felt her limbs weaken. Her baby was with Akhila. It was unimaginable to think what the Kalakeyas would do to them.

Achi was not finished. 'To show how much I detest you all, I have carried this monster here.' She swung Hidumba in the air and his terrified cries sent a chill down everyone's spine. He swung from the rope tied to his legs, from one end of the ship to another, twenty feet above the deck.

'Khanipathi Hidumba, the one who tortured so many children, the devil of Gauriparvat. I, Achi Nagamma, hereby proclaim your punishment.' Achi Nagamma swung the rope in a huge arc and let her end of it go free. For a moment, as if frozen, Hidumba was suspended in the air above their ship, almost at Brihannala's eye level. Then three Garuda pakshis swooped down and tore at Hidumba. For a brief moment, they fought for his flesh, their humongous wings causing massive ripples to hit the ship. Sails got entangled with ropes, and the ship tilted, carrying many overboard. The birds gobbled up what was left of Hidumba, flapped their wings, soared high and vanished into the darkness.

Brihannala screamed in delight. 'Die, all bastards, die!'

Sivagami stood transfixed. All her nightmares were coming true. She heard Jeemotha whispering in her ears, 'This is the time. All I ask is pardon, and I can win you this war.' Sivagami looked at him in surprise. Even at this moment of complete destruction, he had the gall to negotiate.

'Before we all die, I will have the satisfaction of killing you, pirate.'

Sivagami tightened the ribbon sword around his neck, drawing blood.

Jeemotha gasped for breath. 'I too want revenge against Chitraveni. All you need ...' he gulped, '... all you need is to throw a flaming torch into that fleet of ships.'

Sivagami loosened the urumi a bit and Jeemotha said, 'When I repaired their ships, I applied a special keel on the hull of all the ships except this one. They are made with lac. All it needs is a spark of fire.'

For a moment, Sivagami couldn't understand what the pirate meant. From the city, she could hear yells and screams. And then it dawned on her. The pirate had outplayed Chitraveni. This was her chance to finish Kadarimandalam.

Sivagami uncoiled the urumi from Jeemotha's neck. The pirate collapsed, holding his neck. 'You almost killed me,' he cussed under his breath.

Meanwhile, Bijjala saw Mahadeva standing frozen, too shocked to even move, watching his city on fire. Bijjala took his chance and rushed at his brother. Sivagami was expecting this underhanded move from Bijjala. Swiftly, she used her urumi to get hold of Bijjala by his neck. 'A step more, and you are dead,' she said, as Bijjala stood, trembling with fear, the sharp urumi coiled around his neck.

For a moment, Sivagami thought that Mahadeva would use this opportunity to thrust his sword into Bijjala's belly, but then he was Mahadeva. The king flung down his sword and Bijjala cackled, 'Coward. Your lover has saved you, but see what is happening to the city you ruled.'

Sivagami gave the urumi a yank, and Bijjala staggered back. Jeemotha stood up and said, 'Could you spare us the family drama and do what I asked? Otherwise, all my planning will go to waste.'

Without taking her eyes off Bijjala, she yelled at the top of her voice, 'Kattappa, the fire in your torch can save us all. Go and set fire to the Kadarimandalam ships.'

Kattappa had heard the fight going on, but Sivagami had instructed him to not leave his position; he was to wait for them to plunge back into the water after assassinating Chitraveni. He had stood worried, not knowing whether his masters had succeeded in their mission, when Sivagami called out the instruction. Now, he fixed the torch he was holding to the prow of his boat and started rowing towards the fleet of ships.

The Kadarimandalam navy was busy shooting at the Garuda pakshis hovering above as Kattappa rowed in a frenzy towards them.

With rising tension, Sivagami watched Kattappa's boat nearing the fleet of ships. A stray arrow was all that was needed to finish Kattappa and end her only chance of victory over Kadarimandalam. The fate of Mahishmathi rested on the shoulders of a slave rowing a small boat, towards a fleet of warships, with only a torch.

Chitraveni was busy commanding her navy to turn the siege machines and catapults towards the sky. A thousand arrows arced towards the Garuda pakshis, but fell harmlessly into the river. The birds had disappeared into the womb of the sky, and only their screeches could be heard. Their screeches, and the death cries of the Kalakeyas from the city.

Then a boulder fell on a ship near Chitraveni's, breaking it into two. Mast poles cracked, wood splintered and soldiers were thrown into the river. The catapults fired from the ships, but with utter disdain Achi came back, flying so tantalisingly low that the wings of the Garuda pakshi created ripples on the river surface. Then she was joined by the other Garuda pakshis, dropping boulders in a coordinated attack. Spears, stones, arrows were hurled at the birds, but the attack was relentless.

From the crow's nest of Jeemotha's ship, Brihannala tied in chains howled and hooted, 'Amma Kali, give them death. Thandav, thandav, thandav.'

With an admirable calmness, Chitraveni stood at the prow of her ship, giving orders to adjust the catapults. Soon some of the firings started finding their marks. This only angered the giant birds.

Sivagami could see that Kattappa had managed to sneak the boat near Chitraveni's ship. It looked so puny and insignificant; if not for the torch at its prow, it would have been totally invisible. Sivagami stood with bated breath. Near her, Jeemotha leaned against the ship's deck railing and started laughing.

'Five years as a galley slave, Chitraveni. Die you bitch, at the hands of another slave,' Jeemotha hissed.

Sivagami waited for the spectacle that the pirate had promised, but Kattappa didn't move. If anyone in the Kadarimandalam navy saw him, he would receive a barrage of arrows; what was he waiting for, she wondered, worried. The Garuda pakshis screeched as they flew towards the Kadarimandalam navy for the next round of attack. Sivagami looked up at Achi Nagamma. She didn't understand why Achi had not attacked their ship first, instead directing her attack at the queen of Kadarimandalam.

As if reading her thoughts, Jeemotha said, 'Whether you admit it or not, devi, there is no one to beat me with strategy. I sent Chitraveni to another ship, and I got the lucky talisman with this one. That mad old hag Achi will not attack us because—' Jeemotha pointed at the crow's nest where Brihannala was tied, 'no mother would harm her son. You owe me for saving all your lives.'

From the crow's nest, Brihannala kept yelling, 'Kill them all, Amma, kill them all.'

Brihannala's antagonism terrified Sivagami. Had their rule generated so much anger in the people? If people rose against their rulers' injustices, which empire would be left in the world?

Sivagami saw that Kattappa was still waiting for something. With a heavy heart, she thought that she might have sent him to his death.

The Garuda pakshis circled around the fleet of ships. Another loud crash and a wave rushed towards them, making their ship bob in the water. 'Another ship has gone down,' Jeemotha hissed joyfully. 'But what is that fool of a slave waiting for?'

The birds circled above them and vanished into the darkness. The Kadarimandalam navy's eyes were turned to the horizon where the birds had vanished, but they would sooner or later see Kattappa near the ship with a flaming torch.

Sivagami couldn't even move from where she was positioned for she had to keep Bijjala trapped in the coils of her urumi. 'It's a curse, it's a bloody curse to have married such a man,' Sivagami mumbled in exasperation. 'For Amma Gauri's sake, Kattappa, throw that torch and be done with it.'

Yet, the slave waited.

SIXTY-FIVE

# Kattappa

KATTAPPA WAS WAITING for the right moment. The memories of his fight in Gauriparvat came flooding back to him and it required all his will not to throw away the torch, jump into the water, and stay there forever. The screeching sound the Garuda pakshis made as they circled above the ships was sufficient to paralyse him.

He toyed with the idea of carrying out what he had come to do and then making his escape. Rani Sivagami wanted it. Nobody would blame him if he did just that and left. Kattappa understood there was something peculiar with the ships of Kadarimandalam, and despite the pirate literally throwing water on his plan of using the kala lavanam on Jeemotha's ship, there was the possibility that Kadarimandalam's end would be with fire.

But what use was annihilating the Kadarimandalam ships if they still had the threat of the Garuda pakshis to reckon with? If he could time it properly, perhaps he could take down the Garuda pakshis too. Kattappa was waiting for that right moment. He knew that if he got the timing wrong even by a whisker, he would be doing a great disservice to his country. By waiting, he had taken on an enormous burden. If someone from the Kadarimandalam side spotted him and decided to finish him off with an arrow, Mahishmathi would lose the war and he would die with the knowledge that he had let down Sivagami and Mahadeva. He would have let down his country.

The Garuda pakshis were flying very high, and except for the distant screech that echoed in the sky, he could not even make out where they were. The iron balls and the arrows that the Kadarimandalam navy was continuing to shoot vanished into the darkness. And then he saw two of the birds diving towards the ships. Kattappa figured out the pattern. After dropping huge boulders and sinking a ship, the Garuda pakshis needed to fly away and bring bigger stones. But the gap between the two attacks would give the Kadarimandalam navy a chance to regroup or form some other strategy. So, the attack had to be relentless, and Achi Nagamma was timing it well. While two birds went to get boulders, she used the other two Garuda pakshis to create panic in the Kadarimandalam ranks. These birds flew nearer to the deck and pulverised whatever was there in their path. From far above in the clouds, riding the mother Garuda pakshi, Achi Nagamma was raining death and destruction on two empires.

Kattappa's hand that held the torch was sweating in fear and exertion. Despite the din of the battle, Kattappa could hear his heart pounding in his chest. Another two ships went down and Kattappa counted in his mind. If Achi Nagamma was following the pattern he had observed, the next cycle of attack by the two Garuda pakshis would come now.

With a shrill and unearthly cry, two birds swept towards the ships. Despite Chitraveni's best efforts, the Kadarimandalam soldiers fled seeing them; they jumped overboard, flinging their puny arrows and bows. As the birds touched the ships, Kattappa flung the torch high in the air.

Things slowed down as he watched, forgetting even to breathe, as the flaming torch arced in the sky. The wing of one of the attacking birds hit the torch as it dove down, and Kattappa thought everything had gone wrong. The torch was thrown up higher into the sky, and if it missed the ships and plunged into the river, that would be the end of everything. The torch spun in the air and slowly fell on the deck of Chitraveni's ship.

Kattappa started rowing furiously back towards the lead ship. He had done his work, and if he had failed, he decided he would thrust his sword into his heart and die. All his life he had served Mahishmathi, and he had taken a huge risk now. If he had failed, he didn't deserve to live.

## SIXTY-SIX

# Sivagami

SIVAGAMI'S EYES FOLLOWED the arc of the torch as it flew in the air, and then landed on Chitraveni's ship. A moment earlier, she had seen two Garuda pakshis attacking the ship. Leaning against the railing of the deck, Jeemotha tapped her shoulder. 'Your slave is a genius,' he said.

A massive explosion lit the sky and sent twelve-foot-high waves rolling towards them. Mahishmathi city, the river, the jungle on the other side, all became visible for a flash, as if the sun had suddenly made an appearance. Sivagami lost her grip on the urumi as a huge wave hit their ship. Many fell to the deck as the ship tilted. One by one, the entire Kadarimandalam fleet went up in flames.

The two Garuda pakshis rose high, shrieking in pain and fear. Their wings were on fire, and the flames soon spread all over their bodies as they flew towards Sivagami's ship. She closed her eyes, fearing the worst, expecting them to fall on their ship and set it on fire. But the flaming mass of the two

Garuda pakshis plunged into the water on either side of their ship.

Far above them, Sivagami could hear the terrified cry of another Garuda pakshi. Like a curse from the heavens, Achi Nagamma's voice boomed, 'You killed my children. You will all pay with death.' The gigantic Garuda pakshi she was on swooped down till it was a few feet above their heads, and then vanished into the darkness.

From the crow's nest, Brihannala screamed, 'Give them death, Amma. Give them death!'

In the light of the flames that consumed the Kadarimandalam fleet, Sivagami saw Achi Nagamma appear again. As the Garuda pakshi she rode circled above their heads, Sivagami could hear the sound of wings from the jungle side. The remaining two Garuda pakshis were approaching her ship.

Jeemotha yelled at the top of his voice, 'Mad woman! Your son is our captive.'

In answer, Brihannala laughed. 'Amma, you gave me birth, you give me death,' he yelled.

The Garuda pakshis continued to fly towards them.

'No mother would kill her son. She is just posturing. Let us stand our ground,' Jeemotha said.

Brihannala yelled, 'Amma ...'

Suddenly, the dark sky seemed to swallow the birds that circled around their ship. Jeemotha ordered for the anchor to be lifted and the ship moved towards the Mahishmathi dock from the middle of the river. He had assumed command, and the remaining Kadarimandalam warriors on the ship obeyed him without a whimper.

Sivagami could hear the distant shrieks of the birds as Jeemotha took control of the rudder wheel and turned the ship. The galley slaves started rowing, their song rising in rhythm, and the massive ship creaked as it slowly turned towards the Mahishmathi dock.

There was silence now: the birds had vanished and not even their cries could be heard. Maybe Jeemotha was right, Sivagami thought. Achi could not bring herself to kill her son. Sivagami ordered the soldiers to tie Bijjala, and without hesitation they pinned him down. He tried to wriggle out of their grip, and a soldier brought a rope to restrain him.

They were only a few yards from the Mahishmathi dock now. With the annihilation of the Kadarimandalam navy, they had warded off a major threat. Now she had to turn her attention to the Kalakeyas and reclaim the city. The shrieks she could hear from the fort made her worry about the safety of her baby and Akhila.

'Faster,' she heard herself shout, and Jeemotha smiled. 'Rani, this cannot fly. We will be there soon. We are taking a sharp turn and the waters are choppy. The wind—'

At that moment, a blood-curdling shriek ripped apart the sky and before they could recover from it, two massive boulders fell in succession, splintering the ship in the middle.

SIXTY-SEVEN

# Ally

ALLY WAS TRYING hard to control the Kalakeyas, yelling commands for them to stop fighting. The Kalakeyas turned towards her and growled. A Vaithalika elder stepped forward and yelled, 'Enough, you barbarians. What are you doing? Didn't you hear our commander's order to stop?'

The Kalakeya in front of him grinned, showing his stained teeth, and brought down his stone hammer on the elder's head. Ally screamed despite herself.

The Kalakeyas ignored Ally and started pounding on the door, hitting it with their axes and hammers. The door groaned on its hinges and Ally could hear Gundu Ramu's terrified cries.

'Oh God,' Ally thought. She had not reckoned that her beloved Gundu Ramu would be inside the room. How would she stop these barbarians?

Before she could figure out what to do, an explosion from the river rattled the palace, causing everyone to freeze. Even the Kalakeyas paused for a moment. The sight of the two Garuda pakshis on fire, swirling in the sky, made them gasp. Taking advantage of their distraction, Ally moved towards the door, gesturing for her Vaithalika men to defend her when the Kalakeyas noticed her absence.

One of the Kalakeyas gave a yelp of joy and pointed at something in the garden. The Kalakeyas started talking excitedly amongst themselves, and Ally craned her neck to take a quick look over their shoulders. She could see several elephants bedecked with jewels that shone in the light of the explosion. One of the Kalakeyas near her jumped from the first-floor balcony, and the others soon followed, some of them falling on those who had landed before. They scrambled to join their people who had started ripping apart the elephants. Ally turned towards the door and hesitated before it.

Inside the room, Gundu Ramu had heard the sickening thud of a body and Ally's scream, and he suspected the worst. He whispered something in Akhila's ear, but she only gripped his wrists tight and wept in fear. He pleaded with her and reluctantly she stood up. Holding her belly with her left hand, Akhila went towards the cradle and picked up Sivagami's baby. Then she walked towards the door.

Gundu Ramu whispered, 'I will take down the leader and you take the baby and run.' He wheeled himself to the far end of the room, took a deep breath, and rushed forward towards the door. With trembling hands, Akhila moved the bolt and flung open the door, and Gundu Ramu passed her like a storm, his arms stretched out. He pushed the person standing outside and saw the body hit the railing and topple over it. In the next moment, Akhila slipped out and ran.

Gundu Ramu waited for the blows to fall, bracing himself to fight until Akhila had sufficient time to get away. Instead, he saw some men running towards the stairs in the corner and rushing down, screaming and crying. To his bewilderment, he saw they were not Kalakeyas.

Gundu Ramu slowly moved towards the railing and leaned over to see who he had knocked down from the first floor, and with a shock realised it was Ally. Ramu let out a cry of anguish. 'What have I done, what have I done? She came to save me and I ...' He broke into sobs.

A hand pressed his shoulder. Startled, he turned back to see Akhila standing behind him, holding Sivagami's baby. The corridor was empty. The baby giggled and extended his stubby arm towards Gundu Ramu.

Ramu wept, placing his chin on the railing as he looked down at Ally lying on the ground. The Vaithalika men formed a circle of protection around her. Ally stirred and Ramu screamed, 'I am sorry, I am sorry.' He wanted to go down. He wanted to beg her forgiveness. He began to turn his wheeled chair, but Akhila stopped him and pointed out what was happening near the wooden elephants.

'I want a bow and an arrow,' Gundu Ramu said.

---

Keki was prepared to fight the Kalakeyas who had surrounded her for the treasure. 'Get away, brutes. This is mine, this is mine,' she screamed. A Kalakeya's stone hammer cracked open her head. They fell upon her and took everything she had collected, but she had gone to a world where nothing mattered. Neither the precious stones nor the gender to which she belonged.

A Kalakeya boy of sixteen stood apart, watching the madness of his tribesmen. He tried to remind them about the holy book for which they had started the war, but no one listened to him. In disgust, he moved away to prowl the corridors with a handful of his friends.

---

With trembling hands, Gundu Ramu drew the arrow to his ear. Akhila lit the tip of it. Gundu Ramu prayed, 'I thought all my work in making those elephants filled with kala lavanam had gone waste. Amma Gauri, now I know you spared my work for a reason. Amma Kali, be the flame at the tip of my arrow and do your thandav.'

Gundu Ramu let go of the arrow and watched it arc gracefully above Mahishmathi city before it dipped down and fell on the elephant in the middle. It spluttered and sparkled and then an explosion that dwarfed what had happened on the river shook the Mahishmathi palace. Gundu Ramu screamed in terror as he saw bodies of men being flung in the air. Most of the Kalakeya army was annihilated in a moment. The fire didn't discriminate based on caste or tribe. It swallowed everyone in the vicinity. As the shower of death subsided, it rained gems, pearls and diamonds on Mahishmathi city.

---

By now, Ally had managed to sit up. Surrounded by the last of her men, she watched the fire's dance of death and knew she had lost once again. Ally buried her face in her hands and wept. The pain from her broken thigh bone was nothing compared to the wound she felt in her spirit. All their sacrifices had gone to waste. Nothing changed in this bloody world, she thought. It was the fate of her people to lose and be enslaved. Never again, she vowed, would she pray to any God or Goddess. She had no need for a God who was so unfair.

Ally felt a touch on her back and waited for a sword to fall on her neck. Instead, she found she was being embraced. Gundu Ramu sobbed on her shoulder, 'Akka, I didn't know you had come to save me. I am sorry.'

Ally felt she was drowning in shame and guilt, and defeat. She did not have the courage to face Ramu or the world.

SIXTY-EIGHT

# Sivagami

WHEN SIVAGAMI BROKE the surface of the water, she found Kattappa's boat a few feet away. She saw Mahadeva sitting in it, drenched and shaken. Around her, in the water, she could see the destroyed ship. The air was filled with the screams of drowning people and a breeze carried the stink of charred flesh. The light from the fire that had engulfed the Kadarimandalam fleet was still burning bright, causing an eerie golden reflection in the river. It took all her strength to swim towards Kattappa's boat. Sivagami took hold of Mahadeva's extended hand and hauled herself into the boat. As she sat shivering more from fear than the cold, Kattappa started rowing towards the Mahishmathi shore. Sivagami saw that Mahadeva's eyes were searching for someone.

There were hundreds of people swimming towards the safety of the shore; some were holding on to ship debris that floated in the water towards the burning vessels a hundred feet away. Narasimha Varman had certainly been killed, as had

Brihannala, when the massive boulders fell, Sivagami thought. She shuddered at the memory of Achi Nagamma's wrath; she hadn't even hesitated about taking the life of her own son; in fact, she had deliberately dropped the boulder on Brihannala to underline her intention.

Sivagami looked fearfully at the dark skies. Achi could be hovering above them like a God from the ancient tales, a God that could unleash the power of nature, hurl thunder and lightning bolts, or set storms at them.

They were nearing the shore now and Sivagami turned her thoughts to the fight within the fort. She was sure she could tackle the Kalakeyas, provided she was able to rally their army. People were still crowded at the port, watching the dance of death and destruction unfolding on the river.

'Kattappa, why are we going in circles? Take us to the shore,' she said as she realised their boat had turned away from the shore and was once again moving towards the centre. Mahadeva looked at her in surprise, and then it struck her with a jolt. Shame gripped her. Mahadeva was searching for his brother, her husband, the father of her son. She had not even spared him a thought.

'We cannot give up, Kattappa. He must be here somewhere,' Mahadeva said, and Sivagami found her eyes welling up. The man she was ashamed to call her husband, the man who had tried everything in his life to destroy his brother, had disappeared into the heart of the Mahishi river. Yet Mahadeva was not ready to give up on him.

Sivagami turned to Mahadeva. 'Please, our people need us, let us stop this.'

Mahadeva murmured, 'But he is my brother.'

Sivagami could stand it no more and she commanded Kattappa, 'Take us to the shore, now.' Mahadeva sat with his head bent, the responsibility of a king to place his people above family weighing heavily on his shoulders.

They found Jeemotha waiting for them at the dock, drenched, covered in blood, but with a smug grin on his face. 'Did you enjoy the show, devi?' he asked. Sivagami had half a mind to push the pirate back into the water and it took all her will to not do it.

Sivagami drew her sword and cried at the top of her voice, 'Jai Mahishmathi!'

The cry rallied the scattered army and people of Mahishmathi together. And in reply, from inside the fort, came the ululating war cry of the Kalakeyas. Leading their people, Mahadeva and Sivagami rushed inside the fort. And then a massive explosion shook the earth, as Gundu Ramu's flame arrow found its mark.

When the dust had settled and the smoke had cleared, Jeemotha said, 'What a show, my devi, what a bloody good show. Much better than what I had arranged.'

When the Mahishmathi army understood that most of the Kalakeyas had been annihilated, the air rang with cries of 'Jai Mahishmathi'. Energised by the return of their leaders, the people of Mahishmathi were eager for their revenge. They started butchering the few Kalakeyas who had managed to survive the blast. Mahadeva tried desperately to stop the savagery, physically pulling away many of his people from clubbing the remaining Kalakeyas to death. With a sinking feeling, Sivagami understood that, in their bloodlust, Mahishmathi citizens were no different from the Kalakeyas.

'It is not our culture to kill those who are injured, those who have surrendered,' Mahadeva cried, as the mob roared for blood. Sivagami saw a group of soldiers pushing and shoving a bunch of young Kalakeya men towards them. The mob rushed forward, eager to tear them apart.

Mahadeva flung himself between the terrified Kalakeyas and his own men and roared, 'Not a drop of blood more. We have won the war and I will not allow this barbarity.' Seeing their king, the Mahishmathi men hesitated. Sivagami and Kattappa stood on either side of Mahadeva, their swords drawn, daring their own people to disobey. Behind them, the Kalakeyas cowered in fear.

Though she knew they deserved no mercy, Sivagami could understand why Mahadeva was behaving the way he was. He was the one who had learned the duties of kingship from the ancient dharma shastras, unlike his father, who had sharpened his skills in the harsh world of politics. He was displaying what Somadeva had always warned about, allowing conscience and principles to stand in the way of practicality. But the crowd was angry. They wanted revenge.

'We will have a trial and we will hang them. Tie them up,' Sivagami ordered, and before Mahadeva could object, she hurried away. The crowd cheered. Soon the Kalakeyas were tied up in ropes and chains and were paraded through the fort gardens. The Mahishmathi soldiers danced and yelled and calls of 'Jai Mahishmathi' echoed in the air.

---

Kattappa hurried to stop an angry crowd that had surrounded the Vaithalikas near Sivagami's palace wing and was taken aback to see Ally there. She was crying on Gundu Ramu's shoulder. When she saw Kattappa, Ally looked away and said in a flat voice, 'Now you can kill me.'

Kattappa stood before her, silent, tears streaming down his cheeks.

When Sivagami reached them, she took Ally's hand in hers and asked, 'Why, Ally, why? You are my sister born in another womb. We fought together to end the evil on Gauriparvat. I made you queen of the mountain. Yet, you did this to us?'

Ally just shook her head and said softly, 'I lost and you won, sister.' Then, her voice choking with emotion, she continued. 'But you know what, Sivagami? The hero who saved your city is our Ramu.'

Ally held Ramu close and kissed his forehead, and he burst into tears. 'I am sorry you are hurt because of me. I pushed you down.'

Ally said, 'You did right, my boy. I had come to take Sivagami's son hostage.'

Shocked, Sivagami took a step back. 'How could you, Ally?'

Ally smiled at Sivagami. 'Because ... we are sisters.'

Sivagami knew what Ally meant. She had married Bijjala for the sake of her goal. She had killed Thimma, caused the deaths of Raghava and Neelappa to achieve what she thought was right. How could she ever blame Ally for acting the way she had? But then, Ally had brought the war into Mahishmathi and caused the death of so many. How could she spare her?

Sivagami was lost in thought when a pair of hands gripped her feet. 'Kattappa,' she gasped.

The slave was sobbing at her feet. She tried to lift him up but he wouldn't let go. Between his sobs, she heard, 'Spare Ally, spare her, devi. Spare her for me.'

Sivagami stared at Ally, unable to believe what she was hearing. Ally's moist eyes said it all. The man who had given everything to Sivagami, the slave who had killed his own brother, the one who lived for the country, was pleading to spare the woman who had tried to kidnap her infant son. Sivagami was torn. *Amma Gauri, why do you test me like this*, she thought.

The tolling of the bell at the fort abruptly pulled her away from her thoughts. '*Garuda pakshis!*' she heard the frightened screams from the garden, and then a massive boulder crashed into the west wing of the palace, bringing a part of it down.

Achi Nagamma was back.

SIXTY-NINE

# Bijjala

BIJJALA SCREAMED IN terror as the current carried him towards the burning ships. Charred bodies floated by him and the heat was unbearable as he neared the inferno. He took a deep breath and went underwater. Holding his breath, he swam for what felt like an eternity. Breaking to the surface for air at the wrong time meant being caught in the mouth of the fire. Finally, when he could no longer hold his breath, he paddled to the surface and almost got hit by a burning log that was floating by. He went down into the water once again and waited for the burning wreckage to pass. When he broke surface for the second time, he was far from Mahishmathi city. Bijjala knew he had been badly hurt in the attack, his body was racked with pain; but with all his will, he slowly paddled towards the shore and pulled himself up. The prince who wanted to be king lay alone and broken in the dampness of the swamp, fear still throbbing through his veins. Death had sniffed at his back and let him go. Thick, putrid smoke hung in the air. He stared at the river carrying embers of a civilisation destroyed; the waters seemed silent and solemn, like a hearse carrying the dead.

Slowly, memories came crawling like ghosts from a graveyard. They hissed and sneered, laughed and taunted. *How dare that woman keep me ensnared in her urumi?* As the current had carried him away, he had seen Mahadeva and Sivagami in that slave's boat. It seemed like they were searching for someone, and he guessed they were looking for him. His brother wanted to ensure that he was dead. All the years of planning, five years of living like Mekhala's slave, all to no avail. Why was Amma Gauri so partial to Mahadeva?

Bijjala lifted himself up and needles of pain shot through his body. His back was wet and sticky with blood. In the distance, he could see the glow of Mahishmathi, and in the breeze, the war cries waxed and waned. Floating under the water, Bijjala had not heard the second explosion that annihilated the Kalakeyas. All he could hear now was the Mahishmathi soldiers celebrating, and that could only mean one thing—his brother had won, again.

The cries grew clearer as the wind changed, and he could make out shouts of 'Jai Mahishmathi', 'Jai Vikramadeva', 'Jai Rani Sivagami', and like a wounded wolf, he let out a howl. Then he staggered to his feet and limped towards Mahishmathi. He wished he had Keki with him, but that sly eunuch had not returned to the ship after delivering Chitraveni's message to Sivagami. *Everyone has deserted me at the time of crisis,* Bijjala thought bitterly. Only one thought possessed Bijjala now—murder. He wanted to feel the warmth of Mahadeva's blood on his hands. But with no men, how would he enter

Mahishmathi? Walking into Mahishmathi fort would be suicidal. He had to find another way.

And then, an incident from a long time ago flashed in his mind. Bijjala remembered that Mahadeva would sometimes disappear outside the fort. There were tunnels that led from the untouchables' colony into the fort. To avoid detection, he would go around the fort, reach the other side and double back. That would take at least two or three days on foot, and he would need to make sure he wasn't seen by Mahishmathi soldiers. From prince and consort to the queen, he had turned into a fugitive, thanks to Sivagami and Mahadeva. 'Murder, murder,' he kept repeating, as he dragged himself forward and disappeared into the darkness.

## SEVENTY

# Sivagami

'COWARDS, FIGHT BACK. Where are you running off to?' Sivagami yelled, as her soldiers, who had been doing a victory dance a moment earlier, ran for their lives. She tried to stop them, and Mahadeva yelled commands to put up a fight, but no one heeded their desperate cries as boulders rained down upon the city. Sivagami saw Marthanda fleeing with his mercenaries. She grabbed his wrist and said, 'You are the dandanayaka! How can you run away?'

'Devi, how can we fight against such forces of nature? I am not a fool,' he said as he yanked his arm away from her grip and fled.

Half the palace had already crumbled under the assault of the Garuda pakshis. Massive stone boulders lay all around. The most terrifying thing was the pause between the attacks. They didn't know whether the Garuda pakshis had left to bring more projectiles or were just hovering around, waiting to attack.

Whenever Achi Nagamma flew lower, she would yell, 'I accept no surrender, I give in to no begging. I am Kali, the Goddess of death!' That would send waves of panic through the Mahishmathi soldiers. It was just a matter of time before the entire palace would be reduced to rubble. There was no place to hide, nowhere to run.

Sivagami saw a lone figure trying to fire a mahashila yantra in the courtyard. It was Kattappa. He put one of the kala lavanam balls into the hasta, the palm-shaped stone-holder in the yantra, aimed it at one of the birds, set the ball on fire and released it. The ball sputtered and spun in the air, going up barely twenty feet before exploding uselessly. Sivagami ran to Kattappa and Gundu Ramu followed her. Without a word, she loaded another fire ball and, as if reading her mind, Gundu Ramu cranked the catapult. Mahadeva joined them and their desperate defence began.

As if to hinder their efforts, Achi Nagamma appeared that very moment, screaming her war cry. The wingspan of the giant bird she rode on almost covered the entire palace ground. Mahadeva lit the kala lavanam ball and Gundu Ramu let go of the rope on Sivagami's signal. The fireball whizzed and spun towards the bird, but the Garuda pakshi smacked it away with one of its wings. Sivagami saw the fire ball arc over her head and land on the roof of the palace. A moment later there was a deafening explosion and part of the palace crashed down.

Sivagami loaded another ball and shot at the bird, which had flown up higher. It was worse than she had imagined. This time the ball didn't even travel a quarter of the height required to reach the bird. It fell to the ground with another dull explosion. Defeat and death were just a formality now. Nothing could stop the Garuda pakshis. Achi Nagamma would have her way.

Hiding in an attic, Pattaraya, Mekhala and Roopaka watched what was happening in the palace grounds.

'Nanna, what will we do if one of those boulders lands here?' Mekhala cried.

'In the game of chaturanga, luck plays a part as much as skill. Believe in your luck. Sivagami is out there, in the open. If she dies first, then we will take charge. You are still the queen. Why do we care whether Mahishmathi lives or dies? The madwoman cannot keep this attack going forever. She will leave when she has destroyed the city, and then we can rebuild it. Just let them all die like flies. Wait and watch the fun.'

In the palace grounds, Sivagami had used up more of the fire balls but had not been successful with any of them. Achi Nagamma's laughter boomed. 'Your silly contraptions are not going to work. I am Amma Kali, I am the force of nature. Behold my fury.' And she flew higher with the other two birds following in a zigzag pattern, their screeches sending terror waves through the people below.

Night was beginning to give birth to day, and the eastern skies had started bleeding red. The sun would rise on the graveyard of two civilisations. Sivagami was becoming disheartened. When her story would be told long after, the bards would sing about the foolish woman who tried to tame nature, control destiny and thought all she needed for it was some courage, some luck and some determination.

'A position of honour,' Jeemotha whispered in her ears, 'and in return I can win this war for you.'

Sivagami stared at him. Was the pirate mocking her? Jeemotha stood with that irritating smile on his lips. A boulder crashed near him, but he did not even flinch. He walked around the catapult with a smug smile and asked, 'Who made this excuse for a mahashila yantra?'

Gundu Ramu cowered as if he were a child picked on by a teacher. Jeemotha ran his fingers over the catapult, pulled and yanked the ropes that held it, and took a few steps back to study it. Then he turned to Gundu Ramu and said, 'It is not bad for a toy, boy, but in a war field it is useless.'

Another boulder crashed near them, missing them by a whisker.

'Will you give us a break, old witch? Can't you see we are having a conversation?' Jeemotha yelled at Achi, as she flew away in search of more boulders.

When the dust settled down, Gundu Ramu said, 'There were some books in the royal library and—'

Jeemotha laughed. 'Ah, I should've guessed it. Books. A scholar, eh? The one who knows everything and can do nothing? This blasted country is full of people who know what to do but have no clue *how* to do it. What do you say, Sivagami devi? What about my offer?'

Mahadeva stepped forward. 'If you can save Mahishmathi, we would always be grateful.'

Jeemotha ignored Mahadeva and continued to stare at Sivagami. Finally, Sivagami nodded and Jeemotha let out a whistle. 'I had once trusted a woman and she made me a galley slave—'

'Could you please just get on with the work, Jeemotha?' Sivagami snapped.

Jeemotha smiled. 'Once this is over, devi, you should give me a patient hearing. I have so many anecdotes to tell. Now, Mahadeva,' Jeemotha cried, and Sivagami was taken aback.

'Oh, was that not suitable? A low-caste fisherman and pirate calling the king of Mahishmathi by his name?'

'You can call me anything, Jeemotha,' Mahadeva said.

'Of course, I can. I am in command from this moment on, and you, this boy and that slave are all the same to me. All of you will do exactly as I say,' Jeemotha said and burst out laughing. Sivagami looked at Mahadeva, who stood unaffected by Jeemotha's jibes.

'Let us take all these to the sabha. I need to reassemble them.'

'What?' Sivagami was shocked.

'Let the Mahishmathi sabha be useful for once in its life.' Jeemotha laughed. 'Or do you prefer to be squashed under—'

Another boulder fell. Jeemotha shook his fist towards the sky. 'Witch, just you wait.'

Sivagami yelled out for soldiers to come and help, and a few reluctantly emerged from their hiding places. They pushed the catapults to the sabha.

Jeemotha pointed to the top of the catapult. 'Mahadeva, climb there and twist the angle of the hasta like this. Do you think you can do it?'

'I will do it, swami,' Kattappa said.

'Oh slave boy, I know you can manage it easily. I want to see whether this man knows how to do anything other than rule over everyone.'

Sivagami knew Jeemotha was using this opportunity to get back at the royals, making the king work like a slave in his own hall. Mahadeva started climbing the hasta and Jeemotha barked instructions at him. Jeemotha made Mahadeva tighten ropes and chop off some excess weight. Like a sculptor looking at the beauty of his creation, he would step back now and then to observe the contraption he was making. Mahadeva, being Mahadeva, did his work without complaint, while Sivagami fumed.

As she watched, the three catapults merged into one. The arm now extended over a hundred feet. Despite her hatred towards Jeemotha and all he represented, she couldn't help admiring the genius of the man. The contraption was bewilderingly complicated, with its knots and stone weights. How could a man's mind hold so much complexity? And what would he have been, had he not been a pirate?

The answer didn't comfort her. He would have been like her father, Devaraya, and her father didn't survive in the complex world of politics. This man, however despicable he might be, was a notch above her father, for he was a survivor.

'Now, let us have a party,' Jeemotha said, and walked out. Mahadeva started pulling the giant mahashila yantra with the help of the soldiers. Slowly, the contraption inched towards the palace ground. When Sivagami made a move to help push it, Jeemotha stopped her. 'Walk by my side, devi. Had I not been a pirate's son and of the fisherman caste, I would have had the honour of asking for your hand,' Jeemotha said, grinning, and when Sivagami's nostrils flared, he winked at her and said, 'Did you think I would actually do that? I was just trying to charm you. You can use me and throw me like garbage. That's what people like you have been doing to our people for centuries. Don't change it for me. Let our glorious civilisation flourish and enslave more and more of its own people.'

'If you hate us so much, why are you doing this?' Sivagami asked.

'Ah, I am proving a point. The power of a civilisation is not in some obscure sacred texts or in the croaking of priests. It is in the power of knowledge, in the power of science and technology. If a few birds can destroy us, then there is no meaning to all the intelligence we possess. We may be taken aback by the force of nature occasionally, but it is in the taming of her that the future of human civilisation rests.' Jeemotha grinned at her. 'And if you want your country to be truly great, believe in knowledge and not in the accident of birth.'

Sivagami cursed the fate that made her dependent on such a man, but she knew he was right.

Jeemotha looked up at the sky and now, in the light of the rising sun, he could see the birds hovering above them. He yanked a few ropes, adjusted some knots and the next kala lavanam ball was loaded. He gave the honour of lighting it to Sivagami, and then fired it. The ball whooshed high in the air, much higher than what they had expected, and Achi Nagamma was taken by surprise. She deftly evaded the strike though, and the ball exploded high above the birds. Jeemotha let out a cry of triumph. The battle was even now. If she could depend on the earth's pull for the stones, he could depend on his mahashila yantra's propulsion towards the sky.

There were nine balls left, and Jeemotha knew he had to plan each shot carefully. The birds had flown away, and Jeemotha began adjusting the yantra in a frenzy. They knew Achi Nagamma would be back with some new trick. And they saw what it was soon. This time, the three birds appeared from different directions and they didn't know where to shoot. Jeemotha cried, 'Move the yantra—she's aiming for it!' But the yantra was stuck in the slushy ground because of its weight.

Sivagami cried, 'Kattappa!' The slave rushed to the front. He helped Jeemotha lift the wheels as the Garuda pakshis' screeches grew louder above them. Kattappa ran to the other side of the yantra. Using his immense strength, he managed to pull it a few feet just as the boulder crashed at exactly the same spot the yantra had been a moment before.

Jeemotha cursed under his breath. Gundu Ramu had already loaded the next ball and this time Jeemotha himself climbed up the hasta and adjusted the stone holder. He asked Sivagami for the torch and she threw it up. Jeemotha caught it mid-air as he balanced himself on the hasta. He lit the ball and jumped down thirty feet, landing gracefully on the other side while Gundu Ramu fired the catapult. This time, he didn't miss the mark. They cheered when the flaming ball hit one of the Garuda pakshis on its belly and exploded. The bird caught fire and fell, plummeting towards the roof of the palace. Jeemotha patted Gundu Ramu's back and said, 'Congratulations, you aren't just a bookish scholar. You are learning fast. Sooner or later they will hang you.'

The massive bird had fallen where Pattaraya and his daughter were hiding. They scampered out as that wing of the palace caught fire. Their luck had run out. As the fire started spreading, they ran through the corridors blindly, coughing and choking in the smoke and came face to face with a few soldiers who were bringing water to douse the fire.

Pattaraya froze, knowing they were trapped. He cried, 'Mekhala, run and hide, daughter. Don't come out whatever happens to me, and know this—no father has loved his daughter as much as I have.'

Mekhala stood wordlessly as she saw her father running to take on the soldiers. He was unarmed, but the soldiers were caught by surprise. He flung himself upon them, punching, kicking and hitting, while crying, 'Daughter, escape. Don't let all my life's work go to waste by standing there.'

Mekhala leaned on the wall, sobbing. The soldiers quickly overpowered Pattaraya and she saw them coming for her. It was over, but she would never allow them to capture her. Mekhala ran towards the fire, ready to fling herself into its mouth. At the last moment, a hand pulled her away. 'Roopaka,' she gasped.

'This way, my queen,' Roopaka said, dragging her down a staircase. She heard the palace wing crash above her head and dark smoke started curling towards them. They went deeper and deeper into the ground. Mekhala knew she would never see her father again and fought Roopaka. 'Nanna, Nanna is gone. I don't want to live.'

'My queen, remember his words of parting,' Roopaka said as he pulled her along.

She cried, 'No father loved his daughter like my Nanna.'

---

Like a captured wild beast, Pattaraya kicked and bit the soldiers as they dragged him towards Sivagami.

'We will deal with prisoners later. Chain him somewhere like the dog that he is,' Sivagami shouted over the din. The war was not yet over. There were two other birds to bring down. She looked over at the number of fire balls left and let out a gasp.

'We missed, Akka,' Gundu Ramu said sadly.

When the birds screeched above them, he let go of the next ball. It spun towards the Garuda pakshi, and at the last moment, Achi Nagamma managed to manoeuvre out of its way and dropped another boulder on them, killing many who had come to help move the mahashila yantra. Jeemotha cursed; they were now left with only two balls. They couldn't afford to miss again, but Achi seemed to have quickly learned how to evade the ball. They could hear her manic laughter and the unearthly cries of the birds. *Die, die, die*, they seemed to say.

'Axe!' Jeemotha screamed as he ran up the arm of the yantra. Kattappa ran to fetch an axe. He found one lying by a slain Kalakeya soldier and he flung it to Jeemotha. The pirate caught it and he started chopping at the hasta like a man possessed.

They watched as the wood splintered as the pirate worked feverishly. He had split it open vertically and placed the axe handle there as a wedge between the sides. He asked for both balls and Gundu Ramu threw them to him. He placed both in each part of the arm and asked for a flaming torch. Sivagami couldn't understand what the pirate was trying to do. The birds were flying lower, towards them, and Sivagami saw they weren't carrying any boulders. Achi Nagamma was trying to find out what the pirate was planning. The wind from the flapping of their wings shook the mahashila yantra. Jeemotha clutched on to the hasta. When the birds started soaring higher, he asked Kattappa to turn the mahashila yantra in the opposite direction. Kattappa and Mahadeva hurried to follow his instructions.

Some soldiers ran to give a hand. They kept moving the yantra, tracking the trajectory of the birds. Soon there were more than fifty people helping to turn the mahashila yantra. The birds rose higher and higher, and then, quite unexpectedly, Jeemotha fired the mahashila yantra. They watched with bated breath as the two balls streaked higher, spinning in two opposite directions. It was a gamble. They could lose both the balls and then they would have nothing to fight with.

Sivagami's eyes were fixed on Achi Nagamma's bird. She saw one of the balls soaring towards it. Achi dexterously manoeuvred her bird away. Sivagami fell on her knees and wept as the ball exploded above Achi's bird. Suddenly the air was filled with a painful cry as the other bird was hit and caught fire. Its piteous cries reverberated through the skies as it plummeted to the ground.

Mahadeva touched Sivagami's hand. 'It is over, Sivagami,' he said.

Sivagami looked up to see that Achi Nagamma's bird was a dot on the horizon. Jeemotha, drenched in sweat, jumped down and bowed before Sivagami. 'I got both of them. I won the war for you.'

Sivagami looked at him, perplexed.

'The fire ball exploded above Achi, but it injured the bird,' Mahadeva explained. 'One of its wings caught fire. That's why she has escaped with it.'

'She will come back,' Sivagami said.

'Not anytime soon,' Jeemotha said. 'That wing won't heal so easily. By the time she returns, we would have made enough kala lavanam balls. And I can make many mahashila yantras and position them above the fort walls. We can use these catapults to shoot at anything she brings.'

Mahadeva hugged Jeemotha and said, 'Anything you ask for is yours, my friend. You have saved my people.'

Jeemotha remained quiet, waiting for Sivagami's response. She reluctantly nodded. She knew it was dangerous to keep Jeemotha in Mahishmathi. She had to find a way to get rid of him, but only after he had made the yantras. Achi Nagamma would come back, and they had to be prepared.

As if reading her mind, Jeemotha said, 'Your Highness, all I require is a ship, a few soldiers and some priests.'

'Priests?' Mahadeva asked in surprise.

'There are more things out there than one can imagine. There are many lands much larger than ours. Give me a few priests who can lie through their teeth and some holy books. Before the innocent souls on those lands can blink, they will have our holy books and we will have their lands. Religion is the best trade one can have. Not as honest as piracy, but more profitable. All I ask for is the ship and a royal decree that all the lands I step on belong to Amma Gauri or whatever God we choose. I can build a nation bigger than you can imagine. Give me a chance.'

'I don't agree with your cynical worldview, but I will keep my word. You will have your ship and the decree,' Mahadeva said.

Sivagami didn't argue; she had better things to do. It was time to see Pattaraya suffer as her father had suffered. She allowed the spark of pleasure that was throbbing inside her heart to expand and fill her. It was short-lived. She soon learned that Mekhala had come out of hiding to rescue Pattaraya. And while they had caught Pattaraya, Mekhala had escaped their clutches. She knew then that the war was not over.

Sivagami was right and wrong. For Bijjala had found a way to enter the fort, and he was crawling on all fours through the secret tunnel that Kattappa had once used, years ago, to warn Mahishmathi about the Vaithalika attack. The worst was yet to come.

SEVENTY-ONE

# Bijjala

BIJJALA HAD LOST count of the days he had been inside the tunnel. He had expected to come out into the well that was behind Skandadasa's abandoned mansion. However, once he was some way into the tunnel, he realised the flood had closed off many paths and opened others. Disoriented, he had lost his way.

Bijjala was exhausted now, slipping in and out of consciousness. His only thought was to escape somehow. Starvation made him hallucinate; he saw himself sitting on the throne of Mahishmathi, sentencing his brother to Chitravadha; and then he saw their roles being reversed, and the dream turned into a nightmare. Bijjala feared he was going insane. He prowled the tunnels, sometimes on all fours, hungry, angry, screaming, cursing his fate and breaking into sobs.

At one point, Bijjala woke up with a burning fever. His wounds had putrefied and pus oozed from the sores all over his body. Desperately, he scourged again for food. He finally found a small pond in one of the tunnels, with a few fish and tadpoles in it. He managed to catch one using his dhoti as a net. The fish sustained him for a few days, but as time passed, he grew despondent. Would he ever get out of these tunnels? People didn't even know he was alive, let alone trapped underground. This was his end, his fate to die like a rodent under the palace of Mahishmathi. His brother was sitting on the throne that belonged to him, and here he was, surviving on raw fish and drinking stale water, waiting for death to visit. He had to find a way out.

The water had left the tunnels to destroy Mahishmathi city—he just had to find that path. Even if it took years, if he could survive, he would do it. Bijjala screamed into the darkness, 'I won't die like a rat. I will find him, Vikramadeva Mahadeva, and kill him.'

Bijjala tried to calm himself and think. To be able to make his way out, his body had to heal. He decided to rest awhile. In a few days, he had adjusted to the raw fish and water and his body showed signs of recovery. He could feel his muscles growing stronger once again. One day, he spotted something shining at the bottom of the pool. He waded into the water and searched for the light, for he knew what it was. He fished out the Gaurikanta stone. He studied it, and saw that it was dense; if he could fashion a handle for it, it would make a good axe.

Over the next few days, Bijjala scurried around inside the labyrinth, searching for driftwood or branches that had made their way inside. Finally, he found a gnarled branch that lay half-buried in muck.

Using the stone, he started chipping at it, shaping it into a handle. It was hard work and took lots of time, but time was the one thing he had in abundance. He trapped a bat and ate it raw, sparing only the intestine, which he dried. This, he used to tie the Gaurikanta stone to the handle he had fashioned, and he now had a crude but powerful axe that a Kalakeya would have been proud of. Bijjala swung the axe above his head and smashed it against the wall. A portion of the wall crumbled, opening the path to another tunnel running parallel to where he was standing.

Bijjala kissed the axe and howled with joy. His yells echoed through the maze of tunnels. He would smash his way through this labyrinth, and sooner or later he would find the exit. With renewed vigour, he began working his way through the tunnels, only taking breaks to hunt fish or drink some water. He slept little—the thought of reaching Mahadeva, surprising his brother, and then looking into his eyes when he smashed his head in kept Bijjala awake.

SEVENTY-TWO

# Sivagami

'YOU ARE BEING very unfair, Your Highness,' Marthanda cried.

Sivagami jumped from her seat. 'Unfair? You should be hanged, traitor.'

'We did our best, devi,' Marthanda said. 'We are not courageous like the king and you, but some of us came back to lend a hand with the Garuda pakshis. Without us, our respected Jeemotha would not have achieved what he did.'

'Of course, what would I have done without you,' Jeemotha said with a wry smile.

Sivagami gritted her teeth. 'You were nowhere around. You ran away.' Over Marthanda's protests, she continued angrily, 'Your Highness, I want all of them hanged. I want to make an example of these traitors.'

Mahadeva said in a soft voice, 'Sivagami, I agreed to your request against all my principles. I cannot do what you are asking now.'

Sivagami had managed to convince Mahadeva to give Pattaraya the death penalty, but the king had insisted on holding a trial for all the other prisoners. This had dragged on for three months, while he heard every side, consulted ancient dharma sutras, and discussed the various aspects with scholars. Today was the day he was giving his judgement. Except for Gundu Ramu, who sat in his wheeled chair in a corner of the sabha, scribbling hurriedly on a palm leaf, every pair of eyes were turned to the king. Gundu Ramu had finally been able to decipher the language in the holy book of the Kalakeyas, and was now copying out the text before it was returned.

'A king must pardon those who can be reformed,' Mahadeva said. 'Violence should be the last option. Marthanda did not do his duty, but that does not deserve the death penalty. Cowardice is not a crime. I dismiss Marthanda and his regiment from Mahishmathi's service.'

Sivagami sat in her chair, livid at what was unfolding. She could hear Somadeva's laughter ringing in her ears.

Marthanda gave a stiff bow, glared at Sivagami for a moment, and walked away.

Sivagami turned to Mahadeva and said, 'At least expel him from Mahishmathi.'

'This country is for all, devi,' Mahadeva said, trying to control his irritation. 'Who is next?' he asked Gomati.

'Ally and her Vaithalikas,' Gomati said. 'The crime is waging war against Mahishmathi, and attempting to harm the prince and the pregnant queen.'

Ally stood, now recovered from her injuries, but in chains and heartbroken. The sabha waited for the king's decision. Sivagami stared at the floor. Kattappa stood behind the throne, looking into the distance, not even blinking.

'Mahishmathi has been unfair to the Vaithalikas. I can understand the rage your people have for us. I pardon all your crimes,' Mahadeva said, and Ally looked at the king, unable to believe his words. Sivagami raised her head and stared at Mahadeva.

'I promise we will never mine Gauriparvat; the mountain shall remain holy not just for the Vaithalikas, but for everyone in this kingdom. Ally, you had talked about how an ideal kingdom would be one where there are no slaves, no discrimination based on caste, religion or gender. I will try to make Mahishmathi like that; but this is an old kingdom, and it will take time. I am gifting you sixty-four villages towards our northern borders, together called Kuntala Mandala. You establish your kingdom there and be an example for all of us. I know this is no compensation for what your people have suffered for so many generations, but I hope you will accept it.'

Sivagami cried as she heard Mahadeva's words. Ally knelt down, her shoulders heaving with emotion. The Vaithalikas broke into sobs, and with voices choking with emotion, they cried, 'Jai Vikramadeva!'

'Free her,' Mahadeva commanded. Kattappa walked towards Ally amid the thundering cries of 'Jai Vikramadeva', 'Jai Mahishmathi', 'Jai Kuntala'. As Kattappa unchained her, Ally gazed at him, wishing he would say something, that he would meet her eyes, but the slave never looked up. His duty done, Kattappa stepped to the side, waiting for the next orders.

Ally hesitated and Sivagami knew what she wanted. Sivagami turned to her trusted slave and said, 'Kattappa, you are free to go. I free you from slavery, I free you of your father's promise. You deserve better, my brother.'

She had not even consulted Mahadeva, but who knew Mahadeva's mind better than her? She would be sorry to see Kattappa go, she thought, and then, to her surprise, the slave ran to Mahadeva and fell at his feet.

'What sin did I do to be discarded like this, swami?' Kattappa wept, holding on to the king's feet. The courtiers were taken aback, for it was difficult to fathom a slave refusing the offer of freedom. But as Sivagami looked into Kattappa's tearful eyes, she could understand the man who had killed his beloved brother for his country. Ally broke into tears and called out his name. Kattappa refused to get up from his position, remaining prostrated before the king.

Finally, Ally said, 'I would be heartless to make him come with me. He belongs here. There is nothing dearer to him than Mahishmathi.' Without waiting for an answer, she turned and walked away. She paused to give a brief, tight hug to Gundu Ramu, and then marched out into the sun with the Vaithalikas following behind.

Mahadeva lifted Kattappa and said, 'You are going nowhere. You will stay with me, as my brother, serving Mahishmathi.'

Mahadeva had stepped down from his throne to hug the slave as his equal. The people in the sabha stood up to applaud this gesture; the slave's devotion had moved many to tears.

When Kattappa turned to touch Sivagami's feet, she stopped him. 'Anna, you are elder to me,' she said, and leaned down to touch his feet.

He stopped her, 'Rani, no,' he said, and smiled, making Sivagami feel proud and worthless of Kattappa's devotion at the same time.

Gomati read out, 'Kalakeyas.'

Soldiers dragged the chained Kalakeyas into the sabha. They stood mutely, staring at everyone with eyes that held more fear than hatred. Then, a boy, barely sixteen, stepped forward and extended his hand. 'We be like you. Good. Good. Give book. Our book ... holy book.'

Mahadeva smiled. 'Ah, your holy book, of course.' He gestured for Gundu Ramu to come forward. Sivagami watched, emotions overwhelming her. The book held the weight of her destiny. It had caused the death of her parents, it had changed the history of Mahishmathi, and now it was going back to where it belonged, to the Kalakeyas, who didn't know how to read, but who were willing to kill and die for it. Mahadeva ordered for the Kalakeyas to be unchained, and as Kattappa removed their chains, a few of them tried to run out of the sabha. When the guards stopped them, they growled, hurled abuses and tried to fight back.

The young boy continued to stand silently, waiting for the book. No one had stood before the king of Mahishmathi with so much self-assurance. Mahadeva smiled at the boy and placed the book reverently in his hands. The boy stared at it. Then, with utter devotion, he brought the book to both his ears and murmured what sounded like mantras.

Then, without a word of thanks, the boy turned on his heel and ran towards the door to join his companions. Many courtiers stood up, drawing their swords, bristling with anger at this lack of respect towards their king, but Mahadeva chuckled. He called out, 'What is your name, brother?'

The boy paused at the door. He looked haughtily at the king and said loudly, 'Inkoshi. I ... Inkoshi.' The name echoed in the sabha, and Inkoshi's eyes roved the hall and settled on Sivagami's face. A shiver went down Sivagami's spine.

Inkoshi marched out with confident steps, as if he were a conquering monarch, and joined his tribesmen, hooting and howling in their Kilikki tongue. At the sabha entrance, they formed a circle, began a strange ritualistic dance, drew patterns with their index fingers in the air, and together pointed at the king and at Sivagami. They clicked their tongues and bared their teeth, and with a beastly roar that shook the hall, they ran out.

Sivagami felt that Mahadeva had made a mistake by letting the Kalakeyas go. Had it been Somadeva, all of them would have been hanging from the trees that lined the royal highway. Something told her that she would meet that boy again, and Mahishmathi would pay a heavy price for Mahadeva's decision.

'Jeemotha,' Gomati called out, breaking the uneasy silence, and the pirate stepped forward. He stood with his hands on his hips and his lips curled in a derisive smile.

'Oh, am I on trial? Why am I not surprised?' Jeemotha asked.

'No, my friend,' Mahadeva smiled. 'You saved my city. You have made dozens of mahashila yantras. Your crimes are many, but I am a man of my word. I allot you a fleet of seven ships. Go forth and conquer new lands, but I want no share of it. I want no more land, I covet no riches that belong to others.'

'In other words, never come back.' Jeemotha smiled.

'No,' Mahadeva said firmly.

'Well, I was expecting to be cheated once again. You have been more than fair, Your Highness. I accept your terms. Do I get the greedy priests and merchants too?'

'You can take anyone who is willing to go with you, friend.'

Jeemotha gave an elaborate bow. Before leaving, he requested for a word with Sivagami.

'Would you care to join me? We can conquer the world together,' he whispered, and Sivagami waved her hand, dismissing him like he was a pesky fly. 'Good bye, devi. And take care of your king. Good men like him rarely last long. You need to protect him. '

Jeemotha bowed to everyone and walked away. Sivagami watched him leave, relieved. She hoped that, along with him, he would take some of her detractors. Kalicharan Bhatta, for one, and the other priests who objected to Sivagami appearing in court, for they were sure that she was now a widow and had to be confined inside the palace. She lived in dread of Bijjala's death being confirmed. As a widow, it would be difficult for her to even appear in public. Much as she resented the cruel custom, she couldn't go against age-old traditions and fight an entire city.

Mahadeva dismissed the sabha and leaned towards Sivagami. 'Have you considered what I said?'

Sivagami clenched her fist. 'You know what he did to my parents. I have done enough for Mahishmathi that I deserve this small pleasure. Don't ask me to spare Pattaraya.'

Mahadeva said, 'I am not asking you to set him free. He will lie in a dungeon forever.'

'No,' Sivagami said.

'I lived in a dungeon,' Mahadeva said.

Sivagami smiled. 'And now you are king. Put Pattaraya in a dungeon, and soon he will be sitting on your throne.'

Mahadeva said with a sigh, 'I am not enticed by the throne. I hate every moment of this.'

'That is why you are the right man to sit there. And you have made a mistake, Mahadeva, by letting all the prisoners go, especially those Kalakeyas. Your father would not have spared any of them.'

Mahadeva looked at Sivagami and smiled. 'I am not my father.'

Sivagami said, 'You don't understand how difficult it is to try and argue with a saint.'

'I am no saint, Sivagami,' Mahadeva said. 'I am like everybody else. But I don't believe that killing anyone is a solution. Violence begets violence.'

'That is the nature of the world. You can't fight it, Mahadeva.'

Mahadeva shook his head sadly. 'I know you are adamant and I can understand your emotion. But don't expect me to be present when you are killing that old man.'

Sivagami cried, 'But that isn't fair. People should see that the king is punishing the traitor. You can't shy away from your responsibility.'

But Mahadeva had already walked away. Sivagami continued to sit in the sabha, even as it emptied out and darkness crept in. She had done so much for Mahishmathi, and she had to beg for this, Sivagami fumed. But in some corner of her mind, she could understand Mahadeva. Had her father been alive, he might have said the same thing. *You need to protect him*—Jeemotha's parting words echoed in her mind, making her uneasy.

'Sivagami, there is news.' It was Gomati. Her face was grave. 'Spies have informed me that Marthanda and the other soldiers who were dismissed have not left the city. A conspiracy is brewing. We must be careful. With Mekhala still missing, I am worried.'

Sivagami's eyebrows knit in a frown. After a few moments, she said, 'The king says he won't participate in the execution of Pattaraya.'

Gomati gasped. 'But that is so improper.'

'On the contrary, I am now feeling it is for the best. If Mekhala is alive, she must be planning something to save her father.'

'A last desperate attempt.' Gomati's eyes flashed.

Sivagami smiled. 'And how would one save him when the entire Mahishmathi army will be assembled at the Mahamakam arena.'

Gomati frowned. 'If I were in Mekhala's place, I would attempt to kill the king. If I succeed, I would have started a coup. Even if I fail, I would've created enough confusion to give me an opportunity to save Pattaraya.'

Sivagami nodded. 'So, if Mekhala is going to come out of her hiding place, it has to be on the day of Pattaraya's Chitravadha. Let us lay a trap.'

'But what kind of trap? There won't be any king to assassinate, for the king has refused to participate.'

Sivagami smiled. 'Precisely. But she does not know that.'

SEVENTY-THREE

# Achi Nagamma

VAMANA CLIMBED THE hill carrying a basket of herbs he had collected from the Gauriparvat valley. By the time, the old dwarf managed to reach the small landing that lay near the peak, he was exhausted. Though the path was perilous and a single misstep could cause him to fall thousands of feet below, he had been making the climb for herbs every day for the past few days.

Achi Nagamma helped him climb the last few steps and made him sit in his usual place. The dwarf was covered in sweat and grime, and Achi couldn't thank him enough for his efforts. Vamana was an inspiration. He had lived all his life as part of someone's mindlessly cruel game, yet he had remained true to his own self. He'd had no power to fight the system, but had helped so many unfortunate children. And he had done so expecting nothing in return.

Achi sat watching his stubby hands working with surprising assuredness as he ground the different herbs he had brought.

Achi thought about her son, Brihannala. He had served her like no other. He had become a woman for her, and died cheerfully for her cause. The old woman's lips trembled as she thought about the devastating loss. And she had also sacrificed four of her beloved children, apart from Brihannala. She cursed herself for underestimating Sivagami and that pirate Jeemotha.

Vamana called out that the paste was done. She dragged herself over to his side. She pinched the herbal paste and rubbed it between her index finger and thumb. It was finely ground. Taking Vamana's hand, she started climbing up. When she saw the Garuda pakshi lying without moving, her heart skipped a beat. 'Have you also left me, daughter?' she asked in a trembling voice. The giant bird opened one of its eyes and squawked softly. Achi Nagamma put her arms over its beak and started sobbing. 'I am sorry, I can understand your pain. I lost my son, I killed him, but you lost four of them. I am a sinner. Can you ever forgive me?'

The bird struggled to open its eyes. There was no excuse for what she had done to this bird, thought Achi. The Garuda pakshi was the last of its species. Just like Achi Nagamma, the bird too was all alone in the world. They had lost to men's greed and arrogance. It was unfair.

As Vamana applied the balm he had prepared all over the burns on the bird's wing, the Garuda pakshi gave a weak cry of pain. 'It is all right daughter, it is all right. It is for your good,' Achi whispered, and the bird lay calm, soothed by its mother's voice. Later, when the bird had drifted off to sleep, Achi sat looking at Mahishmathi in the distance. Vamana sat beside her, not saying a word.

'It is unfair that Amma Gauri let them flourish and punished us like this, Vamana,' Achi said as she slammed her staff on the ground. Mist crept up from the valley and a cold breeze stung their faces. Winter was approaching, and soon Gauriparvat would be covered with snow.

Vamana said, 'We need to cover her with something, or she will freeze to death in a week or two.'

Achi looked at the shivering bird and said in a flat voice, 'I will be dead before her.'

Vamana sat, thinking about the dreadful loneliness that would envelop him on the mountain when the old woman and the bird were gone. Achi stood up and shook her fist at the mountain. 'Why Amma Gauri, why? I am a sinner, but why did you punish her? Your daughter, the poor mute bird?'

Vamana said in a low voice, 'Amma Gauri doesn't spare anyone. The signs are already there. Sooner or later she will start her dance.'

Achi looked at the dwarf questioningly. Vamana sniffed the air. 'What do you smell? Rotten eggs?' The dwarf clasped his hands as if he were trying to capture something from the air. 'For the last two decades, I have been warning them. Amma Gauri is old, as old as the earth and the stars. For her, two decades is a blink of an eye. If not today, in twenty years or thirty years or maybe a hundred years, she is sure to laugh.' Vamana's voice grew to a whisper, 'And then there would be none.'

Achi Nagamma stared at him, and then said, slowly, 'Why didn't I think of that?'

Vamana snapped his head towards her. 'We think a lot, Amma, and that is the fault of humans. We should stop thinking and just be ourselves.'

Achi Nagamma's despair had vanished. Excited, she knelt before the dwarf and said, 'Tell me, Vamana. How can we force her hand?'

Vamana said in a flat voice, 'There is perhaps one way. I am not sure of it, but I heard a great man once saying it in despair when he came here. Devaraya said that all it would take to end the cruelty of mining was to close the wound in Amma Gauri's heart. Seal the throbbing heart of Amma Gauri, the mouth of the volcano, and Amma would explode in fury ...'

'And then there would be none.' Achi Nagamma's laughter echoed through the mountains. She pointed her staff at Mahishmathi, lying drenched in the blood of dusk, and yelled to the howling wind, 'And then there will be none.'

As night fell, Vamana continued to sit, brooding. Kali seemed to be dancing before him. Her necklace of skulls swung on her bare chest, her hair aflame, her tongue hanging out, she danced with abandon. Wind licked at Vamana with her death-cold tongue. *Amma Gauri, save Mahishmathi and its people*, he prayed. Never in his life had any of his prayers been answered. He was a man forgotten by the gods. No one cared—yet, he prayed.

It started snowing and the mountains echoed with an old woman's maniacal laughter. 'And then ... there will be ... NONE!'

SEVENTY-FOUR

# Mekhala

MEKHALA WAS SITTING alone in the room. Outside, in the next room, she could hear the men who were waiting for her whisper to each other.

'Nanna, give me courage. For the first time, I am going against your advice; you wanted me to lie low and keep out of sight. But I have to try and save you, and I can't see any other way to do that,' she said, allowing herself to cry for some more time. She didn't want the men to see her tears. She was not sure how much she could trust them. They were mercenaries, recently dismissed from the Mahishmathi army. Roopaka had brought them to where she had been hiding.

When she entered the room, the men looked at her, as if judging her, before standing up. She had been their queen, and these men had once grovelled before her; now they needed to be prompted to stand up. But this was not the time to be worried about such things. They needed her and she needed them.

'I am the queen of Mahishmathi,' Mekhala said, and out of the corner of her eye, she could see the smirk on Marthanda's face. She ignored it and, staring at the wall opposite, she said in an even voice, 'All of you will be rewarded once I regain my throne.' She waited for them to voice their gratitude, but they remained silent. The mercenaries had sat back down without her permission and were now leaning back in their seats. She did not feel like this was going well.

She looked at Roopaka and he intervened. 'What Rani Mekhala devi is offering is the position of mahapradhana to the venerable Marthanda.'

Marthanda's lips twitched. 'I am a soldier, and I was the general of Mahishmathi. Why would I want to be someone scribbling some nonsense on a palm leaf? I cannot even hold a stylus.' He raised his palm, splayed his fingers and continued. 'See these calluses. I earned them in battle. So the position of mahapradhana doesn't tempt me.'

Mekhala looked at Roopaka helplessly and he said, 'How about money?' Marthanda looked at his comrades and they burst out laughing.

Mekhala snapped, 'Let us not waste time. Tell me what it is you want.'

Marthanda leaned forward and said, 'Gauriparvat. We will own it and we will hold all the mining rights. I will be the king of the mountain and my colleagues will be the ministers.'

Roopaka said, 'But, Gauriparvat—'

Marthanda leaned back in his chair, crossed his legs and said, 'Now that there is no longer the threat of the Garuda pakshis, I believe it is there for our taking.'

Roopaka was about to argue but Mekhala raised her hand. She said in a weary voice, 'Agreed.' Nothing mattered to her anymore except saving her father.

Marthanda smiled. 'I have stopped believing in the sanctity of spoken words long ago.' He looked at Roopaka and the bureaucrat fished out a palm leaf from his waistband. He looked expectantly at Mekhala, and when she nodded, he scribbled an agreement and passed it on to her. Mekhala started reading out, 'I, Mekhala devi, the queen of Mahishmathi, hereby grant—' but Marthanda snatched it from her hands.

Roopaka asked, 'Don't you want to read it?'

'I have never troubled myself with learning the letters. We live by the sword and our …' Marthanda tapped his head.

'So it is settled,' Mekhala said. 'We will go through our plan once again—'

Marthanda cut her off rudely. 'I know the plan by heart. Tomorrow, when they are going to kill your father, we will be in the crowd among the onlookers. You will be at a vantage point from where you will shoot the king. In the chaos that will follow, we will rush to the Gauristhalam, free your father, and butcher everybody on the pyramid platform. Then we will hail you as the queen of Mahishmathi.'

Mekhala nodded. 'The most important thing is to free my father.'

Marthanda waved the palm leaf before her face and said, 'For us, this is most important.'

The mercenaries walked out. When the sounds of their heavy steps on the spiral staircase had faded, Roopaka cleared his throat. 'Devi, if I may say so, it is risky for you to shoot the king with an arrow. If you miss—'

'I won't miss, not when it is to save my father.' Roopaka opened his mouth to object, but she raised her hand. 'No, I don't want you to do it. It must be done by me. And you have another job, Roopaka. I want you to get me something. I want the most potent poison you can get.'

Roopaka stared at her. 'Devi, you aren't thinking of—'

Mekhala laughed. 'I am not one to take my own life. That isn't what my father taught me. This is to finish off Mahishmathi's royal family, and who better than you to do that admirable task.'

Roopaka felt uneasy. He had betrayed many, caused the death of some, but what Mekhala was asking him to do was unpalatable, even for him.

'You may be wondering what is there for you in this, isn't it, friend?' Mekhala asked. Roopaka hesitated and shuffled his feet. Mekhala put a hand on his shoulder and said, 'The position you have always coveted. When I am queen again, you will be the mahapradhana of Mahishmathi. Or would you prefer to be the vassal king of Kadarimandalam?'

When Roopaka's eyes sparkled, Mekhala knew that any qualms he had about following her instructions had dissolved in his greed.

'I will get the poison,' he whispered, and she patted his shoulder in encouragement. Now all she needed to do was wait for the next day when they would drag her father out and proclaim his death sentence.

SEVENTY-FIVE

# Sivagami

SIVAGAMI LOOKED AT the boy standing before her with affection. She had seen him fighting bravely when the Garuda pakshis had attacked. Gomati stood beaming near him, as if the boy were her own brother.

'What is your name?' Sivagami asked.

The boy replied in a respectful voice, 'Shaktadu, but my friends call me Shakti.'

Sivagami asked, 'Are you aware of the risk, brother?'

Shaktadu said, 'Her excellency the mahapradhana has explained it all to me. I am proud to do this, for my country and also for …' he hesitated. Sivagami waited for him to continue. She couldn't help noticing that the boy had a strong resemblance to Mahadeva, and at certain angles, he resembled Bijjala too. Was her suspicion correct? She didn't want to ask, though, and hurt the boy.

When he remained silent, she said, 'Mahishmathi will always be grateful to you, and I guarantee that nothing will happen to you. The best of our warriors, Kattappa, will ensure that.'

The slave, who was standing silent in a corner, bowed as if in acknowledgement. Sivagami dismissed them and the boy embarrassed her by touching her feet before leaving. When they were alone, Sivagami turned to Gomati and said, 'What do you think?'

'We might have to barricade the crowd some distance away from the Gauristhalam. From a distance, he can pass for Mahadeva.'

Sivagami smiled. 'I am sure you will organise that, but I was asking something else. How come the strong resemblance?'

Gomati burst out, 'If you roam the streets of Mahishmathi, you will find many men and women resembling our king.'

Sivagami shook her head. 'How different his two sons born in wedlock turned out to be. I would grant this, Maharaja Somadeva—may his atma achieve moksha—enjoyed his life to the fullest.'

'And left all these issues for us to solve, while his saintly son sits on the throne and thinks a country can be ruled with a smile and some kindness.'

The two women laughed, and then Sivagami's tone grew serious. 'On no account should Shaktadu's life be in danger. Place men everywhere, and I'm sure we will trap Pattaraya's daughter. And once we capture her, I want to see Pattaraya's face when we give her the punishment she deserves. That should be the last thing he sees before he leaves this life.'

Gomati nodded.

The day dawned with the people of Mahishmathi hurrying to witness another spectacle. Inside the tunnels, meanwhile, Bijjala was trying desperately to escape. He had smashed through most of the labyrinth, but was yet to find a way out. He could feel a cold breeze coming from somewhere, but was not able to locate the source. If only he could place where the breeze was coming from, he knew he would find the way out.

As if from a distance, he could hear cheering and sloganeering. Some event was happening inside the fort. He heard people hailing Mahadeva, and with renewed anger, Bijjala continued to hack at the walls.

SEVENTY-SIX

# Achi Nagamma

IN DISTANT GAURIPARVAT, Achi was supervising Vamana's arrangements. They were standing at the rim of the volcano mouth, and Achi was holding her hand over her nose. The intense stink of rotten eggs seemed to be sticking to her skin. She felt pity for Vamana, who had been toiling for the last few days, erecting a wall of mud and stones around the volcano mouth. In the heat from the volcano, the wall that Vamana was erecting had hardened and become like a rock.

As she did with everything, Achi had meticulously planned what they had to do. She had measured the mouth of the volcano and rummaged through the mountain to find a boulder that was right for the task. Achi Nagamma's only worry was whether her Garuda pakshi would be able to carry the boulder. The bird's wing had only barely started healing; there were now small feathers where her wing had been charred.

Vamana turned to Achi Nagamma and said, 'It is ready, Amma.'

Achi Nagamma nodded gravely and climbed up the steps. Her heart went out to the poor Garuda pakshi. She tried to suppress the sobs that threatened to weaken her as she struggled to climb the hill. Behind her, the mighty waterfall roared and disappeared into the mouth of Gauriparvat. Steam and smoke curled around her as the volcano hissed. Trembling, Achi Nagamma staggered out of Gauriparvat's mouth.

Achi started climbing towards the landing where the Garuda pakshi lay. In the golden light of the rising sun, the mother Garuda pakshi looked majestic. As its mother approached, the bird gave a cry of recognition, and Achi burst into sobs. The breeze dislodged a soft feather from the bird's wing and it floated in front of Achi for a moment, caressing her cheek before it floated towards the valley. The old woman stood watching the sunlight play on the feather. The world was so beautiful, and life so exhilarating.

The bird squawked; her plea to Achi to come over and pet her. Achi threw herself on the bird's neck. In its gigantic ears, which lay hidden between the feathers, she whispered, 'Forgive me, daughter. We do not belong here. Let us fly to a new dawn, where hopefully there will be no greed or ambition. Will you take me there, dear?'

In answer, the bird nudged her with its giant beak. Achi knew that if she hesitated any more, she would lose courage. She turned towards Mahishmathi, now bathed in the glory of the sun's rays. She drew herself up to her full height and cried to the wind, 'So far, you have come seeking Gauriparvat; today, she comes to visit you.'

The mountain breathed in a low rumble. Amma Gauri had spoken her heart. Achi knew it was time. She heaved herself up on the shoulders of the bird. The Garuda pakshi became alert and struggled to its feet. It tried to flap its wings, and gave a cry of pain. Achi leaned forward and whispered into the bird's ears, 'Just do it for me, dear. One last thing for your mother.'

Giving an unearthly cry, the bird soared to the sky. Its charred wing didn't have its earlier strength, but it was powered by the inexplicable love it felt for the woman who was taking her somewhere. With the excitement of a child going out after the rains, the bird circled over Gauriparvat. Achi looked down and could see the mouth of the volcano—the fiery eye of a giant staring at her. From above, Gauriparvat didn't look benevolent like Gauri, it had the fiery face of Kali. Wind screamed in her ears, snow fell in beautiful flakes, glistening like diamonds in the sunlight. It was a glorious day to die.

Achi directed the bird to the boulder and, on her command, the bird lifted it up. The gale became stronger and the bird struggled with the weight, but Achi kept urging her daughter that the time had come to be in a beautiful place. Trusting her mother, the bird rose higher and higher till the mountain's mouth was a pinhole. The clouds hid the mountain and enveloped them in an embrace, whispering the poetry of life in their ears. It was a glorious day to live.

Achi uttered a silent prayer, 'Amma Gauri, here I come, accept me into your womb.'

Vamana looked through the opening above his head. Near him the waterfall roared and vanished into the well of lava, hissing and spouting the smoke that swirled around him.

The old dwarf waited, sitting cross-legged as if in meditation, feeling the throb of the mountain under him.

From far above, the Garuda pakshi dove towards the open arms of Gauriparvat. Vamana could hear them approaching, and he whispered a prayer. 'In my next life, make me a bird or a butterfly, Amma Gauri.'

At that moment, the bird gave a shriek. A flutter of wings, an unearthly cry, and then silence before the wall collapsed with the impact of the boulder. Vamana saw Achi and the bird vanish into the mouth of Gauriparvat and the boulder was wedged at the mouth. Through narrow gaps, the mountain hissed and spewed. The dwarf could feel the anger inside the belly of Amma Gauri bubbling up. Vamana sat waiting for the thandav of Kali to commence.

SEVENTY-SEVEN

# Mahadeva

AKHILA HELD MAHADEVA'S hand. Since that morning, she had been feeling contractions although she was only in her eighth month of pregnancy. She was afraid that she would deliver prematurely. The previous night, an unspeakable nightmare had woken her, and she hadn't allowed Mahadeva to sleep after that. The premonition of something dreadful hung in the air.

Mahadeva sat beside his wife as she moaned in pain, his eyes welling up. Her face went blank sometimes, and she flitted in and out of consciousness. The rajavaidya had assured him that it was normal for some women to deliver prematurely, and since Akhila was nearing nine months of pregnancy anyway, it was not cause for worry. In case of an emergency, the rajavaidya was waiting in a nearby room.

'I can see him ...' Akhila said, gripping Mahadeva's hands and staring blankly.

'Who, my dear?' Mahadeva asked.

Akhila whispered, 'Death.'

'Don't talk like that.'

'Don't leave me. Please ...'

Mahadeva was uneasy. He believed in the law of karma. Killing Pattaraya would cause its own results. Why couldn't Sivagami understand that she would pay the price one day or another? Mahadeva felt he too would pay for the chain of violence being unleashed.

From outside, the cheers from an enthusiastic crowd floated in. Most people just wanted a show—they didn't mind who was getting killed. The same people who had cheered for the Chitravadha of Devaraya were baying for Pattaraya's head. *Will my child grow up in a better world?* Mahadeva looked at Akhila and her swollen belly. She had drifted off to sleep, but her fingers were still wound around Mahadeva's wrist.

The cheering from the Gauristhalam had become louder and Mahadeva heard something that took him by surprise. They were yelling his name, and then there was the unmistakable sound of blaring horns and frenzied drumming meant to be played at the appearance of the monarch. What was happening outside? Sivagami had pulled off some trick. An uncharacteristic fury gripped him and he rushed to the door. Akhila called out in a weak voice, 'Please ... don't go.' With a sigh, Mahadeva shut the door and returned to her side.

Hidden in the attic of Akhila's chamber, Roopaka hurriedly pushed the plank in the ceiling back into place. He had been lying on his belly, watching the royal couple. When he saw the king moving towards the door, he had started to descend, but had to abort his plan when Mahadeva came back. He cursed his own greed that had made him agree to the despicable task that Mekhala had given him. He ran his fingers over the contours of the small vial of poison in his waistband and sighed. Why was the king still with his queen? Wasn't he supposed to be in the Gauristhalam to preside over Pattaraya's execution? Roopaka waited impatiently, trying hard to fight a sneeze.

SEVENTY-EIGHT

# Mekhala

MEKHALA LAY ON her stomach on the slanting roof of Mahishmathi palace. She could see the king's entourage approaching the Gauristhalam. The citizens of Mahishmathi broke into loud cheering, and when Mekhala heard the cries of 'Jai Sivagami devi', her lips trembled with anger. She gripped the bow tightly and drew an arrow from her quiver. Soldiers dragged Pattaraya out and pushed and shoved him through a jeering crowd towards the Gauristhalam.

Mekhala's eyes welled up and she turned her face away, allowing her tears to fall. When she looked again, they were pushing her dear Nanna up the steps that led to the top of the pyramid. Frail and broken, chained like an untamed beast, Pattaraya took each step with deliberate slowness. The crowd roared, 'Traitor, traitor, traitor.' Drums beat loudly, and curved horns blared. Dust rose in thick swirls as the people moved restively. Fathers had their sons and daughters perched on their shoulders. It was a hot and humid day. In the azure sky, eagles circled around.

Mekhala scanned the cheering hordes and she could see that Marthanda and his men were positioned strategically in the crowd. Once again, her eyes went to her father, and she felt her limbs weaken. Then the cheering became thunderous. 'Jai Vikramadeva', 'Jai Mahadeva', 'Jai Rajadhiraja Vikramadeva'.

The king of Mahishmathi descended from his chariot, waved to the crowd, and climbed the steps to sit on the throne. Mekhala frowned. They had put up barricades in front of the Gauristhalam and at least twenty feet separated the people from the ruler. Even the path through which the chariots had arrived had bamboo barricades on either side. It was uncharacteristic of Mahadeva, who loved to walk among the crowd, allowing them to touch him, holding their hands and pinching the cheeks of giggling babies. Why was he being so aloof today?

Mekhala felt uneasy, but pushed her doubts away. Maybe they wanted to ensure maximum security for the execution.

Sivagami raised her arm and the crowd went silent. The soldiers were raising the cage in which Pattaraya was to be hoisted. Sivagami glanced at Pattaraya. He looked like a broken old man and not the villain she had always known him to be. Mahadeva's words came rushing back. 'No one is good or bad. It is the circumstances that make them act in a particular way.'

Sivagami chided herself—she should not be weak now, at this moment. *I am Sivagami and I have lived for this revenge,* she thought. Pattaraya was the last among those who had executed her parents. Taking a deep breath, she held up a palm leaf book and untied the string that bound it. The crowd waited in anticipation for her to read out the crime of the accused, and get on with the entertainment. The cage rhythmically creaked as it swung above Pattaraya's head.

Sivagami glanced towards Shaktadu, who was sitting on the throne. So far, the deception had worked perfectly. His glittering costume had drawn attention away from his face.

Sivagami's eyes scanned the crowd. If Mekhala was alive, this was the moment she would reveal herself. Sivagami started reading out Pattaraya's crimes. 'You, Pattaraya, as bhoomipathi, were once one of the nobles who presided over the unfair killing of the noble bhoomipathi Devaraya and his wife.'

Pattaraya snickered, and that erased any sympathy Sivagami had for him.

With renewed vigour, Sivagami listed out Pattaraya's crimes: how he had killed Skandadasa and then conspired with Kadarimandalam, stolen the Gaurikanta stones and brought down Somadeva. Why did Mekhala not appear, she wondered as she read.

Pattaraya didn't miss Sivagami's agitation. He turned his head towards the king and Sivagami knew that Pattaraya, standing only a few feet away, had seen through the deception. He was about to say something when an arrow whizzed past his ears. A dull thud was heard. Kattappa, standing behind the throne, had brought his shield up to protect Shaktadu, and the arrow had lodged in it. Shaktadu trembled in fear behind it.

Sivagami's gaze followed the path of the arrow. 'There,' she yelled, pointing at the roof. The soldiers that Gomati had kept ready rushed to corner Mekhala.

Pattaraya let out an animal cry. 'Why, daughter, why? Why did you disobey me? Now everything is finished!'

Sivagami stood before him with a victorious smile. 'Your daughter loves you, Pattaraya. Now you two can be in the same place forever.'

Mekhala put up an admirable fight against the soldiers who approached her. She managed to knock over three men and they toppled down from the roof to their death. That angered the crowd and they started baying for her blood. When the soldiers finally captured her, Sivagami heaved a sigh of relief.

'Drag her here,' she commanded.

Gomati whispered in Sivagami's ears, 'What will the king say when he hears that we have hanged a woman?'

Sivagami snapped at Gomati, 'I will tell him about a five-year-old who witnessed a fire swallowing her mother. I will remind him about his favourite law of karma.'

As Mekhala was dragged up the steps of the pyramid, she paused for a moment to glare at Sivagami. Pattaraya stood with his eyes downcast.

Mekhala's eyes scanned the crowd: where was Marthanda? When she spotted him standing in the crowd, a blank expression on his face, Mekhala sneered. She had trusted a mercenary, and she deserved what she was getting.

Marthanda had had every intention of keeping his word, but the same doubts that had assailed Mekhala when she saw the unusual barricade had fired his instincts to wait and watch. He followed the first rule of the mercenary code: save yourself first.

Sivagami raised her arm again and addressed the crowd. 'This evil woman oppressed each of us for five years. On behalf of the people of Mahishmathi—'

Mekhala raised her voice above Sivagami's. 'Beloved people of Mahishmathi. I carry the royal heir of Mahishmathi. I am pregnant.'

A gasp went through the crowd, followed by an agitated murmur. Sivagami looked at Mekhala in shock. Mekhala had thrown her last dice. She thought she had turned the board of chaturanga to her favour. People might despise her, but if they knew that she carried Prince Bijjala's baby in her womb, they would not be happy to see her killed. Mekhala looked at her father, expecting him to appreciate her quick thinking, but Pattaraya's eyes were filled with tears, and he shook his head in dismay.

Sivagami raised her hand, and the crowd's murmuring died down. Sivagami turned to Mekhala and said, 'You are pregnant from my husband. Congratulations. But you don't look pregnant. May I know how many months pregnant you are?'

Mekhala's heart sank. She understood her father's reaction. She didn't answer. Sivagami drew her sword and raised Mekhala's chin with its tip. 'How many months?'

Mekhala mumbled, 'Three months.'

The silence that followed was chilling. Sivagami laughed aloud. 'You heard that, people of Mahishmathi? The queen is three months pregnant.'

A murmur arose. The crowd was getting restless.

'When did my husband leave Mahishmathi?'

'A year ago,' many voices cried from different parts of the crowd.

'Fourteen months back, my dear people.'

The crowd roared. Mekhala fell on her knees and wept. She had made a grave mistake.

With a dramatic sweep of her arm, Sivagami asked, 'So what does that make her?'

'Whore, whore, whore,' the crowd cried in unison, with the customary glee of a mob that finds pleasure in morally judging the high and mighty.

'What is the punishment for a whore?'

'Burn her. Burn the whore.'

Gomati placed her hand on Sivagami's shoulder. 'The king would be furious, Sivagami. Please …'

Pattaraya was weeping loudly. 'Kill me first. Don't let me see my daughter burn. Kill me, kill me first.'

Sivagami shrugged off Gomati's restraining hand and leaned towards Pattaraya. 'Remember this face? A five-year-old child watching her mother being burnt alive, remember that? What do you suggest, Pattaraya? Do you want your daughter to watch you die, or do you want to see your daughter burn? Which do you prefer?'

Pattaraya's eyes flashed in anger. 'You are the most heartless woman I have met.'

Sivagami shook her head and said scornfully, 'I didn't choose this life. Men like you made me like this. And unlike you, I have never killed anyone innocent. This is justice, Pattaraya. The justice of Rani Sivagami devi.'

'If your husband Bijjala comes back, will you kill him too?' Pattaraya asked with a sneer.

Sivagami turned her face away.

Pattaraya hissed, 'Would you dare to be a widow?'

Sivagami seethed with anger, but chose not to answer. She moved away and made a show of consulting with the king. Shaktadu was white with fear, but he acted admirably.

Sivagami turned to the crowd and said, 'The king has ordered the death of the whore first. Soldiers, prepare the pyre.'

As the soldiers fanned the pyre in front of the Gauristhalam, terror-filled memories of her childhood came rushing back.

She could see herself screaming with horror as Rudra Bhatta pushed her mother into the fire. The crowd waited with bated breath and Sivagami caught Mekhala by her hand and took her to the edge of the Gauristhalam platform. As flames danced in anticipation, the heat made Sivagami feel uncomfortably hot. She hesitated for a moment at what she was going to do.

Mekhala said, 'Just like you, I have been a good daughter to my father, yet you are heartlessly killing a pregnant woman.'

Sivagami looked at her. 'You are not pregnant, liar.'

Mekhala did not reply for a moment. Then, with a sudden fury, she turned to her and said, 'I curse you, Sivagami. You will never know happiness in life. My curse will follow you. You will kill the ones you love the most. You will see Mahishmathi torn by internal strife, with brothers killing brothers, mothers killing sons and fathers killing daughters. This is my curse on—'

Sivagami didn't let her complete her sentence. She pushed Mekhala into the burning fire. Her screams and the smell of charred hair and flesh filled the air. Sivagami watched Mekhala burn with a face set in stone. Her fiery eyes reflected the dance of fire as she looked on blankly. Somewhere in her heart, she knew Mahadeva would condemn her actions. She could see Skandadasa looking at her sadly, and Parameswara shaking his head in dismay at what she had turned out to be. And then she heard the laughter of Somadeva.

She waited for the euphoria of revenge to fill her, but all she felt was a hollowness in her heart. She watched soldiers putting Pattaraya into the cage and she raised her hand to stop them. She didn't want the spectacle anymore. Gomati heaved a sigh of relief and asked, 'Are you going to spare him?'

Sivagami shook her head. She knew there was no turning back now that she had started on this path; but at least she would not take pleasure in the cruelty anymore. A weariness was creeping over her. Killing Pattaraya no longer carried the sweetness of revenge, but the distaste of performing an unsavoury duty. Sivagami said, 'We will hang him. That will be quicker.'

When Pattaraya heard this, he let out a laugh. Mahapradhana Gomati announced the king's decision to hang Pattaraya, and the crowd groaned at the disappointment of missing the spectacle of Chitravadha. As the noose fell around Pattaraya's neck, he continued to smile at Sivagami, and she wanted desperately to wipe that expression off his face. She wished he would cry out, curse her, abuse her. She was facing a man who had nothing left to live for. But with his despicable smile, Pattaraya was telling her that she was no different from him.

In order for everyone to see Pattaraya being hanged, the soldiers removed the sides and the top of the cage. They made Pattaraya stand on the bottom plate, and with the noose around his neck, they raised the platform. To hang him, they would pull away the platform, and Pattaraya would swing thirty feet high over the crowd. The people cheered as the platform was raised. There would be some entertainment at least, even if the spectacle was not as gruesome as a Chitravadha. They munched on their roasted chickpeas and chewed on sliced sugarcane and waited.

The chains creaked as the platform on which Pattaraya was standing was hoisted up. The guards adjusted the rope, tested its strength, and then Pattaraya's laughter boomed. He was gazing towards Gauriparvat. 'Fools, stop cheering. All of you are going to follow me in a moment.'

Sivagami ignored him and gave the order for the platform to be pulled away, and Pattaraya's body hung from the noose. His limbs thrashed around for a few moments. They heard the sound of his neck breaking, and that was the end of Pattaraya. The crowd started dancing as if each one among them had won a fortune. They had seen the gruesome death of a powerful man, and even if they lived like rodents for the rest of their lives, this was enough. Once again, Sivagami could hear Somadeva's mocking laugh and his voice. *They don't need their ruler to be noble, my dear. They want rulers to give them a spectacle. They will continue to cheer for you, die for you and hail you as God. Bloody blind devotees; fools; give them what they deserve. Give them theatre and empty promises about good days to come, and you can steal from their begging bowls.* She had never hated Somadeva more than at that moment, for with a shock she realised she had become him.

Just then, an explosion shook the very foundation of Mahishmathi. Somebody screamed 'Earthquake!' and there were yells and shouts—and then they saw it. Gauriparvat was disintegrating before their eyes; it was spewing fire and molten rock was being flung high into the sky, making the mundane theatrics of men look juvenile.

People scrambled to leave the arena, running here and there. A stampede began. The mountain was rushing towards them. Palace walls were crumbling and parts of the fort had cracked. A portion of the fort gate fell down, crushing many people. From the stables, horses bolted and elephants broke their chains, running into the palace grounds and creating even more chaos.

Mahadeva had run out of his chamber when he heard the explosion. He had felt the entire palace moving. It was as if he were in a ship being tossed by a storm, and when he looked towards Gauriparvat, he knew that they all had very little time to live. Ignoring the desperate cries of his wife, he ran outside. He had to save his people. Nothing else mattered.

SEVENTY-NINE

# Gundu Ramu

GUNDU RAMU TOO had excused himself from seeing Pattaraya being killed, and was in the royal library when the explosion occurred. The explosion threw him off his chair and he lay on the floor, trembling with fear. This was the event predicted in the holy book of the Kalakeyas; this was the event that Devaraya had warned about long ago; this was the death dance of Amma Gauri.

Ramu struggled to get back into his wheeled chair, but failed. The earth was still trembling; shelves had fallen, and manuscripts and furniture lay strewn all over. After many attempts, Gundu Ramu finally managed to get into his chair. The walls were swaying and things continued to tumble down around him. It felt like the end of the world, and his teeth chattered in fear. He was trapped in the debris, the path out being blocked by shelves and a part of the roof that had caved in.

Fear paralysed Gundu Ramu and he prayed to Amma Gauri. 'Show me a way, Amma,' he cried. 'You are our protector, you are our destroyer too. Save us, Amma Gauri.' As if in answer, something flashed in his mind. The words in the holy book of the Kalakeyas. Amma Gauri was the protector. Amma Gauri ...

Yes, only she could save them. Pushing himself out of the wheeled chair, Gundu Ramu started crawling towards the door, pulling himself over the shelves. He had to find either Sivagami or Mahadeva, someone who would listen to him.

The scene outside was terrifying. Gundu Ramu had seen Mahishmathi destroyed by the flood and later by the Garuda pakshis, but nothing had prepared him for what was unfolding before his eyes now. The earth seemed to be caving in. In the distance, Gauriparvat continued to explode in short intervals, and it seemed as if the sky itself was melting in the heat. The very air seemed to be boiling, stinging his eyes, burning his skin.

The volcanic eruption had triggered a forest fire that was fast approaching Mahishmathi. Soon the city would be engulfed in flames. From what he had read in the holy book of the Kalakeyas, he knew that even the river would not protect Mahishmathi. Rather, the river would become a conduit, bringing lava from Gauriparvat to the city. The apocalypse that the Kalakeyas had witnessed, the apocalypse that had ended ancient civilisations and changed the course of their world had come visiting once again. Hot winds carried soot, and the air had the taste of ash; the pungent smell of gases made people choke.

But there was perhaps a way to stop it. Even the ancient Kalakeya seer who had written the book had only speculated about its efficacy. The last verses in the book were the laments of the seer that none had listened to him.

Another tremor took down a pillar and it crashed a few feet from Gundu Ramu, showering him with debris. Ramu continued to crawl forward, insignificant, helpless, while the Goddess of death danced all around.

## EIGHTY

# Akhila

ROOPAKA CLAWED AT the floor of the attic as the entire building trembled and swayed. He suppressed a terrified scream with great difficulty. The part of the attic he was on opened up, and he landed hard on the floor. The room was more or less intact, and the king was not there. He saw Queen Akhila writhing in pain and screaming. Sivagami's baby lay in a cradle in a corner of the room, crying. Roopaka scrambled up and stood panting, leaning against the wall and watching Akhila. When the first wave of tremors ended, there was an uneasy calm. Taking out the container of poison from his waistband, Roopaka walked towards Akhila. The queen was in agony; her eyes were closed, and she had not even noticed his presence. Roopaka looked over his shoulder and tipped the poison into a bowl of milk that had been placed near the queen.

Footsteps outside startled him. In his panic, some milk spilt as he took the bowl to Akhila's lips. The queen was yelling with pain, and Roopaka said in a soft voice, 'Drink this, it will ease your pain.'

Akhila's eyes fluttered weakly, and Roopaka added, 'I am the rajavaidya's assistant, Your Highness. He sent this medicine for your pain.' He pressed the bowl to Akhila's lips.

Someone knocked on the door. 'Devi, are you all right?' The rajavaidya had arrived, and Roopaka knew he didn't have much time. He prised open Akhila's mouth and emptied the milk bowl into it. Akhila tried to spit it out, but he held her mouth shut.

Akhila thrashed her legs around, gasping for breath, and the three-legged stool by the bedside toppled, shattering a bowl of fruits. The next moment, the door was flung open and the rajavaidya yelled, 'Soldiers!'

Roopaka sprung away from the bed and tried to climb a table so he could scramble back into the attic, but he couldn't reach it.

'What have you done, you scoundrel?' the rajavaidya screamed and lunged at Roopaka.

Roopaka pushed the elderly man away and took off towards the door, but was confronted by the soldiers the rajavaidya had summoned. At that moment, the earth shook again, and it seemed as if the entire palace was tilting towards one side. Roopaka lost his balance, careened towards the corridor and fell on his back. Seizing the opportunity, he scrambled up and fled, but as if the hands of fate were waiting for him, a beam from the roof crashed down on his head, killing him instantly.

The soldiers ran back into the chambers, hearing the rajavaidya's panicked cries. They saw the queen had stopped moving, and the rajavaidya was sitting on the floor with his face buried in his hands. When the guards came inside, he looked up and said, 'Get the king, quick. She doesn't have much time to live. He has poisoned her.'

The rajavaidya looked at Akhila, who was turning a pale blue. As hope drained out of the old court physician, he continued to sit on the floor, not knowing how he would face the king.

EIGHTY-ONE

# Sivagami

MAHADEVA HAD MANAGED to bring some order to the chaos. He was able to get people to stop running and instead assemble in the open, ensuring that no one was near any buildings as the tremors continued. Sivagami stood by his side, ashamed to face him. Behind the stone throne, Shaktadu sat trembling, hiding from the king. Above them, the inert body of Pattaraya swung in the breeze. The pyre that had consumed Mekhala continued to blaze.

Gundu Ramu dragged himself forward as fast as he could, beseeching whomever he saw to take him to the king. But people were busy saving their own lives or searching for their loved ones, and had no time for him. Finally he reached the Gauristhalam, and Sivagami ran to help him up. Mahadeva raised his fist in the air and shouted, 'Jai Mahishmathi!' Initially, there was some scattered response, but as he persisted, the panicked people rallied behind their leader. Someone cried 'Jai Vikramadeva', and from thousands of throats, the cry echoed. In answer, Mahadeva yelled, 'Jai Mahishmathi,' filling his people with courage and hope.

Someone yelled from the fort, 'The river, look at the river.' Many men rushed to the rampart.

'Look, it is a river of fire. The river is boiling. It is carrying molten lava to the city.' Cries of despair rose and men started running around again.

Gundu Ramu said, 'Your Highness. The only thing that can stop Gauriparvat is Gauridhooli. We need to erect a wall of Gauridhooli metal. It can withstand fire and it can withstand the lava, for it is made of the same material that forms the belly of the holy parvat.'

'How do you know?' Sivagami asked incredulously.

Gundu Ramu said, 'That is the final chapter in the holy book of the Kalakeyas.'

'Bring all weapons made of Gauridhooli. Fast,' Mahadeva commanded, flinging his sword into the pyre burning at the bottom of the Gauristhalam. Sivagami followed, and soon soldiers were bringing every piece of weapon made of Gauridhooli. The flame blazed, melting everything. The molten river was moving swiftly towards their city, and steam from the river now covered Mahishmathi. The heat from the forest fire singed their eyelashes—it was so close to them.

The pile of swords and shields all melted in the blazing fire that had consumed Mekhala only a little while ago. An eerie blue light spiralled up and throbbed. Soldiers screamed, 'It is here, it is here!' They could see the lava rushing through the river and time was running out. But when the soldiers tried to lift the molten Gauridhooli using ordinary metal barrels, it simply dissolved the containers. A sense of panic started building up in the soldiers. How were they going to transport the Gauridhooli?

'Fashion a barrel out of Gauridhooli itself,' Sivagami called out, and the soldiers poured water on a part of the molten Gauridhooli and then beat it into two vats. When they solidified, they used one to pour molten Gauridhooli into the larger one, and Kattappa rushed with it to the fort wall. He emptied the molten metal over the wall and it formed a layer as it cooled.

Soon a chain of men stood from the pyramid to the fort wall by the river. The vat of molten metal was passed through relay and soldiers poured it over the wall, giving it a metal shield.

At any moment, the river of lava would reach the city, but they were ready. From Mahishmathi to distant Gauriparvat, it was an expanse of fire and smoke. For a moment, Sivagami's heart went out to the villages and the tribes that populated the forests. The fire would have annihilated them along with the birds, the beasts, and plants. As usual, it was the powerless and the innocent that paid the price for the avarice of the rich. And once again, human ingenuity was finding a method to tackle the consequences of their reckless acts, protecting the privileged while leaving the less fortunate to the vagaries of nature.

Sivagami stood at the top of the fort, watching the wall being strengthened, as more and more molten metal was poured over it. The lava started nudging at the northernmost edges of the fort. Sivagami watched with bated breath.

She saw that as the lava came into contact with the wall shield, it cooled down and fused with the Gauridhooli, making the fort stronger. She nearly collapsed with relief. She could hear the cheering of her soldiers; they were calling out 'Jai Sivagami Devi', as if she had saved the city.

Sivagami turned towards the people and, raising both her arms, she uttered thanks to Amma Gauri for sparing them. The mountain they had disrespected, exploited, mined and destroyed had just shrugged its shoulders in annoyance and caused impossible destruction. As far as her eyes could see, the land lay barren and charred. It would be in this barren land that an epic war would be fought in the future: the Kalakeyas led by Inkoshi against the Mahishmathi army led by two princes competing for the throne. That story belongs to another place and time.

---

Inside the tunnel, Bijjala lay trapped. He had smashed open many of the walls and was sure that he had found the escape route when the volcanic eruption happened. In the series of tremors that followed, tunnels collapsed and some pathways were blocked. Whatever progress he had made in the past few months had gone in vain and Bijjala started panicking. There were some paths that linked to the river, and as the lava began to sneak in, it filled the tunnels with poisonous gas. Bijjala started screaming at the top of his voice, 'Help me, help me, please—help!'

There was no one to hear his cries.

EIGHTY-TWO

# Mahadeva

MAHADEVA RUSHED TO Skandadasa's abandoned mansion. He had seen smoke billowing from the rear side of it. When he reached, several soldiers had already surrounded the well from which thick dark smoke was emerging. It took only a moment for him to realise what was happening. The boiling river water was flooding the tunnel he used in his childhood to escape to the river.

It would be minutes before the hot lava that they had stopped at the fort walls would find its way inside through the well. He remembered the trapdoor in the well. They had to secure it quickly using Gauridhooli. 'Kattappa, forge a plate of five feet by three feet. Rush,' Mahadeva commanded, and Kattappa ran to fetch what the king wanted.

When Kattappa returned, dragging a sizzling plate made of Gauridhooli metal, he found the soldiers agitated.

'Maharaja Vikramadeva has entered the well,' they said.

Kattappa called out into the smoke, 'Swami, the plate is ready.'

'Lower it,' Mahadeva's voice echoed from the depths, followed by a bout of coughs. Kattappa could see his outline in the dry bottom of the well.

'Fast, Kattappa,' Mahadeva cried and coughed again. 'The old door is rusted. Fast.'

Kattappa hoisted the Gauridhooli plate on his shoulders and was about to descend, when he saw Mahadeva pressing his ears to the rusted trapdoor. A jet of scalding hot water shot out.

'It is him,' Mahadeva said, 'Bijjala is trapped inside,' and he frantically started to punch and kick the rusted door. It fell apart and the smoke thickened, blinding Kattappa for a moment. When the smoke cleared, there was a yawning gap on the floor and Mahadeva had disappeared. Leaving the soldiers to hold the Gauridhooli plate, Kattappa leapt down into the well and entered the tunnel.

The smell of rotten eggs assaulted him. His eyes stung; choking and coughing, he waded through the knee-deep water that had started to get warm. He knew the tunnel headed towards the river; he had once used it. He went through the twists and turns of the tunnel. A faint golden light illuminated the walls, and it was getting brighter by the moment. The river was carrying lava through the tunnels, and he could encounter it any moment.

The cry of a man screaming for help echoed and from somewhere in the labyrinth, Mahadeva answered, 'I am coming, Anna.'

Kattappa was covered in sweat. The water level was increasing and getting hotter. The glow on the tunnel walls became brighter. Bats screeched above his head and flapped around in confusion. From various pathways, smoke curled out, choking him. Coughing and panting, Kattappa called out for his master.

'Kattappa, I am here,' Mahadeva's voice echoed. Kattappa was unable to locate the direction from which it was coming. Water had risen to his waist now, and the tunnel was filled with steam and smoke.

'Swami, swami,' Kattappa called out frantically. A hand grabbed him and pulled him to the side. Mahadeva pointed to Bijjala trapped under the debris of a tunnel wall that had collapsed.

'Help me free him.'

Bijjala was sitting with his back to the wall, pinned from his waist down under a pile of big rocks. Water had reached his chin.

'I will drown, help me,' he cried piteously. Kattappa and Mahadeva tried to push away the debris and pull Bijjala out, but he still couldn't move.

Far ahead, they could see the molten lava sizzling and the golden glow became brighter. They could hear the lava now, slithering like a serpent, spitting, and hissing, sticking out its tongues of fire. Kattappa's toe struck Bijjala's crude axe lying buried in the water. He lifted it up and started smashing at the debris that trapped Bijjala.

'Slave, the fire is here, it is here, it will kill me,' Bijjala cursed and screamed in panic. Just as the stream of lava was stretching its fingers to grab them, Kattappa managed to break away the last of the stones and Mahadeva pulled his brother out. Without even waiting to thank them, Bijjala hurried forward. In his scramble to get away from the lava, he pushed

Mahadeva. Instinctively, the king put his right palm down to break his fall and screamed in pain as it came into contact with lava. Kattappa yanked Mahadeva out of the lava's way and they ran towards the trapdoor, following Bijjala. Behind them, the fire snake advanced relentlessly. Bijjala was the first to emerge out of the trapdoor, and a moment later, Mahadeva and Kattappa came out. The well was thick with smoke.

'Get the plate fast,' Mahadeva yelled to Kattappa, and the slave shouted up to the soldiers to throw down the Gauridhooli plate. It crashed through the thick curtain of smoke and landed with a clang, startling Bijjala who sat panting on the ground.

The lava had reached near the trapdoor and Mahadeva and Kattappa lifted the heavy plate and slammed it on the frame of the trapdoor. To their horror, it did not fit properly, and toppled inside. Scalding water shot out.

The next moment, Kattappa saw Mahadeva plunge into the tunnel. Before he could react, Mahadeva had hoisted up the Gauridhooli plate and shut the gap from inside. 'Hold on, Kattappa, don't leave it,' Kattappa heard Mahadeva cry.

'No, no,' Kattappa cried, but Mahadeva held the plate firm. The slave knew what his king was doing. He was sacrificing himself for his people. He heard the screams of Mahadeva as the lava reached him. Through the tiny gap between the plate and the frame, he could see the lava climbing up Mahadeva's legs. Yet the king, with unwavering resolve, held the plate over his head. Fighting his tears, Kattappa held the door firm, pressing down from above.

Slowly, the lava covered Mahadeva and reached the plate. It spilt through the small gap, oozed a little, and fused the door to the frame. The Gauridhooli plate had managed to stop the lava once again, but Mahadeva had paid its price.

Kattappa gave an animal cry of anguish. It should have been he, Kattappa, who made that sacrifice—not the king. He had failed in his duty.

The man who had had a heart as soft as a flower would now become part of a rock. Smoke cleared and the soldiers who were watching from the mouth of the well saw Kattappa crying. They knew what had happened. Mahadeva had lived and died for what he believed. He had lived and died for the people of Mahishmathi. Mahadeva Vikramadeva, the great soul, had died without seeing the face of his child or even knowing his wife was dying.

Bijjala sat looking at the Gauridhooli door with a smug smile. He couldn't believe his luck. Nothing stood between him and the throne of Mahishmathi now. The grin on Bijjala's face enraged Kattappa, and for a moment he forgot that he was a sworn slave of Mahishmathi. His duty was not to judge the princes but serve them whether they were devils or Gods, whether they were noble or evil, but he had witnessed something beyond human understanding and he couldn't help himself. He grabbed Bijjala by his hair and pulled him up as the soldiers lamented the death of Mahadeva.

Bijjala screamed and hurled abuses, and struggled to free himself, but the slave continued to haul him up by his hair, climbing like a lizard up the well wall.

When he reached the top, he saw Sivagami standing with an ashen face. Kattappa flung her husband at her feet and cried out, 'Our maharaja has gone, devi.'

Sivagami collapsed to the ground. Kattappa said, 'It was to save your husband that our king died.'

Sivagami sat leaning against the wall of the well. She didn't cry, she didn't say a word. She stared straight ahead as Bijjala lay in a heap at her feet.

'It was for this scoundrel that—' Kattappa started again, and then stopped. What was he saying?

The king had died to save his people. That Bijjala was trapped there and the king had tried to save his brother too was immaterial. Had it been anyone else, even this worthless slave Kattappa, Mahadeva would have done the same thing.

Kattappa squatted before Sivagami and beat his bald head with both his hands and cried, 'Kill me, I am a sinner. I couldn't save him, he died for all of us. He died for all of us. I have failed.'

Bijjala hissed, 'I will have your head for humiliating me.'

Kattappa ignored him and continued to cry. His king was gone.

Through his tears, Kattappa saw some soldiers approaching Sivagami and whispering something to her. Sivagami stood up, her face pale with shock. She hurried after the soldiers. They had been sent by the rajavaidya to inform Mahadeva that his pregnant wife was dying.

EIGHTY-THREE

# Sivagami

SIVAGAMI BURST INTO the chamber of the queen and rushed to Akhila. The rajavaidya slowly stood up, tears in his eyes. Sivagami patted Akhila's cheeks and shook her gently. 'Wake up Akhila, wake up.' Her voice broke. 'Sister, wake up, please …'

In a corner, Gundu Ramu sat, crying. The rajavaidya said in a grim voice, 'Roopaka poisoned her.'

Sivagami grabbed the rajavaidya by his shoulders and yelled, 'What do you call yourself a vaidya for, if you cannot save her.'

The old vaidya stammered, 'It is the will of Amma Gauri that the queen has to die, and with her the unborn child.'

Sivagami didn't know what to do. One part of her felt like destroying everything, killing everyone and bathing in blood. The other part of her wanted to be in a prayer room, asking for forgiveness for all her sins. She wished she could exchange her life for Akhila's. The wheel of karma seemed to be rolling relentlessly. She shook Akhila again, as if that could wake her up, and her foster sister, the one who had always loved her, smiled weakly at Sivagami. She struggled to open her eyes and Sivagami pressed her little sister to her bosom.

Akhila whispered, 'Save my child, Akka.'

The queen of Mahishmathi and the baby in her womb were dying before her eyes and there was nothing they could do. Sivagami broke into sobs and then Gundu Ramu touched her shoulder and said softly, 'Akka, there is a story.'

Sivagami slapped Gundu Ramu with the back of her hand and yelled, 'Fool, is this the time to tell a story?'

Gundu Ramu shrank back as if stung, but he continued between sobs, 'Long ago, in Pataliputra, Emperor Chandragupta's wife was poisoned when she was pregnant. The vaidya said the mother and the child could not be saved. But Acharya Chanakya saved the baby and he became the Emperor Bindusara later.'

Sivagami stared at him. Gundu Ramu, tears running down his face, continued. 'Acharya Chanakya cut open the queen's belly and took out the baby.'

For a moment, no one said anything. Sivagami felt Akhila's grip on her hand tighten. She was struggling to say something. Gathering all her strength, Akhila said, 'Just save my baby.'

There was no time to waste. Sivagami took the dagger from her waistband with trembling hands. She closed her eyes, allowing the gravity of what she was about to do to sink in. Sivagami had killed Thimma, caused the death of Bhama, and later, Raghava. And now ... This was how she was repaying Thimma's kindness. *Cursed is my life*, she thought, and her lips quivered.

Gundu Ramu said softly, 'Time is running out, Akka.'

Through her tears, Sivagami could see the colour of Akhila's skin change for the worse. 'Amma Gauri, help me,' Sivagami said, as she touched Akhila's belly with the tip of the dagger. 'F—forgive me, sister.' And with that she tore open her sister's belly.

As Akhila screamed, Sivagami took out the baby covered in blood and placenta. For an anxious moment, the baby didn't cry. Sivagami waited, praying, terrified, not daring to take her eyes off the baby. Mahadeva's and Akhila's son, orphaned at birth, let out a sudden scream, cradled in his aunt's arms. Sivagami pressed him to her cheek, feeling his warmth, tears of joy falling from her eyes, and thanked Amma Gauri. *You are my son,* she whispered in his ears, and from the cradle in the corner, Sivagami's own son woke up and bawled.

Sivagami smiled, hearing the two princes of Mahishmathi crying. At that moment, all the tragedies that haunted her felt far away.

She made the baby kiss his mother's cheeks for the first and last time. Akhila looked serene, trusting that her son would be safe in her sister's hands. 'Be happy, sister, wherever you are now, with my ... your Mahadeva.'

Sivagami lifted her son from the cradle and held both babies in her arms. She kissed them both, her two sons, the princes of Mahishmathi.

EIGHTY-FOUR

# Epilogue

JEEMOTHA'S SHIP WAS approaching Kadarimandalam. Standing at the prow with Kalicharan Bhatta, he could see that the city was burning. Had there been riots after the annihilation of the Kadarimandalam navy? He had heard the explosion of a volcanic eruption and now he could see the horizon darkening and an orange glow in the northeast sky.

As his fleet of ships approached the ancient port city, he thought of trying his luck in Kadarimandalam. If he played his game well, perhaps he could become king. Though he had no intention of staying there forever, it would always be an advantage to have a famed port as his base.

Immersed in his thoughts, Jeemotha had not been paying attention to guiding his ship, and it was only when it jerked and tilted to one side that he realised that they were grounded. Cursing, he rushed to the prow of the ship, wondering what his deputy had done. They were in the middle of the river, where the waters were deep. Why had they been grounded?

As he looked seaward, Jeemotha's eyes expanded in fear and astonishment. *Why has the river gone shallow? Where is the sea?* As far as his eyes could see, there were sand dunes. It was as if he had strayed into a desert. The sea had withdrawn beyond the borders of the horizon. And Jeemotha knew what that meant.

He screamed orders for his men to disembark and run for their lives. But none of his men moved. Crowded on the decks, they were all staring at the sky. Then he saw it. The sea was rushing back to the land. Like a fist that had withdrawn before giving a punch, the sea had curled into itself. Like a monster from some nightmare, it now towered as high as a mountain and was rushing towards Kadarimandalam. Jeemotha knew this was the end, not only his, but of the ancient city of Kadarimandalam.

The sea's fist gave a mighty punch to the port and then embraced it in its thousand arms. It smashed everything in its way as it rushed landward. It flung Jeemotha's ships high into the air, juggled them and smashed them together, splintering the ships into many pieces.

All that Jeemotha remembered was getting sucked into the arms of the sea as it went back, drawing the city of Kadarimandalam to its bosom. Much later, when Jeemotha awoke, he found that he was floating on a plank. He didn't know how he had managed to get hold of it. Around him floated the debris of a broken city. Countless stars blinked at him from the sky, as if they had crowded around to entertain themselves by mocking his plight. Below him, the sea heaved gently like a sleeping beast, calm and serene. Jeemotha didn't know how far he was from the shore, but he was thankful to be alive. It was a miracle that he had survived, and he let out a howl of laughter.

This was his home, this was his country. He belonged to the sea, she was his mother. If she had spared him, she must have some plans for him. Instead of fighting her, Jeemotha decided that he would surrender himself to her. *Let her take me wherever she wants,* he thought. It was better to go away from this accursed land where the only thing that mattered was which caste you were born into. In any other country, he would have been a celebrated genius, but having been born a fisherman's son, he had had to live as a pirate. He could never be anything more in this blasted land. By the position of the stars, he calculated that the sea was taking him west. Perhaps he would end up in the land of the barbarians with yellow hair and ghostly pale skins. Wherever he landed, he knew, he would fight his way to the top. Perhaps he could teach them a thing or two about ships, and who knows, one day, he or maybe someone of his blood, many generations hence, would return to the land of his birth. The fools would probably not have learnt to treat humans as humans even then. They would still be quibbling about which caste was high and who had to bow to whom. And such fools would become slaves to anyone who wandered by. For now, he had a plank, a sea that held him in its bosom, and the vast skies above. In some stories written to glorify kings and queens, he was just a low-caste pirate, unscrupulous and sly. In his epic, however, he was the hero. Jeemotha, the king, knew that the future belonged to him and his ilk.

Sivagami walked towards the throne with determined steps. On either arm, she cradled the two princes. The sabha was in full attendance. She sat on the throne with both babies in her lap. She had never wanted to be queen of Mahishmathi, but the hand of destiny had placed the crown of thorns on her head. It was her fate that she had to rule it, and rule she would, until Amma Gauri willed it.

Looking around the sabha, Sivagami announced, 'The river Mahishi brought us life and death, but we have resurrected. Henceforth, the river will be known as Jeeva Nadhi, the river of life.'

When the cheering in the sabha had died down, they brought her husband to her in chains. He had not lost his arrogance.

'When are you going to hang me, Sivagami?' he asked, knowing well she would not dare. The moment she killed him, she would be a widow, and the conservative society of Mahishmathi would never allow her to rule. As queen, she toyed with the idea of putting an end to such deplorable customs, but that would involve suppressing rebellions. And she had had enough bloodshed for many lives. She was ruling on behalf of a man who had abhorred violence. It would be a dishonour to Vikramadeva Mahadeva. It was strategic to allow Bijjala to live, but to think that he would walk free without any punishment after causing so much pain to everyone was unthinkable. There had to be justice, and she had to make an example of him.

'So is it Chitravadha or a mere hanging, my wife?' Bijjala asked with a smug smile.

Before she could answer, she had another challenge to face. Marthanda and his group of mercenaries stormed into the sabha. Marthanda flung a palm leaf at Sivagami's face. 'Gauriparvat is ours, and we are taking it,' he said. Sivagami knew that the mercenary dared to act like this thinking he could bully her into getting his way. She was a woman, with no men to support or advise her, was his thinking.

Sivagami roared, 'Kattappa!' and like always, that call was answered immediately. From the balcony above, Kattappa jumped down to land gracefully in front of Marthanda. Before the mercenary could react, Kattappa's Gaurikhadga, the last of the swords made of Gauridhooli, severed his head cleanly. The rest of the mercenaries took to their heels. Sivagami snapped her fingers and soldiers captured the fleeing mercenaries. She made a gesture of slicing their throats, and the soldiers obeyed, butchering Marthanda's men. Her message was loud and clear. It was Maharani Sivagami devi on the throne of Mahishmathi.

Sivagami cocked an eyebrow and glowered at Bijjala. His smile had vanished. 'Are you going to kill me?' Bijjala asked in a frightened voice. The change in tone was pitiful.

With a contemptuous smile, Sivagami said, 'Six years back, I had come here with enough treasure to last many generations. Your brother had advised against it, but like a fool, I brought all the Gaurikanta stones. And you sold this city to Kadarimandalam. At that time, I had made a vow when you raised your hand against me.'

Bijjala staggered back. Sivagami's lips curved in a cruel smile. 'I am not going to kill you, for you don't deserve death. You are nothing but a fool, and to remind you and the people of Mahishmathi that the queen is fair, but doesn't spare anyone who works against the people, I shall punish you. You will be made a living example of how a prince should not behave, how human beings should not behave. This is Sivagami's justice.' Sivagami paused, allowing her words to sink in.

'Kattappa ...' Sivagami nodded to her faithful slave.

Kattappa gave a curt bow and walked towards Bijjala, who started trembling.

'Kill ... kill me. Don't humiliate me like this. Slave, don't touch me, don't,' Bijjala screamed, as Kattappa gripped Bijjala's right hand. The same hand he had used against Sivagami in the sabha years ago. Using the ancient knowledge of marma vidya, Kattappa twisted his hand and snapped it. Bijjala screamed in pain and then he fainted. With a wave of her hand, Sivagami gestured for soldiers to take him away.

Kattappa bowed. 'He will never be able to use the hand, Maharani.'

Sivagami nodded. An uneasy silence hung in the sabha. She knew she had shocked everyone with her ruthlessness. She reminded herself that Mahadeva could afford to be gentle, for he was a man. If she allowed herself to be gentle, they would think she was only a weak woman.

One of the babies whimpered, and she looked at the two boys in her arms. For a moment, she forgot she was the monarch of Mahishmathi. She was their mother. Sivagami had not given them names so far. As per the prevalent belief, princes did not get a name until they were a year old. To name them before they turned one was considered as challenging destiny. But Sivagami had challenged destiny enough. It was time for Amma Gauri to show her some compassion, she told herself.

'Kattappa,' Sivagami called the slave and he stepped forward.

'You are the mama for these two, my brother. Name them.'

Kattappa's eyes filled up and his lips trembled with emotion. Her own eyes filled with tears as she handed over her son. Kattappa raised the baby to the courtiers and whispered his name three times in his ear. Then, for the courtiers to hear, he announced, 'Ballaladeva.'

The sabha erupted in cheers. 'Jai Prince Ballaladeva,' they cried. When the cheers died down, Kattappa took the other baby. The orphan stared at the slave, and he pressed the baby to his chest, allowing memories of the kind Mahadeva to wash over him. Sivagami touched Kattappa's shoulder and he shuddered. Kattappa looked at the baby, ran his fingers over the infant's face, and whispered his name thrice.

Sivagami said, 'Say it aloud to the world, Anna.'

Kattappa raised the baby as the courtiers cheered and shouted, Gundu Ramu the loudest among them. The faithful slave, the mama of the baby, said in a voice that boomed in the Mahishmathi sabha, 'Baahubali.'

The sabha of Mahishmathi roared in one voice that shook the very earth, 'Jai Prince Baahubali.'

Sivagami sat on her throne, took both the babies in her arms and smiled at them. 'I am holding this crown till you grow up, my darlings,' she whispered. She had suffered enough in life and caused enough suffering too. She looked down at the faces of the two innocent babies in her lap, and prayed, 'Let there be no more wars in the future, let there be no more strife. Let the better between my two sons be the king of Mahishmathi and let the other serve his brother like how Lakshman served Lord Ram.'

## And then …

# Acknowledgements

THIS BOOK SERIES is a tribute to the vision of a great director, artist, and human being, Sri S.S. Rajamouli. *Bāhubali* is a landmark film in the history of Indian cinema, and the sheer scale of it is mindboggling. One can only wonder at how much effort would have gone into making such a classic. Taking the responsibility of working on a prequel of such a story was a daunting task. Had it not been for the absolute freedom, encouragement, and kindness shown by S.S. Rajamouli, this book would never have been possible. I am indebted to him for life, for the trust he has shown in me.

Sri K.V. Vijayendra Prasad is one of the greatest living screenplay writers in the Indian film industry. Sri Prasad, who is S.S. Rajamouli's father, has penned many classics, among which *Bāhubali* happens to be one. My first meeting with him is still etched in my mind. It was his story I was going to rework and expand, and I was apprehensive about how he was going to take it. He was grace personified and the tips and advice he gave me on writing are more precious to me than anything I have ever achieved. I consider him my mentor and this book is my humble tribute to his art.

Prasad Devineni and Shobu Yerlaggada, the producers of *Bāhubali*, the film, and promoters of Arka Media, deserve special mention for their unstinting belief and trust in my skills as an author. *Bāhubali* has gone much beyond being a great film. It has become a global brand. I hope I have lived up to their expectations and hopefully added some more sheen to the brand. Having worked with many producers in the past, I can vouch for the fact that people who give complete freedom to the writer are rare to come by. Thank you, gentlemen, for being there to support and encourage me whenever I was assailed with self-doubt.

I have to thank the kindness of Gautam Padmanabhan, CEO of Westland. He is more a friend than my publisher, and it was he who advised me to shelve the book I had been working on and take up the *Bāhubali* trilogy. His enthusiasm gave me confidence. Now that I have wrapped up the series, I will resume work on *Devayani*. It would have been my fourth book, but now it will be my eleventh.

I should thank my editors Deepthi Talwar and Sanghamitra Biswas. The map was designed by Vishwanath Sundaram, the graphic designer and VFX artist of Arka Media. He was assailed by two perfectionists, S.S. Rajamouli and yours truly, for every minute detail, and he has done amazing work. Thank you for the great piece of art.

Krishna Kumar, Nidhi, Shweta, Arunima and Satish Sundaram of Westland deserve special mention for all the public relations and sales-related work they have done for me. I'd like to thank Rajinder Ganju for the inside layout of the books, and Aparajitha Vaasudev for the cover design.

I am grateful to the press and TV journalists too for the extensive coverage of the book.

My friends often say that my better half Aparna deserves a Nobel Prize for tolerating me. Thank you for being there, my dear. It may be a great trial to live through my mood swings, but after more than fifteen years, I am sure you are used to it. My children Ananya and Abhinav have been my greatest critics and inspiration. They bring me down to earth from my flights of fantasy. And my pet dog Jackie deserves a special mention, as he was the one who often heard my stories during our long walks together.

My extended family has always stood by me, even when I wrote books that challenged their beliefs and convictions. They have been my source of inspiration from childhood. My siblings Lokanathan, Rajendran and Chandrika, my in-laws, Parameswaran, Meenakshi and Radhika, and my nieces and nephew, Divya, Dileep and Rakhi, have always made our family get-togethers lively with many debates about the Ramayana and Mahabharata.

My friends for more than three decades, Rajesh Rajan, Santosh Prabhu and Sujith Krishnan; other friends like Sumit Balan, Sanju, Prasant Menon and Nissar all deserve special thanks for keeping me inspired. My batchmates of EEE 1996, from The Government Engineering College, Trichur, especially Cina, Gayatri, Ganesh, Malathi, Maya, Aji, Mathew, Gopu Keshav, Anjali, Bala Murali, Brinda and Habibulla Khan, all deserve my heartfelt gratitude.

My special thanks to all the readers of my books. Your words of criticism and praise and your suggestions have been my inspiration and the reason I continue to write.

Blessed by the sacred Gauriparvat, Mahishmathi is an empire of abundance. The powerful kingdom is flourishing under its king, who enjoys the support and loyalty of his subjects, down to his lowly slaves. But is everything really as it appears, or is the empire hiding its own dirty secret?

Orphaned at a young age and wrenched away from her foster family, Sivagami is waiting for the day she can avenge the death of her beloved father, cruelly branded a traitor. Her enemy? None other than the king of Mahishmathi. With unflinching belief in her father's innocence, the fiery young orphan is driven to clear his name and destroy the empire of Mahishmathi against all odds. How far can she go in her audacious journey?

From the pen of masterful storyteller and bestselling author Anand Neelakantan, comes *The Rise of Sivagami*, the first book in the Bāhubali: Before the Beginning series. A tale of intrigue and power, revenge and betrayal, the revelations in *The Rise of Sivagami* will grip the reader and not let go.

Political intrigue is astir in the land of Mahishmathi. After the failed coup staged by the Vaithalikas, Sivagami finds herself elevated to the position of bhoomipathi, from where she can more ably pursue her burning goal to avenge her father's death. Meanwhile, there is a tussle between the two sons of the maharaja of Mahishmathi: both for the crown and Sivagami's affections. And behind the scenes, a wily, skilled player of the political game moves the pieces to topple the king, Somadeva.

Will the maharaja—usually able to match wits with the best of them—prevail? Or will one of his many enemies finally be able to best him at this game of Chaturanga?

Set against a backdrop of ambition, love, loyalty, passion and greed, the second book in the Bāhubali: Before the Beginning series is a twist-a-minute page-turner—riveting and deeply satisfying.

www.ingramcontent.com/pod-product-compliance
Lightning Source LLC
LaVergne TN
LVHW041604070526
838199LV00047B/2130